About the Authors

Monica Richardson writes adult romances set in Florida and the Caribbean. Under the name Monica McKayhan she writes adult and young adult fiction. She currently has nine titles in print. Her YA novel, *Indigo Summer*, was the launch title for Mills & Boon's young adult imprint, Kimani TRU. *Indigo Summer* snagged the #7 position on the Essence bestsellers list and appeared on the American Library Association (ALA)'s list of Quick Picks for Reluctant Young Adult Readers. To schedule an appearance, book signing or interview with Monica, please email publicity@monicamckayhan.com

Fiona Brand lives in the sunny Bay of Islands, New Zealand. Now that both of her sons are grown, she continues to love writing books and gardening. After a life-changing time in which she met Christ, she has undertaken study for a bachelor of theology and has become a member of The Order of St. Luke, Christ's healing ministry.

Marion Lennox is a country girl, born on an Australian dairy farm. She moved on, because the cows just weren't interested in her stories! Married to a 'very special doctor', she has also written under the name Trisha David. She's now stepped back from her 'other' career teaching statistics. Finally, she's figured what's important and discovered the joys of baths, romance and chocolate. Preferably all at the same time! Marion is an international award winning author.

Island Escapes

Island Escapes: Moonlit Liaisons

MONICA RICHARDSON

FIONA BRAND

MARION LENNOX

MILLS & BOON

First Published in Great Britain 2021
by Mills & Boon, an imprint of HarperCollins*Publishers* Ltd,
1 London Bridge Street, London, SE1 9GF

www.harpercollins.co.uk

HarperCollins*Publishers*
1st Floor, Watermarque Building,
Ringsend Road, Dublin 4, Ireland

ISLAND ESCAPES: MOONLIT LIAISONS
© 2021 Harlequin Books S.A.

Second Chance Seduction © 2016 Monica Richardson
Keeping Secrets © 2018 Fiona Gillibrand
Miracle on Kaimotu Island © 2013 Marion Lennox

ISBN: 978-0-263-30258-5

MIX
Paper from
responsible sources
FSC C007454

This book is produced from independently certified FSC™ paper to ensure responsible forest management.

For more information visit: www.harpercollins.co.uk/green

Printed and bound in Spain
by CPI, Barcelona

SECOND CHANCE SEDUCTION

MONICA RICHARDSON

This is dedicated to my readers who have fallen in love with the Talbot family.

Chapter 1

Edward stood across the room from her and admired long, lean legs, a round butt and perfectly exhibited breasts. Her hair was short and sassy, not long and flowing as when they were together. She smiled at the gentleman in front of her and then pushed her bangs out of her face. Edward was in awe of her for a moment. This wasn't the woman he remembered. No, this lady was self-assured and sexy—not the timid young woman that he once knew.

She finally looked his way and gave a nod of acknowledgment. It was her idea that they meet at her downtown office instead of her West Palm Beach home. He noticed that she was becoming increasingly uncomfortable with him visiting her space, even if it was for a good reason. The last few times, she'd suggested that they meet at a park or a restaurant to facilitate the exchange. Things had become much more impersonal, against his wishes.

She gave him a smile and headed his way. The smile, he remembered. It was genuine and wholesome—not to mention gorgeous. She led the way, and he followed her to a beautiful office with art that adorned the walls. The walls were painted in warm hues of orange—Savannah's favorite color. He immediately recognized the portrait of the colorful Eiffel Tower, an urban piece that they'd picked up when they honeymooned in Paris. He sat in the leather wingback chair and stared at the woman who sat across from him. He picked up the framed photograph from her desk—the one of their daughter, Chloe. *His girls*, as he used to call them.

"I talked to my mother the other day."

"Really?" He leaned back in the chair and glanced at Savannah's face. Tried to read her expression at the mention of her mother.

"Yes." Her face was blank.

It seemed that she was trying to shield her emotions from him, but he knew her all too well. He knew that her relationship with her mother had been strained and was the reason for many years of inner turmoil for Savannah.

"What was that conversation like?" he asked.

"It was long and—" a subtle little smile appeared in the corner of her mouth "—and genuine, actually."

"Really?" He was surprised.

"I'd like to go to London and spend some time with her."

"Okay, that's nice. A week or so?"

"Maybe longer."

"What about your job?"

Savannah exhaled and leaned her head against the back of the leather chair. "They're downsizing. Letting some people go. This is actually my last few weeks here."

"Savannah, I'm sorry." Edward crossed his leg over the other one. "What will you do? Have you been putting your résumé out there?"

"I'd like to look for a job while I'm in London."

"You're thinking of relocating there?"

She nodded a yes.

"What about Chloe?"

"She would go, too," she stated matter-of-factly. Like it was the most normal thing in the world to take a man's child clear across the world.

He took in a deep breath, gathering himself before he spoke again. But he could feel his anger boiling. His daughter meant the world to him, and he couldn't imagine her living in another state, let alone another country. He couldn't fathom the thought. Wouldn't. No. It was out of the question.

"You're not moving to London with Chloe." He was calm, but emphatic.

"Not right away, I know."

"Not at all!"

"You're being unreasonable, Edward."

He sat up in the chair. "How do you propose I see my daughter if you take her to England, Savannah? Are you going to fly her here for my weekend visits? And what about Christmas and summer breaks?"

He'd already found it difficult to manage a week without seeing Chloe's little face. He couldn't even imagine not seeing her for longer than that.

"We'll figure something out."

"We'll figure something out?" he asked. "She's just as much my daughter as she is yours, and I won't allow it."

"You're telling me what you won't allow? What gives you the right?"

"I have rights when it comes to my daughter. And I will exercise them if I need to."

"Are you threatening me?"

He stood. Headed toward the door. "It's not a threat, Savannah. It's a promise."

Their marriage had ended in divorce after a short eighteen months. It was the one thing that Edward had failed at. He'd excelled in college and breezed through law school. He'd run for mayor, and lost—but had landed a position on the West Palm Beach City Commission. A place where he could actually make a difference for the people in his community. However, the mayoral campaign had robbed him of his marriage. A newlywed with a pregnant wife at home, he'd gotten too caught up in his career. Not to mention he'd spent too much time with his beautiful campaign manager. Although he'd never cheated on Savannah with Quinn, the closeness of their relationship had caused more of a disturbance than his new marriage could take.

One of the best things about Edward's marriage to Savannah, though, had been their daughter, Chloe. He needed his daughter like the air he breathed. He needed to see her every single day. They'd become the best of friends. In her five years of life, he was astounded at the things that she knew. He didn't want to miss one single moment of her life. But now Savannah threatened to take it all away. He wouldn't allow her to do it. Couldn't.

"What do you want from me, Edward? Do you want me to put my life…my career on hold again?"

"This is not about your career, or mine for that matter. This is about our daughter. If you want to go to London to make amends with your mother and build a new career, that's fine. But don't take Chloe away from me. She's all I have."

"I couldn't leave her here. I won't," she said. "This is something I have to do, Edward. I'm sorry."

It seemed that he'd been dismissed.

"Get yourself a good lawyer, Savannah," he spat, and then stormed out of her office.

He needed air.

He walked briskly and managed to make it to the parking garage, loosened his tie and pulled a set of keys from his pocket. He collapsed into the driver's seat of his sedan and sat there for a moment. Listened while Omar Sosa's Afro-Cuban rhythms soothed his senses. He hated fighting with Savannah, but it seemed more frequent lately. Not long ago, they'd debated over which private school to send Chloe to and which curriculum would be better suited for her. They'd argued about whether to place her in a karate class or ballet. A week ago they'd argued about something as simple as Chloe's bob haircut. He thought she was too young for such a grown-up style. She was a kindergartner, for Christ's sake. He'd been active in every decision about his daughter, but not the one where Savannah planned to take her thousands of miles away. It seemed unfair.

He pulled out onto Clematis Street and breezed through the yellow light. His heart ached. He scrolled through the address book on his phone and looked for Jack Wesley's phone number. He didn't want to involve his attorney—in fact he'd only said it to get Savannah's attention—but he needed to know what his rights were regarding his daughter.

"JW!" Edward exclaimed. "How the hell are you?"

"I'm making it," Jack said. "Trying my best to keep a good law practice and maintain a happy marriage all at the same time."

"Well, I can't help you in that area, bro. I failed tremendously at my marriage."

"You failed because you didn't put in the effort. Savannah was a good woman."

"All of that is neither here nor there."

"Do you miss her?" Jack asked.

"What? Of course not," Edward lied. He would never let his friend know that he regretted every moment since Savannah left. "She has her life and I have mine."

"Right," a skeptical Jack said.

"I didn't call you to talk about my failed marriage to Savannah. I need some advice regarding Chloe."

"What about Chloe?"

"Savannah's trying to take her to London...to live! Can you believe that?" Edward asked. "I need to know what my rights are."

"Have you had lunch already?"

"Not yet."

"Meet me at the little chicken and waffles spot on Okeechobee in thirty minutes."

"Bro, fried chicken and waffles? How about something a little healthier?"

"You're still on that kick," Jack stated. He sighed. "Have you completely given up meat?"

"No, of course not. I've traded red meat and pork for chicken, fish and tofu. I'm just eating healthier, man, that's all."

"I see. You choose, then."

"Darbster. Dixie Highway."

"Do they have anything that resembles meat?"

"Tofu." Edward laughed.

"Ah, man."

"Keep an open mind," said Edward. "I'll meet you there in thirty minutes."

Edward hit the end button on his phone. Turned up the volume on his music. He was anxious to speak with Jack. Surely he would receive some good advice from his old friend. Jack would tell him exactly how to go about keeping his daughter in the country. He felt better already, less helpless. Cocky, even.

He slid into the booth at the restaurant and gave the menu a quick scan. He already knew what he wanted—it was a place that he frequented often. He ordered his usual meal and then ordered something for Jack.

"And bring two glasses of water, please," he said to the female server.

He raised his hand when he saw Jack walk through the door. His friend looked worn, as though he needed a vacation. He removed his suit jacket and slid into the booth across from Edward. Gave him a strong slap of the hands and a handshake.

"Good to see you."

"Likewise." Edward grinned. "I took the liberty of ordering for you."

"And why would you do that?"

"Because I know this isn't your kind of place," Edward said, "but you'll be thanking me later."

"You think so?"

"I know so."

Soon the server arrived with two piping-hot plates of food and set them down in front of the men. Jack frowned at the sight of his.

"Don't knock it until you try it," said Edward.

"I'll try to keep an open mind."

"Good," Edward said, and then went on to explain what transpired at Savannah's office earlier.

"You overreacted, bro." Jack frowned as he picked over his meal. He pushed the tofu aside and managed to get the vegetables into his mouth. "But you do have rights regarding your daughter. The question is, are you up for a fight with Savannah?"

"I can't let her take Chloe away without a fight."

"Perhaps you two can work something out without involving the courts. Summer is approaching. Maybe you can convince her to let Chloe spend the summer with you. You'd deliver her to London safe and sound in the fall, just before school starts. Maybe you can get her again around Christmastime or spring break."

"That won't work," Edward said emphatically. "I need to see her at least once a week. And besides, we have a custody plan that says I get her every week. She can't just wake up one morning and decide she wants to move to the other side of the earth."

"Well, if you're not in agreement with the move, then Savannah must file a petition for relocation with the court. The family court judge will take into consideration what's in the best interest of the child. Stuff like how Chloe's relationship with you will be impacted if she takes her away. Also, how the move will impact her mental, physical and emotional development."

"Okay."

"And whether or not the relationship with you can be preserved…kind of like the arrangement that I suggested in the beginning."

"Can't be preserved," Edward said.

"Then once she files, we have a short deadline to object to the move," Jack said. "I'll get the paperwork started as soon as I return to my office so we'll be ready."

"You're a lifesaver, man." Edward smiled. Exhaled.

"We'll have to contend with a court hearing. Maybe even a trial, if it goes that far." Jack sipped on his ice water. "Are you up for that?"

"What choice do I have?" Edward said. "I'm up for it if she is. She started this whole thing."

"I'm just asking, because I know it's been a long, hard road for you and Savannah in the past. I was just wondering if you're willing to go down that road again."

"I don't want to fight with Savannah again. It was a painful time."

"I remember. I was right there with you."

"Yes, you were. You've been a great friend."

"I just hate to see you go through that again. And you two have finally gotten this co-parenting thing down."

"Right. We have."

"You've made it through some tough times. Not to mention that whole bogus engagement thing Savannah had with her corny boss." Jack grinned. "If you can make it through that, you can make it through anything."

"Don't remind me of that fool."

Jack laughed. "You were so jealous."

"I wasn't jealous!"

"You were beyond jealous. I knew then that you were still in love with that woman."

"What?" Edward denied Jack's claims. "I'm not in love with her. I do love her *in a family sort of way*...kind of like I love my sisters."

"Yeah, I don't think you love Savannah like you love your sisters." Jack laughed. "But if that's your story..."

"That's my story." Edward laughed, too. "And I'm sticking with it."

"Maybe you should just move to London, too," Jack said.

"Go to hell!" said Edward.

"I'm only kidding, bro. I know this is a serious situation for you." Jack wiped his mouth with a cloth napkin. "Let me see what we can work out. Perhaps we won't have to go to court at all."

"That would be great."

Savannah had surprised him with the divorce. She'd claimed that she needed to get away and had gone to Georgia for a lengthy visit with her father. After several long weeks, instead of returning to their home in Florida as Edward had anticipated, Savannah had decided to stay in Georgia with her father. Soon she'd had Edward served and completely caught him off guard. And if divorcing him wasn't enough, she asked for alimony and child support. She wanted the family home and asked that he continue to pay the mortgage until she was gainfully employed. He wouldn't be blind-sided by her again.

In fact, when he was done reading Savannah her rights, she wouldn't know what hit her.

Chapter 2

Savannah was young when she married Edward. Her pregnancy had been difficult, and Edward had insisted that she stay home with Chloe for her first two years.

"I'll take care of us," he'd said.

"What about my career? My goals?" she'd argued. "I have dreams, too."

"Give me time. When I'm mayor, you can go back to work."

It was too much for Savannah. She'd become invisible to him. He'd stopped coming home at a decent hour. She was alone more times than not, and she'd become lonely. She'd even suspected that Edward and his campaign manager, Quinn, were more than friends. She'd cried too many tears. Begged Edward for a reprieve.

"I can't focus when you're on my back all the time," he'd complained.

Finally, her father convinced her to come to Georgia for a visit. "You and the baby," he'd said. "That way you can figure things out."

Savannah, Georgia, had been her home for most of her

life. She was named after the city with cobblestone streets and Spanish moss hanging from ancient trees. Her father, a decorated officer in the military, had retired there—it was his home. He'd met Savannah's mother while stationed in Germany. Nyle Carrington had taken the train from London to Germany for a weekend getaway with girlfriends, and returned to her home in London engaged to a US soldier. They dated for a short time, and soon, Frank Carrington's wife-to-be was pregnant with their new bundle of joy. When Savannah was two, her father's tour of duty was over, and the couple moved to his home in Georgia. Nyle found life difficult in the States, and soon returned to London, leaving Frank behind to raise their toddler alone. She sent cards and gifts for birthdays and Christmas, and occasionally she returned for short visits. Each visit, she'd promise to stay. She'd fill Savannah's head with stories of her home in London and promises that the next time she came, she'd take Savannah back to London with her. Instead, Savannah would awaken the next morning or return from school, only to find her mother gone again. By the time Savannah reached puberty, she'd given up any hope of having a normal relationship with her mother. She'd resolved that Nyle would never be a part of her life. And once she was an adult, she'd cut off all communication with her.

Until now.

Nyle was aging and needed Savannah in her life. She was remorseful and admitted that she hadn't been the best mother. She wanted to meet her only grandchild and realized the importance of having Savannah and Chloe in her life now. Savannah by all rights could've turned her back on the woman who'd abandoned her, but the truth was, she needed Nyle, too. Her life had been incomplete for so long, and she was ready to be a whole person. She wanted Chloe to know her grandmother and to learn about the history and her family in London. She needed to give their relationship a chance.

Conversations with her mother had become more frequent. They talked every day the way mothers and daughters were supposed to. They experienced moments that Savannah had only dreamed of in the past. They talked about Savannah and Chloe coming for a long visit—maybe even permanently. With Savannah's company downsizing, it seemed like the opportune time.

Nyle invited her to share her flat until she found her own place. Savannah would leave Chloe in Florida with Edward until the school year ended. She'd go there and get settled before coming back for her daughter. She was an experienced designer and already had an interview lined up with a prominent company. Her plans seemed perfect, flawless. And the anticipation of reuniting with her mother was all that mattered now. It was important to her, and she couldn't see why Edward didn't understand. He knew the history of her relationship with Nyle. They'd had plenty of conversations about it. She'd cried on his shoulder more times than she cared to remember, and he'd comforted her, given her encouragement. Loved her all the more. She expected him to be the one person who understood this burning desire. But instead, he was the one giving her grief.

"Have you had lunch?" Jarrod walked into her office as he often did, without knocking, and plopped his medium frame down in the chair opposite her desk. He studied her with those light brown eyes and gave her that bright smile that she loved so much. He was nicely built with dark curly hair and a strong physique that he worked for at the gym too many times a week, in her opinion. He was always sharply dressed.

"No time," she said.

"You have to eat," said Jarrod. "Why don't we go grab a bite?"

"I can't. I have a ton of work to finish up here."

"I'm giving you permission to take a lunch break." Jarrod laughed. "I'm the boss. And frankly, you're a workaholic."

"I have a meeting with a buyer this afternoon, and I want to be prepared."

"I appreciate your commitment to this company, Savannah. Even in the wake of my selling it."

"I love my job."

"And you're damn good at it." He smiled. "Which reminds me. I just got off the phone with an old colleague of mine, Herman Mason. His company specializes in women's fashion. One of the largest in England. I got you an interview."

"Are you kidding? Herman Mason?"

"I told him you were my best fashion designer, and he's very interested in meeting with you when you arrive in London," he said.

"Jarrod! I don't know what to say."

"Say that you won't embarrass me. Show him what you got." He smiled. "It's the least I can do, considering I can't keep you around here."

"I appreciate it. More than you know."

Jarrod became more comfortable in his seat. "I heard the commotion that went on…earlier…with your ex. Is everything okay?"

"Everything's fine."

"You need me to rough him up a little bit? Teach him a lesson?" Jarrod grinned at his own joke.

Savannah laughed inside. She knew that Jarrod could never stand up to Edward. Not physically. Not otherwise. The two were very different. When she met Jarrod, she wanted something so different from Edward that she'd gone to the other extreme. Jarrod was doting, gave her all the attention she wanted and needed—and sometimes more than she wanted. He wasn't afraid to share his feelings. Edward was a man's man. He would never admit to anything, and was hardly ever available to her. The two were like night and day. Both were gentlemen and loving, but Edward would rough Jarrod up if given half a chance.

"That won't be necessary. Edward's harmless."

"I know you still have a thing…for him…"

"Don't start, Jarrod. Please."

"It's why we didn't work out, isn't it?"

"We didn't work out because we just weren't meant to be." Savannah kept the conversation light. She knew that the tone had the potential to change—fast. "I appreciate everything you've done for me. You're a great friend."

Jarrod stood, headed toward the door. A slight smile danced in the corner of his mouth. "So I've been placed back into the friend bucket."

Savannah laughed. "Yes."

"Anything for you and Chloe."

Jarrod disappeared before Savannah could say another word. She did appreciate him, in spite of the fact that their whirlwind fling hadn't lasted. He was the first man she'd dated after the divorce. He'd romanced her and given her all the attention that a woman desired from a man—the attention that she'd desired from Edward. He'd even fallen in love with Chloe, and would've made a wonderful stepfather. When he'd asked Savannah for her hand in marriage, it seemed the only logical next step—except for the fact that she didn't love him. She thought he was a nice catch, a successful man any woman would be happy to have. But she didn't feel for him the things that he felt for her. He didn't care if she didn't love him—he wanted her anyway. She would grow to love him, he'd told her.

"Love is overrated anyway," he'd insisted. "People put too much emphasis on it. Successful marriages aren't built on love, they're built on commitment."

That way of thinking didn't sit well with Savannah. She needed love, and she wouldn't settle for anything less. He was devastated when she broke off the engagement, but it didn't stop him from trying to change her mind every chance he got.

Jarrod knew fashion inside and out. He'd been in the business a long time and had taught Savannah much of what she knew. His company had taken the industry by storm. But suddenly it was on a downward slope. Sales had fallen and the business was suffering. He needed to downsize, and as much as he wanted to retain Savannah, he couldn't afford to keep her. Soon Jarrod's Fashions would be owned by someone else.

Savannah shut the door to her office to avoid any other interruptions. She took a seat at her drafting table, her sketches scattered about. She thought of Edward. Wanted to call and smooth things over with him. Her decision to go to London hadn't been meant to hurt him. She wanted him to understand her need to connect with her mother. They'd come a long way since the divorce. They'd become more than just co-parents—they were friends. And she didn't want to jeopardize their friendship. But it was her time. He'd always come first in their marriage—his career, his feelings, his everything. It was the thing that had torn them apart. She'd taken a backseat for long enough. Now it was her time to do the things that made her happy.

She'd already anticipated that Edward might not be amenable to her idea of relocating with Chloe. Her income wasn't as adequate as Edward's and she didn't have attorney friends to assist her. She'd already done her research and learned that there were forms that needed to be filed whether

Edward agreed or disagreed with the move. So she'd already downloaded the necessary forms for both scenarios. She'd hoped that they could come to an agreement and that the decision would be consensual. However, Edward had been all but tolerable. The news was sudden, and he needed time to absorb it. Soon, he would see that he'd overreacted. But if not, she would take him to court.

Chapter 3

Edward sat sunk back in the leather seat of his car and watched as youngsters hopped into their parents' vehicles. The petals of a plumeria flower rested against the leather seat, right next to a plastic bag filled with Laffy Taffy, Nerds, Milk Duds and Skittles. He watched for Chloe. Expected her to rush to his car as she had every single Friday afternoon—her thick ponytails would be flying in different directions, the plaid skirt that she wore would be twisted in the back, and she'd offer him the biggest snaggletoothed smile that he loved so much.

Surely she remembered it was Friday. And not just any Friday, but the one on which her favorite movie came out at the theaters. They would smuggle the bag of candy into the auditorium in her backpack. They would order a large bucket of popcorn and a large Coke to share, and they would sit in the middle of the theater. Not too close to the screen, but not too far in the back. Right in the center.

Miss Jennings marched out of the school, a row of kindergartners following close behind. Edward sat straight up in his seat. He didn't want to be caught slouching as he scanned the row of children in search of his daughter. When he saw her, he smiled. Her ponytails flew in opposite directions, just as he'd suspected. She rushed to the car when she spotted him, Miss Jennings following close behind. Chloe pulled on the door handle and hopped inside. Miss Jennings stuck her head inside.

"Hello, Mr. Talbot." She gave him that same flirty smile that she always gave him.

The first time he saw the smile, he thought he was mistaken. Thought it was innocent until the time she gave him a raise of the eyebrows followed by a slip of her phone number during a parent-teacher conference. He never called. Feared that it would be a conflict of interest, dating his daughter's teacher. Not to mention, she wasn't his type.

He'd dated a few women after the divorce. Freda was the attractive psychologist that he'd met at a conference. She was the total package—beautiful, smart, independent. A nice catch, but she was too bossy. She wanted to dress him and mold him into what she wanted him to be, and he wasn't that type of man. He had his own agenda. Miranda was conservative and laid-back, accommodating. Too accommodating for his taste. She was the total package, too—beautiful, smart, independent—but there was no mystery. He'd managed to find something wrong with every woman he dated.

"Hello, Miss Jennings." Edward was cordial.

"Her homework is in her backpack," she said.

"Thanks."

"Have a great weekend, Chloe. I'll see you on Monday."

"Bye, Miss Jennings!" Chloe exclaimed before shutting her door. "Hi, Daddy!"

"Hello, Princess." He tapped the side of his face until she leaned over and kissed it.

"How was school?"

"Awesome!"

"For you, madam." He handed her the single yellow flower.

She smelled it and then stuck it into her hair. "It's pretty, Daddy. Thank you."

"You're welcome."

"You got the goods." She grinned wickedly as she peeked into the plastic bag filled with candy. She fastened her seat belt.

He knew that he shouldn't let her ride in the front seat. She was supposed to be buckled up in her car seat in the back, but some days he made an exception. And this was one of them.

"I got the goods." Edward smiled as he pulled out of the school's parking lot.

Chloe stuffed the bag of candy into her backpack. "What time does the movie start?"

"Four o'clock," he said. "If we hurry, we can make it before the previews are over."

"Cool." She toyed with his stereo until she found her favorite satellite radio station. She sang along with Katy Perry.

The theater was crowded. It seemed that every child in America had shown up for the premiere of the movie. Edward purchased tickets and then the two made a bee-line for the concession stand. He held on to Chloe's hand.

"How's your mommy doing?" he asked as they stood in line.

"She's fine," said Chloe. "She misses you."

"Really? How do you know?"

"She talks about you all the time."

"Really," he asked, and tried to seem unfazed by her remarks. But he couldn't help prying. "Like what?"

"I don't know, Daddy. Just saying stuff like 'your daddy and I used to listen to this type of music' or 'your daddy really likes this kind of food.'"

"I see," said Edward.

"Do you still love her?"

"I will always love your mom. And you. We're always going to be family."

"Even when we move to London?"

"Your mom talked to you about London?"

"She said we're going to live with her mother, Nyle."

"How do you feel about that?"

"I don't want to go, Daddy. Please don't make me go. If we go there, I won't get to spend the weekends with you anymore."

"Don't worry, baby. You're not going anywhere." Edward kissed Chloe's hand. "I'll make sure of it."

He intended to speak with Savannah about filling his daughter's head with her fantasies of moving away. As soon as the movie was over he'd confront her.

At home, Edward poured himself a glass of Merlot and began to prepare a vegetarian Caribbean meal for two. Being reared in the Bahamas, he'd learned his way around a kitchen. Growing up in a large family with three sisters and a mother who could cook, he was spoiled. Never had to worry about cooking. But after marrying Savannah, he was forced to become a great cook, considering his wife could barely boil water. He would call home to his mother in the Bahamas and she'd equip him with her recipes.

After his father's heart attack scare, Edward had become obsessed with his diet—only feasting on fish and chicken and incorporating more vegetables into his diet. He insisted on healthy eating in order to prevent heart disease and other ailments that bad eating caused. He needed to be healthy for his daughter, and he wouldn't compromise that. He visited the gym every other morning, if for nothing more than a run on the treadmill.

"You think you can break up the broccoli?" Edward asked Chloe.

"I can do it." She stood on a step stool in front of the kitchen's island with the granite top.

"Good!" He pulled her ponytail. "You do the broccoli and I'll cut up the peppers and onions."

He headed into the living room and tuned the stereo to his Afro-Cuban playlist. He could hear his phone ringing in the kitchen.

"Daddy, it's Mommy!" Chloe called from the kitchen.

He grabbed it from the granite countertop and answered it. "Hello."

"Hi." Savannah's voice was sweet in Edward's ear. "What's Chloe doing?"

"She's preparing vegetables for our dinner," Edward said. "We're making a vegetarian gumbo."

"Yum. You always were a great cook," said Savannah. "The movie was great, I hope."

"It was fantastic," Edward said. "Your daughter fell asleep midway through, but I enjoyed it."

Chloe laughed, and so did Savannah.

"She's so bad at movies."

"The worst." Edward laughed. "Would you like to speak with her?"

"I actually called to speak with you. I'd like to talk to you about London."

"There's nothing more to talk about." Edward was calm for Chloe's sake.

"I would really like your blessing, Edward. I would hope that we could come to an agreement about it."

"That won't happen," he said, and then smiled at Chloe,

who was listening intently. Edward stepped outside onto the back deck where he could speak freely. "I haven't changed my position on this, Savannah."

"Would you really deny me the opportunity to connect with my mother? You of all people know how important this is for me."

"Then *you* should go to London and connect with your mother. But leave Chloe."

"I can't leave my child, Edward. You know I would never leave her."

"Then you won't be going. Because she's not going!" He was adamant. "I would never agree to that."

Savannah was quiet for a moment. "Then I don't have a choice. I'll have to petition the courts. I don't want to, Edward, but you're leaving me no choice."

"Do what you have to do, Savannah. But know that I will fight this."

"I know that you already have your bulldogs lined up," she said, referring to Edward's lawyer friends.

"I've already consulted with counsel. Yes."

"Fine."

"And just so you know, Chloe doesn't want to move to London. Have you considered that?"

"You've been talking to her about it?"

"She brought it up," he said. "Apparently you've been filling her head with this bullshit."

"How dare you discuss this with her without me."

"You've created this, Savannah! So deal with it."

"I will!" she yelled and hung up.

Edward stood on the deck for a moment, trying to gather himself before going back inside. If Savannah was looking for a fight, she'd surely found one.

After dinner, he tucked Chloe into her bed.

"Are you mad at Mommy?"

"No, sweetheart. I'm not mad at your mommy," he lied. The truth was, he was furious with his ex-wife. "Now get some sleep. You're in charge of the pancakes in the morning."

"Me?"

"Yes, you."

"Good night, Daddy."

"Good night, baby." He kissed her forehead.

He poured himself another glass of Merlot and plopped down on his leather sofa. Turned on CNN to find out the latest goings-on in the world. He leaned his head against the tan leather and thought of Chloe. He didn't know what he would do if a judge found that she'd be better off in another country. He wouldn't survive without her, and thinking about it took his breath away. He blocked it from his mind. Thought about work instead, and before long his eyes grew heavy. He gave in to the fatigue.

When he pulled up in front of Savannah's home on Sunday afternoon, his emotions got the best of him. Usually, she'd suggested that the drop-off take place somewhere else, but this time she wanted him to drop Chloe at home. In the past, when he'd dropped Chloe off there after his weekend, he would at least walk her to the door. Occasionally, Savannah would invite him inside for a cup of coffee and a quick chat. But today he wasn't in the mood to stand on her doorstep, and even less in the mood for a conversation with her. He sat in the driver's seat of the car, leaned over and kissed his daughter.

"I love you, sweetheart," he said.

"Love you, too, Daddy. You're not coming in?"

"No, not today, baby. I'll wait here until you go inside."

Chloe hopped out of the sedan and skipped to the front door of the two-story traditional brick home. The home that he and Savannah had shared before the divorce. The one that he still made mortgage payments on. She rang the doorbell and within seconds Savannah appeared in the doorway. She took Chloe's backpack and gave her a strong hug. She glanced toward the car, as if waiting for Edward to step out of the car or at least wave. He refused to do either of the two, and as a result she ignored him, too. She grabbed Chloe's hand and went inside, shutting the door behind her.

He sat there for a moment. Part of him hoped she'd return and at least beg him to come inside, start a fight or something. He needed to engage with her, even if it was negatively. With a long sigh, he slowly pulled away from the curb. They'd reached an impasse. And the only logical move was to allow the courts to make a decision. They'd been down this road before, allowing the system to decide the fate of their family. They had vowed never to do that again, to allow a third party to come into their lives and make decisions for them. They were educated and reasonable, and fully capable of deciding what was best for Chloe. However, they had broken yet another promise. They had all but started a war.

Chapter 4

Savannah sat in the third row of the auditorium, a wide grin on her face as Chloe glided across the stage, dancing on her toes to "Für Elise." She'd been practicing the routine for months, forcing Savannah to watch as she stumbled over her own feet too many times. But tonight she was graceful and poised, and she beamed with pride. Savannah lifted her phone into the air as she recorded the event. The seat next to her was empty. She'd saved it for Edward in the event that he made it on time. She hadn't spoken with him in days. It was obvious that he was still bitter about their last encounter.

She looked around the auditorium and then took a quick glance at the door. She searched for him and finally spotted him standing at the back of the auditorium, his tall frame leaning against the wall. She always thought that Edward was a handsome man with a wonderfully built physique, light brown skin, a nicely trimmed goatee and a Bahamian accent that drove women wild. His tie was loosened a bit, and he looked exhausted. It appeared that he'd made it there in the knick of time, just moments before Chloe's performance. Their eyes connected and she smiled, gave a subtle wave. He nodded a hello. She pointed at the empty seat next to her, but he kept his eyes focused on the stage—pretended not to see the gesture. Edward could be stubborn. And so could she.

After the recital, she searched for him again, but he was nowhere in sight. She couldn't believe that he would leave without saying goodbye to Chloe, or at least letting her know that he'd been there. A light breeze brushed across the palm trees as she and Chloe stepped out into the night air. Edward stood near the door, waiting for them outside. Savannah exhaled. She was glad he was still there. When Chloe spotted him, she rushed over to him.

"Daddy!"

He lifted her into his arms and kissed her cheek. "Hey, sweetheart."

"Did you see? I didn't make any mistakes."

"You did good."

"Hello, Edward." Savannah gave him another warm smile.

"Savannah." He was cold.

They walked toward Savannah's car as Chloe filled his ears with everything that had gone on over the course of her day.

"Sweetie, why don't you sit in the car and wait for Mommy? Let me have a word with Daddy," Savannah said.

"Okay."

Savannah unlocked the door, got inside, started the engine and turned on the air-conditioning. Chloe hopped into the backseat and snapped the seat belt around her booster seat. Savannah got out and shut the door behind her.

"About the other day—" she began.

"Don't even worry about it. It's okay," he interrupted.

"Edward, I don't know how to fix this."

"What are your plans, Savannah? Are you moving to London or aren't you?"

"I am."

"Then what is there to fix?"

"I'm not trying to hurt you. I'm just trying to do something for me for a change."

"Without regard for your daughter...or me," Edward argued. "Doesn't it concern you at all that she'll be so far away from her father? You women are all the same. You want a man to step up to the plate and be a good father, but then you won't let him."

"Don't try to make this about all women or send me on a guilt trip."

"If you're feeling guilty, then maybe it's your own conscience." He walked toward the rear of her car and beckoned for Chloe to let her window down. "Good night, sweetheart. I'll see you this weekend."

"Good night, Daddy."

He walked past Savannah and headed for his car. "Good night, Savannah. Drive safe."

She stood there. She'd been dismissed, and she didn't like it one bit.

She drove home, her heart beating fast. Edward had a way of getting under her skin. She glanced into the backseat, gave Chloe a warm smile. Didn't want her daughter to notice that she was uneasy or angry. She bought Chloe a Happy Meal from McDonald's and headed home.

When she stepped into the house, it felt stuffy from the Florida heat. She walked across the shiny hardwood into the kitchen and opened a window to let in some fresh air. She loved the home. She and Edward had it built to their own specifications. The hardwood had to be raisin-colored, and the ceilings had to be yea high. Edward had been very specific about the dimensions of the backyard and the square footage of his man cave. Almost immediately after the divorce, his man cave had been transformed into her home office. She'd painted the walls a soft pink as a tribute to her heartache.

Chloe rushed upstairs to her room and Savannah pulled the last load of laundry from the dryer.

"Chloe!" Savannah called. "Chloe, come and get your sneakers off the stairs, please."

The phone rang as she made it halfway upstairs. She headed back downstairs to the kitchen to grab her phone. "Chloe! Your shoes."

"Mommy, can I have an ice cream, too?" Chloe stood in the doorway of the kitchen.

"Give me a minute," she said and picked up the telephone receiver. "Hello."

"Savannah," the caller whimpered on the other end.

"Nyle?" Savannah dropped the basket of clothes onto the tile floor. "What's wrong?"

"They put me out."

"Who?"

"My landlord. Put me right out onto the street. I have nowhere to go."

"What? Why would they do that?"

"I don't know, Savannah. Times have been hard. I missed a couple of payments. All I know is that all of my stuff is out on the street, and I have nowhere to go."

"What about Aunt Frances? Why don't you go there?"

"We don't get along very well. I've burnt my bridges with her. She won't let me stay."

"Maybe I can talk to her."

"I don't know, Savannah," said Nyle. "When are you moving here?"

"I'm working on it." Savannah sighed. "I need some time to wrap things up here."

"I'll be homeless by the time you get here."

"Maybe you can just come here for a while. I'll send you a ticket." Savannah thought that was a perfect idea. It would resolve her problems with Edward, and at the same time give Nyle a place to go.

"I can't. I have to live in London. It's my home," Nyle said. "It's why your father and I…our marriage didn't survive. He wanted me to live in the US."

"He wanted you to live in the US because it's where he was…where your child was."

"I know you blame me for leaving you, sweetheart. But he wouldn't allow me to take you."

Nyle's story suddenly sounded eerily familiar. Edward was giving her the same resistance that her father had given Nyle. Only Nyle was willing to leave without her daughter. Savannah wouldn't make that sacrifice. She wouldn't leave without Chloe. Of that, she was certain. She would fight him.

"I can send you money to help you get into a place. It's the best I can do."

"I just need a deposit and first month. After that, I can make it on my own. And I promise to pay you back as soon as you get here. I promise."

"I'll wire you some funds in the morning," Savannah said. "Do you have somewhere to go until then?"

"I'll see if my neighbor will let me crash on her couch for the night."

"Good. I'll talk to you tomorrow, Nyle."

"Kiss Chloe for me," she said.

"I will."

"I can't wait to meet her," Nyle said. "I'll talk to you tomorrow."

She was gone, just as she had always been during Savannah's life. She felt the emptiness and yearned for her mother's presence. Leaving Florida would tear her and Edward apart, but she needed to be in London—to right the wrongs of her past. She needed it like the air she breathed.

Chloe stood in front of her, sneakers in hand. She grabbed her daughter's face in her hands and kissed her forehead.

"Are you okay, Mommy?"

"I'm fine, baby."

She was all but fine.

Chapter 5

Edward leaned back in his chair as he was winding down his call. He spun around and gazed out the window at the view of the marina from his office. He quickly jotted down a few notes and then looked up. Quinn was standing in his doorway. He held his finger up to her and she gave him a smile. He admired her curves in the dress she wore. She was a beautiful woman with a five-foot frame, dark flawless skin, braids and the deepest of dimples.

Quinn had been his biggest fan, the cheerleader who supported his every venture.

He finished his call and then hung up.

"What's up?" he asked.

"We're all headed over to Bailey's for a drink. It's Martin's birthday. The big four-o. Can you believe he's that old?"

"Doesn't look a day over thirty-nine," Edward teased.

"You're coming, right?"

"I'm gonna pass. I have a lot to finish up here," said Edward. "And not really in a celebratory mood."

"Really? Why?"

"Just not feeling up to it today."

"You want to talk about it?"

"Not really. No."

"If you don't want to talk about it, then you have to at least come have a drink. It would be rude not to." Quinn smiled. "Come on, dude. I'm not taking no for an answer. Leave your car and I'll drive."

Edward contemplated her offer. The truth was, he needed to unwind. The entire work week had been trying. He was grateful for Friday, although his Monday morning hadn't gone well at all. He hated fighting with Savannah. He felt as if he needed to protect her, yet he was always hurting her. He was stuck in a hard place. He wanted her to be happy, but not at the cost of losing his daughter. She was all he had. Sure, he'd graduated from one of the most prestigious law schools in the country, Harvard. He'd been at the top of his class. He had practiced law at one of the top law firms and had almost won the mayor's office. He had a gratifying career as a council member and soon he'd make a decision to run for the senate. And although he'd failed at being a husband to Savannah, with fatherhood he'd been given a second chance to make things right. He wouldn't gamble with that.

"Fine. Give me like twenty minutes to wrap things up," he said.

"I'll meet you in the lobby in thirty."

Quinn had loved Edward from the moment they'd started working on his mayoral campaign. And he knew it. She had placed her own career on hold to support his. A paralegal in the prosecutor's office, she'd always been ambitious. It didn't surprise him one bit when she landed a job in the mayor's office. He knew that she loved him, but he never acted on it. He also knew that he would never love her the way she wanted him to. Not the way he loved Savannah. He would never commit to her. Not even sexually. He felt that a sexual relationship with Quinn, even after his divorce from Savannah, would violate everything he loved and honored. His reluctance only made her try harder, and having Edward in her life and her bed had always been her one ambition. But he kept things at arm's length. He enjoyed her friendship and never gave her any reason to think there would be anything more. In fact he'd always told her that he loved their friendship just the way it was; didn't want to tarnish it. He'd always made it clear that he wasn't interested in her that way, and he respected her too much to give her false hope.

His six-foot-two frame sank into the passenger's seat of her Mercedes coupe. He moved his seat all the way back and reclined. "Please drive the speed limit today," he warned.

"Excuse me. I always drive the speed limit." Quinn smiled and adjusted the volume on her music.

"And no rap today…"

Before he could finish his sentence, Nicki Minaj's vocals permeated the car. Obscenities drifted into the air as Quinn let the convertible top down and pulled out of the parking garage.

"Buckle up," she said and then zoomed down Okeechobee Boulevard.

When they stepped into the bar, their colleagues had already snagged a table near the window. John Palmer raised his glass into the air to get their attention. The birthday boy was on the dance floor with a tall, sexy woman. Dollar bills were pinned to his shirt. Quinn took a seat at the table and Edward made his way to the bar, where he ordered a round of drinks for his colleagues. At the table he began to feel the music and bob his head.

"We should dance." Quinn leaned in and tried to speak over the music.

"If it isn't Edward Talbot," Martin interrupted.

"Happy birthday." Edward gave him a strong handshake, ignoring Quinn's offer. "What are you, like fifty now?"

"Minus ten, bro," said Martin. "And I'm sensitive about it, so no jokes."

"You should be glad to see another year," Edward said. "What are you drinking?"

"Vodka tonic. And not the cheap stuff. I want top-shelf." Martin laughed.

"You got it."

"I'm glad you came out to celebrate with me. I feel pretty honored," Martin said. "Take a walk with me to the bar."

Edward excused himself and followed Martin to the bar. "What's up?"

"The election year is fast approaching. What are you doing about the Florida Senate race? Are you running or what?"

"I'm still undecided."

"You should run. You can win this," said Martin. "You should've won mayor. No doubt you were the most viable candidate."

"I appreciate that, but I'm happy in my current position."

"Should you decide to run, I'm willing to invest in your campaign. I'm there for you, like you were for me when I ran for city commissioner."

The mayoral campaign had cost Edward his marriage. He'd been gun-shy about running for any office higher than the one he held as city commissioner. His current position as city commissioner required less of his time and allowed him to spend more quality time with Chloe. He liked it that way.

"I appreciate the support," said Edward, "and should I decide to run, you'll be one of the first to know."

Edward's phone vibrated in his pocket and he pulled it out, looked at the display. Savannah was calling. He was happy to see her smiling face on the screen of his phone, because she certainly hadn't been smiling when he saw her in person. She'd had a change of heart, he hoped. Perhaps she was feeling a bit of sorrow—much as he was feeling about their last interaction. A reprieve was exactly what they needed.

"Excuse me, Martin. I need to take this," he said and then walked as far away from the music as he could get. He answered the phone. "Hello."

"Edward?" the sweet voice on the other end asked.

He could barely hear and decided to step outside the bar. He stood on the patio. "Hello. Savannah?"

"Edward, I'm at St. Mary's with Chloe."

"Oh my God! What happened?"

"Her asthma again. She was running a pretty high fever when I picked her up from school. She's been complaining of chest pains. So I brought her to the emergency room."

"Has she seen the doctor?"

"Not yet. We're waiting."

"I'm on my way," Edward said before hanging up.

Unfortunately, Chloe had battled with asthma for most of her life. It usually flared up in the spring when pollen was high in Florida. She suffered so much and so often that it broke his heart. And every incident and flare-up became more serious than the one before, and it devastated him that he couldn't fix it. He was her father, her protector, and he couldn't protect her from her illness.

As soon as he hung up the phone, it dawned on him that he hadn't driven. He found Quinn and appealed to her to drive him back to his car.

"The hospital is closer," Quinn said. "I'll just take you there."

Edward wanted to protest. The last thing he wanted to do was show up at St. Mary's with a woman Savannah had accused him of seeing for years. But Quinn had been correct. The hospital was a closer drive, and he needed to get to Chloe as quickly as possible. He hopped into the passenger seat of Quinn's convertible and she drove him to the hospital. She pulled into an empty space in the parking lot.

"Do you need for me to wait for you? Or come inside?"

"No. I'll be fine."

"You want me to come back and pick you up?"

"No, I'll manage. It will probably be late. I'll just grab a taxi."

"You sure?"

"Absolutely. I'll be fine." He opened the car door. "Thanks a lot for driving me."

"Call me if you need me," she said.

Edward walked into the emergency waiting room. When he didn't see Savannah and Chloe, he inquired at the front desk and was informed that she'd just gone back to see the doctor. He was allowed to join them. Savannah looked frantic and defeated, but her eyes lit up when she saw Edward. He went straight for Chloe and kissed her forehead.

"Hi, Daddy," she weakly said.

"What's going on with my favorite girl?" he asked.

He'd always called Savannah his favorite girl, too. He hoped the comment would get under her skin.

"I don't feel good," Chloe whined.

Savannah cleared her throat. "The doctor thinks it might be asthmatic bronchitis. They're going to do a test called Spirometry test, which will measure her lung function."

He nodded and acknowledged her statement, but didn't really look her in the eyes; he was too embarrassed about their last conversation and still a bit angry. He took note of how beautiful she looked in her two-piece blue business suit, but tried to keep his attention focused on his daughter.

Hours passed before they received the results of Chloe's Spirometry test that confirmed that she indeed had asthmatic bronchitis. The doctor handed Savannah a prescription and gave Edward a strong handshake. They were given instructions on how to care for Chloe and then sent on their way. It was late, and Edward felt exhausted as they took the silver elevator down to the first floor.

"Where'd you park?" Savannah asked.

"I actually left my car at the office. I caught a ride over from the bar with a coworker. We were celebrating Martin's birthday," said Edward. "I'll just grab a taxi."

"Do you need a ride?" Savannah asked.

"Would you mind?"

"No. Not at all." She pulled her keys from her purse. Held them in her hand. "I'm right out front."

"I don't want to take you out of your way, so you can just drop me off at home. I'll take a taxi into the office in the morning," Edward said. "Besides, you need to get this one home as soon as possible. Get her to bed."

"We have to fill her prescriptions first."

Edward climbed into the passenger seat of Savannah's practical four-door sedan. It was one that she'd purchased after their breakup. He'd offered her the family SUV after they'd parted, but Savannah had complained that she wanted something a little more economical.

"That Lincoln Navigator, although very nice, is a gas guzzler. I want something that gets good gas mileage—a nice little Toyota or something." She was the levelheaded one and way more practical than Edward. She'd kept him grounded. It was what he loved about her.

They'd traded the Navigator for a fully loaded Toyota.

She toyed with the buttons on the stereo until she found something mellow. She seemed nervous. She and Edward had become friends and co-parents for Chloe over the years, but it had been a long time since they shared such a small space together. He tried to lighten the mood by commenting on her music.

"What is it we're listening to?' he asked, and then switched to a hip-hop station.

"Who listens to that?"

"Normal people." He smiled and then looked out the window.

They stopped by the drugstore, and soon Savannah pulled up in front of Edward's home. Waited for him to step out of the car.

"Daddy, I'm hungry. Can you make me your special soup?" Chloe asked before her father exited the car. "It'll make me feel much better."

Edward gave Savannah a knowing grin. "It's really late, baby. Mommy can grab you some soup on the way home."

"Please, Daddy," Chloe sang. "I want *your* soup."

"What do you think?" Edward asked Savannah.

"I don't know." Savannah was hesitant.

"Please, Mommy," said Chloe.

"She's pretty convincing," Savannah stated, and put the car in Park. "I guess it'll be okay. Your soup is pretty easy to make."

"I have all of the ingredients here," Edward said. "I just need you to cut up the papaya for me. If you don't mind."

She'd always helped Edward prepare his papaya soup— a Bahamian recipe that he'd prepared on many occasions. It was Chloe's favorite, and Savannah's, too.

"Okay, Chloe." Savannah sighed. "But then we're going home and getting you medicated and in bed."

Edward stepped out of the car first and opened the back door for Chloe to hop out. He picked her up and she wrapped her legs around him. He carried her to the front door. Savannah locked up the car and followed. Something inside Edward felt joy that they were staying. Maybe he would have an opportunity to talk to Savannah about London again, and this time he'd convince her to stay or at least consider leaving Chloe with him.

Chapter 6

Savannah chopped the papaya while Edward sautéed onions and melted butter in a saucepan. Caribbean music drifted through the air. She could count on one hand the number of times she'd entered Edward's home, and never past the living room. She'd picked Chloe up from there a few times and was always careful not to invade his space. In particular, she didn't want to run across a loose earring or a pair of women's panties. She usually stayed in her place.

"Care for a glass of wine?" Edward asked Savannah.

"Sure."

He turned the fire down low and then opened a bottle of Riesling. Poured two glasses and handed one to Savannah. After cutting the papaya, she took a seat at the kitchen's island and sipped on wine. She watched as Edward combined the ingredients of his soup together. As it simmered, he took a seat across from her.

"Aside from Chloe's trip to the ER, how was your day?" he asked.

"It was going pretty smoothly," she said. "It changed everything when I found out that my baby was sick."

"I know what you mean. My heart sank when I got your phone call."

"I knew you'd want to know that she was sick."

"Thank you for calling me."

"I'll always let you know what's going on with her. You're her father, and I know that you love her."

"I love her very much."

"How was *your* day?" Savannah changed the subject before Edward brought up the move.

"It was a pretty good end to the work week."

"So it's Martin's birthday." Savannah smiled. "I like Martin. He's a good man."

"He is a good man," said Edward. "He offered to help with my campaign should I decide to run for the senate."

"Are you considering it?"

"Somewhat."

"That's good." Savannah took a long sip of her wine. "Why the hesitation?"

"Chloe, of course," he said matter-of-factly. "I'm aware that a campaign might take up too much of my time, and I want to make sure she's my priority."

Savannah wanted to say that with Chloe moving to London, he'd have more time on his hands to pursue his political ambitions, but she avoided any conversation about London. The mood was very casual and friendly. She didn't want to bring up anything that would start an argument. Instead of responding, she just nodded.

"I'm not keeping you from anything, am I?" he asked. "Did you have plans tonight?"

"Yeah, Chloe and I had plans to watch *Sofia the First* for the umpteenth time. Then I planned on watching her fall asleep and I'd be watching it by myself." Savannah laughed.

"Yeah, I've seen *Sofia the First* more times than I'm

willing to admit. And I also won't admit that I actually liked it." Edward laughed and then went to the stove, stirred his soup. "I think it's ready."

Edward pulled three ceramic bowls from the shelf. Ladled soup into each one. He placed a bowl in front of Savannah. "Taste."

Savannah took the spoon and scooped a spoonful into her mouth. Closed her eyes. "Mmm. Just as I remember."

Edward grabbed a spoon, put it into her bowl as if it were a perfectly normal thing to do and tasted the soup. "Not bad."

"I'll go get Chloe." Savannah put down her spoon. She hopped down from the bar-height island stool and went into the den.

Chloe lounged on the sofa and was sound asleep. She considered waking her, but decided against it. Her daughter seemed too peaceful. She walked back into the kitchen where Edward was already enjoying a bowl of papaya soup.

"She's asleep, huh?"

"Yes. And I didn't want to wake her."

"Let her sleep," he said. "Sit down and enjoy your soup."

Savannah did as Edward suggested. The two of them ate soup and enjoyed light conversation. When they were done, they cleaned the kitchen together.

"It's late. We should probably get going," Savannah said.

"Yes, it is late, and I don't like the idea of you two driving around West Palm Beach at this hour. Why don't I tuck Chloe into her bed, and the two of you just spend the night? Go home in the morning." Edward suggested.

Savannah wanted to protest. Not because she didn't want to stay, but she needed Edward to know that she wasn't the passive young girl that he remembered from before. She had changed. She was a strong woman now, with a mind of her own, and she wouldn't give in to his every whim.

"No, we're going to go." She stood her ground.

"Do you really want to load Chloe into the car and then unload her when you get home?" he asked. "She's asleep, and not to mention she's sick."

He had a point.

Savannah exhaled. "I suppose it would be easier to stay here, get a good night's sleep."

"I have fresh bedding and could prepare the guest room for you."

Initially, Savannah thought the evening would be awkward, considering she and Edward were in the middle of a battle. Not to mention, she'd just filed a petition to take Chloe out of the country. The papers would arrive at his office on Monday. She contemplated the drive home and decided that spending the night would be a wiser choice.

"Fine," she said.

Edward carried Chloe to her bedroom, and Savannah followed. She found pajamas in the chest of drawers and undressed Chloe, while Edward disappeared down the hall to prepare the guest room for her. She tucked her daughter beneath the covers, kissed her. Edward stepped back into the room, pulled the covers up to Chloe's chin.

"Good night, sweetheart," he said.

"Good night, Daddy."

"You missed the soup," he told her.

"I'm sorry, Daddy, but I was really sleepy," she said.

"Well, get some sleep, and we'll have breakfast in the morning."

"Are you spending the night, too, Mommy?"

"Yes." Savannah gave her daughter a warm smile. "I'll be in the room right down the hall if you need me. Okay?"

"In Daddy's room?"

Savannah glanced over at Edward, who had a light smile in the corner of his mouth. "No, baby, in the guest room."

"Okay," said Chloe. "Good night, Mommy."

"Good night, baby. I'll see you tomorrow." Savannah stood, kissed Chloe and followed Edward to the door.

Edward turned off the light and pulled the door, leaving it cracked a little.

"You can sleep in Daddy's room if you want," Edward teased.

"No thanks," Savannah said, and playfully rolled her eyes.

"Your bed is ready, then…whenever you're ready for it," he said. "Can I get you a T-shirt or something to sleep in?"

"Sure. That would be nice."

Edward disappeared into his bedroom and returned with his favorite Harvard T-shirt.

"Thanks. I remember this shirt. It's a little faded," she teased.

"It's gotten a lot of use," he smiled. "You should feel honored that I let you wear it."

"I do. Nobody's ever been allowed to touch this shirt. I wasn't even allowed to wash it with the other laundry back in the day." She giggled, took the shirt and headed toward the guest bathroom to put it on.

"That's right! And you should handle it with care," he said.

"I will." She gave him a wink before popping into bathroom.

In the small powder room, she took a curious peek into the medicine cabinet. She wasn't sure what she was looking for, but felt the need to be nosy. Wondered if she'd find an extra toothbrush or evidence that someone had been there for any length of time and left something behind. It was exactly what she'd avoided before, but suddenly her curiosity got the best of her. The cabinet was virtually empty, with the exception of a small bottle of Tylenol. She grabbed a washcloth from the linen closet and washed her face, then stared at her reflection in the mirror for a moment. Her day had been long, and her evening with Chloe at the emergency room had been trying. Spending the night at Edward's place wasn't the norm, but the thought of driving home after her rough day had been an exhausting thought. She was grateful for his offer, but wouldn't get too comfortable. She just needed to get through the night, and then she'd be on her way in the morning.

She walked past Edward's master bedroom. The light was on and the door was ajar. She took a quick peek as she crept past. His room was immaculate with a masculine-looking comforter on the king-size bed. She remembered that Edward had always been a neat person. It was one of the things that they shared in common. She never had to clean up behind him. His California king bed was neatly made, and everything seemed to be in its rightful place.

She wanted to catch the news before retreating to the guest room for the night, so she made her way into the den area. Edward, wearing a pair of pajama bottoms and a crisp white T-shirt, lounged at one end of the sofa, the remote control in his hand.

"Oh, I'm sorry. I didn't know you were still up. I wanted to catch the news before I turned in. If you don't mind," Savannah explained.

"I don't mind at all. I always watch the news myself before bed," said Edward. "I still have trouble sleeping."

"Still?" She plopped down at the opposite end of the sofa.

"I'm up way past midnight every night and then up at the crack of dawn every morning. I usually get less than six hours."

"That's not very healthy. Particularly for a man who is more health-conscious than anyone I know."

"It's not healthy, but it's my reality." Edward stood. "I'm going to have another glass of wine. You care for one?"

"Sure," she said.

He disappeared into the kitchen and then returned with an open bottle of wine and two glasses. He handed her a glass and poured wine into it. She curled her feet beneath her bottom, made herself at home.

"What a trying day," she exclaimed as she took a sip of wine, then leaned her head back and sighed.

"Chloe gave us quite a scare with that high fever."

"I was pretty scared when I received the phone call from her school. She's my baby."

"Mine, too," he reminded her. "After the divorce...you know...well, she's all I have."

"I know how you feel about your daughter, Edward." She wanted to clear the air, address the elephant in the room. "And I'm not trying to hurt you by taking her away. I'm just trying to do something for me—something to make me happy for a change."

"I get that, Savannah," he said. "I don't like it, but I get it."

"I've put my life...my dreams on hold for so long. It's my time."

"I get it. It was all about me...always. My career destroyed our marriage, robbed us of our family. If I could go back and change it, I would."

Savannah was shocked by his words. She'd never heard Edward admit that he was wrong—let alone that he would change his actions if given a chance. After she'd filed for divorce, he had begged her to stay, but she'd always been convinced that he only begged because he thought it was something that a man should do. That she had bruised his ego. That a breakup would blemish his political ambitions.

"What would you have done differently?" She was really curious.

"It wasn't a good time for me to run for mayor, I admit. Not as a newlywed with a pregnant wife. I would have waited until our marriage was more mature, able to handle the campaign."

"I could've been more understanding," she admitted. "You were certainly young and ambitious. I was just so damn insecure."

"You were beautiful. *Are* beautiful. What would you have to be insecure about?"

"For starters, I weighed a ton when I was pregnant." She giggled.

"You were beautiful when you were pregnant."

She blushed at his comment, but said, "Your campaign manager was slim and beautiful, and very much into you."

"Quinn?"

"Yes, Quinn." She said, "Don't act like you're surprised."

"She was my friend. Still is."

"And in love with you! Don't forget that part," said Savannah. "She had more access than me. And I was jealous of her. She had more of you than I did."

"She was the last person you needed to worry about."

"But I did. I worried."

There was an awkward moment of silence.

Edward looked her square in the eyes. "I'm sorry."

"It's okay. Water under the bridge." She stood, finished her wine and placed the glass on the coffee table. "Now we have Chloe, and she's our focus."

"And we have to do what's in her best interest. Whatever that is."

"And we will."

"If you leave with Chloe, my life will be empty," he said. "And not just because Chloe's gone. But you. Truth is, I'll miss you, too, Savannah."

Tears almost welled in her eyes. She headed out of the room before he saw her vulnerability. She needed to be strong. "Good night, Edward."

He sighed. He was losing her already, just when he'd gotten her to open up. "Good night."

Savannah made her way to the guest bedroom. She shut the door securely behind her and stood with her back against it. For the first time in years, those old feelings had returned—myriad emotions of love, anger, jealousy and fear. She felt confused. She had long moved on since their breakup, but couldn't understand what she was feeling at that moment. She had used her father's home in Savannah, Georgia, as her refuge—a place to heal and get over Edward—and she thought she had.

After graduating from art school in Georgia, she'd landed a job in Florida, and decided that it was time to move back to Florida and face Edward again. Her daughter needed a father and she wanted to make their co-parenting work. She had even found romance again—with a man who promised her the world. Though he wasn't Edward, whom she was still madly in love with, she accepted his proposal of marriage. She wanted a better life for Chloe and for herself. And even though it hadn't worked out with him, she was sure that she had recovered from Edward. Until now.

She walked over to the bed, pulled the covers back. She shut off the light and climbed into bed. She just needed to get through the night. Tomorrow she and Chloe would go back to their normal life—the place where she could rid herself of whatever it was she'd just felt after her conversation with Edward. She closed her eyes tightly and prayed for sweet dreams, not the ones that used to haunt her so many nights before.

Chapter 7

Edward flipped the wheat pancake and browned the other side. He checked on the turkey bacon that sizzled in the oven. He warmed maple syrup in the microwave and cut up fresh honeydew melon and pineapple into chunks. The kitchen table was set for three. He was determined to surprise Savannah and Chloe with breakfast. He hoped that he could make up for upsetting her. She'd obviously been bothered by their conversation the previous night. He'd made so many mistakes with her. He knew that he had gotten it all wrong before, but he wanted to make things right. And hopefully, in the process, he could convince her to stay in Florida.

The part of Savannah's heritage that was white and black Caribbean was the part that had always connected with Edward. Her mother was a white Londoner and her father's ancestors had hailed from the Dominican Republic. Their Caribbean roots had transcended all. From the moment Edward saw her, he knew he would make her his wife. He wanted her. He loved her. But he was young—and life had become overwhelming. Though his father,

Paul John Talbot, had been the perfect role model, Edward had completely ignored his teachings. The signs were all there—that his marriage was ending—but he didn't see them. Not until Savannah had completely relocated to Georgia with their infant daughter. And even then, he thought she was being unreasonable and was confident that she would return home soon. It wasn't until he was served with an order for divorce that the reality hit like a ton of bricks. His marriage was over.

He should've fought harder, made more sacrifices, but he was cocky—blamed her for everything. She should've been more understanding of his career, of his need to succeed. Didn't she know that everything he did was for their family? Yet it hadn't been enough. In his mind, she'd been the selfish one, ungrateful even. He had regretted every moment since then. Everything he thought she'd been, time had proven him wrong.

"Good morning." Savannah was completely dressed in the business suit she'd worn the day before. The strap of her purse securely on her shoulder and keys in hand, she stepped into the kitchen. "Chloe's getting dressed. We're headed home."

"But I cooked breakfast. At least stay and eat."

Savannah looked around at all that he'd prepared and seemed to contemplate his offer.

"Please. Be a shame to waste all of this food," said Edward.

"Okay. We'll eat, but then we have to go."

Savannah placed her purse in the empty chair and took a seat at one of the place settings. Edward brought piping-hot food over to the table and placed it in the center. Chloe came into the room. She wasn't her usual bubbly self as she gave her father a hug.

"Good morning, sweetheart," Edward said, and picked his daughter up. "How do you feel?"

She laid her head on his shoulder. He took a seat at the table, placed her on his knee.

"She's still feeling a little crappy," Savannah explained.

Edward touched her forehead. "She's still warm, too."

"I just gave her some Tylenol," Savannah said.

"Daddy made pancakes," Edward said. "Aren't you hungry?"

"No. I just want to lie down."

"Maybe she should just stay here," said Edward.

"She has a bed at home."

"I know she has a bed at home, but she has one here, too." Edward stood. "I'm going to tuck her back in."

Savannah sighed as he stepped out of the kitchen. He carried Chloe to her room and placed her in the bed, removed her shoes from her feet. Her head hit the pillow and she immediately closed her eyes. He kissed her forehead and pulled the covers over her. When he returned to the kitchen, Savannah had begun to make her plate.

"I have to get home, shower and change. Maybe I'll come back and pick her up a little later."

"Leave her. She's fine," Edward said. "Why don't you go home and grab some more clothes. Come back. We can fire up the barbecue grill later, cook some fish…"

"I don't know about that, Edward."

"I need to be near her. But I can't take care of her by myself when she's sick. I need your help."

Savannah cut her pancakes into little squares, and placed two pieces of turkey bacon on her plate. "Okay. I'll come back. But just for the night. We have church in the morning."

"Excellent." He sat down at the table across from her and made himself a healthy helping of pancakes and fruit. He looked forward to her return.

With a baseball cap placed backward on his head and a chef's apron tied around his waist, he took a quick sip of his Heineken beer. Edward carefully flipped the thick fillets of mahimahi on the grill.

"So you two are just going to sit there lounging while I slave over a hot grill?"

"I made the fresh lemonade." Savannah smiled. Her legs were crossed and stretched across the lounge chair as she took a sip from her glass.

"And I helped Mommy." Chloe sat on the lounger next to her mother.

"Yes you did, sweet girl." Savannah toasted her glass against Chloe's plastic Doc McStuffins cup.

"Well, maybe you can come over here and help your dad cook this fish," said Edward.

Chloe giggled, and Savannah did, too.

"Oh, you think this is funny?" Edward placed the spatula down next to the grill and made his way over to Chloe, picked her up and slung her over his shoulder. He raced around the yard with her as she laughed heartily.

"Mommy, help me!" she exclaimed.

Savannah laughed and raised her glass in the air.

"Mommy can't help you now, kiddo." Edward continued to race around the yard. Then he placed Chloe into Savannah's lap. "Here, Mommy, help your daughter!"

He was beside himself with joy. He had his two favorite girls in one place for an entire evening and it felt good. He stepped into the house and grabbed a casserole dish to place the fish on. Went into the living room and found some music on his iPad. He played his Caribbean playlist and turned the volume up so that they could hear it in the backyard.

He peeked his head out the back door and asked Savannah, "Would you like a glass of wine?"

"I'd love one," she said.

He poured her a glass of Chardonnay, handed it to her.

"I would like a glass of wine, Daddy," said Chloe.

"And you will get one. In about twenty years." Edward laughed. "But until then, would you like another cup of lemonade, madam?"

"Yes," Chloe groaned.

He stepped into the kitchen. When his cell phone lit up, he walked over to the counter where it lay charging. He noticed a text message from Jack.

Call me when you have a minute. I have some news to share.

He made a mental note to call Jack once his phone was fully charged, poured Chloe a cup filled with lemonade and stepped back outside. The evening couldn't have been more perfect, with mild weather and palm trees blowing in the wind just before sunset. He glanced at Savannah lounging in her chair and noticed how beautiful she looked. Dressed in a pair of capri pants and a strapless shirt, her bare feet gave him the indication that she was comfortable.

"They're playing our song," he said to her.

As the lyrics of Gregory Isaacs's "Stranger in Town" drifted through the air, Edward remembered a time when he and Savannah loved each other.

"I love that song," she stated.

"Dance with me," he said.

"Edward, I don't feel like dancing…"

Before she could finish her protest, he'd already pulled her up from the lounger.

The two of them moved to the music, just as they had so many times before. He grabbed her hand and spun her around. He placed his hands on her small waist and got lost in the Caribbean rhythm that would forever be their song. As he pulled her close, he took in the moment.

While the nighttime drew near, the three of them enjoyed mahimahi and vegetables on a candlelit patio. Edward and Savannah laughed about the good times and told Chloe funny stories. After the mosquitoes began to bite, Savannah helped him take dishes into the house.

"I'm going to help Chloe get her bath," she told Edward. "She had a good afternoon, but she's feeling a little warm again."

"Okay, I'll finish cleaning up here."

Savannah and Chloe disappeared while Edward loaded dishes into the dishwasher. After he placed leftovers into plastic containers, he went into the living room. He found some soft music. Then he turned the television on ESPN, but muted it. He collapsed onto the leather sofa. Savannah returned and took a seat at the opposite end of the sofa, just as she had the night before. She wore a two-piece pajama set—a silky button-up shirt with matching shorts. Edward found it difficult to peel his eyes from her. The scent from whatever she'd bathed in caressed his nose.

Savannah stretched her feet onto the leather sofa. Edward moved closer and placed her feet on his lap, began to rub them. He squeezed her arches, heels and toes. She leaned her head back against the back of the sofa, closed her eyes. He knew she enjoyed the feel of his fingertips between her toes; she always had. He rubbed her ankles and then moved up to the calves of her bare legs.

"I remember those foot rubs, sensual and wonderful," she whispered.

He moved closer, placing her long legs in his lap. His fingers brushed against her face, caressed her chin. His breathing changed and his nose touched hers.

"I've missed you," he whispered.

She was silent, just stared into his eyes. He leaned in for her lips.

"Mommy." Chloe's voice startled them. She climbed onto the sofa, plopping herself between them.

"What's the matter, sweetheart?" Savannah asked.

"I can't sleep," Chloe whined. "Can I stay in here with you and Daddy?"

"Of course you can, baby." Edward said it, but wished his daughter's timing hadn't been so wrong.

He gathered himself, got his hormones under control. He hoped that once Chloe had fallen asleep, he could pick up where he left off with Savannah. He wanted to kiss her lips so badly. He tried not to let his desires overshadow his daughter's need to be near them. He tuned the television to the Disney Channel and gave Savannah a smile.

Soon Chloe's head rested against his chest, her eyes tightly shut.

"I think she's asleep," he whispered to a sleeping Savannah.

He carefully carried Chloe to her bedroom, tucked her into bed. When he returned to the den, he gently touched Savannah's shoulder. "Savannah," he whispered.

Her eyes opened slowly. "Yes."

"Why don't you go on to bed?"

She gave him a smile and then headed for the guest bedroom. Edward turned off the music, the television and the lights and headed to his bedroom. He took a quick shower and tried to rid himself of thoughts of his ex-wife

and what he'd wanted to do with her before he was interrupted. He slipped into a pair of pajama pants, climbed
into bed. He lay there in the darkness wondering what
would have been had he kissed Savannah. The time he'd
spent with her had been pleasurable, and he was grateful
for it but didn't know where it was leading, if anywhere.
She was leaving the country soon. However, he couldn't
help thinking that he'd never stopped loving her. A wave
of familiar emotions suddenly flooded in, and he wondered if she'd ever stopped loving him.

Sunday morning, and Savannah had obviously forgotten all about church because she was still there, and still
wearing those sexy silky pajamas. He tried not to stare,
but couldn't help wondering what it would feel like if he
slipped his fingertips beneath those silky shorts. Thoughts
like that had plagued him all night, and he hadn't been
able to shake them.

By the afternoon, the trio had found themselves strolling
along Jupiter Beach. Edward lifted Chloe onto his shoulders.
Savannah carried a picnic basket filled with California rolls, a
fresh garden salad, a bottle of chilled wine, and a small bottle
of fruit juice for Chloe. After finding the perfect spot, they
stretched their oversize beach towels out onto the sand. Edward opened the bottle of wine with a corkscrew and poured
it into wineglasses. Then he opened the bottle of fruit juice
and handed it to Chloe. It was these times that he missed
with Savannah—simple Sunday afternoons on the beach,
away from the static of the world. The beach was where he
and Savannah had planned their lives together—their next
steps, their wedding.

After stopping by Savannah's for a change of clothing
and picking up Edward's car from his office, they ended
up at his home again. He didn't know how he did it, but

he'd managed to convince her to spend yet another night. Chloe rushed into her bedroom, and Savannah took her business suit and overnight bag to the guest bedroom. Edward headed for the shower to wash the sand from his legs and feet.

The weekend had been enlightening. It felt good to have his family underneath one roof, even if it was short-lived. He began to toss the what-ifs around in his head. What if he could convince Savannah to stay in the country? What if he could have her back in his life, his home, his bed? What if he had never lost her in the first place? He washed his hair and his chest before stepping out of the shower.

As Savannah stood in the kitchen cutting into the flesh of a watermelon that they'd picked up at the market, Edward crept up from behind, wrapped his arms tightly around her waist. He planted a trail of kisses onto her neck. He hoped he hadn't overstepped his bounds, but he needed to feel her in his arms. She turned to face him, wrapped her arms around his neck. His lips touched hers, and he kissed her shamelessly. Finally and deeply.

"I've wanted to do that all weekend," he whispered.

"And I've wanted you to."

Edward's emotions and hormones ran rampant. There were so many things he wanted to say, but didn't know how to put them into sentences. Instead he just held her close. Besides, it was too soon for her to know all the things he'd been thinking—it was best to keep his thoughts to himself. She didn't need to know that he had thought of her every single day since she'd left, and had actually contemplated ways of winning her back. She didn't need to know that he had beat himself up about losing her, and that he hadn't found anyone who made him feel the way she had. He had managed to find something wrong with every single beautiful woman who had crossed his path, and he hadn't understood why until now. His hand moved from the center of her back and caressed the roundness of her behind.

She pulled away from his embrace.

"What's wrong?" he asked.

"Too much, too soon." She wiped his kisses from the corners of her mouth in a slow downward motion.

"I'm sorry. I just thought…"

"I'm going to check on Chloe," she said and then left the kitchen without another word.

Edward exhaled, leaned his back against the granite island. He'd blown it with her—been too hasty. He'd been thinking with the wrong head.

Chapter 8

"What the hell do you mean, you spent the weekend with Edward?"

"Shhh." Savannah pressed a finger against her lips, a wide grin on her face. She walked around her desk and shut the door. "I don't want everyone in the entire office to know."

When Maia first met Savannah in art school, she was going through the divorce with Edward. Maia had been the one to observe her during the most vulnerable time of her life.

"What was that about?"

"Chloe was sick, and we were caring for her...*together.*"

"What else were you doing *together*?"

"Nothing!" Savannah couldn't help blushing.

"You're lying," said Maia. "Girl, you are blushing."

"No seriously. Nothing happened."

"Not even a kiss?" Maia asked.

Savannah smiled. Averted her eyes from her friend's.

"You kissed him!" Maia laughed. "Savannah, what is going on? Just last week you were taking his ass to court because he was giving you a hard time about leaving the country with Chloe."

"I know," said Savannah.

"Now you're playing house with him?" Maia asked.

"It was unexpected. Chloe got sick. Edward showed up at the hospital. He needed a ride home. Things just sort of happened."

"You still love him, don't you?"

"I'll be the first to admit that I have unresolved feelings for Edward. I need closure if I'm ever going to move to London."

"Well, you won't get closure by spending the weekend at his house. You're setting yourself up. He had his chance with you, sweetie, and he blew it. I say chalk it up as a loss and move on."

Savannah paced the floor. "I've been thinking. Maybe I can pull back the petition…just for a little while."

"Oh no," Maia groaned.

"Just temporarily…"

"Haven't you already filed it?"

"Yes, but if I call the courthouse, maybe I can intercept it before Edward is served today."

"Savannah!"

"I'm not saying that I won't file the petition. I just want to hold off until…"

"Until what, honey? Until he breaks your heart again?"

"You're being so cynical."

"I'm a realist. I'm that friend who tells you the truth when others won't." Maia stood, walked toward the door and opened it. She quickly switched the conversation. "So are we doing Chinese for lunch or what?"

"Chinese is fine." Savannah searched the internet for the phone number of the Palm Beach County Courthouse.

"Fine," Maia said. "And Savannah…"

Savannah was busy jotting the phone number on a sticky note.

"Savannah Carrington!"

"Yes, Maia."

"Just be careful, honey." Maia held both hands over her chest.

"I will." Savannah gave Maia a gentle smile, one that let her friend know that she need not worry.

As soon as the door was pulled shut, Savannah picked up the phone and dialed the phone number. She attempted to work her way through the teleprompts to get to a live person, and quickly grew frustrated and impatient. Didn't they know she'd had a change of heart? The weekend with Edward had been unexpected, and caused her to rethink things. He'd kissed her with those soft, delectable lips that she remembered all too well. He'd wrapped those strong arms around her so tightly, and his tongue had explored the inside of her mouth causing a tingle between her thighs. She'd wanted him, but her good sense told her to run away.

After being placed on hold for the third time, she hung up the phone. Holding the receiver against her chin, she flipped through the internet again.

After a light tap on the door, Jarrod walked in without invitation. "Are you free for lunch?"

"Plans with Maia."

"Cancel them. We're celebrating."

"Celebrating what?"

"Are you serious right now?" he asked.

She *was* serious. And distracted. She didn't have time for Jarrod's riddles. And he was becoming increasingly annoying.

"I'm serious, Jarrod. And I'm really busy right now," she said. "So if you don't mind…"

He moved closer, came around to her side of the desk.

He grabbed the telephone receiver from her hand and hung it up.

"It's my birthday," he said softly.

"Oh, Jarrod. I completely forgot." She smiled. "Happy birthday."

He grabbed her and pretended to dance to imaginary music.

"Let's go dancing after work." His lips brushed against her earlobe.

She didn't even see Edward as he appeared in her doorway. By the time she saw him, he was standing on the opposite side of her desk. He threw a yellow envelope onto her desk.

"I was served with your petition today. At my office of all places," he said. "I guess you're still going through with this…this ridiculous idea of moving to London and taking Chloe with you."

"Edward… I…" She pulled away from Jarrod's embrace.

"I hope you're happy!" He said, "It sure looks like you are."

"This is not what it looks like, Edward."

"I don't really care. I just care about my daughter. If you want a fight, I'll give you one. I'll see you in court!"

She plopped down and sank into her leather chair. She was speechless. She'd had a change of heart, at least for the moment—only Edward didn't know it. Their weekend together had somehow penetrated her soul, had her reconsidering her idea of moving away. She'd spent the entire night thinking about Edward and wondering if there was any hope of reconciliation. But now…

"Jarrod, I know it's your birthday, but I'm sorry, I can't have lunch with you today. Or go dancing with you this evening."

"Are you seeing him again?"

"No."

"Because I know how much he hurt you before." Jarrod moved to the other side of her desk and went toward the door. "I wouldn't want him hurting you again."

"You don't have to worry."

"Good. I'll take a rain check on lunch and dancing." He pointed a finger at her. "This time."

She exhaled when he finally left and pulled the door shut behind him. She covered her face with both hands.

Zumba was a challenge, particularly since exercising was the last thing that Savannah wanted to do. But she was committed to the class. She danced to the sounds of Pitbull as she attempted to keep up with her energetic instructor. She and Maia had splurged on fried chicken instead of Chinese food for lunch, and she needed to burn the extra calories.

Maia grinned at Savannah and wiggled her behind to the music.

"Snap out of it, chica!" Maia yelled over the music.

"I can't. I'm torn."

"You said it yourself. Your mother needs you, and it's time you did something for yourself anyway. Isn't that what you said?"

"I know it's what I said, Maia, but it's not that simple now."

"It *is* that simple. Edward had his chance to have his family around, and he threw it all away for a campaign that didn't even pan out."

"He could've won," Savannah defended him. "In fact he only lost by a small margin."

"Defensive, aren't we?" Maia giggled. "Had he kept his focus on the campaign and not on that beautiful little campaign manager, things might've turned out different."

Savannah ignored Maia's comments and continued to sway her hips to the music. She'd thought the same thing in the past—that Edward and Quinn had been much too close for her comfort, but she would never admit it to Maia.

Savannah tossed her gym bag over her shoulder as she bid Maia a good-night. "I'll see you tomorrow, girl."

"Take care, Savannah." Maia, with a pink baseball cap backward on her head, waved and headed toward her two-door coupe.

Savannah sat in the driver's seat of her Toyota, checked her cell phone for missed calls. Edward had called and then texted—I'm sorry about barging into your office today. I was out of line.

"Apology accepted." She didn't hesitate to call back and tell him that. "Edward, I'm sorry. I tried calling the courthouse to at least delay the petition."

"Have you had a change of heart?"

"I don't know what my heart is feeling right now, but until I'm sure, I want to delay it."

"Listen. This weekend I'm headed to the islands. It's my parents' wedding anniversary, and they're having this big celebration at the Grove. My parents would love to see Chloe…and you, of course. You know they still love you very much…" he said. "Anyway, you don't have to give me an answer now. Sleep on it, and let me know sometime this week."

Savannah was silent. Didn't know what to say. He'd caught her off guard.

"Okay."

"I think it would be a great opportunity for Chloe to see my parents before the two of you head off to London…if that's what you decide to do."

"Edward, I…"

"Just think about it and let me know."

She didn't need to think about it. She'd already made

her decision, but she told him, "I love your parents. I'll let you know."

"Great. Sooner is better so that I can purchase tickets."

"I'll sleep on it. Call you in the morning."

She would make him sweat, at least for the night. And tomorrow she'd go shopping for a party dress for her former in-laws' anniversary party.

Chapter 9

As the jet soared above the clouds, Chloe closed her eyes and held on tightly to Edward's hand.

"We're almost there, baby."

He glanced over at Savannah. Her head was leaned against the back of the seat, and her eyes were closed tightly also. He suddenly remembered her fear of flying as well. He reached over Chloe and touched Savannah's shoulder. She opened her eyes and gave him a warm smile. He massaged her neck and shoulder and tried to help her relax. He held on to both of them until the wheels of the jet finally hit the pavement.

The Bahamas was a beautiful eighty-six degrees, and Edward breathed in the fresh smell of the ocean. He loved his home and visited frequently. The three of them sat in the backseat of a taxicab as the driver took them to his family's B and B. As the car pulled up in front of the Grove, Edward pulled twenty-five dollars in Bahamian currency from his pocket and handed it to the driver. He usually held on to his Bahamian dollars for his frequent visits to the islands.

"Thank you, sir," he told the driver before ushering Savannah and Chloe out of the vehicle. "Keep the change."

"Thank you," said the Bahamian driver as he popped the trunk and assisted with their luggage.

Savannah admired the architecture of the historical homes that had been transformed into a B and B. There were three of them, lined along the ocean right there together. She thought they were beautiful and elegant, and she couldn't wait to see the inside. Edward struggled with their bags.

"Well, well, well, if it isn't Edward Talbot," said Jasmine as they approached the lobby. "Oh my God, Savannah, is that you?"

"Jazzy!" Savannah gave Edward's sister a strong hug.

"You look so gorgeous, as always." Jasmine smiled genuinely. "And who's this little lady? This can't be little Chloe!"

Edward hugged his sister. "This is Chloe. Chloe, say hello to our Aunt Jasmine."

"Call me Aunt Jazzy."

"Hi, Aunt Jazzy," Chloe said softly.

Jasmine, with her long natural hair and perfectly sized body; it was no wonder she'd snagged a few modeling gigs while living in L.A. She grabbed Chloe in her arms and kissed her cheek. "You're so pretty. I don't think I've seen you since you were in diapers."

Savannah remembered the time that Edward's mother and sisters had come for a visit, just a few days after she'd given birth to Chloe. They'd been helpful—preparing meals, cleaning house and changing soiled diapers. They'd kept a watchful eye on Chloe while Savannah slept. It was during that visit that she'd fallen in love with them.

Although Edward traveled back and forth between the islands on business, he hadn't had a chance to take Chloe along. He'd had intentions of it, but the time never seemed right. He regretted not allowing her to connect with his family, but now was as good a time as any.

"It's been such a long time, Jazzy. So good to see you. You look great."

All of Edward's sisters had been fond of Savannah. They all loved her like family, and that hadn't changed with the divorce. In fact, Edward had been concerned that if he'd brought someone new home, he'd have trouble with the women in his family.

"Where is everybody?" Edward asked.

"Alyson and Samson are flying in from Miami later tonight. Nate got in last night. Whitney's flying in from Texas tomorrow morning, and Denny will be here tomorrow night. That's everybody."

"Great. Everyone will be here for the celebration," said Edward. "Where are our quarters?"

"I have you set up in the Symonette Room," Jasmine said.

"And Savannah?"

"Oh, you're not sharing quarters?" Jasmine smiled.

"No," Savannah interjected. "Chloe and I will need a separate room, thank you."

"Oh, I wasn't aware of that. I'll have to check and see if we have an extra room available. We're pretty tight this weekend."

"Are you kidding? I told you I was coming," Edward said.

"Right! You told me that *you* were coming." Jasmine walked over to the front desk, logged on to the computer. "Just give me a second."

"This is a bit inconvenient," Savannah whispered to Edward. "Perhaps Chloe and I can bunk at your parents' home."

"She'll find us something," Edward assured her. "Don't worry."

Jasmine looked up from the computer. "I don't have one single room available, guys. I'm sorry. Everything's booked for the entire weekend."

Edward sighed. "You and Chloe can take the Symonette Room. I'll bunk at my parents' for the weekend."

"I can try to find you a rollaway bed, big brother. How about that?" Jasmine asked.

Edward shrugged. "I'm going to stay at our home in Governor's Harbour."

"The Symonette Room is one of our more spacious rooms. And it has the best view. Quite romantic, too." She cleared her throat. "Should be plenty of space for the three of you."

"I'm sure my old room at home will do just fine." Edward gathered the luggage.

"Okay, suit yourself." Jasmine moved from behind the desk, reached her hand out to Chloe. "And you, young lady...how about you come with me? I spotted some ice cream in the freezer earlier today. Would you like some?"

"Yes!" Chloe exclaimed.

"And we'll have to do something about this hair." Jasmine ran her hand across Chloe's thick mane. "Maybe some plaits."

"That would be nice," Savannah said, laughing. "I don't know what to do with Chloe's hair! It's just a thick bush."

"It's okay. Auntie Jazzy will take care of it." Jasmine grabbed Chloe's hand and headed for the kitchen. "Let's go for ice cream."

Savannah and Edward climbed the wooden, refinished stairs to the Symonette Room.

"I'm sorry that I won't be staying on Harbour Island with you and Chloe for the weekend, but I'll be just a phone call away. I swear this wasn't preplanned. I thought Jazzy understood that we would need separate rooms."

"It's okay. We'll make the best of it." Savannah walked over to the window and took in the view. "Very nice. This place is awesome. It's much more than I'd imagined."

"I can't take the credit. Jasmine and her husband, Jackson, spearheaded the entire project."

"It's so hard to believe that Jazzy is married now. I still see her as your baby sister. She's all grown up."

"And Jackson is a good man. He's one of my best friends, so I don't have to worry about her."

"Good." Savannah smiled. "Because we all know that you're a worrier."

"I'm not a worrier, I just like to protect the people that I love."

"You can't save everyone," Savannah said.

"I'll sure try," Edward said. "I think we should head over to Governor's Harbour to my parents' house. I'm sure they're anxious to see Chloe."

"I'm sure they are," said Savannah. "I just need to freshen up a bit."

"Fine. I'm going to walk the property a bit and visit with Jazzy. Just let me know when you're ready."

"Okay, I'll meet you in the lobby."

Edward's childhood home smelled of Bahamian spices. He loved coming home. Although he enjoyed living in Florida, there was nothing like his home on the islands. A place where he and his five other siblings were reared. Edward was born in Key West, but the family moved to Eleuthera when he was a small boy. His parents moved to the islands to care for his ailing grandfather.

Edward, the oldest of the bunch, was a precocious young man. His father, Paul John, had hopes that his oldest son would follow in his professional footsteps and study medicine, but Edward had plans of his own. He was more interested in law and politics and had already immersed himself in an upcoming local election by the time he'd graduated from Harvard. Changing the laws was just as dear to Edward's heart as being a father.

Edward and his siblings had inherited three historical homes from their grandparents, which had been transformed into the B and B on Harbour Island. Even after the Grove was completed and operational, Edward still had no intention of moving back to the islands to help run it. However, he'd been instrumental in the renovation and obtaining funding for the family's business. He was happy that his sister Jasmine had taken a lead in making the Grove the extraordinary property that it was. It had quickly become one of the most sought-after properties on Harbour Island, which was why there weren't any vacancies for his weekend visit with Savannah and Chloe.

"Where is everybody?" Edward asked loudly.

"Oh my goodness, Edward Talbot! You're here." His mother, Beverly, rushed from the kitchen wiping her hands on the end of her apron. "Oh, my! Who is this little young lady?"

Beverly Talbot was an older version of Edward's sister, Whitney, with medium brown skin and a slender body that didn't represent that of a middle-aged woman. Wisdom hid behind those eyes, and her smile was the same one that Edward owned.

"This is Chloe." Edward grinned with pride. She'd been his greatest achievement. "Chloe, give your grandmother a hug."

"Oh, you're just so precious." Beverly gave the girl a tight squeeze. "And Savannah, you're just as pretty as I remember."

Savannah embraced Edward's mother. "Hello, Mrs. Talbot. So good to see you."

"I believe you used to call me Mother. That still works just fine for me." Beverly placed her hand on Savannah's cheek. "So, the three of you will be staying here, yes?"

"No, Mother, just me," Edward interjected. "Savannah and Chloe will be staying at the Grove."

"What!" said Beverly.

Paul John Talbot came into the room wearing a pair of dingy coveralls and carrying a wrench. "I heard the voice of a little person in the house."

"Pop, what are you fixing on now?"

"Bathroom sink is clogged," Paul John stated. "And you must be Chloe. They told me they were sending someone to help me with the plumbing. Are you the help?"

Chloe grinned and shook her head no.

"No? You mean you don't know how to fix the bathroom sink?"

Chloe shook her head again.

"Well, then. I guess I'll have to do it myself." He pretended to walk away and then turned back to Chloe. "Can you fix anything?"

"Um." Chloe placed a finger against her cheek. "My Barbie's arm came off one time and I fixed it."

"Well, there you go! That qualifies you to fix a sink then."

Chloe shrugged her shoulders. "Okay."

"Say hello to your grandfather, Chloe," said Edward.

Paul John gave his granddaughter a handshake, then turned to Savannah. "Good seeing you, Savannah. I'd hug you, but I'm much too dirty."

"Good seeing you, too, Mr. Talbot." Savannah giggled.

"You all must be hungry," Beverly said. "Come on into the kitchen and get something to eat."

Savannah and Chloe followed Beverly into the kitchen, while Edward took his bags down the hall to his old bedroom. The room was just as it always was when he visited home, with fresh linen on the bed and his favorite chocolates in a candy dish on the dresser. He opened the drapes and let some sunshine in, unpacked his bag. When he finished he made his way into the kitchen where Savannah and Chloe were scarfing down fish and grits.

"Where's Nate? Jazzy told me he's here," Edward said to his mother.

"Nate's already up and running about the island. You know he's not one to sit still for too long."

"Right. He might be at the beach catching some waves on his board."

"Maybe," Beverly said. "Why don't you sit down and have a bite to eat, son?"

Edward didn't waste any time fixing a plate and sitting down at the kitchen table across from Savannah. He listened while she chitchatted with his mother, and suddenly his mind wandered. He wondered how he had allowed Savannah to slip away. His mother had always had her opinions about everyone, but she'd loved Savannah genuinely. His entire family had embraced her in the past, and it was clear that she was still very dear to them. Even his sister Alyson, who was fond of very few people, loved Savannah.

"Is anybody home?" the voice in the living room asked, and then Alyson appeared in the doorway of the kitchen. She'd lost a few extra pounds since Edward had last seen her. Marriage had done her well. Though she struggled with her weight, she was still just as beautiful as all the Talbot women. "You're all in here feeding your faces!"

"Hello, dear. We didn't hear you," Beverly said.

"Obviously." Alyson walked over and kissed her mother's

cheek. "Oh my goodness, Savannah! You look fabulous. What are you doing here? You and Edward back together again?"

Savannah stood and gave Alyson a strong hug. "It's good to see you, Alyson. And no, we're not."

"Did I miss something, big brother?" Alyson blew Edward a kiss.

"You haven't missed anything. I just wanted everyone to see Chloe...and she's been a little under the weather, so I invited Savannah along to help me look after her."

"Didn't you get married recently?" Alyson asked Savannah.

"No," Savannah said sweetly. "I was engaged, but things didn't quite work out for us."

"Well, that must've been good news for you, big brother." Alyson grinned at Edward and then turned to Savannah. "He was beside himself with grief when he thought another man was going to take you away. Showed up on my doorstep."

"Alyson!" Beverly exclaimed. "Behave."

"What, Mother? You know it's true." Alyson kept going. "I thought I was going to have to give him a sedative."

"You just don't know when to quit, do you?" asked Edward.

Alyson rolled her eyes, ignored his question. "And this must be my beautiful niece."

"Yes, this is Chloe," Savannah stated.

Alyson squeezed Chloe's shoulders.

"Where is my brother-in-law?" Edward asked. "He needs to come and get you under control."

"From what?" Alyson giggled. "Samson's getting our bags out of the car."

"I'm right here!" Samson exclaimed. "Is she misbehaving again?"

"As always." Edward stood and gave Samson a strong handshake. "Good to see you, bro."

"Likewise," said Samson as he moved around the table to Beverly and kissed her cheek. "Mother, good to see you."

Beverly placed her palm against Samson's face. "Are you hungry?"

"Famished, Mother."

Beverly shook her head and looked at Alyson. "You have to feed this man, dear."

"Samson knew I was a busy woman before he married me," Alyson said.

"So because you're busy, he can't eat?" asked Edward. "Is that what you're saying?"

"Mind your business, Edward," Alyson warned.

"Like you minded yours earlier?" Edward asked.

"It's certainly not that she can't cook," Beverly said. "I taught them all very well."

"It's that she won't," Edward mumbled.

"Okay, okay," said Alyson. "It's true. I don't cook that often. However, Samson is a pretty good cook himself, so we get by."

Edward ignored Alyson and turned to Samson. "Samson, this is Savannah, by the way. Savannah, meet Alyson's husband, Samson. I honestly don't know how he puts up with her."

"Pleased to meet you." Savannah giggled and reached her hand out to Samson. "I didn't know that you got married, Alyson."

"Yeah, it wasn't a big to-do. Just a little justice of the peace type of thing."

"She refused to do it the right way. She knows the Talbots are a celebratory bunch," said Beverly. "We were looking forward to a big to-do."

"You know I don't like making a big fuss of things. Spending all sorts of unnecessary money."

"We can still have that beautiful ceremony…whenever you want, Alyson," said Samson.

"No need." Alyson grinned and held her hand out to show Savannah her ring. "This rock is beautiful enough."

"It is. Very beautiful." Savannah smiled. "Congratulations to you both."

Alyson waved her hand in the air to brush off the sentiment.

"Thank you," Samson interjected. "A pleasure meeting you, Savannah."

"And this is our daughter, Chloe," Edward said.

Chloe was a mixture of Edward and Savannah, but more Edward. She had his smile and his long, slender frame. With thick hair and bright, inquisitive eyes, she had the ability to charm everyone around her.

"Well, aren't you beautiful." Samson smiled and then took Chloe's small hand in his, kissed the back of it. He removed his fedora from his head, turned to Alyson. "I'm going to drop the bags in our room. Can you fix me a plate?"

"Yes, can you at least fix the man a plate?" Edward instigated. "And I'd like a cold beer while you're headed that way."

Alyson groaned, but then gave Samson a gentle smile. "Of course, sweetheart."

When she handed Edward a beer, he smiled. He loved being at his childhood home. He glanced at Savannah and Chloe. There was nothing more important than family.

Chapter 10

Contemporary Caribbean music and laughter filled the Talbot home. Edward crossed one leg over the other, reclined in the easy chair in the corner of the room and took a sip of his wine. Denny peeked his head in the screen door, a wide grin on his face.

"Oh my word!" Beverly exclaimed. "What are you doing here?"

"I can leave if you'd like." Denny gave his mother a wicked grin and then removed his duffel bag from his shoulder and set it down.

"Get in here, boy!" Beverly demanded. "I didn't even know you were coming."

"I thought I would surprise you. That's why I swore Jazzy to secrecy." Denny hugged his mother tightly and kissed her cheek.

"And she was able to keep that secret?" Edward asked.

"I guess so. Mother didn't know I was coming."

"Good to see you, young man!" Edward grabbed his brother in a headlock.

"Hello, Savannah." Denny gave her a warm smile while

being playfully choked by Edward. "Surprised to see you here."

"Hello, Denny. I can't believe you're all grown up now." Savannah sat on the sofa next to Chloe, her hand resting beneath the bowl of her wineglass. "You were just a young boy the last time I saw you."

"Are you and this old guy back together?"

"No!" Edward and Savannah said it in unison.

"Okay! I was just trying to figure out what was going on here." He moved from Edward's grasp and then turned to Chloe and smiled. "You must be Chloe. I'm your Uncle Denny."

"Hi," Chloe said softly.

Denny turned to his oldest sister. "Alyson, good to see you."

"You're not AWOL, are you?" Alyson asked with a raised eyebrow.

"Of course not." He kissed his sister's cheek and then shook Samson's hand. "I'm on leave."

"Good to see you, Denny," said Samson.

"Hey, Pop." Denny hugged his father, after which he went back to the door and opened it just a bit wider. A young woman followed him inside. "Everybody, this is Gabrielle. Gabby for short."

"Hi." Gabby was dressed in military fatigues, her hair in a ponytail and a cap on her head. She gave the family a slight wave of her hand.

Everyone was too shocked to speak.

"Hello, Gabby." Paul John Talbot was the first to say something and shook her hand.

"Does Sage know that you're home?" Alyson asked Denny about his high school sweetheart, the girl he'd vowed to marry as soon as he returned from boot camp.

"I haven't spoken with her," Denny said nonchalantly.

"Have you introduced Sage to Gabby?" Alyson continued.

"No, Alyson, I haven't!"

"It's very nice meeting you, Gabby," said Beverly Talbot. "Why don't you come in and have a seat?"

"So, obviously you're on the force, too," Edward stated. "Did you train with the navy SEALs as well?"

"Yes, sir, I did," Gabby said.

"Sir?" Edward said. "She called me sir."

"Because you're old," Denny said. "She's respecting her elders."

"Watch it, boy."

"Gabby's from San Diego, California," Denny exclaimed.

"You're a long way from home, aren't you?" Alyson asked. "How did you wind up in the Bahamas, and with my baby brother…who is engaged?"

"You're engaged?" Gabby turned to Denny.

"Not anymore," Denny stated, and then through clenched teeth said, "Alyson, please."

"You're not engaged to Sage anymore?" Beverly asked. "When did that change?"

"I haven't quite told her." Denny became uncomfortable. He grabbed his brother by the arm. "Edward, can I see you in the kitchen for a minute?"

Edward followed Denny into the kitchen.

"Are you telling me that you haven't broken things off with Sage?" Edward whispered.

"I didn't know how to tell her in a letter or over the phone that I'm seeing Gabby now," said Denny.

"I have to tell you, you did that all wrong, boy!" Edward said. "You can't bring a new girl home when you haven't told your old girl that she's been dumped. I thought you loved Sage."

"I do… I mean I did." Denny rubbed his head in frustration. "It's just that I finally got away from the Bahamas for the first time…and there were just so many options."

"Girls everywhere, huh?" Edward smiled.

"Everywhere! Have you seen Gabby?"

"She's cute," Edward admitted. "But Sage is a good girl. She deserves to be treated so much better. She at least needs to know that she's been replaced. You should know better."

"You're judging me?" Denny asked. "The way you treated Savannah?"

"I admit, I wasn't the best husband. But I regret losing her. There! I said it," Edward admitted. "I regret losing her. I needed to hear myself say it aloud."

It was the first time he'd admitted it to someone other than himself.

"You're serious? You still love Savannah."

Edward shrugged his shoulders. Didn't admit or deny loving Savannah. "All I know is when you find a good woman, you should do everything in your power to keep her."

Denny sat at the kitchen table, frustration on his face. "Gabby has so much to offer. She's beautiful, ambitious…"

"Sage is just as beautiful. Maybe not as ambitious, but the grass isn't always greener on the other side, Denny," said Edward. He patted him on the shoulder. "You got your hands full, boy."

"What should I do?" he asked, and grabbed Edward, who was trying to leave the kitchen.

"I don't know. What do you want?"

"I want them both."

"Boy, you're losing it," Edward said. "This is a recipe for disaster."

"I know." Denny sighed.

"If I were you, I'd go rescue Gabby. Your sister can be a beast."

"You're right." Denny stood quickly and rushed into the living room where Alyson had already started giving Gabby the third degree.

Edward shook his head and hoped that his brother made it out of his predicament unharmed, but he wasn't confident that he would. He took a look at his watch. "I think I should get you and Chloe back to the Grove," he told Savannah.

Savannah smiled and stood.

"I'll drive you to the water ferry," his father offered.

"Thanks, Pop. That would be great," Edward said as he leaned in and kissed his mother's cheek. "I'll be back shortly. Just want to get these ladies to their room safe and sound."

"Should I wait up?" his mother asked.

"No. Don't worry too much. I'll call you when I'm headed back," he promised.

"Fine. I'll save you some coconut cake."

"That would be nice."

He gave his brother one final cautionary glance before walking out onto the front porch.

At the Grove, he carried Chloe up the stairs. Her head rested against his shoulder. She'd fallen asleep on the short drive from the water taxi to the Grove. Savannah unlocked the door to their room and Edward gently laid Chloe onto the queen-size bed. He removed her shoes and then kissed her forehead. He stepped out onto the balcony and gazed at the stars. Savannah followed.

"It's a beautiful night," he told her.

"It is. And this is a beautiful place. Thank you for inviting me," she told him.

"My pleasure."

"It was so good seeing everybody."

"They all still love you very much."

"And I them." She smiled at him. "Poor Denny. What's he going to do with two women?"

"What do you mean, poor Denny? He got himself into this mess." Edward chuckled. "And now he's got to figure his way out of it."

"He's young and foolish," she said.

"Yes! He's going to learn the hard way what it means to lose someone he loves. He'll regret it for the rest of his life."

"You sound like an authority on the matter."

"I am." He looked at her. "I lost you."

For a brief, uncomfortable moment she was silent, and he wished she would say something.

"I think we both sort of lost each other," she finally resolved.

His fingertips brushed against her face and he moved closer, waited for her to stop him, but she didn't. He wrapped his arms around her shoulders, pulled her into him. His nose gently touched hers, and then his lips kissed hers. She wrapped her arms around his waist, caressed his back. As the waves from the ocean crashed against the shore, his tongue danced against her mint-flavored mouth.

He still loved her. He knew it, and so did the universe.

Chapter 11

Savannah opened her eyes and noticed the moonlight as it reflected against the wall. Edward's arms were wrapped tightly around her waist, and she breathed in his cologne. His chin rested against her neck as light snores escaped from his lips. He'd fallen asleep right there, and she moved closer into him, snuggled closer.

They'd talked until the wee hours of the morning until they were both too tired to continue the conversation. They talked about what their relationship had been and where they'd both gone wrong. They'd become reacquainted in a matter of hours. Conversations like this one had never occurred in their marriage. He'd been too busy nurturing his career. And she'd given up on them much too soon. He'd needed her more than she ever knew.

After they'd both grown tired of talking and gazing at the stars from the balcony, Edward decided to stay on Harbour Island.

"It's late, and the water ferry isn't running any more tonight. Maybe I can just crash in that chair in the corner," he'd said.

"Or maybe you can just snuggle with us here in the bed. There's plenty of room," Savannah had suggested.

And so he did. He'd kicked his Dockers casual shoes from his feet and stretched across the bed. She'd taken a quick shower and changed into a pair of knit pajamas with the shortest of shorts. When she came back into the room Edward had removed his shirt and was relaxed, eyes closed as he listened to Caribbean music on his iPhone. She climbed into bed between him and Chloe. He smiled and then turned off the lamp. She'd rested her head against his chest, and he held her tightly.

Now she was awake, taking in the moment. She felt safe in his arms—as though she still belonged there. As though she had never left them. She closed her eyes, pulled his arms tighter around her and intertwined her fingers with his.

Morning came suddenly, it seemed, and she felt alarmed as if she'd overslept. She felt the empty bed next to her. Edward was gone, and so was Chloe. When they both came through the door carrying breakfast—a tray filled with an omelet, fresh fruit and a glass of freshly squeezed orange juice—Savannah sat up in the bed.

"What is all of this?" she asked.

"We brought you breakfast, Mommy!" Chloe exclaimed.

"Yes, you did," Savannah said. "It looks delicious."

"Raquel cooked it," said Chloe.

"Raquel?" Savannah glanced at Edward.

"The Grove's cook." He set the tray on her lap. "She's the best."

"Aunt Jazzy was downstairs, too," Chloe said. "She's taking me shopping and to the market today."

"Oh, she is?" Savannah smiled at her daughter.

Edward interjected, "I told Jasmine it was okay to spend the day with Chloe. Are you okay with that?"

"Of course."

"Good. Because I thought you and I would go sailing. My cousin Stephen has a powerboat and I have something I want to show you," he said. "So eat up and then get dressed."

Savannah smiled at the thought of a surprise. She noticed that Edward was wearing fresh clothing. "You changed clothes."

"Pop brought my suitcase over this morning."

"Well, that was sweet of him," said Savannah. "Your father is a gem."

"The apple doesn't fall far from the tree," Edward boasted.

"You're right." Savannah smiled, then had a sip of her orange juice, took a forkful of her omelet. "I'll be quick."

They traveled across the ocean as Edward's cousin Stephen steered his powerboat, *Sophia*. He was quite fond of her, and used her to transport tourists back and forth across the ocean. It was how he made his living—giving people memorable experiences. And when Edward had called him for a favor, he was happy to oblige. She liked Stephen. He had a gentle spirit with a bright smile. She thought he would've been a perfect catch for her friend Maia. Someone to tame her. It was their first time meeting, but before long, he and Savannah seemed like old friends.

Savannah took in the beautiful turquoise waters. She could actually see the rainbow of fish species as they swam beneath the clear water. She reclined on the leather seat in the port of the boat, while Edward relaxed in its bow and chatted with his cousin. The wind brushed against her face, and her shades shielded her eyes from the sunshine.

She wore a two-piece yellow bikini underneath her mesh cover-up. A smile danced in the corner of her mouth as she watched Edward.

She took in the curve of his chin and his strong jaw. Those lips that she'd spent the evening kissing only hours ago. His strong arms that had wrapped tightly around her as they gazed at the moon from their ocean-side patio. Her heart had fluttered, something that hadn't happened since the first time Edward's lips met hers—long before they were married. Back then she'd fallen for him quickly and hard. They were both hopeless romantics. It was another thing they had in common.

Stephen started to navigate the boat to shore, toward a private island in the middle of nowhere.

"Where are we?" Savannah asked.

"My little hidden jewel." Edward gave her a wide grin.

"You mean my little hidden jewel," said Stephen.

"Can I just have this moment, please?" asked Edward, and then with a lowered voice said, "I'm trying to impress the lady here."

Stephen lifted his hands in surrender and then turned to Savannah. "It's his little hidden jewel."

"Well, whomever it belongs to, it's beautiful." Savannah smiled.

Stephen dropped an anchor to steady the boat and then climbed out. He assisted Edward as he disembarked from the boat. Edward grabbed Savannah by the waist and lifted her out. She pressed her body against his to balance herself, and her face met his for a moment. Her feet gently touched the sand, and he let her go. Edward grabbed a backpack and a red cooler from the boat and carried them to shore.

"Follow me," he told Savannah.

"I have a family that I need to pick up and take back to

Harbour Island. I'll be back shortly," said Stephen. "Enjoy your time here."

"Okay, man," Edward said.

"He's leaving us?" Savannah asked as she rushed to catch up with Edward.

"We'll be fine." The confident Edward grabbed her by the hand.

She followed, her nerves easing just a little bit more with each step. Edward's confidence was one of the things that she loved about him. He had the ability to allay her fears.

Seagulls tiptoed along the island's coast and thousands of little baby crabs played hide-and-seek in the sand. Edward grabbed wood and placed it on an old grill, started a fire. He pulled fresh fish, lobsters and shrimp from the red cooler and placed them on the grill. He chopped fresh onions, potatoes and mangoes and seasoned them with a Bahamian rub, then placed them on the grill. He set the cooler on an old picnic table.

"Where did you get all of that?"

"Stephen is a diver and caught the fish. He bought the lobster and shrimp at the market."

"Wow, that's impressive," she said. "I should definitely introduce him to Maia someday."

"Your snooty friend Maia?"

"She's not snooty," said Savannah. "She's okay."

"She's not his type. She hates men."

"She doesn't hate men."

"Okay, correction. She hates me," Edward said.

"She's just protective. That's all."

"Okay, whatever," Edward said as he removed his sunglasses from atop his head, pulled his T-shirt off and placed them on the picnic table. He slipped flip-flops from his feet. "Now, while that's cooking, let's go for a swim."

Savannah found herself staring at his arms, chest and abs. Edward had always been in great shape, and the most attractive man she knew. She felt a tingling between her thighs and willed her eyes to look somewhere else.

"Ready?" he asked.

"Not really." Savannah tiptoed across the sand. "There are baby crabs everywhere."

"It's okay, they won't harm you. But just in case..." Edward lifted Savannah into his arms, cradled her and carried her toward the ocean. He picked up his pace and began to run.

"What are you doing?" She laughed and held on to his neck. "Oh my God!"

"Relax." He laughed, too.

"Don't dunk me!" she warned. "I'm not kidding, Edward."

"I'm not going to dunk you." He grinned.

"I mean it! I just got my hair done."

"I'm not going to dunk you."

He placed her gently in the water and she planted her feet just below the surface. She removed her cover-up and tossed it into the sand, walked out into the ocean until the water covered her midsection. Edward rushed into the water with a splash, went for a swim. He crept up behind Savannah and grabbed her. She turned to face him. He picked her up and she wrapped her legs around his waist. She could feel his hardness between her thighs, and it turned her on. She missed him and felt safe in his arms. He held her close and danced about in the water.

They played in the water and laughed. It was natural being with Edward. As if they had never missed a beat— as if divorce had never entered their lives. They stared into each other's eyes.

"Better go check on the food," he whispered.

"Right." She gathered herself and hopped down from his waist.

The two of them headed for the grill, where Edward flipped the seafood with tongs. He pulled a bottle of wine from the cooler and placed it on the table along with two wineglasses. He opened the wine and poured Savannah a glass, handed it to her.

"Here you go, madam," he said. He pulled two disposable plates from the cooler and placed grilled seafood, potatoes and vegetables on each one. "One for you and one for me."

"It smells wonderful."

"I know how much you like seafood. So I cooked all of your favorites."

"Thank you." She blushed.

She took a seat at the table, and Edward sat across from her. They ate and sipped Chardonnay. Edward found soft Caribbean music on his phone.

"So how many women have you brought to this private island and romanced their panties off?"

"What?" Edward laughed and choked on his wine. "This is my first time here."

"You seem to know your way around all too well for it to be your first time."

"It was a carefully thought-out plan to impress you," said Edward. "Is it working?"

She smiled. "I have to admit that I'm quite impressed."

He reached across the table and held on to her hand. "I'm glad."

After dinner, they both cleaned up the mess. The sun began to set and Edward spread two large beach towels on the sand. They sat there facing the ocean. Savannah pulled her knees into her chest and closed her eyes. It was a beautiful night, she thought.

"Thank you for coming to the Bahamas with me. It meant so much for my parents to see Chloe."

"Thank you for inviting us," said Savannah. "This place is gorgeous. This little private island of yours...the one you've never been to before."

"I swear." Edward moved closer. "You're so beautiful."

He reached for her waist, and his lips found hers. She would've pulled away, but she couldn't will her body to move—and her lips defied her. His hand caressed her smooth, silky legs. He lay on his back and then pulled Savannah on top of him. His hands rested against the roundness of her butt. His fingertips found their way beneath the fabric of her bikini bottom, dipped into the sweetness between her thighs. She moaned. His kiss took her breath away. His tongue danced against hers.

He flipped her over onto her back and removed her bottoms. She didn't fight it. Couldn't. He kissed her belly button, then moved down and kissed her inner thigh. His tongue danced inside her, and her toes curled. She remembered the way he'd kissed her there in the past—remembered all too well. His mouth moved upward and nibbled on her breast through the fabric of her bikini top. He loosened the string from around her neck and removed her top, placed her nude breast into his mouth. It sent electricity through her.

He pulled her legs open with his knee and moved his lips back up to her mouth. He removed his trunks with one hand, and when he sprang free, he placed himself inside her. Savannah breathed deeply with the first thrust. She moaned and took in every thrust thereafter. She'd missed him so much. Hadn't found any man who made her feel the way Edward had. Her body shook with desire, and then his. She resisted her urge to cry, couldn't understand why she was so emotional during that moment. He was making

her weak again when she'd worked so hard to be strong—
to remain in control. She was slowly losing it.

They lay in the sand until they finally saw the lights
from *Sophia* in the distance.

"I guess we should get dressed," Edward whispered.

"I guess we should," said Savannah.

She sat up and searched for the pieces of her bikini. She
glanced out into the ocean. Didn't want to leave.

Chapter 12

Stephen tied a rope from the cleat of the boat to the dock. Edward climbed out of the boat and then helped Savannah out. He held on to her small hand, a slight grin on his face. He was gaining control of their awkward situation. His goal was to romance her until she no longer wanted to move to London, or at least until she'd agreed to leave Chloe with him. She was playing into his plan. His chest stuck out, his jaws tight. She was just about where he needed her to be.

"It was a pleasure meeting you, Savannah," said Stephen. He gave her a gentle smile. "I can't wait to meet little Chloe. I hear she's adorable."

"It was a pleasure meeting you, too, Stephen. And I'm sure you'll see Chloe before we leave the island."

Stephen hugged and kissed her cheek. He gave Edward a thumbs-up behind her back. Savannah had managed to charm every one of his family members.

"Okay, let's get out of here. Get over to the Grove and pick up Chloe. I'm sure that Jazzy is ready for a break."

"I bet she is, too," Savannah agreed. "Chloe can be a handful."

"I'll see you both at your parents' anniversary party to-morrow night." Stephen gave Edward a strong handshake. "Love you, bro."

"Love you, too," Edward said. "And thank you for today."

"Always." Stephen hopped back into the boat.

Edward and Savannah slid into the backseat of a taxi-cab, headed for the Grove. He watched her as she stared out the window, reminisced about their afternoon together.

"Are you okay?" he asked.

She gave him a light smile. "Yes."

"Any regrets?"

She shook her head no. "You?"

"None."

As the cab pulled next to the curb, Edward stepped out and walked around to Savannah's side of the car and opened her door. He reached for her hand and she stepped out. He handed the driver a Bahamian bill and the two of them walked into the Grove.

Edward peeked his head into the kitchen. "Hello, Raquel," he greeted the Grove's cook.

"Hello, bebby. How are you?" she asked in her Baha-mian accent.

"I'm great. Have you seen my sister Jasmine and her little sidekick?"

"Oh, you mean Miss Chloe?" She giggled. "The two of them left about an hour ago. Jazzy said she was headed home to Governor's Harbour."

"To my parents'?"

"Yes."

"Okay, thanks, Raquel."

"Can I fix you and the missus some supper?" she asked.

"That would be nice. Maybe something light. Thank you."

"I think there's some conch salad in the fridge. Can I fix you some?"

"That sounds wonderful," said Edward as he pulled his cell phone out to call Jasmine.

He stepped away from the kitchen.

"Yes, Edward," Jasmine answered on the second ring.

"What's up?" he asked.

"We're on Governor's Harbour," Jasmine said.

"Are you coming back, or do you want us to come there and pick up Chloe?"

"Leave her. She's in pajamas and watching movies with her uncle Nate. She would be disappointed if she had to leave now."

"May I speak with her?"

"Of course," she said, and then yelled Chloe's name in his ear. "Here she comes."

"You couldn't hold the phone away instead of yelling in my ear?" Edward asked.

"Sorry." Jasmine giggled. "Did you have a good time with Savannah today?"

"It was okay," he tried to appear nonchalant about the evening.

"Do I hear wedding bells?" Jasmine asked.

"What? No!"

"Are you telling me that it's completely out of the question?"

He looked at Savannah, who was hanging on his every word. "I'm telling you that I'd like to speak with my daughter, please."

"Here, sweetheart. It's your daddy," he heard Jasmine say.

"Hi, Daddy." Chloe's voice was music to Edward's ears.

"Hello, sweetheart. What are you doing?"

"I'm watching a movie with Uncle Nate," she explained. "Can I spend the night? Grandpa promised me hot chocolate and pancakes in the morning."

"Wow. Hot chocolate *and* pancakes? Who could say no to that? Let me just see if it's okay with Mommy." Edward gave Savannah a glance. She nodded a yes. "Mommy says it's okay."

"Yay!" Chloe exclaimed.

"Now, let me warn you… Grandpa's pancakes probably aren't as good as Daddy's…"

"Stop it." Savannah laughed.

"…but you should still be polite and eat them all up," Edward continued. "And tell him how good they are."

Chloe giggled. "Okay, Daddy."

"Mommy and I will see you in the morning."

"Okay, Daddy. I love you."

"I love you more," Edward said.

"Tell her I love her, too," Savannah whispered.

"Mommy loves you, too," Edward said.

"Love you, Mommy!" Chloe exclaimed. "Daddy, can you give her a kiss for me?"

"I certainly will." He glanced over at Savannah and winked.

He'd give her a kiss, but not the kind that Chloe referred to. His kiss would mean something different. He became aroused at the thought of it. As much as he wanted to believe that the afternoon had been about convincing her to change her mind about taking Chloe to London, he knew there was much more going on in his heart than he was willing to admit.

They feasted on conch salad and conch fritters while relaxing in the cabana. Edward leaned back in his chair and took in the light Bahamian breeze. He sipped on a Bahamian beer, while Savannah drank her second sky juice.

"That's my mother's favorite drink, you know. Sky juice," Edward stated. "She drinks them more often than I'd like her to."

"I can see why. They're delicious," said Savannah. "Never had one before."

"Careful. They sneak up on you," Edward said.

"Wouldn't you love for that to happen?" Savannah flirted.

"Do you think that I took advantage of you on the beach?"

"Didn't you?"

"I thought we were two consenting adults, enjoying each other."

"It was very emotional for me," Savannah admitted. "It's been a long time since we…you know…have been together. The setting was perfect and it was just so damn romantic!"

"So had there been a less romantic setting…"

"I think it was inevitable, no matter the setting." He knew that she was becoming inebriated. "I was drawn to you from the beginning."

"From the beginning of what?" Edward laughed. He knew that he shouldn't discuss these things with her while under the influence, but he found satisfaction in knowing her true feelings.

"Since the beginning of time, silly. I've loved you and wanted you since the moment I met you. That never changed."

Edward was startled by her announcement.

"You divorced me!" he stated.

"Because you didn't have time for us—me or our daughter. And because of Quinn."

"She's never been more than a friend, Savannah. I swear to you."

"You said that," she proclaimed. "I just never felt like Chloe and I were your priority."

They were flirting with danger by discussing such a painful time. The Bahamas was not the place for old wounds, and this was not the time. He wasn't willing to move backward after he'd made such strides.

"Maybe we should go upstairs, and I'll run you a hot bath."

"Maybe we should," Savannah agreed.

She stood and stumbled. Edward rushed to her side, grabbed her, and escorted her back inside and up to her room. He gently placed her on the bed. He went into the bathroom and started the water in the bathtub. When he came back into the room she was struggling to remove her shoes. Finally kicked them to the floor.

"You okay?" he asked.

"I'm fine." She laughed and then curled into a fetal position.

"I'm running you a hot bath. Do you have some bubbles or some smell-good stuff somewhere?"

She pointed across the room, at her bag.

He unzipped the outer pocket in search of her bath products. No luck. He looked inside, and came upon her cell phone. She'd forgotten to turn it off. He'd warned her that international rates would be astronomical. He grabbed her phone to turn it off and noticed a text message from a Florida exchange.

I can definitely get a passport for your daughter. We don't need her father's consent. Call my office when you return to the States and we'll discuss it. Enjoy the Bahamas!

He tossed the phone back into the bag. He was livid. He glanced over at Savannah as light snores escaped from her mouth. She was soundly sleeping, but he wanted to shake her. He took a seat in the Georgian-style wing chair in the corner of the room, watched her as she slept. His mind raced as he tried to decide how he would confront her. He needed an explanation. Did she really think that she could go behind his back and get Chloe a passport without his consent? She had a lot of nerve.

He went into the bathroom and shut off the running water. He left the room and decided he needed to go for a walk. He went through the lobby and past the kitchen.

"Can I get you and the missus anything else tonight, Mr. Talbot?" asked Raquel.

"No thanks, Raquel. She's sleeping."

"You need some hot tea?"

"Something stronger."

"It's that bad?" Raquel gave him a knowing grin. "Drinking is only a temporary fix for things."

"It's all I need," he stated and then headed for the cabana. "Good night, Raquel."

"Good night, bebby."

He stopped at the bar and asked for a vodka and grapefruit juice. The bartender slid the glass in front of him and he paid with a Bahamian bill.

"Keep the change, Deuce," he told the Rastafarian bartender.

"Thank you, sir." Deuce slipped the extra bills into the tip jar on the bar.

Edward headed toward the darkness of the beach. He plopped down into a chair and sipped on vodka. He found a relaxing Caribbean playlist on his phone and leaned his head back. Fell asleep while listening.

* * *

"What are you doing out here?" Jasmine was standing over him.

The sun stood in the corner of the sky and beamed down on his face as he struggled to open his eyes.

"What time is it?" he asked, realizing he'd been there all night.

"Seven thirty."

"You're here early," he stated as he straightened in the chair.

"Your daughter's an early riser, dude. Little girl was up at the crack of dawn having pancakes and chocolate milk with your father."

A smile crept into the side of Edward's mouth. "Where is she now?"

"She's inside with Savannah," said Jasmine. "Did you two have a fight?"

"No. Why do you ask?"

"Because she didn't know where the hell you were, and then I find you out here asleep on the beach!"

"She got a little tipsy last night. Passed out. So I came out here to clear my head."

"And you're okay?"

"I'm fine." He stood, grabbed his empty glass, wrapped his arm around his sister's shoulder.

"Whatever's going on, you can talk to me about it," she said. "I'll listen and only offer advice if you ask for it."

He decided that he needed an ally. A confidant. "She's trying to take Chloe away from me. She's moving to London to be with her mother, and taking Chloe with her."

"Seriously?" Jasmine gave Edward a puzzled look. "Can she do that?"

"She's taking me to court to petition for it."

"Then what are you two doing here together? I'm confused."

"I wanted Chloe to see all of you, and thought it was the perfect time with everyone being home," he said. "And I brought her along to try to convince her not to go, or to leave Chloe with me. I can't live without my daughter, Jazzy."

"She's the air you breathe. I know that. Everyone knows that."

"It doesn't matter. Her mind's made up."

"I know Savannah. She's a good person. She loves you, and she knows that you love Chloe. She'll do what's right."

He needed Jasmine's optimism, though he wasn't convinced that things were that simple. He wasn't sure that Savannah would surely do what was right. If she was able to get a passport for Chloe without his consent, she could probably get her out of the country without his knowledge as well.

Chapter 13

The Grand Room was decorated in royal blue and silver. White lilies adorned the room. It reminded Savannah of her wedding day. She'd insisted on bouquets of calla lilies for her bridal attendants. Her favorite flower was expensive, but Edward had promised that she could have whatever her heart desired.

Edward had been a handsome groom, wearing a black tuxedo with a silky gray vest and gray tie to match. He was young back then. They both were. But they'd matured over the years. This weekend, they'd found each other again. At least Savannah thought they had. She wasn't sure which direction their relationship would go once they returned to Florida, but she knew that it wasn't the same as it had been before coming to the Bahamas.

She watched as Edward held a glass of champagne in the air, offered a toast to his parents on their anniversary. He was their oldest child. Beverly Talbot had been pregnant with him before the couple married. They had a beautiful love story and Savannah loved listening to it, especially when Beverly Talbot told it.

Edward's father, Paul John, had attended Howard University in Washington, DC, where he met her. She was a young student, and they hit it off right away. While Beverly studied to become a teacher, Paul John studied medicine—and in between studying, the two fell in love. After graduating from medical school, Paul John applied for residency at a hospital in Key West, and landed the opportunity with flying colors. However, this opportunity posed a problem for his new girlfriend. Beverly, who'd always called the District of Columbia her home, was offered a position to teach at a prestigious school in Maryland. It appeared that this was the end of their four-year love affair. It seemed logical that they pursue their own separate careers—after all, opportunities didn't fall out of the sky, and there were no guarantees that they'd receive them again. Neither of the two wanted to hinder the other's progress.

Confident that he'd made the most practical decision, Paul John took a train back to Key West, leaving Beverly behind. He managed to bury himself in his work during the first several months of his residency, yet his heart still longed for her. When she showed up in the emergency room of his hospital, bags in tow and with a swollen belly, he was happier than any man could be. His life changed completely that night, and the anticipation of marriage and fatherhood had him on top of the world.

It appeared to Savannah that he remained on top of the world, even until this day—their thirty-seventh wedding anniversary. Savannah wished that she and Edward could've had such a story. She wished their marriage had withstood the test of time, and that they could proudly stand before Chloe one day and celebrate their thirty-seventh wedding anniversary. But things hadn't turned out quite the way they'd anticipated. In fact, their union hadn't even lasted two years. And for that, Savannah felt ashamed. She tried not to focus on her and Edward's discrepancies, but instead glanced over at the beautiful lady of the hour.

Beverly Talbot looked stunning in her silver gown, her hair in a perfect bun atop her head. Her makeup was flawless. She'd sacrificed so much for her family, and Savannah admired her former mother-in-law. She'd been the strong woman in Savannah's life after her own mother had abandoned her. Beverly Talbot had been the voice of reason on the other end of the phone many days before and after she and Edward divorced. Savannah loved her.

Tears welled in her eyes as she listened to Edward and his siblings speak with such admiration and respect for their parents. She only wished that her and Edward's love had been long-standing. Suddenly it occurred to her that they'd given up much too easily. When things got tough, she ran to her father's home. She wondered what would've been had she stayed and made it work.

A Caribbean version of Etta James's "At Last" began to play. Paul John grabbed Beverly's waist and moved her toward the dance floor. He drew her close and began to dance slowly to the music. Jackson grabbed Jasmine by the hand, and the two held each other close. Samson spun Alyson and then wrapped his strong arm around her shoulder. The couples moved to the music. Edward glanced at her from across the room. He hadn't rushed to her side as she'd expected him to. In fact, he'd been standoffish for most of the day.

He finally made his way over to her. "Care to dance?" he asked.

"Sure," said Savannah as she took his hand. She turned to Chloe, who was seated at a table. "We'll be right back, baby."

As they danced close, she breathed in his scent, and thoughts of their lovemaking rushed through her mind.

He looked down into her eyes, and she stared into his. He wore a sensible blue tuxedo, and his goatee was perfectly trimmed. The smell of his cologne danced against her nose.

"I thought you'd never ask," she told him.

"You look beautiful," he whispered.

She'd found the charcoal-gray after-five gown at a local bridal boutique in Palm Beach. It was a must-have and the price tag had caught her eye, marked down by 70 percent. The back revealed bare skin, and the split up the side unveiled long, sexy legs. Edward grabbed the small of her back, and she rested her face against his neck.

"Thank you. You look very handsome."

He smiled. "I do my best."

"It's our last night here in the Bahamas. What are we doing tonight?"

"I think I'm going to spend the night in Governor's Harbour, at my parents' house," he said. "Need to spend some time with everyone before we all part ways. No telling when I'll see them all again."

"That sounds great. Do you think there's room for Chloe and me?"

"Um…yeah…" He was hesitant, and that caught her off guard. "I think there's room."

"You sure?" she asked.

"Yeah, I think there's room."

"Good! Then we'll come, too," she exclaimed.

She loved the Talbots and couldn't wait to spend another evening with all of them.

"Pardon me, big brother." Edward's younger brother Nate approached. "Can I cut in?"

"No, you can't cut in!" Edward teased.

"Why not?" Nate asked. "You afraid she might think I'm a better dancer, or much better-looking?"

"Neither of the two."

"Then step aside, chump." He pushed Edward aside and grabbed Savannah by the waist. "I need a dance with this beautiful lady while the night is still young."

"Hello, Nate." Savannah kissed his cheek. "So good to see you."

"You, too! You're looking beautiful as always," he said. "I didn't believe them when they told me you were here on the island! And with Edward."

Edward lifted his hands in surrender and exited the dance floor.

"He invited Chloe and me for the weekend...for your parents' anniversary party. I'm so happy for them."

"Yeah, me, too. They have plenty of years in. That's a long time to be with one person."

"When are you going to find that special woman to spend your life with?"

"I don't know if she's out there, sis. I've had too much pain."

"Of course she's out there! You just have to look for her."

"What about you? You doing okay?"

"I am."

"You and my brother getting back together?"

"I... We're just really good friends," Savannah stated. In her heart she felt that she and Edward might be moving toward something more than friendship, but she didn't want to be presumptuous.

"I want you both to be happy. So whatever that means, I'm down for that."

"Thanks, Nate."

She had grown fond of Edward's brother Nate over the years. He'd come to live with them briefly one summer during his college days. He thought he wanted a career in politics and decided to shadow his brother. He quickly became bored with following Edward around town, and headed back to Atlanta to what he considered a much more exciting life.

There were a number of lonely nights he'd kept Savannah in good company with games of Scrabble and watching multiple episodes of *Family Feud*. He'd resented his brother for making more time for his career, and not enough for his wife and newborn child—thought that Edward was a fool for squandering his marriage. He'd have given anything to have a woman like Savannah in his corner.

"You'll always be my sister-in-law, no matter what," Nate said. "My brother's a fool if he doesn't get you back in his life. And I'll tell him that to his face."

Denny tapped Nate on the shoulder. "My turn, bro."

"I'm still dancing," Nate protested. "Go dance with Jazzy or Alyson."

"I don't want to dance with them. I want to dance with Savannah."

"Where's your little GI Jane?"

"She went back to the US. She got all pissed off about Sage."

"Well, what did you expect? A parade?" Nate asked, and then continued to dance with Savannah. "You have a lot to learn about women."

"This from someone who doesn't have a woman." Denny grabbed Savannah by the hand.

Nate sighed, and then worked his way outside to the cabana, where Edward had gone just moments before. After dancing with Denny, Savannah made her way back to the table where Chloe waited patiently.

"Hey, baby, are you okay?"

"Yes, Mommy," said Chloe.

"Hey, Savannah." Edward's sister Whitney approached. Whitney wore her natural hair in an up-style. She wore a short evening gown that boasted her curvy figure and long lean legs. Her brown skin was like her mother's, and her smile lit up the darkest of rooms. Though she was an elementary school teacher, she looked nothing like the stereotype. "How are you?"

"Whitney!" Savannah exclaimed. "Great seeing you."

"You, too. They told me you were here." Whitney smiled. "You look good."

"So do you."

"My flight just arrived about an hour ago. So I am exhausted! Jet lag is a beast," Whitney said. "Is this Chloe?"

"Yes."

"Hello, beautiful," she said to Chloe.

"Hello."

"Isn't she gorgeous?" Jasmine asked as she walked up. "Come on, sweetie. Let's go get punch and cake. Lots of sugar!"

"This is what she does," said Whitney. "She fills your children up with sugar and then sends them home with you. I can't wait until she has kids of her own."

"Well, you might not have to wait long for that." Jasmine gently touched her stomach.

Whitney stared at her sister with an open mouth. "What are you saying, Jasmine Talbot?"

"Yeah, what *are* you saying?" Savannah asked.

"Well…" She smiled shyly. "I don't know for sure, but I'm late."

"What?"

"I have an appointment on Monday. And I'll know for sure then."

Whitney grabbed her sister in a strong embrace. "I'm so excited."

Savannah glanced across the room at Jasmine's husband,

Jackson. He looked at the trio speculatively. Wondered what the excitement was about.

"Shh. Jackson doesn't know yet. Nobody knows, except for you two. And I want to keep it that way until I know for sure."

"My lips are sealed," said Whitney.

They both looked at Savannah.

"Mine, too."

"No revealing anything to Edward," Jasmine warned.

Savannah made the motion of zipping her lips. "Mum's the word."

"Where is my big brother anyway?" Whitney asked.

"I think I saw him at the bar," said Jasmine. "Chloe and I are going for cake and punch. Chloe, my lady."

Chloe hopped up from her chair, locked arms with Jasmine and followed her across the room.

"I should go say hello to my parents first," Whitney said. She gave Savannah a hug. "It was great seeing you."

"You, too."

Savannah made her way out to the cabana bar to find Edward. Stood next to him. "Care if I join you?" she asked.

He motioned for her to take a seat next to his. "Where's Chloe?"

"With Jazzy, of course."

"Those two are joined at the hip. They've grown quite fond of each other. Can't wait until Jazzy has kids of her own." He chuckled.

Savannah laughed at the thought, too.

"What are you drinking?" Edward asked.

"Sky juice."

Edward gave her a sideways look. "Sky juice, huh?"

"It's grown on me."

"You and my mother," said Edward. "Deuce, give the lady a sky juice."

Deuce nodded, and Savannah followed Edward's gaze to the mounted television.

"Soccer." she smiled.

She fondly remembered Edward insisting that their local cable company carry the Bahamian channels so that he could watch soccer on the weekends. They never did, and he never recovered.

"I have to come to the Bahamas to see it."

"I remember the letter that you wrote to the corporate offices of Time Warner that year."

"I wanted them to know that I was serious!" Edward laughed. "American men have Monday Night Football. There are more Bahamian men in Florida than people realize. Why couldn't we have a soccer channel?"

"You're great at fighting for causes. You should've taken it further."

"It was a lost cause." He sipped on his Bahamian beer. "Just like a lot of other causes that I fight for."

She felt there was an underlying message in his statement, but she chose to ignore it. Deuce slid the glass of gin with coconut water in front of her, and she took a long sip.

"Mmm. That's good," she said.

"Edward Talbot!" The voice was loud. Whitney shook her hips as she headed their way. "Hey, big brother."

Edward smiled and shook his head. "Can you be any louder?"

"Are you hungover?" Whitney smiled.

"No, I'm not hungover." Edward stood and gave his sister a strong hug.

"I see that you and Savannah are hanging out again. What does that mean?" She sang the last few words.

"It means that she's here…enjoying the Bahamas. And our parents' anniversary party."

"With you." Whitney smiled. "Are we reconciling?"

"No." Savannah and Edward said it at the same time.

"Okay. We'll see," said Whitney. "My brother's a good man, Savannah. You should give him a second chance. And just so you know, Edward hasn't brought any other woman here to the Bahamas…since you two…you, know. Split. I don't think he's even had any…"

"Enough!" Edward exclaimed.

Savannah and Whitney giggled.

"Okay, I'm leaving," said Whitney. "But you think about what I said, Savannah Talbot. Is your name still Talbot? Or did you go back to your maiden name?"

"Goodbye, Whitney," said Edward.

"I'm leaving." Whitney laughed. "But I need a drink first. Deuce, give me a glass of Merlot, please. And put it on my brother's tab."

Deuce nodded and poured Whitney a glass of wine. She grabbed it and bid the couple a good night, walked back inside.

"I'm ready to head over to Governor's Harbour," Edward said. "Do you need to pack a bag or something for you and Chloe?"

"Yes, I'll go up and do that now." Savannah slid from her bar stool. She grabbed her drink. "I'll be back shortly."

"I'll be right here waiting."

She sashayed toward the Grand Room, hoped that Edward was watching her walk away. She turned around to see. He was.

Chapter 14

Edward decided that he wouldn't spend the last night of his trip stewing over the text message he had run across on Savannah's phone. He'd let it go, just for the night. He'd address it with her the moment they were back in Florida, though. But for the night, he would enjoy his family.

George Symonette's voice filled the house, along with the smell of johnnycakes and fresh seafood. Bottles of wine were lined up on the coffee table, and Edward's mother and father danced in the middle of the floor. Edward removed his Calvin Klein loafers from his feet and leaned back on the sofa. Chloe hopped onto his lap. He sipped on a Bahamian beer and watched as his family enjoyed their time together.

"Where's Samson and his guitar?" Beverly Talbot asked. "I want him to play something."

"Yes, that would be great," said Jackson.

"Jackson should sing," Edward insisted.

"Alyson, go tell your hubby that Mom wants a selection," said Whitney.

"Go tell him yourself." Alyson waved her hand in the air and leaned back in her father's easy chair. "He's out on the front porch sulking. We had a fight in the cab on the way over."

Whitney huffed and headed for the porch. "I don't know how he puts up with you."

"I don't know how I put up with him." Alyson tossed her hair. "And I don't know where he's sleeping tonight, because he's certainly not sleeping with me."

"Sweetheart, he has to sleep with you. We're limited on space. And since Edward and Savannah can't sleep together, we need all the room we can get." Beverly Talbot smiled at Savannah and Edward. "Sorry, babies, but we're Baptists, and you're not married anymore, and we can't have you sleeping in the same bed. Now, if you decide to remarry..."

"Mother, it's okay," Edward interjected as every eye in the house landed on him. "We're good."

Savannah smiled sweetly, embarrassment written on her face.

They were both relieved when Samson came into the house with his guitar.

"What would you like to hear, Mother?" he asked.

"Oh, I don't know. Something sweet. A love song," said Beverly.

"Something a little more contemporary than George Symonette," Nate suggested. "No offense, Mother and Pop."

"None taken," said Paul John.

Beverly rolled her eyes at her son. "Fine. Something a little more contemporary."

"Something by Beres Hammond," Jasmine suggested.

"These American boys don't know anything about Beres," Nate teased.

Jackson turned to Samson. "Let's show them what these American boys do know."

Samson sat on the edge of the sofa. His acoustic guitar rested on his leg, and his fingertips began to fret the strings. He began to play the tune of Beres Hammond's "I Feel Good." Jackson started to sing the lyrics. Samson closed his eyes. He didn't see that Alyson's demeanor had changed, and she was hanging on to every word of the song. When he opened his eyes, he smiled at her. Edward bobbed his head and looked over at Savannah, who was consumed by the lyrics as well. He gave her a warm smile.

The duo began to play "Stranger in Town."

"Isn't that your song, Edward?" Nate asked. "Yours and Savannah's?"

"Yes! Get up, you two, and dance!" Whitney insisted.

"Not right now," said Edward.

"As good a time as any," Jasmine said.

"Oh, come on." Beverly Talbot grabbed Chloe in her arms and pulled her son up from the sofa.

Edward and Savannah began to dance. She moved her hips to the music.

"She moves like she's Bahamian!" Jasmine said. "Work those hips, girl."

Jasmine and Denny danced together, and Whitney pulled Alyson up from her chair and the pair danced. Alyson's bad attitude slowly dissipated as the music resonated through her body. She smiled at her husband as he played his guitar and as Jackson sang the lyrics of the Bahamian love song.

It was these times that Edward loved and missed most about home. Times like this gave him life—wrongs were righted during these visits home. He gave Savannah a slow spin and then pulled her close. He looked into her eyes and wanted to kiss her lips at that moment. Had to remember where he was. He didn't realize that the entire family was watching him as he watched her.

* * *

After the women were settled in their beds, the men sat on the front porch, a bottle of Bahamian beer in each one's hand as they told lies and laughed about the good things and complained about the bad. Caribbean music played lightly on an old radio. The moon was brightly situated in the corner of the dark sky, stars played hide-and-seek, and the smell of the ocean swept along with the wind every time it decided to blow.

"Sir, you and Mrs. Talbot have been married for longer than I've been on this earth," said Samson. "How did you do it?"

"Forget it," Nate said. "You're married to Alyson. There's no hope for you, boy."

Laughter filled the porch.

"It's not easy, son, but there is hope," Paul John said. "You put up with things that you don't always want to put up with. You love them when they're unlovable. You smile when you're hurting inside. You agree when you don't want to. You make it work."

"And you don't bail when things get tough," Nate said, and then glanced at Edward.

"Are you speaking to me?" Edward asked.

"Just in general," Nate said. "When you have a good woman, you don't bail on her."

"Why don't you just say it, Nate? Whatever it is that you need to say. Obviously you have something you need to get off your chest," said Edward.

"I was speaking in general, but since you brought it up, I think you squandered your relationship with Savannah."

"For your information, she divorced me. She ran off to Georgia to her father's house and didn't come back!"

"She ran off because you weren't showing her any attention. You were too occupied with your career and that damn campaign manager of yours. What was her name? Quinn?"

"I'm sorry. How is this any of your business?"

"It's not."

"Good. Then let it go."

Nate waved his beer in the air. "It's gone. But if I were you, I wouldn't let her get away a second time. She clearly still loves your ass. I can't imagine why, but she does."

"You were letting it go, remember?" asked Edward.

Nate waved his bottle of beer in the air again. "Gone."

"And what makes you think she still loves me anyway?" Edward pushed. "Did she say something to you?"

"She didn't have to. The world can see that you both still love each other." Nate stood. "Anybody want another beer?"

"I'm good," Jackson said.

"Bring me one," said Samson.

"None for me," Denny said. "I have an early flight."

"You, Pop?" Nate asked.

"No, son, I'm done for the night," said Paul John.

"Edward?"

"What is it with you and Savannah, anyway? Do you want her?" Edward stood. "You've always had this little thing for her. This little crush. So let's just get it out there in the open. Would you like a roll in the hay with my ex-wife, Nathan Talbot?"

"What are you talking about?"

"I'm talking about this little obsession you've always had for her."

"Pop, get your son. Please tell him to sit back down before I have to drop him."

"Nobody's dropping anybody," said Paul John.

"Don't talk to Pop as if I'm not standing here. Talk to me. I'm right here."

"To answer your question, no, I'm not interested in Savannah or any other woman. As a matter of fact, I'm not interested in women at all, big brother. And it's been that way for some time. So you have nothing to worry about."

A disturbed Edward sat back down. "What?"

"There. It's out there. Nobody has to speculate anymore. It's right out there in the open," Nate said.

Every man on the porch was left speechless as Nate went inside. Slammed the screen door behind him.

"I know he's not saying what I think he's saying," Edward said. "What do you do with that information, Pop? How do you deal with that? Aren't you going to demand that he come back and explain himself?"

"He's my son, and I love him. That's how I deal with it," said Paul John.

"That doesn't disturb you one bit? He always gets away with stuff. Always has."

"I don't necessarily agree with any of your lifestyles. You or your siblings, but I love each of you, in spite of yourselves. Individually. Nothing can change that."

Edward reclined in his seat. Took a long sip of his beer. Paul John Talbot didn't get excited about much, Edward knew that, but he wanted his father to get excited this time—to chastise Nate for once. They were Baptists, as his mother was always so quick to remind him. Yet Nate's revelation had gone unchallenged.

"There was some truth about what he said about you, though. It's clear that you still love Savannah and that she still loves you. What will you do with that, son? That's the question." Paul John stood and then walked into the house.

Chapter 15

Edward's head bounced against the leather seat. He fought sleep and wanted to be awake to think things through. He needed a plan, and he needed to come up with it long before the wheels of the jet hit the runway. He had to know which direction he was going to take this relationship with Savannah. His plan for romance in the Bahamas had been successful. But he wasn't sure if he'd romanced her enough to keep her from leaving the country.

When he married Savannah, his mother had insisted that he give her the family ring—the vintage ring with the oval emerald in the center. Tiny diamonds danced around the outer edge of the center stone. It was the ring that his grandfather, Clyde Talbot, had given his bride when they wed. His grandmother had worn it until her death.

"You're Clyde Talbot's oldest grandchild," his mother had told him. "Your father and I want you to give it to Savannah when you propose."

"Are you sure? It's an expensive ring, and a family heirloom. That's a lot of pressure."

"Your grandfather would want you to have it," Beverly had insisted.

He'd taken the ring. And when he'd proposed to Savannah, he explained the significance of it. Her tears were an indication that she understood. She had been honored to wear his grandmother's ring and promised never to take it for granted. She would live up to its legacy, she swore. And she had.

After the divorce, she'd returned it. Placed it in his hand right there at the courthouse. "Thank you for letting me borrow this," she'd said.

He had returned the ring to his mother, hoped that one of his other brothers would have better luck in love. However, during this visit, he'd built up the nerve to ask for it back.

"You're going to ask her again?" his mother had asked. "I knew."

"I should never have left," he'd told his mother.

"You're right." She'd placed her hand against his face. "I told you that."

"I'm not made of the same stuff my father is made of, Mother. He's much stronger than I am. Braver."

"He's no stronger or braver."

"I failed her. And my daughter. And I need to make it right."

His mother placed the emerald in his hand and then closed his fingers around it. "I don't want this ring back, Edward Talbot. Not unless I outlive Savannah. Which I pray doesn't happen."

"I hear you, Mother."

"Don't go back for the wrong reasons, either. Go back because you love her, and only that. And if you love her, then Edward, give it everything you have to make it work this time."

"I will."

* * *

He glanced over at Savannah as the plane soared to new heights. Her head rested against the window and light snores crept from her lips. He stared for a moment. Wondered what her dreams were made of. When the time was right, he was going to ask her to be his wife again. He was ready to start anew, give their family a chance. He could see himself loving Savannah again. They'd connected in the Bahamas, and his family already loved her to death. Her father might not be so welcoming, but he would deal with him. Edward would respect the man regardless.

He'd even forgiven Savannah for attempting to get a passport for Chloe under false pretenses and without his consent. He'd also forgiven her for filing the petition for relocation and having him served at his downtown office. None of it would matter once they were married.

He pulled into the driveway of the home that used to be his and turned off the engine. He got out, reached for a sleeping Chloe and pulled her out of the backseat, then followed Savannah to the door as she unlocked it. He took Chloe to her room and placed her in bed. He tramped back down the hardwood staircase and then unloaded their luggage from the trunk, placed it next to the stairwell.

"You need me to take it upstairs?" he asked.

"No, I think I can manage from here," said Savannah. "Thank you for a lovely weekend."

"Thank you for coming along."

"Chloe and I both had a wonderful time with your family," she said. "And the beach. I particularly enjoyed the private island and the beach."

"Hmm. I'm glad." He smiled. "Let's get together this week. I'd like to take you out to dinner, talk about some things. You think you can get a sitter for Chloe…maybe Friday?"

"Yeah, I think so."

"Good." He kissed her cheek and then gently kissed her lips. He held on to her hand. "I'll give you a call later."

"Okay."

Their hands lingered together for a moment. He looked at her ring finger, caressed it. It looked like it needed a little bling. The beautiful stone would look good there, just as it had before. He let her go and almost skipped to his car. He'd give it a week. Be sure he was making the right decision. With all things considered, he would be an engaged man by Friday night.

Edward hit his garage door opener as he pulled into his subdivision. The first thing he noticed was the red Mercedes with the top dropped, parked in front of his house. Quinn stepped out when she saw him pull into the driveway.

"I just took a chance and picked up your favorite!" She held a white plastic bag in the air. "Thai."

"How did you know what time I'd be here?"

"I just said I took a chance." She giggled. "I got Thai basil shrimp, spicy curry chicken, green curry tofu for the weird guy who prefers to not eat meat."

"The weird guy, huh?"

He decided to leave his bags in the trunk. He'd grab them later. Instead he walked in through the garage with Quinn close on his heels. She wasn't hesitant about going straight to his kitchen. She pulled two plates from the shelf and grabbed two forks and two wineglasses.

"Don't be shy. Make yourself at home," he said sarcastically.

"Don't mind if I do." Quinn prepared a plate of green curry tofu for Edward. "So how was the trip?"

"Nice."

"Your parents' anniversary party was spectacular?"

"Wonderful," said Edward, "and it was great seeing my family. All my sisters and brothers were there. I took Chloe *and* Savannah, too."

"Really? I didn't know that Savannah went." Quinn's demeanor changed a bit. "Something I need to know?"

"No."

"Wow, you took her to the Bahamas. That's different," Quinn said as she made herself a plate. She walked over to Edward's wine rack, grabbed a bottle of Chardonnay. "Where's the corkscrew?"

"Top drawer." Edward sat at the island in the kitchen, a plate of Thai food in front of him. He grabbed a fork and dug in. "This is good."

"I know it is. The best damn Thai food in Florida." She found the corkscrew and opened the bottle of wine. Poured two glasses.

"I'm thinking about asking Savannah to marry me again," he stated.

"Yeah?" She pretended not to be alarmed by the news. "What makes you think she wants to remarry your behind?"

"Because I'm a good man. And I'm her baby's daddy—" he rubbed his chin "—and I'm fine as hell."

"You are all of those things," she said, "but that doesn't necessarily warrant a marriage proposal, Casanova."

"No, it doesn't. But love does. I realized that I still love her, and I think we can make this work." He pulled the emerald out of the pocket of his shirt and showed Quinn. "My mother gave me the ring back, and I'm going to propose."

"Wow! That's, uh…" She cleared her throat, took a drink of her wine. "That's deep. A lot must've happened on that trip."

"A lot did." Edward finished the helping of food and

took a gulp of wine. "I'm going up and hop in the shower. I'm really tired and want to just unwind."

"Sure, I will—I'll just finish up here and clean up my mess," said Quinn. "I'll let myself out."

"You sure?" he asked.

"Of course. No worries. Go take a shower."

"Okay, cool. Maybe I'll see you at the office tomorrow," Edward said as he headed to his bedroom. "Or maybe I won't."

"You will! Because you're a workaholic!"

"I'll be there," he replied.

He knew that Quinn would be bothered by his news about Savannah, which was why he gave it to her straight, no chaser. She needed to know sooner rather than later. Plus he needed to hear himself say it to her. Somehow that made it real. In addition, he knew that it was necessary for their friendship to change if he had any hopes of a future with Savannah. He would slowly disconnect from her. She would chafe at it, but he had to do it. He couldn't risk losing Savannah again. He had to fight for them with all of his might this time.

Chapter 16

The moment Savannah lifted the black suitcase to carry it upstairs, she knew that it wasn't hers. It was too heavy. Edward had gotten their luggage mixed up again. She had his suitcase, and he had hers. They'd had matching luggage for years, and she'd sworn that she was going to buy something brighter in color, not the drab black leather bag that she'd owned for too long. She needed her bag—her toiletries, makeup and other unmentionables were inside. She called his cell phone. It went straight to his voice mail.

"Shoot," she whispered.

She slipped a pair of sandals onto her feet and loaded a sleepy Chloe into the backseat of her car.

"We have to go see Daddy," she explained to her five-year-old. "He took the wrong luggage. I promise we'll be back soon, and you can get back into your comfy bed. Are you hungry?"

"Yes," said Chloe.

"Maybe we'll grab a pizza on the way back."

"With pepperoni?"

"Whatever you want, sweetie. Now buckle up."

Savannah drove across town to Edward's neighborhood. She hoped he would answer his phone—save her the trouble of unloading Chloe and coming inside. He could just bring the luggage out to the car, and make the switch without her having to lift a finger. She was drained, and wanted nothing more than a long, hot shower and to hop into a pair of sweats and a T-shirt. She had a long day ahead of her. It was time to pack up her office and prepare for her future. She'd decided to put London on hold for a bit, at least until she determined what it was that she and Edward were doing. She felt as if they'd reconnected, bonded, and perhaps they had a chance at a real future. She owed it to herself and Chloe to at least find out.

She pulled up in front of his house and noticed the red Mercedes parked out front. He had company. She dialed his number again. It rang this time.

"Hello," said the female voice on the other end.

"I'm sorry, I must have the wrong number."

"Who are you looking for?"

"Edward Talbot."

"You have the right number."

Her hands shook, and her heart beat rapidly. "May I ask who this is?"

"It's Quinn."

She'd suspected that it was. "Is Edward available? He mixed up our luggage again, and I just need to get my bag."

"He's showering right now," she said. "We were about to turn in for the night. Can I give him a message?"

She was enjoying this. Savannah could hear the satisfaction in her voice.

"No. None." She quickly hung up. Sat there for a moment to gather her emotions.

She hated him at that moment. They'd been in town for less than a few hours and Quinn was already in his home, and obviously in his bed, too. Tears threatened to fall from her eyes, but she willed them not to. She wouldn't cry over Edward again. She had no more tears for him. She couldn't for the life of her figure out why he would drag her all the way to the Bahamas, seduce her and then break her heart again. And she didn't want to know. She just wanted to forget that Edward Talbot existed.

She pulled into her driveway and sat there for a moment, a pepperoni pizza in the passenger seat next to her and Chloe asleep in the backseat. Those tears that she'd willed not to fall earlier were much stronger than she thought. They had a mind of their own, and slowly crept down the side of her face and burned her cheeks. She turned her head and looked out the window. Here she was feeling this way again. She pulled her cell phone out again. Pulled up the text message from Maia's friend at the State Department. Responded.

Change of heart. I will need that passport for my daughter after all.
ASAP! When can we meet?

She wiped tears from her eyes, got herself together and then stepped out of the car. She reached into the backseat of the car.

"Let's go inside, baby," she said to Chloe and lifted her out of her car seat. "Mommy's got pizza."

After eating and putting Chloe to bed, she cleaned the kitchen. Her cell phone buzzed and she looked at the screen. Edward had the nerve to call. Had he finished loving his girlfriend and now wanted a conversation with her? She ignored the call and poured herself a glass of wine instead. She started the dishwasher and then climbed the stairs to her bedroom. She turned on her stereo and listened to Jill

Scott serenade her with an appropriate song, a remake of Billie Holiday's "Good Morning Heartache," while Chris Botti accompanied her with his horn. She drew a hot bath, climbed in and relaxed her head against the tub.

She tossed and turned all night, and even when the sunlight flashed across her face in the morning, she wanted to lie there just a little longer. Unfortunately, she needed to get Chloe dressed and ready for school, so wallowing in her misery was not an option. She needed to drop Chloe off and then head over to her office to pack up her things. Staying in West Palm Beach was no longer in the cards. She needed a one-way ticket to London by week's end. She pulled herself out of bed.

"Let's go, sweetheart. In the shower you go," Savannah told Chloe.

"Can I stay home today, Mommy?"

"Are you sick?"

"I'm really tired."

Savannah felt her head for a fever. They'd had a long weekend, and Savannah concluded that she was just tired from their trip to the Bahamas.

"Okay, kiddo. You can hang out with Mommy today. I have to go to my office and pack my things. And I just need for you to behave. Okay?"

"Okay," she said. "Are we going to see Daddy today, too?"

"I don't think so, honey. I'm sure your dad has to work."

"Can we see him after he gets off work?"

Savannah sighed. How was she going to avoid Edward for an entire week? "We'll see."

Maia stood in the doorway of Savannah's office. A tight blue dress hugged her ample hips.

"So…we're back from the islands."

"Yes, we are."

"And did we have a good time?"

"We did indeed."

"Did we get some of that big, fat, sexy…"

"Maia! Chloe's here."

Chloe popped up from behind her mother's desk, a Barbie doll in her hand.

"Damn, I didn't even see her over there." Maia covered her mouth. "Hi, sweetheart. How are you?"

"Hi, Maia." Chloe waved.

"That's a cute little Barbie you have there." Maia smiled sheepishly. "What's her name?"

Chloe shrugged. "Barbie."

Savannah dug into her purse for some change, pulled out four quarters.

"Baby, why don't you run down the hall and get something out of the vending machine. Let Mommy talk to Maia." She handed Chloe the change.

"Okay." Chloe left the office and closed the door behind her.

"I'm headed to London this weekend," Savannah whispered.

"What?" Maia said. "What about your text message? You said that you and what's his name had found love again…or some nonsense. And you were considering putting London on hold for a while."

"That was before."

"What happened?"

"We weren't back in the country two hours and that tramp was already at his house, in his bed."

"What!" Maia's eyes grew large as she eased her behind into the chair across from Savannah's desk. "How do you know?"

"Her car was parked in front of his house. Plus I called

him, and she answered his cell phone. Said that he was in the shower and the two of them were about to go to bed together."

"She was lying!"

"She wasn't lying."

"She has wanted him since the beginning of time. You know that. She would do anything to get rid of you and get her claws into him."

"I, um…" Savannah hadn't considered that Quinn might be lying. But how did she have access to his phone? And more importantly, why was he in the shower while she was there? She didn't care anymore. She'd cried herself to sleep the night before, and she didn't have any more tears for Edward Talbot. It was time to get down to the business at hand. "I need you to take Chloe for me."

"What!"

"Just for a few weeks. Just until the end of the school year and until I get settled in London."

"Savannah, are you insane? I don't know anything about taking care of a five-year-old."

"You just have to make sure she gets to school every day. Feed her and put her to bed every night. Chloe's easy to care for and she knows our routine very well."

"And what happens when her father calls and demands to see her?" Maia asked. "Savannah, why don't you just leave her with Edward for a while…at least until you get settled?"

"I don't know."

"He'll take better care of her than I will. Trust me. I don't even have pets or plants, for Christ's sake!"

Savannah plopped down in her leather chair. This wasn't going to be as easy as she thought. But Maia had a point. Edward was good with Chloe. He would take great care of her, at least until the end of the school year. And once she got settled in London with Nyle, she'd come back for her daughter.

The door opened and Chloe came back in.

"I might give him a chance," said Savannah.

"How about giving him a chance to explain, too." Maia stood, headed for the door.

"Now you're on his side?"

"Never," Maia said. "But you should at least hear his side of the story."

"Now you're pushing it."

"Am I?" Maia asked. "Check in with me before you leave."

"I will."

Savannah continued to place pictures and other personal items into the cardboard box. Leaving was proving to be much harder than she'd anticipated.

Chapter 17

Edward refused to leave Savannah's house until he saw her pull up. He'd been worried sick, wondering if she and Chloe were okay. He'd been calling her cell phone and work phone for two days, and so far she hadn't picked up and hadn't returned one single call. He saw her sedan in his rearview mirror as she crept down the street. She pulled into the driveway and he stepped out of the car. He went to his trunk and grabbed the black leather luggage that belonged to her.

He stood on the lawn, his arms folded across his chest, waited for her to get out of the car. Chloe wasn't in the car, and his heart beat rapidly. Where was his daughter?

"Hey." He frowned, although a feeling of relief rushed over him. At least she was unharmed, but he was still a bit angry that he hadn't heard from her and she hadn't returned any of his calls or text messages. "Where's Chloe?"

"She's having a playdate with one of the little girls from our church." She grabbed a box from the front seat of her car.

"Let me carry that for you."

"I got it. Thanks."

"I brought your bag. We got the two mixed up the other night." He grabbed the bag by its handle.

"I know."

"Is something wrong here?"

"You tell me."

"I've been calling you for the past two days, and you haven't picked up, haven't returned any of my calls," he said. "What's going on?"

"I've been busy." She placed the box on the ground and opened her front door.

"Why aren't you using the garage?"

"The garage door opener went out last week."

"It's not safe. You should be pulling into the garage instead of going in through the front door," he stated as he followed her into the house. "I'll fix it."

"It's okay. I won't be here long anyway. Leaving for London very soon."

"What? When were you going to tell me?"

"I wasn't." She set the box down at the edge of the stairs, went to the corner and grabbed his luggage by the handle and wheeled it toward him. "But then I realized that I need your help. Chloe's got a few more weeks of school left…"

"Six weeks," Edward added.

"Anyway, I don't want to pull her out of school. So I'd like for you to take her, just for a few weeks until school's out and I get settled. Find a place…"

"Why are you leaving? I thought…" He chose his words carefully. "I thought you might reconsider after…"

"After what, Edward? After you made me believe that we could really have a future together?"

"We *can* have a future together," he insisted.

Had she figured it out? That in the beginning, his intentions had been to romance her into staying?

"We can't have a future!" She raised her voice. "Not when you're still seeing other people and sleeping with them! I'm not into casual sex, and I won't be your side chick."

"What in the hell are you talking about, Savannah?"

"I'm talking about Quinn."

"Not that again."

"Yes, that again!" She looked at him in disgust. "So, for your information, I'm not interested in a future with you, Edward Talbot. I am fine with my life…just the way it is. The only thing I need from you is a father for my child. I need for you to care for her until I come back for her in a few weeks."

"I haven't given you permission to take her away," said Edward.

"I don't need your damn permission! If I wanted to, I'd take her in the middle of the night without your knowledge. But I'm being respectful here," she stated.

"We have joint custody, so you do need my permission!" he exclaimed.

"We're going to London, with or without your blessing."

"And how will you obtain a passport for her? With the help of the criminal who texted your phone while we were in the Bahamas?"

"Were you spying on me? Sneaking around, checking my phone?"

"Answer the question. Is that what your plans are?"

"No. You'll sign the application. You and I will both sign the application," she said.

"What makes you so certain that I will?"

"Would you really deny your daughter the opportunity to live with her mother? She would be miserable without me, and you know it. No one can take care of Chloe better than me. Of course, you're her father, but a girl shouldn't be without her mother. I know that firsthand!"

It was true and he knew it. Savannah had grown up without her mother, and it had nearly destroyed her. She'd never been a whole person, and he'd always felt bad for her. He didn't want that for Chloe.

"When are you planning to leave?" he asked.

"End of the week," she said.

It felt as if the wind had left his soul. "End of the week?"

"Friday evening. And I'll be back to get her the minute that school's out. I should be settled by then."

"And once you come back for her, and the two of you are settled in London, how will I see Chloe?"

"I'll send her to you on breaks and during the summer. Not Christmas. I need her during the Christmas holidays. But you can have any other holidays you want."

Edward felt deep sadness and an aching in his heart. What had caused Savannah's sudden change of heart? He was sure when they had returned from the Bahamas that her intentions had been to stay in Florida. They were supposed to be engaged by the end of the week, not moving to London. This was all wrong.

"Fine." His voice cracked and he tightened his jaw. He wouldn't show her his emotions. He would shield his hurt and anger. "Will you sell the house?"

"Yes. I have the card for that real estate agent that we met with before. I'll get in contact with her."

"I'll work with her to get it on the market. She can call me for showings and such."

"Thank you." She remained in her professional mode. "That will help me quite a bit. Not to have to worry about that."

"I'll continue to pay the mortgage until it sells." He looked around at the home they'd built from the ground up.

"That's very generous, Edward. And I appreciate everything that you do for Chloe."

"And for you, Savannah. I do them for you as well. I love you both." There. He'd said it. He loved her. He walked toward the door, felt like he couldn't breathe. He stood there for a moment, his shoulders sunken. He felt defeated, but the words he was about to speak would be the hardest ones he ever had to say. "I don't know what happened between Sunday and today, but I'm sorry for whatever it was. And I hope that you'll be very happy in London. I won't give you any trouble about taking Chloe. As long as I can still see her during breaks and holidays, as you've promised."

"You'll see her. We can go before a judge and get it in writing."

"I'll have Jack draw something up," he stated.

"Fine."

He grabbed his luggage, walked out while he was still able. Headed straight for his car and didn't turn around. He popped the trunk and tossed the bag inside. Slid into the driver's seat, started the car and sat there for a moment. He was numb. Felt as though he couldn't move. He grabbed the steering wheel tightly and shook it. He glanced at her door. She'd already closed it.

He drove to Jupiter Beach and pulled into the lot. He needed some air, to breathe, to think. Still wearing slacks and dress shoes, he got out of the car. He didn't even bother to remove his expensive tan-and-brown loafers. He walked through the sand and didn't care. He didn't care that he smelled rain, or that thunder roared and lightning flashed across the sky. Beachgoers were packing up their things and heading for their cars. People were pulling their Jet Skis in from the ocean.

A few raindrops pattered against his face. He kept

walking until the sky opened and a flood of rain poured over him. He didn't care. He needed to cry, and this was the perfect time to do it. This way the trace of his tears could be concealed by the raindrops. And he did it. He cried. Long and hard.

Chapter 18

Trying to reconnect with Edward had been a mistake. For Savannah, there had always been a void in her life that only Nyle could fill. Reconnecting with her mother was something that she needed. London was also the perfect place to nurture her career in fashion design. She and Edward had connected in the Bahamas, but she wasn't willing to change her plans. Not this time. It was time for her career and her own plans. As hard a decision as it was to leave Chloe, she didn't have many choices. She wasn't certain of her own future in London, and wouldn't bring Chloe along until she had some level of stability. She vowed that once she found a job in fashion and a place, she'd come back for her daughter. And she didn't have a huge window of time; six weeks would fly by.

Before Savannah boarded her flight to London, tears streamed down her face. She stared out the window as she waited for them to announce that they were boarding, rain pouring down outside. It had rained all week, and she wondered if it was washing away her past, giving her a fresh start. She wanted to be excited about her venture, but the truth was, she was sad. Leaving Chloe had been brutal, and watching her daughter cry as she pulled away in a cab had been pure torture. She only hoped that she could manage without her.

She knew that Edward was a good father, but he'd never had Chloe on his own. Though it was only temporary, there would be sacrifices that Edward would have to make, and she wasn't sure that he would be able to make them—ones that he hadn't made in their marriage. He would have to get his priorities in order. She wasn't so sure that Edward could manage that. But deep in her heart, she hoped that he could—for their daughter's sake.

Once she was situated in the leather seat on the plane, she knew there was no turning back. It was real. In about fourteen hours, with a two-hour layover in Atlanta, she'd be there. She'd be knocking on her mother's door and staring into her eyes. She hoped they would bond quickly, and that it wouldn't be too awkward. She hoped to be employed soon and living on her own. Thanks to Edward's paying her mortgage since the divorce, she had been able to save up a nice little nest egg—one that would get her through until she was able to land a new job. And not just any job. She wanted to work at one of those London fashion design companies that she'd only read about in magazines. She had gained a great deal of experience in the fashion industry since working for Jarrod. Her resume was polished and she was ready to take the industry by storm.

She placed her phone on airplane mode, leaned her head back against the seat and closed her eyes. Whispered a little prayer for safe travels.

"First time in the UK?" asked the handsome man in the seat next to hers.

"I was there when I was a baby. I don't remember it, though," she said.

"Business or pleasure?" he asked in his British accent.

"A little of both."

"How long are you staying?"

He was full of questions, she thought.

"Indefinitely," she said. "I'm relocating."

"Well, welcome home," he held his hand out to her. "I'm Rolf."

"Savannah." She shook his hand.

"Already found a place to stay?" he asked.

"With my mother," she said.

"Ooh. Mommy dearest. My condolences."

"What's that supposed to mean?"

"Nothing. Your mother is probably a very sweet woman and easy to live with." He laughed. "Mine, on the other hand…a piece of work."

"I don't really know my mother," she said. "Long story."

"Well, if you find yourself in the market for a place to stay, I have a two-bedroom flat for rent in South Kensington. You can walk to museums. Seven minutes to the Tube…"

"The Tube?"

"The rail station," he said, handing her a business card. "I usually rent it out short-term, but I'm open to a long-term renter. Give me a call if you'd like to see it."

"Thanks. But I think I'll be okay." She slid the card into a pocket on her cell phone case.

"Great. Let's hope." Rolf gave Savannah a gentle smile and then plugged his earbuds into his ears, began to listen to music on his iPad.

Savannah opened the photo gallery on her phone. Looked at pictures of Chloe. She'd only been away from her daughter a short time and already had separation anxiety. She didn't know how she'd make it through the next few weeks without her. The pilot finally leveled the plane and Savannah relaxed in her seat. She reached into her leather

backpack and pulled out the romance novel she'd packed
for the trip. Romance was definitely not on her mind, but
she needed something to help pass the time. Before the
second chapter, she'd already begun to doze.

Nyle was supposed to pick her up at the airport, but left a
text message that something had come up. She gave instructions on how to get to her place, and to go ahead and take care
of the taxi—she'd be reimbursed the moment she arrived.
The Peugeot E7's engine hummed at the curb of Heathrow
Airport, and Savannah slid into the backseat of the black cab.
She gave the driver Nyle's address and relaxed on the right
side of the car behind him. He glanced at her in the rearview
mirror, his face expressionless. She looked away and took in
the picturesque views of the city.

While she was used to driving on the right side of the
street in America, the Londoner taxi driver maneuvered
the car along the left side—much like the drivers in the
Bahamas. In fact, the British and Bahamians had quite a
bit in common, Savannah thought, remembering riding on
the opposite side of the street when she visited the Bahamas. Though the queen of England was not involved in the
day-to-day business of the Bahamas government, she was
still its queen.

Visiting Buckingham Palace was definitely on Savannah's
list of things to do. She wanted to get all of her touristy type
things out of the way before she became a permanent fixture.
But for now, she needed a long, hot bubble bath or at least a
shower. And just as her stomach growled, she wondered if
Nyle had a nice meal waiting, too. She was exhausted, but
excited about being there and thrilled to meet the woman
who gave her life. All of the anger and hostility that she'd
felt in the past had suddenly been replaced by intrigue and

curiosity. She still hadn't completely forgiven her, but she was open to other emotions.

Savannah paid the driver with cash and found herself on Nyle's doorstep ringing the bell for much longer than she thought necessary. Wasn't the woman expecting her? It seemed she should've been standing with the door wide open, waiting for her daughter with outstretched arms. She thought that Nyle should've met her at the cab and helped her carry her bags inside. After having no luck with ringing the bell, she knocked.

"She stepped out for a moment," yelled the neighbor from the doorway of her flat. "Said she'd be back shortly."

"Are you freaking kidding me?" Savannah mumbled under her breath. But then gave the red-haired neighbor a wave. "Thank you."

"You're the daughter, eh?"

"Yes, ma'am."

"You're pretty like her. You're not licentious, too, are you?"

"Licentious?" asked Savannah.

"A loose woman," the neighbor said. "Like your mother."

"I'm not loose. But thank you for asking," said a tired Savannah to the busybody neighbor. She seemed to have a few loose screws.

She glanced down the narrow street and knew that the woman rushing down the block toward her was Nyle. With a grocery bag in one hand and a cigarette in the other, she was easy to recognize. She walked like Savannah. Had the same build, but just a bit more developed. She wore black leather pants that were much too tight for a woman her age, thigh-high boots and a black leather jacket. Her brown hair was shoulder-length and a pair of red-lensed glasses covered her olive-colored face. She was attractive and definitely had her own style.

"Have you been waiting long?" Nyle asked as she approached, a huge smile on her face. Her teeth were starting to brown. Undoubtedly from the cigarette smoking.

"Not very."

"Look at you! You're stunning," she said. "You don't look anything like your photographs. Isn't she stunning, Harriett?"

"Gorgeous," the busybody neighbor, Harriett, murmured through a raspy, cigarette-filled cough. "Did you bring the smokes?"

Nyle reached into her pocket and pulled out a package of cigarettes, tossed them to Harriett. "You should smoke the herbal ones. They're free of nicotine, and strawberry-flavored."

"What would be the point?"

Nyle ignored her. She didn't hug Savannah but wrapped an arm around her shoulder as if they were old friends who hadn't missed the past thirty-plus years together. "Let's go inside and catch up."

Savannah looked around at the beautifully decorated flat and thought that the money that she'd sent Nyle had been put to good use. White leather furniture, and glass fixtures were everywhere. A fuzzy rug was the focal point in the center of the room, and intriguing art adorned the walls.

"Nice place," Savannah said thoughtfully.

"Thanks. But I can't take the credit. Godfrey has quite the style." She placed the grocery bag in the kitchen and then plopped down on the sofa.

"Godfrey?"

"My boo," she said. "Isn't that what you youngsters are calling them these days?"

Savannah shrugged. Still standing. Purse on her shoulder. "I can't say that I use that term. So this isn't your place?"

"It's Godfrey's place. He lets me bunk here while he travels the world. He's very well off," said Nyle, and then she quickly changed the subject. "How's your father?"

Savannah wondered just how long she'd known Godfrey, and why she hadn't rushed to him for refuge when she was put out on the street. And what Nyle had done with the rent money she'd wired to her. She wanted to ask, but decided to let it go.

"Daddy's doing well," Savannah said. "He's retired now."

"Gorgeous military man. Ex-military man. He swept me off my feet, Frank did. He was always so grounded. Regimented. Not like me. I was a free spirit," she said. "Sit down."

Savannah slid onto the edge of the white leather chair. "Thank you."

"You're so polite. Just like him. You're nothing like me. You have my good looks, though." She smiled. "But nothing else. He did well with you."

"Yes, he did."

"Tell me about yourself. I know over the phone, you told me that you went to college in Florida."

"Florida State. And then I went to art school in Savannah."

"You were named after that city, you know. Such a beautiful place. Those cobblestone streets… Go on." She giggled. "I interrupted."

"I have a degree in fashion, and before last week…a job."

"You've definitely come to the right place. London is the fashion capital of the world."

"Not anymore. It's New York now."

"Whatever," said Nyle as she lit another herbal cigarette. "It's a close second. A good place to plant your feet in the fashion industry."

"Right."

"I used to be in fashion myself. I was a model in my younger days. I've graced the covers of *Vogue* and *L'Officiel* magazines."

"Seriously?"

"You didn't know?" she asked. "It's why I couldn't take you along. It's why your father and I parted ways. I was traveling too much, trying to pursue my career. He didn't understand."

"You mean you chose your career," Savannah said matter-of-factly.

"I wanted to bring you here to England, with me. But your father wouldn't allow it."

Savannah became uncomfortable with the way the conversation was headed. She wasn't ready to face the past just yet. She was tired. And hungry. And not at all ready for truths about her childhood. She wasn't ready to defend her father, nor let Nyle off the hook for her misgivings either. She needed a good night's rest before she contended with the heavy issues.

"Is there somewhere I can freshen up?"

"Yes, of course. Follow me." Nyle led the way down a long hallway.

She flipped on the light in one of the bedrooms. "This is where you'll be sleeping. You can place your things in here. And the toilet is just down there on the right."

"Thanks," said Savannah.

"I'm going to prepare something to eat for us. We'll have Cumberland pie. Have you had that before?"

"No. Can't say that I have."

"Good. You'll love it." Nyle placed a gentle hand on her daughter's cheek. "I'm glad you're here."

"Me, too."

"And when you're done…freshening up…you can tell me all about Chloe, and Edward. If you want to talk about him. I know he's the ex. So we don't have to talk about him at all, if you don't want to. But Chloe… I want to know all about her."

"I'll tell you all about her once I get settled."

"Fantastic." She smiled.

Savannah took note of how beautiful Nyle was. She could picture her face gracing the cover of fashion magazines once upon a time. She wanted to talk to her about life, and catch up on all that they'd missed, but for now—she needed a moment to catch her breath. And sleep.

Chapter 19

Edward struggled to get the rubber band around Chloe's thick ponytail. The center part was crooked, and the second ponytail was more flyaway than the first one, but he'd managed to complete the task. He'd combed Chloe's hair. He was happy that it was Saturday and she didn't have school. At least he'd have the weekend to practice before Monday morning.

"There!" he said with pride. "It's not quite like Mommy's, but it's done. Go look in the mirror."

Chloe hopped down from the kitchen bar stool and rushed down the hall to the bathroom. Edward cleaned up the mess he'd made with ribbons, bows and other hair products. He grabbed the remote control for his stereo and turned the volume up. Washed his hands and began to season the orange roughy he and Chloe had picked up at the farmers' market. His cell phone rang.

"Hello."

"It's me." Savannah's voice was music to his ears. "How are things going?"

He tried to hide his excitement. "Everything's fine."

"Where's Chloe?"

"She's in the bathroom looking at her hair. Daddy combed it today."

"Oh, Lord."

"What? I did a good job. She looks great."

"Well, let me ask her for myself," said Savannah.

"How was your trip?" Edward asked. "I'm glad you made it safely."

"It was long and tiring. When I made it to Nyle's place, I was exhausted and hungry."

"What's she like?" he asked in an almost-whisper, as if Nyle could hear him.

Savannah giggled. "Somewhat eccentric. Pretty, though."

"I understand why you needed to go, Savannah. I do. I know how important this is."

"Thank you. I needed to hear that."

"Let me get Chloe," said Edward as he walked to the bathroom where Chloe stood on the toilet and gazed at her hair in the mirror. "Sweetheart, your mother's on the phone."

"Mommy!" Chloe exclaimed and then hopped down from the toilet. She grabbed the phone from Edward's grasp.

Edward walked out of the bathroom. Gave them a bit of privacy and an opportunity to catch up. He hoped that Chloe wouldn't resort to crying again after hanging up the phone. She had cried the entire day before and most of the night. She was more attached to Savannah than he imagined. He guessed that every girl felt that way about her mother, but it left him helpless.

He stepped out back and placed charcoal briquettes in the grill, fired it up. Chloe rushed outside and handed him the cell phone and then bolted back into the house.

He looked at the screen and realized that Savannah was still on the line.

"Hello."

"She's sad, but she'll be okay later," Savannah explained. She was tearful. "I miss her like crazy. I hope I can do this."

"She'll be fine. You don't have to worry, Savannah. I promise I'll take great care of our daughter."

"I know. And I'll be okay," she sniffed. "I'm just fatigued and emotional."

"Get some rest, and visit with your mother. We'll give you a call in a couple of days and check on you," said Edward. "Let's not run up your phone bill. Hit us up on Facebook."

"Okay."

"I'll post pictures of Chloe every day, so that you can feel like you're a part of her routine."

"Okay." She smiled. "Thank you."

"My pleasure. Now go get some rest and check your Facebook page later. I'll post pictures of her hair."

Savannah laughed through her tears. "I can only imagine what it looks like."

"Like I told you before, it looks great. You'll see," he said. "Now I have to go. Gotta get this fish on the grill."

"Okay. Kiss her for me."

"I will. We'll talk soon."

Edward wanted to ease her anxiety as best he could, and when he hung up he felt as if he'd been successful.

He and Chloe sat in front of the television, ate fish and watched a Disney movie. He wanted to ignore the text message that he received from his colleague, asking if he'd completed his part of the report for Sunday morning's presentation. The mayor was meeting with one of the city's top officials for Sunday brunch, and she needed her talking points. He hadn't finished them. He'd rushed out of the office on Friday and headed straight for Chloe's school because he needed to be on time picking her up. He'd completely forgotten about the report and the meeting.

"Damn," he mumbled under his breath.

He glanced over at his daughter, dressed in her *Sofia the First* pajamas. He hated the thought of loading her into the backseat of his car and dragging her into the office on a Saturday night, but he didn't have much of a choice. Duty called. He'd have completed the report using his laptop computer, but he needed access to the files in his office.

"Baby, we're going to take a ride," he told her.

"Where?"

"To Daddy's office," he said. "I need for you to go find some shoes and to pack some toys into your backpack."

"Okay, Daddy." She rushed down the hallway and was back in a few moments.

He pulled out of his Delray Beach subdivision and zoomed down Atlantic Avenue, then pulled onto Interstate 95 toward downtown West Palm Beach. The sun was already beginning to set as the palm trees swayed in the wind, and he hoped to be back soon and have Chloe in bed at a decent hour.

In his office, Chloe sat in a chair and spread her toys out across his mahogany desk. He pulled files from the cabinet and began flipping through their pages, turned on his computer. He plugged numbers into an Excel spreadsheet, then found music on his iPad.

When he glanced at the clock again, it was well after midnight. Chloe had since curled up and fallen asleep. He leaned back in his chair. Exhausted. He grabbed his cell phone and pulled up the camera, snapped a shot of Chloe's hair, then logged into Facebook and sent it in a message to Savannah. She immediately replied.

What took you so long? And where is she?

At my office. I had work to finish up.

On a Saturday night?

Yes.

It's after midnight!

He'd made a mistake, snapping the photo at his office. He knew that Savannah would worry about things that she had no business worrying about. But she was the one who'd left him in this predicament.

We're headed home now.

It wasn't completely a lie. All he needed was another thirty minutes or so and he'd be homeward bound. He put the finishing touches on his report, pulled charts and graphs into his spreadsheet, and saved the document. After this, he shut down his computer. He glanced over at Chloe and a wave of guilt rushed over him. She was supposed to be at home tucked into bed. What type of father kept his little girl out until the wee hours of the morning? He brushed sleep from his own eyes, turned off the music and then lifted Chloe into his arms. He turned off the lights and carried her out to the parking lot.

Chapter 20

Savannah ordered porridge with a fruit salad, while Nyle went for the full breakfast with eggs Florentine and American-style pancakes with fresh fruit and maple syrup, and steak frites. She insisted on a Bloody Mary to top it all off. Snagging a table at Balthazar London was usually very difficult, but for Sunday morning brunch they had no problem. The French brasserie was a perfect imitation of New York's version of the restaurant, with red awnings, red leather banquettes, huge antiqued mirrored walls and mosaic floors.

Savannah watched in awe as Nyle ate as though there was no tomorrow. It had been her idea that the two eat there. Nyle insisted on treating Savannah to a nice English meal at her favorite brunch spot. She spent the entire meal catching Savannah up on all that had taken place in her life over the years. She shared the story of how she met Godfrey, the man she'd been in a relationship with for the past few weeks.

"He's a wonderful lover," she stated, "but he's never home. Always traveling abroad. The flat is his. I just lay my head there."

"Does he know that I'm staying there?"

"Of course."

"Are you sure?" Savannah pressed.

Nyle gave a nod. "We're two ships in the night. Our paths rarely cross."

"Why do you put up with that? Why not find a man who has time for you?"

"I like him," she said. "And I enjoy the time to myself when he's gone."

"I guess if it works for you both. How does he feel about it?"

She laughed. "He has the nerve to be jealous."

"Will you ever marry?" Savannah asked.

"Doubtful. We're fine this way. Why fix something that isn't broken?" Nyle asked. "Marriage is overrated anyway. I've been down that road before, and so have you. Will you ever remarry?"

"I don't know. I suppose if the right man comes along." Savannah finished her porridge. "Edward and I spent some time together in the Bahamas recently. I thought we might reconcile, but it didn't really work out."

"Why not?" asked Nyle.

Savannah looked at her mother. Wasn't ready to share everything with her just yet. They needed to build trust.

"Timing."

"What does that mean? You weren't ready or he wasn't?"

"Neither of us. "

"Another woman?"

"Where did you get that idea?"

"It's obvious. You seem scorned," said Nyle. "Was he not worth fighting for?"

"We're not married anymore. We both have moved on," said Savannah. "Now let's drop it."

Nyle raised her hands in surrender. "It's dropped."

After the server brought the check, Nyle grabbed it from the table and then dug into her purse. "I thought I had a few bloody pounds in here. I must've left them on the table at home."

"Don't worry about it. I have my MasterCard." Savannah grabbed the check from Nyle. "I'll take care of it."

"I'll give it back as soon as we get home."

"No worries," said Savannah, and she paid the check.

The pair hopped into the backseat of a hackney carriage. Nyle slid in first and hugged the driver from behind. "Where the hell have you been, you ornery man?" she asked the blond-haired older man.

"I've been bloody working!" The driver glanced at Savannah in the rearview mirror, and then gave Nyle a wide grin.

"This is my daughter," Nyle explained.

"Wow! Really. She's just as beautiful as you are," he said. "You don't look old enough to have a daughter that old."

"Savannah, this is Xander. Xander, Savannah."

"Pleasure meeting you, Savannah," said Xander. "You're not from here, are you?"

"No."

"Will you be staying long?"

"I hope so."

"Savannah has relocated from the US."

"I see," Xander said as he glanced at Savannah again. "Welcome. I think you'll find it a wonderful place to live. What part of town are you looking at?"

"She's living with me for the time being," Nyle explained. "At least until she gets her feet grounded."

Xander slammed on the brake to avoid hitting the car in front of him. He was distracted—too busy staring at Nyle in the rearview. When he pulled up in front of the Design Museum, Savannah exhaled. His driving made her nervous. Savannah and Nyle hopped out of the car. They took in the industrial and fashion design that the museum had to offer. They shopped for jewelry and had coffee at the little café that overlooked the Thames. They talked about fashion, and when they were done taking in the exhibitions, they walked out and found Xander, who was waiting with the car running. They visited three more museums.

Nyle had Xander stop at a liquor store, where she sent him in for a bottle of wine. And soon he pulled the car in front of Nyle's flat. Savannah opened her purse to look for a few pounds to pay for the cab ride. Nyle placed a hand over Savannah's and shook her head no. She snapped her purse shut.

"Thank you, Xander," Nyle said.

"My pleasure." Xander gave Nyle a wink in the mirror and waited for the ladies to exit the cab.

Savannah stepped out first and waited for her mother. Nyle whispered something to Xander, patted him on the shoulder and then exited the cab. Xander grinned at whatever was said and then slowly pulled away from the curb. Nyle hooked her arm inside Savannah's as they walked up to the front door.

"What a fun day," she exclaimed.

"I enjoyed it," Savannah agreed. "You and Xander must be pretty close."

"We're old chums," said Nyle as she unlocked the door. "Now let's get that bottle of wine opened, kick our shoes off and have some girl talk."

The thought of it sounded good to Savannah. She went to her room and pulled flannel pajamas out of her bag. She hadn't completely unpacked. There was still some reservation from before, but she was starting to relax a bit more. She removed her underwear from her luggage and placed it in the top bureau drawer. She then put her socks and shirts in the middle drawer. She hung clothes in the closet. She grabbed her toothbrush and pajamas and headed down the hall to the bathroom. Turned on the shower. She desperately needed a shower.

As the water cascaded over her naked body, she thought of Edward. His touch and the way he had kissed her lips and made love to her on the beach. She missed Chloe, but had to admit that part of her missed Edward, too. She admitted that to herself, though she had no intentions of admitting it to anyone else. She wished with all her heart that she could get him out of her head. She had presumed that once she arrived in London, she could actually rid her thoughts of him. She didn't expect to think of him more.

She dried herself off with a thick towel and sat on the edge of the tub. Grabbed her cell phone and logged on to Facebook. Edward had posted pictures of Chloe, and Savannah smiled as she scrolled through them. She even smiled at the selfie that Edward and Chloe had taken together, both of them sticking their tongues out and crossing their eyes. They appeared to be having fun together, and Savannah's heart was filled with envy.

"Nice photos," she typed.

We're watching a movie.

Shouldn't she be preparing for bed?

No. We're about five hours behind you.

Savannah had forgotten about the time difference.

Did she complete homework? Make sure she has a bath. And make sure she brushes her teeth.

We got this. How was your day with Nyle?

Surprisingly wonderful. We're about to have wine and girl talk.

That should be fun.

Maybe.

Well, don't worry about us. We're good. Go have fun and we'll talk tomorrow.

Okay. Gn.

Gn Savannah.

She washed her face, brushed her teeth, and slipped into her pajamas. When she opened the bathroom door, loud music resonated through the flat—Jimi Hendrix sang "Purple Haze" and the stench of marijuana drifted in the air.

"Is she serious?" Savannah whispered to herself.

She walked to her room and grabbed her bathrobe, wrapped it around her body and tightened the belt. She crept down the hall and into the living area to see what Nyle was up to. She peeked around the corner and Nyle was sitting in the easy chair in the corner of the room, a glass of wine in one hand and a joint in the other. She took a long drag from the joint and leaned her head back in slow motion. Xander had returned and was sitting across the room from Nyle. Laughter filled the air.

So much for girl talk, Savannah thought. She walked back to her room, pulled the door shut and sat in the middle of the bed. She took a novel out of her backpack and started to read.

Chapter 21

Edward was having a hard time balancing his career and Chloe. Handling her alone had become a challenge, but he would never give Savannah the satisfaction of knowing that.

He pulled into the parking lot of the elementary school. Chloe and Miss Jennings sat on the steps. He hopped out of the car and rushed toward them.

"I'm so sorry, Miss Jennings. I had a late meeting," he explained.

"How are you, Mr. Talbot?" Miss Jennings's usual flirty smile wasn't there. She had an edge of disappointment in her voice. "We've been waiting for almost an hour."

"I'm sorry. I promise it won't happen again," he said, and grabbed Chloe by the hand. He threw the strap of her backpack over his shoulder.

She gave him a smile. "Please see that it doesn't, Mr. Talbot."

He smiled at her brown face and hoped she realized that he really *was* sorry. She gave him a look of disappointment, one that she might give one of her kindergartners when they misbehave. He was grateful that she hadn't read him his rights or threatened to take some action.

"Her mother is away, and I'm doing this on my own."

"I understand," she said. "Her homework is in her back-pack."

"Thanks."

"And don't forget to bring her cookies for the celebration tomorrow."

"Cookies?" Edward asked.

"Yes. Each of the kids is bringing a snack for our little celebration. They have to prepare it themselves...with the help of a parent, of course. There was a note about it in her backpack last week."

"I didn't see it. I missed it," said Edward.

"I told you about it, Daddy," Chloe said. "But you were working."

"It's okay," Edward told Miss Jennings. "We'll bake cookies."

"Well good, then. I'll see you tomorrow, Chloe, bright and early. And don't forget to complete your homework assignment."

"I won't, Miss Jennings."

"Good night, Mr. Talbot." She gave him a semismile that time.

"Good night, Miss Jennings." He gave her a genuine one.

Chloe snapped her seat belt on as Edward pulled out of the parking lot.

"Daddy, you were so late! All of the kids were already gone, and I thought you weren't coming," she whined. "Did you forget about me?"

"Of course not, sweetheart. I would never forget about you. Daddy just had a late meeting and it was hard getting here. Traffic was a son of a b...traffic was bad." He reached into the backseat and grabbed her small hand in his. "I promise to do better. Okay?"

"It's okay, Daddy."

"Forgive me?"

"Yes." She smiled. "Can we go for ice cream now?"

"After dinner," he said. "We gotta figure out how to bake these cookies. Or maybe we could just buy some already baked ones at the Piggly Wiggly. We can put them in a plastic container and everything. Pretend. You don't tell, I won't tell."

"We can't pretend, Daddy. We have to bake them for real."

Edward huffed. "Okay."

Edward rushed to the hardware store. He needed to repair the kitchen sink, which had leaked water all night. The leak would damage the wood in the cabinet, not to mention send his water bill into orbit if he didn't repair it right away. He dropped by McDonald's and grabbed Chloe some chicken nuggets. A feeling of guilt rushed over him. He'd promised himself that he would take better care of her, and at least feed her a healthy diet. She'd eaten frozen fish sticks the day before because he'd run out of time, and pizza the day before that. All thoughts of healthy food had gone out the window.

After patching the leak, Edward and Chloe found themselves at Piggly Wiggly, making it through the automatic doors in just the knick of time. Chloe was already sluggish and winding down, and Edward worried that she wouldn't stay awake long enough to see the cookies to their fully baked state. But Miss Jennings had insisted that the children prepare them themselves.

"I know it's past your bedtime, sweetheart, but you have to stay awake," he warned as they rushed through the express lane. "You have to bake these cookies."

"I know, Daddy."

He grabbed his receipt from the freckle-faced cashier and

picked Chloe up. Carried her to the car. She was sound asleep by the time they pulled into the garage. Edward sat in the car for a moment. He sighed. Wondered how Savannah managed to do all of this by herself—keep house, manage a career and take care of Chloe. All of it was next to impossible for him, yet she made it seem effortless.

Chloe stood on a step stool and placed little squares of chocolate chip cookie dough on the pan. Edward heated the oven, and then placed the cookie sheet inside. He set the timer and then grabbed the television remote, flipped to ESPN, relaxed on the leather sofa. Chloe rested her head in his lap. The cough he'd heard that morning and the night before had returned. She shivered.

"Are you cold, sweetheart?" he asked.

"Yes."

The weather had been mild, and he hadn't turned on the air conditioner for days. Chloe was shivering uncontrollably. He grabbed a throw from the linen closet and wrapped it around her. He felt her forehead, and it was warm.

"You have a slight fever," he announced to her, and went to the bathroom in search of the Children's Tylenol.

"I don't feel good, Daddy."

"What's hurting?" he asked.

"I'm tired," she said. "And my throat hurts from coughing so much."

Savannah would know what to do in situations like this. He wanted to reach out to her, but didn't want to alarm her. Chloe needed Tylenol for the fever and cough syrup for the cough. He found the Tylenol in the medicine cabinet, but not the cough suppressant.

He went to the kitchen and placed the teakettle on the stove. Perhaps a hot cup of tea would do the trick. His phone rang, but he ignored it. Instead grabbed two mugs and two tea bags from the pantry. His phone rang again and he looked at the screen. *Quinn*. He didn't have time to humor her, but he answered anyway. Placed her on speakerphone.

"What's up?" he asked.

"Did you hear the news?"

"What news?"

"Whitman dropped out of the election."

"What?" he said. "No! We need him in the race."

"He's out, dude," said Quinn. "You know what that means, right?"

"What?"

"You have to run," she said. "Stop straddling the fence and make a decision. Just do it."

"I can't right now. Too much going on."

"Oh, right. You're reuniting with Savannah," she said. "How's that going, by the way?"

"It's not." He was frustrated and annoyed. "Quinn, I can't talk right now. I have a sick child and I need to get to the store for a bottle of cough syrup."

"I can drop by the store and grab a bottle of cough syrup for you."

He thought for a moment. As much as he wasn't up for Quinn's company, he hated the idea of dragging Chloe out to the store again even more. The thought of her bringing cough syrup was actually quite appealing.

"That would be great," he said as he pulled burned cookies out of the oven.

"I'll be there shortly."

Quinn held on to Chloe and rocked her to sleep. The coughing had ceased, the fever had gone down and Edward exhaled. He'd panicked, but somehow Quinn had saved the day, and he was grateful.

"I think she's ready for bed now," said Quinn.

Edward stood and lifted Chloe into his arms. He took her to bed and pulled the covers up to her neck. He turned on the humidifier and put the lights down low, then left the door ajar just a bit so that he could hear her. When he returned to the living room, Quinn had made herself comfortable, remote control in hand and flipping through the channels.

"Thank you," he said.

"My pleasure." She smiled.

"You're good with her."

"She's sweet." Quinn made herself at home as she usually did, went into Edward's kitchen and located a bottle of Merlot. She opened it. "Want some wine?"

"Yeah, I'll have a glass." He followed her into the kitchen, pulled two glasses from the cupboard.

"I'm really surprised that Savannah would rush off to London, and leave her daughter like that. Especially when Chloe's not in the best of health," Quinn stated.

"It's not like she just abandoned her. She left her with me, her father."

"I'm not knocking your parenthood, but girls need a mother," she said. "Seems kind of irresponsible."

"She's definitely not irresponsible. She's a great mother."

"Well, you're defensive. Especially since it seems she abandoned you, too," she said. "I thought you were about to propose, and then suddenly she's gone."

"I don't know what happened. I tried calling her that Sunday after we returned from the Bahamas and she never returned my calls. So a few days later I dropped by…" Edward took a sip from his wine.

"To switch the luggage."

"Yeah." A frown on his face, he stared at Quinn. "How did you know that?"

"Know what?"

"That I went there to switch our luggage."

"You told me."

"I never told you that."

"You're mistaken. You told me that you had her luggage and she had yours."

"I never told you that, because I didn't even realize it until the next day. By that time you were long gone. When I opened the suitcase in search of my shaving cream the next morning…" He gave Quinn a look of skepticism. "You have something you want to tell me?"

"No." She wrapped both hands around the bowl of her wineglass, her fingers intertwined.

"What did you do?"

Quinn sighed. "Okay. I might've have answered your phone when you were in the shower."

"You what?" He became angry.

"Savannah called that Sunday when you were in the shower."

"And you answered my phone? Did you also delete the call?"

"I was trying to help you, Edward! You were talking marriage, and proposing…and I know that you're not ready to go down that road again. First of all, if it didn't work the first time, what makes you think that it would work now?"

"Are you out of your mind?"

"No, I'm quite sane," she said. "And did I mention that you should be running for the US Senate…not running around chasing your ex-wife?"

He was livid. Stood and paced the floor. He wanted to make sure he maintained control. He would never strike a woman, but the thought sure crossed his mind. "You have to leave."

"Edward." She giggled. "Don't be silly. It's me, Quinn."

"I'm trying not to throw you out, so I would advise you

to get your ass up and walk out that front door without saying another word to me."

"You're serious?"

He breathed deeply. She was trying his patience. His jaws were tight.

"Damn, you are serious." She finally got it, stood, an inquisitive look on her face. Grabbed her glass of wine and slammed it. She headed for the front door, opened it.

He waited until he heard the door shut before he exhaled. He immediately pulled his cell phone out of his pocket. He needed to reach out to Savannah, explain and apologize profusely. The phone didn't ring. Instead he got her voice mail, and anxiety got the best of him.

He needed to get to her, plead his case. Right the wrongs that Quinn had created. She must've thought him to be a terrible liar and a cheat. He needed her back in the States, so that he could tell her how much he loved her and needed her in his life. He needed to make her his wife and give her the ring that once belonged to her. He was going crazy! A million thoughts rushed through his head.

Chapter 22

Savannah forced her eyes open and glanced at the digital clock on the nightstand. It took her a moment to remember where she was, but she still hadn't quite grasped why she was hearing loud, argumentative voices. She sat straight up in her bed, flipped on the lamp.

"I need you to leave!" a male voice yelled.

Savannah stood, grabbed her robe and wrapped it around her body. She cracked the door a bit and listened.

"I don't have anywhere to go," she heard Nyle say.

"That isn't my problem, now is it?"

"Godfrey! Let me explain."

"I don't need your bloody explanation!"

Savannah crept out of the room, down the hall and into the living room. Xander was standing there in his powder-blue boxer shorts and a white T-shirt that barely covered his large, hairy stomach. A fitted sheet covered Nyle's naked body. Godfrey quickly moved the shotgun from Xander and pointed it at Savannah.

"Hey!" Nyle yelled. "That's my daughter."

Savannah held her hands high in the air. Godfrey moved the gun back to Xander. "Out!" He told him.

Xander reached for his trousers.

"No!" said Godfrey. "Leave them."

"I need my bloody trousers!" Xander complained.

Godfrey cocked the shotgun. "I said leave them!"

Xander rushed toward the front door of the flat and went out into the darkness, half naked.

Godfrey lowered the gun. "I'm leaving. And when I return, I expect you to be packed and gone," he told Nyle.

Within seconds, he was gone. Savannah stared at Nyle. Her eyes begged for an explanation.

"It's okay. No problem," said Nyle.

"What do you mean, no problem?" Savannah asked. "It's after one o'clock in the morning and we're being thrown out on the street?"

"We'll go to Aunt Frances's for the night. Once Godfrey calms down…"

"He doesn't look like he's going to calm down!" Savannah said.

"He will," Nyle explained. "He loves me. He's just really, really mad right now."

"You were sleeping with another man in his home! How will he recover from that?"

"He will." Nyle dropped the sheet, revealing her naked fiftysomething-year-old body that looked more thirtysomething. She began to retrieve her clothing from the floor. "Let's pack an overnight bag."

"I'm packing everything," Savannah said in a huff, and returned to her room.

The pair caught a taxi to Whetstone and pulled up in front of a two-story brick terraced house. They stepped out of the car, bags in tow, and walked up to the door. Before they could knock, the door swung open. An elderly woman stood in the doorway, bent over just a bit, an apron tied around her waist. Her gray hair was pulled back into a ponytail. Her olive face was much like Nyle's.

"Why am I not surprised by your shenanigans?" she asked.

"I don't need your judgment. Just a place to rest my head for the night," Nyle said. "And for my daughter."

"Just for the night, and not a moment longer," said Aunt Frances. "You must be Savannah. You're much prettier in person."

"Thank you." Savannah gave her a half smile. She was still appalled by the events that had led her to this woman's doorstep. "And thank you for letting us stay for the night."

"Come inside. Are you hungry?" She directed her question to Savannah only.

"No, ma'am. Just tired."

"Fine. I'll show you where you'll sleep."

Savannah followed Aunt Frances through the cluttered space with dull hardwood floors and an old brown sofa in the living room. They reached a small bedroom toward the back of the house, and Aunt Frances motioned toward the twin-size bed in the corner.

"Here you are, dear."

"Thank you," Savannah responded and dropped her bags onto the floor. She felt defeated.

"There's a powder room just down the hall."

Savannah nodded her head yes, and within a few seconds Aunt Frances was closing the door behind her. Savannah slipped into a pair of pajamas and then tucked herself beneath fresh-smelling sheets. She wanted to check her Facebook page to see if there were any new postings from Edward. She wanted to talk to him and tell him about everything that had gone on, but her phone had long since died and she hadn't packed her charger. The first chance she got, she needed to find a store that sold mobile phone accessories.

Savannah stared at the ceiling. Wondered how she'd ended up in this chaos called Nyle. She was still quite angry, but giggled at the thought of Xander leaving the flat wearing nothing more than his powder-blue boxers—at gunpoint, nonetheless. She exhaled and before long, sleep captured her and she gave in to it.

Daylight crept through the window and jarred her awake much too soon. Savannah opened her eyes and stared at the ceiling for a moment, tried to grasp where she was. She grabbed her purse and searched inside, found the business card that she'd received from the handsome stranger on the plane—Rolf. She grabbed her robe and wrapped it around her body. Tiptoed out of the room, her bare feet touching the cool floor. Aunt Frances sat at the kitchen table, a newspaper in front of her, reading glasses at the tip of her nose.

"Good morning," she said without even looking up.

"Good morning," said Savannah.

"Coffee is over there." Aunt Frances pointed at the coffee-pot on the countertop. "Cups are in cupboard."

"Thanks," Savannah said. "Is there a phone I can use?"

Aunt Frances pointed toward the cordless phone in the corner of the room. "No long-distance calls."

"This is local." Savannah gave her a smile and reached for the phone.

"I mean it. No long distance," Aunt Frances reiterated.

"Yes, ma'am," Savannah simply said and then retreated to her room, dialed Rolf's phone number.

"Yeah," his husky voice answered.

"Rolf?"

"You've got it!"

"We met on the flight from Atlanta to London. Sat next to each other on the plane."

"Savannah," he stated emphatically.

"Yes. You remember."

"Yes, of course," he said. "How's your stay been so far?"

"Well...not so good. Which is why I'm calling. I'd like to see if that flat of yours is still available?"

"Absolutely! When would you like to see it?"

"Right away. Today," she said.

"Fantastic. I can meet you there this afternoon. Say around two?"

"Okay."

"Great. Grab a pen and write down the addy."

She did. Found a pen in the top drawer of the antique chest. She wrote down the address of Rolf's rental property.

"Okay, I got it," she said.

"Take the Tube to the South Kensington station. It's a short stroll from there. The weather is mild, so you should be okay."

"I'll be there at two. Thank you."

Savannah returned the phone to its place in the kitchen.

"If you want breakfast, you'll have to cook it yourself," Aunt Frances said. She hadn't moved from her spot at the table, and she continued to stare at the newspaper. "There's eggs in the refrigerator. Meat. Bread."

"Thank you, but I usually skip breakfast."

"What's your angle here, dear?"

"My angle?"

"Did you come here expecting a happily-ever-after with your mother? Because you certainly won't get it," said Aunt Frances. "She's not capable of doing anything normal. There's not much hope for her, you know?"

Savannah glanced into the living area and noticed that Nyle was on the other side of the wall, listening. She felt sorry for her mother at that moment, and wondered if what Aunt Frances said was true. She wondered if there was any hope for Nyle. After all, she wasn't getting any younger. Savannah averted her eyes as Nyle stepped into the kitchen.

"Morning, ladies," she said and went to the cupboard, grabbed a mug. She poured a cup of coffee.

"Good morning," said Savannah.

Aunt Frances glared at Nyle over the top of her glasses.

Savannah escaped from the kitchen and rushed back down the hall to her temporary quarters. She gathered her underwear and toiletries and retreated to the powder room for a shower. The pipes squealed as she turned on the water. She glanced at herself in the faded mirror and wondered how she'd ended up in this place.

Savannah stepped from the underground train and onto the platform at the South Kensington station. She walked the few short blocks to Rolf's flat, stood outside and waited for him. She was happy to see the black sedan pull up and park in front of the white brick property.

"Been waiting long?" Ray-Ban shades covered Rolf's face.

"Just got here."

"Well, let's go inside."

Shiny hardwood adorned the elegant Victorian flat. A beautiful tan leather sofa and matching chair, glass tables, and stainless appliances made the space look spectacular.

"I'm sure I can't afford this," she stated. "It's already furnished."

"No worries. I'll work with you."

"You do realize I don't have a job, right?" she asked. "I have a couple of months rent, but no job."

"I'll tell you what… I might be able to help. I know that your background is fashion, but I think I might have something that can get you by for a bit." He pulled his wallet from the inside pocket of his blazer. Handed her another business card. "Drop by here. Dr. Abbott. Tell him I sent you. Wear business attire."

She studied the card. "What type of work?"

"It's a receptionist position. It's quite busy, so you'll need to keep up."

"Answering phones?"

"And arranging appointments for a busy doctor. Billing. Things of that nature," he said. "It's a paycheck, right?"

She smiled. "Right."

"I'll take a deposit, but won't charge you rent until you get your first paycheck from Dr. Abbott. However, you're free to move in today if you'd like."

She studied his face. "You're serious."

"Yes."

"You're too kind."

"No smoking and no pets," he warned. "The place rents for nine hundred fifty pounds, but for you rent is six fifty, due on the first, but no later than the fifth."

"How much is that in US dollars?"

"About a thousand US dollars per month."

"I think I can handle that." She grinned.

"I'll draw up a contract," he said. "Is your deposit in cash?"

"Yes. I can switch the currency if you need me to."

"No worries. US dollars are fine."

"Thank you, Rolf. Thank you so much."

"My pleasure." He pulled a single key out of his pocket. Handed it to Savannah. "Welcome home."

In only a few days, she'd snagged her own flat and a new job. Things were quickly looking up.

Chapter 23

Savannah lit a scented candle and found some nice music on the stereo. She'd spent her Saturday morning picking up a few items at a yard sale that she found just a few blocks away. The space couldn't be more perfect, and she tried to make it feel warm, but it felt nothing like home. She missed her house that she and Chloe shared in West Palm Beach. She missed her daughter and their strolls along the beach. She missed picking her up from school and arguing over what to prepare for dinner and helping with homework. She even missed Edward, even though she told herself that she didn't.

She placed an arrangement of fresh flowers in the center of the wooden table and tacked secondhand curtains on the windows. She unpacked her clothes and hung them in the closet, placed her underwear in drawers. She enjoyed her time alone before Nyle returned from picking up groceries. Nyle had settled in, too. She'd claimed the bedroom at the end of the hallway—the one closest to the bathroom. Savannah was reluctant to cohabitate with her again, but knew that her mother had nowhere else to go. She was her only hope. That didn't stop Savannah from reading her the rights—no smoking, no pets and no scandalous behavior, she warned.

It wasn't long before Nyle was banging on the door, her arms filled with bags of food. Savannah let her in and then grabbed the bags, placed them in the kitchen on the counter.

"You bought a lot of stuff."

"Storm's coming," said Nyle. "I want to make sure we have the things that we need."

"That was thoughtful."

"Savannah, I cannot tell you how sorry I am…about all that has gone on," Nyle said. "I promise to make it up to you."

"Don't worry about it," said Savannah. "But I don't want to come home and find you in bed with some random man. I have a five-year-old daughter who will be here soon."

"You don't have to worry about that." Nyle pulled out one of her herbal cigarettes.

"And I said no smoking," Savannah reminded her.

"They're herbal. Not a drop of nicotine in them."

Savannah shook her head no, and Nyle put the cigarette away. In a huff, she started to unpack the groceries. "I'll get dinner started."

Savannah began to help put groceries away in the cupboards and refrigerator. She hoped that she and Nyle could start over again, pretend that nothing ever happened. She wanted this thing to work out, but the truth was, she was afraid to shut her eyes around the woman. She could barely be trusted.

"I almost forgot." Nyle had changed into a pair of the shortest of shorts and a cropped top. Her hair was pulled back into a ponytail. "I picked up a charger for your phone."

Savannah exhaled. "Thank you! Thank you very much."

"I know it's been torture for you, not being able to check in with your little girl."

"I've been going crazy!" Savannah rushed into the bedroom and retrieved her phone, plugged the charger into the wall behind the sofa in the living room.

"You're a good mother. I can tell," Nyle said out of the blue. "A lot better mother than I ever was."

"I made it my business to be in Chloe's life. It's always been my goal."

"You must really trust your ex-husband, to leave your daughter with him."

"I do. He's good with her. He loves her just as much as I do."

"I know you don't like talking about him," said Nyle. "But what went wrong with you two?"

Savannah sighed. Nyle insisted on knowing about Edward, and she wanted to keep her at bay. But then realized that the only way that the two of them would ever get to know each other was to talk about things—things that might be uncomfortable.

"Edward was married to his career. When I was pregnant with Chloe, he was running for mayor. He was never home, always on the campaign trail, and always with his beautiful campaign manager. He barely made it for Chloe's birth."

"Hmmm, another woman," said Nyle. "I bet she wasn't as beautiful as you."

"He claimed that they were just friends. And that nothing ever happened between them."

"But you don't believe it."

"I didn't know what to believe. All I knew was that he hadn't made our marriage a priority. So I rushed to Daddy's house. Hired a lawyer and divorced him."

"Did he fight for you?"

"I think his fight was more about saving face. He was

a political figure, and he didn't want the embarrassment of a divorce."

"But over the years, you two have become friends."

"More like co-parents," said Savannah. "We both have a lot of love for our daughter. We've agreed to be civilized for that reason."

"How does he feel about you moving his daughter to London? How will you pull that off?"

"It wasn't easy, convincing him that this was the right thing to do."

"Is it? The right thing? Because I have to tell you…you don't seem very happy here at all."

Savannah looked at her mother's eyes. Tears threatened to fill hers. Had she been that transparent?

"I know that I've been a terrible mother, Savannah. And I know that you're here looking for all those things that I deprived you of. I know that I left a horrible void in your life. And I'm sorry," Nyle said. "I'm just a rotten person. And I don't know if that will ever change."

"What do you mean?"

"Don't expect too much from me. I'm too old to change." Nyle chuckled. "Don't destroy what you have, the beautiful life that you have, looking for something that might never be."

"What are you saying? It was a mistake to come here?"

"I'm saying that you shouldn't expect too much." Nyle headed into the kitchen. "I'm having a Bloody Mary. You care for one?"

"Sure. Why not?"

After dinner and several Bloody Marys, the women sat in the center of the hardwood floor. Tears filled their eyes as they discussed the difficult issues that they'd avoided until then.

"I hated you," a drunken Savannah revealed. "All of

my friends had mothers who took them shopping and did their hair. I needed you, and you weren't there."

"I know," said Nyle. "My mother did the same bloody thing to me. She wasn't around either. Ran off with some man when I was five. Left me with Aunt Frances to raise me. And I gave that old woman hell!"

"What happened with you two, anyway?" asked Savannah.

"I don't wanna talk about it."

"Oh, come on! I just poured my heart out to you," begged Savannah. "Give me the goods."

"Savannah, I don't want to talk about it."

"What did you do to burn your bridge with Aunt Frances?"

"I didn't do anything!" Nyle exclaimed. She sighed and leaned her head against the edge of the sofa. Her hair was a wild mess on her head. "I'll never forget it as long as I live. I was young, slender like you, beautiful. I was a student at Westminster. Third year. Building my modeling career. Her boyfriend, Felix, came on to me. He'd been drinking… stumbled into my room late one night…"

"Where was Aunt Frances?"

"She worked nights. She was a nurse," Nyle said. "When I told her about it, she didn't believe me. Accused me of being loose, taunting him…"

"Did you? Taunt him?"

"No. He was a disgusting human being. And I did not taunt him. I was promiscuous. I admit that. But I was selective, and I wasn't at all interested in him. Which is why he wanted me so bad." Tears rolled down the side of her face. "She hated me after that. He didn't want her… he wanted me, and she couldn't live with that."

"What happened? Did she ever figure out the truth?"

"He left her for someone else, and she became a bitter old woman. She still blames me, you know."

"Did your mother ever come back?"

Nyle wiped tears from her eyes. "She died when I was seventeen. Committed suicide. Can you believe that? She bloody killed herself!"

Savannah slid across the floor and moved closer to her mother. She grabbed Nyle's hand and held on to it tightly. "I'm sorry."

"You should run away from me as fast as you can. I have nothing in my past but heartache and pain. And nothing good in my future," she said. "You heard what Aunt Frances said about me. It was the truth."

"You never had a chance. You weren't equipped to be a mother," said Savannah. "No one equipped you. Everyone abandoned you."

"Who equipped you?" Nyle asked Savannah.

"No one really. I watched Edward's mother, and I just had instincts. I didn't have a devastating childhood. I was very much loved by my father. And I was just so determined to be a better mother than…"

"…than me."

"It was my driving force," Savannah whispered. "Sorry."

"No apologies necessary. I'm happy that you found hope, Savannah. That you were able to give your daughter what she needed. I never was able to do that."

Savannah rested her head against her mother's bosom. For that moment, she felt as if she truly had a mother.

Chapter 24

Three weeks and Savannah had a new job as a receptionist. It wasn't the job she'd been looking for but it was a job nonetheless. And she had her own flat, and was finding her way about town. But her life wasn't as complete as she thought it would be once she arrived in London. The idea had been to find a career in fashion. And she was grateful to Jarrod for setting up the interview for her with one of the top fashion companies. However, it had been days since she'd met with Herman Mason, and she hadn't received a call back. She feared that she'd be a receptionist much longer than she'd intended to. She also missed Chloe like crazy. She missed their life together—*in Florida*. She missed Maia and her other friends. And though she hated to admit it, she missed Edward.

She looked forward to her daily Facebook chats with him. She'd begun messaging him before and after school. He would post pictures of Chloe and keep her abreast of what they were having for dinner and what homework assignments they were working on. Eventually, the before-and-after-school chats became more frequent. She found herself chatting with Edward throughout the day. The chats weren't just about Chloe, but had become more personal. Soon they'd begun to vent about their workdays. She hoped he hadn't detected the loneliness in her messages.

"Hey, Savannah. We're going out for drinks after work. Why don't you come along?" Mel, her red-haired coworker, stood in front of her. Mel had dipped into the restroom and changed from her professional garb into a short miniskirt with fishnet panty hose.

"No, I'm going to pass." Savannah removed her headset and checked her watch.

"Oh come on. You know you need a break," said Sunny, the chocolate-faced girl who had been so sweet to her since her first day. "I'll drive you home afterward."

"Just a couple of drinks," Mel encouraged.

Savannah sighed. She hadn't taken in any nightlife since arriving in London. And she wasn't in any hurry to get home to Nyle.

"Okay," said Savannah. "I'll go. But just for a little while."

"Great!"

She dialed her home phone. Called Nyle to let her know that she would be late. "I'm going out with the girls for a little while," she told her.

"Where?"

"What's the name of the place?" She held her hand over the receiver and asked Sunny.

"We'll probably hit a couple," Mel interjected, "but we'll start with Dirty Martini for happy hour."

"So we're club-hopping?" Savannah asked. "I thought we were going for a couple of drinks somewhere."

"We're going to Dirty Martini. St. Paul's location," Sunny said as she shushed Mel. "You'll scare the poor girl off."

"We're going to a place called Dirty Martini," Savannah told Nyle. "St. Paul's location."

"I've heard of it. Have a good time, and be careful," said Nyle. "I'll put you a plate up."

"Thanks," she said.

Savannah noted that Nyle almost sounded motherly. A light smile danced in the corner of her mouth as she grabbed her purse and joined Mel and Sunny at the huge silver elevators.

"This is going to be so much fun!" Mel exclaimed. "Lots of cute guys!"

"Savannah's not interested in cute guys," Sunny said. "She has a guy."

"Ex-guy," Mel corrected her.

"She still loves him," said Sunny. "Isn't that right, Savannah?"

They had been discussing her life as if she weren't standing there.

"We're still close friends. Co-parents to our daughter, if you will."

"Seems like a bit more than co-parenting, darling. You're messaging with him too many hours in the day."

"So he's a friend with benefits, eh, Savannah?" Mel asked.

"Just friends, no benefits."

"If you say so, darling." Mel hooked her arm inside of Savannah's as they walked toward Sunny's compact car. Mel hopped in and stretched her legs across the backseat. Savannah got in on the passenger's side and fastened her seat belt. Sunny blasted her stereo.

The music bounced against the brick walls, and bright lights spanned the room. They managed to snag a corner booth and each of them slid into it. They laughed and talked over the music.

"First round of drinks on me," Sunny said. "What are you having, Savannah?"

"Maybe a glass of wine," said Savannah.

"Are you kidding me?" Mel asked. "No way! You can't come to a place called Dirty Martini and not get a dirty martini!"

"I don't want a martini." Sunny missed her protest, because she'd already headed to the bar.

When she returned, Sunny placed the cocktail in front of Savannah. "Drink up," she said.

"Unwind," Mel said as she sipped on a vodka tonic. "And cheer up. You look like you've lost your best friend."

A tall, handsome man approached the table, whispered something into Sunny's ear. He grabbed her by the hand and pulled her onto the dance floor.

"Well, he was yummy." Mel gave Savannah a wide grin. She held her glass in the air. "Cheers, my friend."

Savannah lifted her glass and toasted with Mel. "Cheers."

"What are we cheering?" asked a blond-haired gentleman as he approached the table. "Is it someone's birthday?"

"We're cheering my friend's arrival to London."

"You're new here?" he asked.

"Yes," Savannah shouted over the music.

"Welcome!" he said, and held his hand out to her. "I'm Louis."

"Hello, Louis. I'm Savannah, and this is Mel."

Louis and Mel shook hands.

"Would you care to dance, Savannah?"

"No, thank you." Savannah gave him a smile. "But my friend Mel here is dying to dance."

"Well, we can't have her dying, now can we?" he asked, and held his hand out to Mel.

Mel gave Savannah a squint of the eyes and a tightened fist behind Louis's back as she followed him to the dance floor. They disappeared into the crowd and Savannah eased her legs onto the leather seat. She sipped on her drink and sat with her back against the wall. She hoped that it wouldn't be a long night, but she was already ready to go. She pulled her cell phone out of her purse and logged in to Facebook. She hadn't heard from Edward in two days. They'd argued about something frivolous and had ended their conversation on a bad note. And he hadn't responded to her message from the night before. She missed him, and hoped he would get past it.

When Sunny returned, Savannah slid out of the booth.

"I need to go to the little girls' room," she said.

"Do you need me to go with you?" Sunny asked.

"I think I'll be fine." Savannah made her way through the crowded nightclub.

She found the restrooms, but there was a long line to get in. So she snagged a place behind a girl who was yapping on her cell phone. The line slowly inched along, and Savannah became impatient. What was she doing here, at this club, in this line, in this country? Why wasn't she at home—her real home—in her warm bed, reading a bedtime story to her child? She'd even rather be arguing with Edward over Chloe's hair, or what extracurricular activities she should participate in. Nyle was right—she was homesick.

"Are you here alone?" someone whispered in her ear.

"No, I'm not," she said sternly without even looking around.

"Are you here with your man?" whispered the intruder.

"No."

"Well, can I be your man?" The voice then sounded familiar.

She turned to face her intruder and found Edward's beautiful eyes looking back at her. He wore blue jeans and a gray cashmere sweater. He had a fresh haircut. She loved when his hair was freshly cut. It made him look so handsome. Her mouth dropped open at the sight of him. And then she cried. Tears crept down the side of her face.

"Not happy to see me?"

She wrapped her arms tightly around his neck, buried her face in his chest. "What are you doing here?"

He didn't respond. Instead he hungrily kissed her lips. "You want me to leave?" he asked.

"No," she whispered, and tears continued to fill her eyes. Whatever they'd argued about two days ago had quickly dissipated. She didn't care about anything or anyone else before this moment. "I'm so glad you're here."

She didn't want to let him go.

"Are you still in line?" asked the woman behind her.

She motioned for the woman to go ahead of her.

"What are you doing here? When did you get here? How did you find me? Where's Chloe?" She asked Edward a million questions.

"She's with your mother," he said.

"You left her with Nyle?"

"She seemed harmless," said Edward.

"We have to go," Savannah said, and grabbed Edward's hand. She led him through the crowd and back to the table where Mel and Sunny sat.

"Well, he's a cutie," Mel said. "You find him in the toilet?"

"This is Edward," Savannah said. "Edward, this is Mel and Sunny. We work together."

"Pleased to meet you both," Edward said.

"No wonder she's still in love with you. You're drop-dead gorgeous!" Sunny said.

"Scrumptious." Mel smiled, licked her lips and gave him a wink.

"We're gonna go," said Savannah, and then she turned to Edward. "How did you get here?"

"Some dude named Xander. He's a friend of your mother's." Edward pointed toward the door. "He's waiting outside."

"Not Xander," mumbled Savannah.

"Who is he?"

"I'll explain later," she said. "Ladies, thanks for inviting me out. It was fun. And I'll see you both on Monday."

"Will you?" Mel asked with raised eyebrows.

"I don't know," she said. Honestly, she didn't know how much more of the job or London she could take.

"Do you have a brother or cousin, or someone who bears a strong resemblance to you?" Mel asked Edward.

"Let's go." Savannah slid her hand into his.

She felt more content and happier than she had in weeks.

Chapter 25

Edward tried to hand Xander a twenty-dollar bill, but he turned it down. Savannah gave Xander a look of skepticism, and Edward wondered what had happened to make her treat him so rudely. He stepped out of the cab and then reached for her. He placed his hand gently around her waist. He wasn't sure how she would react to his showing up unannounced, but he was grateful for the welcome that he received. He'd taken a chance, scrambling for Chloe a passport at the last minute and purchasing two expensive airline tickets. And even as he and Chloe had boarded the flight, he still felt uneasy.

He had tightened Chloe's seat belt around her waist and then secured his. He listened as the flight attendant gave instructions on what to do—and what not to do—in case of emergency. He glanced out the window. It was starting to rain, and he wasn't looking forward to the long flight. But he was looking forward to seeing Savannah. It had only been a few weeks since she left, but it felt like a few months.

He knew that he was taking a chance by coming, but he

needed to fight for her. Finally. If that meant that he had to fly clear across the world to let her know what he was feeling, then he was willing to do that. He needed to let her know how much she meant to him, and that she was wrong about Quinn. He slid his hand into the pocket of his jeans, pulled the emerald out and gave it a quick glance. He was going to get his woman.

Edward and Chloe had slid into the backseat of a hackney cab and he'd given the driver the address that Savannah had given him in case of emergency. She and her mother had been ejected from one place, and she was renting a flat somewhere. The cab pulled up in front of the white brick place, and Edward stepped out and lifted his bags out of the trunk.

"Thank you," he told the driver and gave him a hefty tip and a strong handshake.

He and Chloe stood at the door and rang the bell. When the door swung open, he was surprised to see the beautiful woman who stood on the other side. She was an older yet beautiful replica of Savannah. Her skin was more ivory-colored, but her features were very much like his ex-wife's. He couldn't stop staring.

"Hi, I'm…"

"Edward!" she said before he could finish his sentence.

"Yes."

"Come inside." She gave him a hug and kept smiling. "I'm Nyle."

"I figured," said Edward.

"And you're Chloe!" Nyle gave her a wide grin.

"Hello," Chloe said, and held on to her father's waist.

"Oh my! Did Savannah know that you two were coming?"

"No," Edward said. "We're here to surprise her."

"Boy, she'll be so surprised. And so happy to see you. I think she's quite miserable here."

"She is?" Edward asked.

"She's a good sport. She wanted to make this thing work, she really did. But she's terribly homesick. She needs you two more than she needs me."

"Where is she?"

"She went out for drinks after work."

"She has a job?"

"Yes. Something temporary, just until she lands something permanent."

Edward and Chloe stood in the middle of the floor.

"Sit down. Take a load off," said Nyle. She grinned at Edward. "You're way more gorgeous than I imagined."

"So are you," Edward said.

"Well, aren't you a sweet one. No wonder my daughter's in love with you."

"She's in love with me?" he asked. "Did she tell you that?"

"She didn't have to. Anyone could see," Nyle said. "Do you love her?"

Edward felt uneasy discussing such an intimate subject with someone he hadn't known for more than five minutes. But he couldn't bring himself to lie. "I do love her."

She squealed. "Yes! I knew it. If she loves you, and you love her, then what's the problem?"

Edward unbuttoned the top button of his cardigan. "There's no problem."

"Well, you don't have to talk to me about it." Nyle smiled. "Why don't you go tell her? She's at a place called Dirty Martini. It's a club where the youngsters hang out. Not far from here, and I have a friend who can drive you there."

It hadn't taken much convincing before Edward was in the backseat of a cab and headed to get his woman. There was some reluctance to leave Chloe with Nyle, but he didn't have a choice. He hoped that Savannah wouldn't be too upset about his rash decision. But he was prepared for anything, even if she turned him away.

Now as they stepped into her flat, the aroma of onions and garlic filled the home. Nyle stood at the stove stirring a pot of something, and Chloe stood on a step stool beside her. Savannah obviously hadn't picked up her mother's cooking skills, Edward thought. But he hoped that Chloe would. She tossed vegetables into the pot that Nyle stirred. They were both singing the lyrics of an Adele song. Edward and Savannah stood in the doorway for a moment and observed the duo. When Chloe finally spotted her mother, she hopped from the stool and into Savannah's arms.

"Mommy!"

"Oh, little girl, I've missed you!" Savannah showered her face with kisses. "What are you doing?"

"Me and Gigi are making lamb soup!"

"You and Gigi?" Savannah glanced at Nyle.

"Sounds much more glamorous than Grandmum."

"What else have you and Gigi done today?" Savannah asked.

"We danced." Chloe waved her hands in the air.

"I see," said Savannah. "I've missed you so much!"

"Missed you, too, Mommy."

"Now this is the first smile that I've seen in weeks. You two have made her happy again." Nyle smiled gently. "Why don't you two go find something to do? Let Chloe and me finish dinner." She pushed them both out of the kitchen. "Go. Go have some fun."

* * *

Edward and Savannah did just that. They started with a walk to the Tube and hopped onto it.

"Where are we going?" Edward asked.

"I don't know. Anywhere!" She smiled.

They took the Tube to one of London's rooftop bars. They sipped martinis at the legendary Dukes Hotel bar, and then took the Tube to one of London's oldest wine bars and snagged a table in the dark cave-like bar. A candle burned in the center of the table. They grabbed a wine list and ordered a bottle of Riesling, with a cheese plate to share. Edward couldn't help gazing at the beautiful woman who sat across from him at the table. His eyes wouldn't leave her.

"You're staring," she reminded him.

"I can't help it." Edward reached into his pocket and pulled the engagement ring out. He needed to do this sooner than later, couldn't afford any more missed opportunities. "I love you, Savannah. I never stopped loving you. My heart was ripped apart when you left, but I didn't have the guts to tell you that I couldn't live without you."

Savannah covered her mouth as she hung on every word.

"I don't care about Quinn. I never have, and if she makes you uncomfortable, she's history. I just want my family back." He looked her deeply in her eyes. "Savannah Carrington, will you marry me? Again?" he asked.

The ringing of her phone interrupted their moment. Savannah looked at the screen. "I have to get it. It's Nyle."

"Give me an answer first."

She held her finger in the air and answered the call. "Hello."

"Savannah, it's me. Chloe's running a really high fever,

a hundred and five, and I think I should take her to the emergency room. She doesn't look good."

"Yes, yes, you should take her. Where's the nearest hospital?"

"Chelsea and Westminster."

"We'll meet you there," said Savannah. She hung up. "Chloe's running a fever of a hundred and five. We have to go!"

Edward took care of the check and the two rushed outside and hopped into a cab.

Chapter 26

When they arrived at the hospital, Aunt Frances greeted them in the waiting room.

"Aunt Frances!" Savannah exclaimed. When she didn't see Nyle, she suspected that her mother had ditched Chloe and disappeared again. It was her style. "What are you doing here?"

"Nyle called me. She was frantic," said Aunt Frances.

"She pawned Chloe off on you?"

"No, dear. She's in there with her right now. She hasn't left her side." Aunt Frances pointed. "Down the hall on the right."

Savannah didn't wait for the room number. She quickly trotted down the long hallway with shiny buffed floors. Edward struggled to keep up. She peeked into every room until she found her daughter's. Chloe was sound asleep, but Nyle was next to her bed. She stood when they walked in.

"The doctors managed to get her fever down. Her bronchitis has progressed into pneumonia. They're going to keep her."

"Oh my God! Her bronchitis was cleared up weeks ago." She turned to Edward. "Did she get sick again?"

"I wanted to tell you, but I didn't want you to worry." Edward gave her a sheepish look.

"How could you not tell me?" She stormed toward the door, "I need to see the doctor."

"He's gone for the night, honey. He'll be back in the morning," said Nyle. "But you can speak with her nurse."

Edward covered his face. "I shouldn't have brought her here. She wasn't well enough to travel. This is my fault."

"I shouldn't have left her," Savannah said. "What mother leaves her child?"

"Both of you can stop," said Nyle. "It's nobody's fault. You both just need to focus on getting little Chloe well."

Edward wrapped his arm around Savannah, pulled her close. "I'm going for a cup of coffee. Can I bring either of you something back?"

"No, thank you," they said in unison.

After spending a few days at the hospital, Chloe's condition seemed to worsen. Both Nyle and Savannah refused to leave her side. It was there that the mother-daughter duo began their hard conversations, as Savannah described to her mother how she'd let her down.

"Each time you left, you took a piece of me with you."

"I'm sorry."

"I hated you. I didn't respect you. I pretended you were dead."

"I deserved that." Nyle sat up in the uncomfortable chair that she'd been sleeping in for days. She stretched her legs.

"But then something clicked when I got older. I felt like I was incomplete without it. Felt like I needed to come here and…complete myself. Like somehow, you would make me a whole person," said Savannah. "When all along, I was already complete. I already had everything that I needed."

"I'm glad you came anyway," Nyle said.

"So that you could humiliate me by getting me thrown out onto the street in the middle of the night?" Savannah spat. "You're too old for your shenanigans."

"You're absolutely right."

Nyle apologized to Savannah for not being a good mother, or a mother at all, for that matter. And she promised that her behavior would change. Chloe had somehow touched her heart, and she wanted to be a better example for her granddaughter.

"Something happened to me when little Chloe walked into that door the other day," said Nyle. "I hope that you will allow me to love her."

"What about loving me?" Savannah stood in a huff. She stormed out of the room.

She needed to breathe. She had just unleashed a lifetime of emotions and thoughts onto Nyle in a matter of days. Suddenly she felt a sense of release. Exhaled. How dare her—wanting to love Chloe! She didn't deserve the privilege, and Savannah wouldn't allow it. She would deny *her* this time. She'd been on the receiving end of Nyle's grief; now it was her turn. Make her feel what she'd endured her whole life—wanting to love someone, but not being allowed to do so.

Within a few days, Chloe's condition had progressed a bit and she was out of the woods. Finally, the doctor thought she was getting better, and she would be released from the hospital with a prescription for antibiotics and an order for plenty of fluids and rest. Nyle wanted to stay with her on her last night.

"Why don't you leave her with me for the night. She's doing much better, and you two could use a break," Nyle told Savannah and Edward. "Go enjoy this romantic city. There's nothing wrong with finding love a second time."

Savannah was hesitant at first. She'd already told her-

self that she wouldn't allow Nyle to spend any quality time
with Chloe. But the truth was, she needed a good night's
rest—something other than being cramped in a leather
chair in the corner of a hospital room. And she needed to
be alone with Edward—badly.

"If anything goes wrong, anything at all, you call me,"
Savannah warned. "If she coughs funny, I wanna know
about it."

"I promise."

"Okay." Savannah gave Nyle a half smile. "We're leaving."

She kissed Chloe on the forehead and explained that she
would be there first thing in the morning to take her home.

"Are you okay if Mommy leaves?" she asked.

"Is Gigi staying?"

"Yes. She's going to stay with you."

"Okay." Chloe almost smiled. She was comfortable
staying with Gigi. The two had become old chums by the
end of the week.

"Try to get some rest," said Savannah. "I love you."

"Love you, too, Mommy."

Edward tapped his cheek for Chloe to kiss him. She
did. "See you in the morning, sweetheart," he told her.

He managed to pry Savannah away from the room and
get her into a cab.

At Savannah's rented flat, they sipped on some aged
wine, a bottle that Savannah had saved for a special occasion. Savannah spread a blanket on the living room floor
while Edward placed wood in the fireplace. He lay on the
floor and beckoned for Savannah to join him.

"Come here, love."

She collapsed onto the floor and found safety in his
arms. His lips met hers and he lifted her shirt, placed his
cold hand against her skin. He squeezed her right breast.
He pulled her shirt over her head and then unhooked her

bra. He slowly unbuttoned her jeans and pulled them off, slipped his fingers beneath the elastic of her panties and sank them deep into her sweetness. She moaned.

He buried his face in the crease of her neck and gently kissed her shoulder. He left a trail of kisses between her breasts before taking one between his lips. He licked her nipple and then kissed the other one with the same tenderness. He nibbled on her navel and planted kisses between her thighs. When she felt his tongue dancing, she curled her toes. He savored the taste of her and drove her crazy. He moved his lips back up to hers and kissed her tenderly. He eased himself inside her and made love to her on the floor in front of the fireplace.

She hadn't given Edward an answer to his marriage proposal. She had been too afraid. Afraid that they were rushing into things, that their lives would be too complicated or that they would fail at marriage again.

"I want you to come home," Edward whispered. "We can make this work."

"What makes you so sure? It didn't work the first time."

"I was young and stupid. But now I get it. Now I'm ready to make the sacrifices," said Edward. "I never stopped loving you, Savannah. But I didn't realize it until we were in the Bahamas."

"What about Quinn?"

"She told me what she did. She answered my phone and lied about what was going on. Nothing ever happened between us, Savannah. Not ever. You have to believe me," he said.

She searched his eyes, as if looking for the truth. "I believe you."

He exhaled. He needed to hear those words.

"What about the campaign?" she asked.

"I don't want to run for office. Not if it means compromising my family. You and Chloe are my family. And baby, I choose you."

"Really?"

"Yes, really," said Edward.

"I choose you, too," she said.

He vowed to give her whatever she wanted just to have her in his life. He kissed her lips. "I'll take care of you. Protect you."

"You promise?"

"I promise."

"Then, yes. I will marry you again."

The ramifications of their love, they would consider later. But for now, he had her, and she had him.

Chapter 27

Chloe had finally left the hospital, and Savannah had already made the decision to return to Florida. There were a few loose ends she needed to tie up before leaving London. She needed to visit the doctor's office where she worked, turn in her notice of employment termination and say goodbye to her friends—the ones Edward had met at the club that night. She also needed to meet with the fellow whom she'd rented the flat from, to end their rental arrangement.

As soon as Savannah left to tend to her errands, Edward, Nyle and Chloe had prepared a traditional English meal, and finished it. By midafternoon, Nyle had given Edward a hard lesson in the game of bridge. He was the king of spades and knew bid whist like the back of his hand, but bridge was a game he had never played. As he sat there, he knew that he hadn't quite mastered the game. Chloe, with a baseball cap turned backward on her head, kept score.

The music was loud as a British rap artist spewed his lyrics, and Nyle sipped on a Bloody Mary. She laughed long and hard when Edward lost yet another hand.

"Okay, off with the pants!" she said.

"I'm not taking my pants off, Nyle. This isn't strip bridge." Edward sipped his Bloody Mary. "I'll take off a sock."

"A sock?" Nyle pouted. "That's it?"

"That's it."

"What do you think, madam?" she asked Chloe.

"A sock is fine." Chloe covered her mouth and giggled. She sipped apple juice through a straw.

"Okay, fine," said Nyle. "Off with it."

Edward removed his trouser sock, slapped it onto the table. "There!"

By four o'clock, the trio had become old friends. The music was so loud and they were so engaged in the game of bridge, they didn't even hear Savannah walk through the door.

"Edward?" she asked.

Edward stood, barefoot and shirtless.

"Mommy!" Chloe yelled and rushed into Savannah's arms.

"Hi, baby. Looks like you're feeling better," said Savannah. "Edward, what's going on?"

"We were just playing a game of bridge."

"Nyle, you've been smoking in the house," Savannah said.

Nyle gave her a sheepish grin. "I'm sorry, darling."

Savannah sighed. "I quit my job today, and I called Rolf and told him that I'd be moving out of the flat. What will you do?"

"Oh, don't worry about me. I'll go soften up Aunt Frances. That old woman won't let me sleep on the street."

"I'm going to pack my things."

Edward put his shirt back on, buttoned it and followed Savannah to her bedroom, tapped on the door. He pulled the door open. She sat on the edge of the bed. When he walked in and shut the door behind him, she stood and busied herself around the room.

"Savannah. I know when you walked in…it looked like…"

"Like you and Nyle were having a pretty good afternoon, and you were half naked in my living room."

"I like her. She's cool." Edward laughed, but then dropped his smile when he saw that Savannah was not amused.

Tears burned Savannah's eyes. "It was a mistake coming here."

Edward grabbed her and held on to her. Kissed her tears away. "I don't think it was a mistake. I think it was necessary for you to come here, spend some time with her."

She looked at him with surprise. "I don't know."

"None of us is perfect, Savannah. She was a lousy mother, but she's an okay person. And she loves you. Loves Chloe, too."

"I know."

"Don't judge her too harshly." He pulled her close to him. Wrapped his arms tightly around her. His lips found hers. His tongue danced against hers. He grabbed her face in his hands and looked into her brown eyes. "She's a trip, though. You know that, right?"

"You don't know the half of it," said Savannah. "She's a piece of work."

"Yes."

"She damn near charmed you out of your drawers."

"She didn't charm me out of my drawers."

"Almost."

Edward kissed her lips again. He was glad to have her

back in his arms and his life. And soon they would share the same home again. He knew that, with love, they could handle most anything.

Chapter 28

Leaving London was bittersweet for Savannah. She and her mother hadn't bonded as she'd hoped, and she wasn't sure that they ever would. But Nyle and Chloe *had* connected. It was the first time her mother had displayed anything maternal, and she almost hated to separate the two of them.

"I'll come visit," Nyle told Chloe.

"You promise?" asked Chloe as she held on to her Gigi.

"I promise, little one. Don't you worry."

It was the same promise that Savannah had heard from Nyle her entire life. Chloe would be just as disappointed as she'd been as a child. Waiting for Nyle to return, but she never would.

"If you happen to be in the States, look us up." Savannah gave her mother a quick hug and broke away just as quickly. Tears filled her eyes, but she hid them. She knew that this would be the last time she'd pursue her mother again. She had finally accepted that Nyle Carrington would never change, and that she would never be the mother she needed in her life. She had come to terms with that.

"I'll do that," said Nyle.

Edward lifted their bags out of the trunk and set them at the curb. He glanced at their airline tickets and then at his watch. "We should get going if we're going to make our flight."

Nyle hugged Savannah, then Edward. She gave Chloe a strong hug and then lit an herbal cigarette. She hopped into the front seat of Xander's cab and let the window down, rested her chin on the door.

As he pulled away from the curb, she yelled out the window. "Go make me some more grandchildren. I need about five more like her!"

"Bye, Gigi!" Chloe yelled.

"Bye, my little Chloe. Be sweet!" she hollered back.

"I will."

Savannah watched as the hackney carriage disappeared into traffic. She shook her head, and a slight smile danced in the corner of her mouth. She sighed and followed Edward through the airport's automatic doors.

The plane ride home didn't seem as long as it had coming. She and Edward laughed and discussed the antics of Nyle. Savannah wondered how she would survive without someone there to keep her in line. She hoped that she would manage to get her life together. They talked about their future together and what it would look like.

"I don't want another wedding. Do you?" asked Savannah.

"I want what you want."

"I think we can just go to the justice of the peace," she said.

"I don't care about the formalities, I just want you." Edward grabbed her hand and held on to it.

"Maybe we can have a barbecue or some little get-together. Invite our friends."

"Okay."

"I need to call my daddy," said Savannah. "Let him know."

"He won't be happy for us. He still blames me for hurting you the first time."

"He just wants what's best for me. And once he sees how happy I am, he'll be happy for us."

Edward looked at her. "I should call him. Tell him myself. I called him the first time...asked him for your hand in marriage. I'll call him again."

"You sure?"

"No. But I'm a man. I can do this."

Savannah placed her hand gently against his cheek. "You are a man. My man."

Edward leaned over and kissed her lips. "I can't wait to call my parents. They'll be thrilled. They love you."

"And I love them." Savannah smiled.

"We should plan another trip there. Soon."

"I'm always up for a trip to the Bahamas," she said.

They discussed their finances and taking the house off the market. They would remain in their dream home—the one they'd built together the first time around. It was a perfectly good house. Edward would sell his house instead.

Savannah was thrilled to see the Florida palm trees that she'd missed so much. She inhaled the moist air and breathed in the smell of the ocean. It was great to be home. Edward took the scenic route and then pulled the car into the driveway of their home. She appreciated the thought of *their* home. They would soon be a family again, and living under one roof. He would be her man again, her husband, her lover. She looked at the emerald on her finger and smiled.

"Take Chloe in and get her settled. I'll get the bags," he said and stepped out of the car.

Savannah helped her daughter out of her seat and led her into the house. She started her a warm bath and found a pair of pajamas. She tucked Chloe into bed and turned off the light. She rushed to her bedroom and ran her own bath, squeezed bubbles into the tub. She laid out her favorite pair of lace panties—a pair she'd picked up at Victoria's Secret months ago, but had never worn. She didn't even know why she bothered. But tonight she was glad she had. It would be her first night with Edward in their home.

She lit a few candles and then turned down the lights. She stepped into the tub and relaxed against the porcelain, closed her eyes and listened as Marvin Gaye's "Let's Get It On" filled the master bathroom. When she heard the light tap on the door, she opened her eyes as Edward walked in.

"Care if I join you?" he asked.

"Not at all," she said. "Where have you been?"

"Caught the end of the game. Thought I'd come and see what you were up to."

He shut the door, and when he returned he was completely naked. Savannah admired the beauty of his chiseled, well-endowed body. She'd missed it. Those strong arms had always held her close, kept her safe. Those legs had braced her when she'd found herself on top. She'd rested her head on that chest more times than she could count. And what lay between his thighs had given her so much pleasure.

He stepped into the bathtub and took a seat behind her. He wrapped his arms tightly around her and caressed her breasts, pinched her tender nipples. He squeezed shower gel into his palms, lathered it, and caressed her. This time he gently planted kisses against the back of her neck. She moaned when his fingertips found their way between her legs, danced there until she couldn't stand it any longer.

"Welcome home," she whispered.

"It's so good to be home," he said.

She relaxed her head against his chest, and he wrapped his arms tightly around her. He held her until Marvin finished singing about sexual healing. She turned around in the tub and washed his chest, arms and parts that belonged to her again. She kissed his lips and rested her behind on his hardness until she felt him inside her, wrapped her legs around his waist. He grabbed the roundness of her cheeks and squeezed.

She loved him again. In fact, she'd never stopped. And all things were well again in the Talbot household.

Chapter 29

The first thing Edward wanted to do was take Savannah and Chloe to his parents' home on Eleuthera, Bahamas. Show them off. Let everyone know that they'd been right all along—he *did* still love Savannah, and they were a family again. When they heard the news of the engagement, they insisted on a celebration in the couple's honor at the Grove. It was a happy time for the Talbot family.

Savannah wore a navy blue after-five dress with a one-shoulder silhouette. Edward wore a navy tie that accented his gray suit. The Grove was beautifully decorated in navy and silver, and crystal lights beamed throughout the Grand Room. White roses were sprinkled about, and silver candles burned on every table. A traditional Caribbean meal was prepared—baked cod, conch fritters, conch salad and Edward's favorite papaya soup. Raquel had captured his recipe down to the smallest ingredient.

Music filled the Grand Room, and Edward stood next to his two favorite girls. He beamed with pride and his heart was filled with joy. His life would be different—his family had become his priority, and his career had taken a backseat.

He was a new man. All the Talbots were in attendance. Even Denny had flown in early that morning. He held on to Sage's hand. Edward was happy to see that his younger brother had manned up and patched things up with his ex-fiancée. He knew that a good woman was a rare commodity, and losing one was unacceptable. Edward could attest to this, and he didn't want to see his brother endure the same pain.

When Edward saw Nate, he went over to him.

"Little brother." He reached for Nate's hand.

Nate embraced him. "I'm sorry."

"Water under the bridge," said Edward. "You only spoke the truth."

"I'm glad you got your girl," Nate said. "Happy that you found love again."

"What about you? Will you find love again?" asked Edward.

"Probably not. But I'm okay with that. I'm happy to be alone."

"No one should be alone. It's a lonely world out there," said Edward. "Maybe you'll find a woman...*or not*...someday."

Edward was in denial about his brother's sexuality. He'd chosen not to think about it.

"Maybe."

Jasmine's voice interrupted their moment. She grabbed the microphone and tapped on it to see if it was on.

"Hello."

"I think it's on," Edward told her.

"I'd like to make an announcement," she began. "Where's Jackson?"

Jackson raised his hand in the air as if he were in an elementary school classroom.

"Come up here, babe."

Jackson maneuvered his way through the crowd and stood next to Jasmine.

"We would like to announce that we are with child..."

Jackson looked shocked. It was the first he'd heard of it. "We are?" he asked.

She grabbed his hands in hers and placed them on her stomach. "I don't mean to steal your moment, Edward and Savannah."

"It's okay," said Edward. "Congratulations."

Jackson grabbed Jasmine in his arms, lifted her in the air. He beamed with pride as Jasmine grabbed his face in her hands. She kissed his lips. Edward remembered what that moment felt like—the moment when he first learned that Chloe was growing inside Savannah's stomach. He had rushed out and purchased a soccer ball and a baseball glove, had the glove engraved with the Talbot name. He had plans of teaching his son the basics of soccer. He would encourage him to follow his footsteps in politics. He felt a bit of disappointment when the doctor announced that his son was a daughter instead. He even walked out of the room to gather himself. When he returned and held that little girl in his arms, he felt better. But the first time she peered into his eyes and gave him a half smile, his heart melted. Chloe had him doing her every bidding since that moment.

"Just hope it's not a girl," Edward whispered to Jackson. "You're doomed if it is. She'll have you wrapped around her skinny little finger before you know what's going on."

"I'm confident that it's not a girl," said Jackson. "I don't make girls."

Edward's laughter caught the attention of his sister.

"What are you two over here laughing about?" Jasmine asked.

"Nothing," the two of them said in unison.

Edward finally retrieved the microphone from his sister. He offered a toast to his bride-to-be. He talked about how lucky he was to have her back in his life, and he meant every word of it. He looked at his parents. His father held on tightly to his mother's waist. Their love was a true example of what it was supposed to look like. If he could keep Savannah contented for that many years, he would die a happy man. He held his glass in the air, and so did everyone in the room.

"Cheers!" he said.

"Cheers!" the crowd repeated.

He kissed Savannah's lips, and everyone applauded.

After the toast, Edward glanced across the room and spotted a familiar face in the midst of the crowd. Nyle raised a champagne flute into the air, a wide grin on her face. He gave her a wink. Savannah spotted her, too, and he watched as she sighed deeply. He had to admit it was good seeing Nyle, and he knew that Savannah would feel the same way. Although things hadn't worked out for her in London, he knew that she still loved her mother and had hopes of salvaging some type of relationship with her. Perhaps there was hope for them after all.

Everything in Savannah's life seemed to be falling right into place. She'd even been successful at finding work with another fashion design company in Florida, and Edward was happy about that. He'd assured her that she didn't need to work, that he would take care of them. But Savannah loved her career, and fashion had been her lifeline. She wanted to work.

Chloe had already reconnected with her Gigi and the two were engaged in a conversation. At that moment, he knew that whatever Nyle had missed with Savannah, she would regain through Chloe. The two had become friends. He knew they would. And he knew that she had been excited about his and Savannah's newfound love, which was why he'd sent her an airline ticket to the Bahamas. He wanted her there to share their moment.

"She's coming to stay in Florida with us for a little while," he whispered to Savannah. "Is that okay?"

She gave him a genuine smile and a nod. A tear crept down the side of her face.

"I love you," she whispered in his ear.

"I love you more."

Edward gazed in her eyes and made a note of how happy she looked at that moment. Her heart was full, and so was his. He'd managed to snag the woman of his dreams and sweep her off of her feet—*again*. Which only proved that love really was sweeter the second time around.

* * * * *

KEEPING SECRETS

FIONA BRAND

To the Lord, who says, "Come to me, all you who are weary and burdened, and I will give you rest...for I am gentle and humble in heart, and you will find rest for your souls."
Matthew 11:28–29

Many thanks to Stacy Boyd and Charles Griemsman.

One

The discreet vibration of his cell interrupted Damon Smith's stride as he jogged the hard-packed sand of his private island in New Zealand's Hauraki Gulf.

The conversation was to the point. His younger brother, Ben, was quitting. He would not be in the office tomorrow, or in the foreseeable future.

Reason? He had run off with Damon's pretty blonde personal assistant.

Jaw locked, Damon turned his back on the glare of the setting sun. An icy breeze cooled his overheated skin and flattened his damp T-shirt against the tense muscles of his back, but he barely noticed. For an odd moment sensory perception seemed to fall away and Damon was spun back in time. Almost a year to the day, when another PA, Zara Westlake, had run out on *him*, leaving her job *and his bed*.

Zara. Damon frowned at the image that instantly surfaced. Dark hair, direct blue eyes, finely molded cheekbones made more intriguing by a scattering of freckles. A faintly tip-tilted nose and a firm jaw, all softened by a quirky, generous mouth, which added a fascinating, mercurial depth to a face that was somehow infinitely more riveting than conventional prettiness.

The wind gusted more strongly, the chill registering, as an old wound in his shoulder and another at his hip—both courtesy of his time in the military—stiffened and began to ache. Grimly, Damon dismissed the memories of Zara, annoyed that they still had the power to stop him in his tracks, despite his attempts to put the brief fling in its proper perspective.

After all, their involvement had lasted barely a month. On a scale of one to ten, given that he had once been married for seven years, it shouldn't have registered. Especially since Zara herself, with her usual trademark efficiency, had made it crystal clear she had only ever been interested in a short, very private affair.

"We're in love," Ben helpfully supplied now.

The words *in love* made Damon's jaw tighten. They echoed through a childhood he preferred to forget, one Ben had no knowledge of because he had been lucky enough to be born after the untimely death of their father. Ben had never been around to experience Guy Smith's infidelities or his corrosive temper, the long nights when Damon and his mother had borne the brunt of that temper, and the scars.

"In love." He tried to keep the distaste out of his voice, and failed.

The words dredged up memories of the beautiful women who had hung at the edges of his father's life, expensive women who had demanded diamonds, exotic holidays and credit cards with dizzying limits that had eaten away at the family fortune. Guy Smith had claimed to be "in love" a number of times despite his marriage. When the money had finally run out, his latest mistress had left him. He had ended up in a bar, drunk enough to make the mistake of picking a fight with someone who could hit back. He had been found unconscious on the street the next morning, and had died of a fractured skull on the way to hospital.

When Adeline Smith had gotten the news of her husband's death, she had broken down and cried, but the tears had been ones of relief. Damon, at ten years old, nursing two cracked ribs and a broken jaw courtesy of his attempt to protect his mother from Guy's red-faced fury when he'd discovered they were broke, hadn't shed so much as a tear. Life had been gray and drained of hope. In the instant he heard his father had died, it had felt like stepping out of the shadows into blazing light. Six months later, Ben had been born.

Now, as Ben's only close family, Damon had to tread carefully. His brother hadn't endured the experiences that had shaped Damon. Ben didn't understand how destructive out-of-control emotions could be, and he carelessly fell in and out of love on a regular basis. In a way, Ben's cavalier approach to relationships was an uncomfortable reminder of their father. Although, thankfully, Ben had none of their father's meanness.

Flexing his stiffening shoulder, Damon paced the hard-packed sand of the curving bay, which was punctuated by dark drifts of rock at each end. He forced himself to concentrate on his brother's latest crisis, which this time impacted Damon directly.

For the past eighteen months he had been training Ben to help run their family's sprawling security empire. The one his mother, with the help of her brother, Tyler McCall—Damon's uncle—had pulled from the financial fires of near bankruptcy. Unfortunately, *like their father*, Ben had proven to be spectacularly disinterested in Magnum Security. It was a fact that Damon would have gotten a great deal more done if Ben had not been in the office. His assistant, Emily, however, had been smart, intuitive and almost as efficient as Zara.

With effort, he shook off a further raft of memories and refocused on the problem at hand: saving Ben from himself and retrieving Damon's assistant. Emily was significantly involved in a crucial deal he was working on. At this juncture, it would be nearly impossible to replace her.

"Walk me through this. I didn't think you even liked Emily."

"How would you know? You've had your head buried in the McCall takeover for weeks."

Damon could feel his blood pressure rising. "So has Emily. If you will recall she's my PA."

Although, to put a fine point on it, he had never appointed her to the position. Emily was a temp, the third temp he had employed over the past year while continuing to interview numerous candidates, both male and female, some with impressive degrees. Unfortunately, not one of them had possessed the exacting qualities required for the position. Qualities that had been oddly defined in Zara and which he had not realized he needed until she left him.

"Uh, not any longer. Check your email and you'll find Emily's resignation."

A boarding call echoed through the phone, informing Damon that Ben and Emily were already at the airport.

Damon kept a lid on his frustration. He could live with the inconvenience of losing Emily. What really worried him was what was happening to Ben. The partying and dating aside, he was becoming immersed in the darker, undisciplined passions that had overtaken their father. Passions that had even extended to Tyler McCall, who had become the CEO of Magnum Security and the boys' guardian following Adeline's death from cancer when Damon was fourteen and Ben just four. As stable as Tyler, an ex-SEAL and intelligence expert had seemed, in his late forties he had fallen for a spectacularly beautiful model, then died along with her in a car accident on the romantic Mediterranean island of Medinos.

Damon's chest tightened at the memory of the loss that, four years ago, had hit him hard. Tyler had been the father Guy Smith should have been. He had been a safe haven for both Damon and Ben until he had been ensnared by Petra Hunt, an aging model turned A-list party girl.

To lose Tyler, whose watchwords had been *reliability* and *common sense*, to the kind of liaison that had gone hand in glove with Damon's father's degenerate lifestyle… It had, to put it mildly, shaken Damon.

Damned if he'd let Ben fall into the same trap.

Damon's fingers tightened on the phone. Technically, Ben had not run off with Emily yet; they were both still at the airport. There was a chance to nip the relationship in the bud if Damon kept his cool. "Don't board the flight. I can be at the airport in an hour—we can talk this through."

"There's nothing to talk about," Ben said curtly. "Emily and I have been seeing each other for the past month. Long enough to decide that this is something special."

"You're only twenty—"

"Old enough to make my own decisions. Last I heard,

I could go to war at eighteen if I wanted. You were younger when you married Lily."

Damon's brows jerked together at the mention of his ex-wife. "The two situations don't equate."

"Why? Because Lily left you?"

For a vibrating moment Damon was confronted by a past he took great pains to avoid thinking about, because it highlighted the singular difficulty he had with relationships. There hadn't been one thing wrong with Lily. She had been beautiful, intelligent and sweet-natured and he had *liked* her, all good reasons to choose her as his wife. Unfortunately, he had never been able to give Lily the two things she had decided she wanted from him *after* the wedding. First, that he would fall in love with her. Second, that he would give her the children she had decided were now a deal breaker.

There was a loaded pause. "Or is it because you slept with your assistant last year," Ben asked softly, "and you've suddenly decided *that's* a forbidden sin?"

Damon stopped dead in his tracks. Flashes of the stark, heated passion Zara had unlocked in him, and which he had constantly failed to control, rushed back at him, making his chest tighten. "How could you know about that?"

Zara had insisted they keep the liaison secret. She had made it clear she couldn't work for him if people knew they were involved. Damon had complied even though he hadn't liked the condition. It had smacked of his father's illicit affairs. Emotion might be a no-go area, but Damon preferred to keep his sexual relationships straightforward and aboveboard.

Ben's tone was impatient. "Zara is Emily's agent. Emily put two and two together."

Damon's stomach tensed as more memories of Zara

surfaced. In every way, Zara was his ex-wife's polar opposite. Exactly the kind of woman he usually took care to avoid, because of the subtle, locked-down sensuality that was just a little too interesting. Zara had been dark and curvaceous, where Lily had been blonde, athletic and slender. The differences hadn't stopped at physical appearance. From the first moment, Zara had been a vivid, fascinating mixture of efficiency, quirky humor and unexpected passion.

Their connection had blindsided them both.

"The two situations are not the same."

"Right on to that. What Emily and I share is more than just convenient sex."

An image of Zara lying in bed, dark satiny hair spread over the pillow, blue eyes veiled with mysteries and secrets, assaulted him. Convenient sex? There had been nothing convenient about it. The words that sprang to mind were more along the lines of *hot*, *reckless*.

Addictive.

The same brand of intense, unruly passion that had ruined his father and Tyler and which had kept Damon awake nights because he had vowed it would never control him.

A clarifying thought that made sense of Ben and Emily's elopement suddenly occurred to Damon. He could kick himself for not thinking of it before. "Emily's pregnant."

Ben made a sound of disbelief. "Emily's not the one who got pregnant."

Not the one who got pregnant.

The words seemed to hang in the air. Suddenly, like a piece of a puzzle falling neatly into place, Zara's abrupt exit from Damon's life, her disappearance for months, made perfect sense.

She had left because she had been pregnant. With *his* child.

Damon sucked in a deep breath and tried to think, tried to orient himself. He felt like he'd been kicked in the chest.

If Zara had had a baby—and by now, over a year on, the baby would be four months old—why hadn't she told him?

Admittedly, they hadn't known each other long, six weeks in total.

Long enough to get messily involved and for Damon to break a whole list of personal rules.

Long enough that he'd had trouble forgetting her. That he'd broken his last intact rule, a rule that should have been inviolable. Instead of letting Zara go and regaining his equilibrium, *his distance*, when she left town, he had gone after her.

He had tracked her to a small cottage in the South Island city of Dunedin. On the verge of knocking on her front door, he had abruptly come to his senses. He had known that if he walked through that door they would be in bed within minutes. Added to that, if he continued an affair that had become dangerously irresistible, he risked becoming engaged to and marrying a woman who was the exact opposite of the kind of wife he needed. A passionate, addictive, unpredictable lover who had made it clear she had no interest in a committed relationship.

Disgusted with the obsession that had clearly gotten an unhealthy grip on him, he had walked away. The only problem was, he had not been able to stay away. Months later, when he had discovered Zara had opened her own employment agency in town, instead of steering clear, he had requested that his office manager ditch the large, established firm that usually fulfilled their employment needs and start using Zara's agency.

His fingers tightened on the cell. "How long have you known that Zara had a baby?"

Ben made an exasperated sound. "Right at this moment I'm not sure if you're burying your head in the sand out on that fortress island of yours or if you really didn't know. If Emily was expecting my child, *I* wouldn't be afraid of fatherhood."

Fatherhood.

Damon stared bleakly at the misty line where sky met sea. Unwittingly, Ben had gone straight for the jugular, exposing a truth Damon had no wish to confront. The whole issue of fatherhood was something he usually avoided, because it entailed facing a past he had gone to a great deal of trouble to bury and forget. It meant coming to grips with another relationship for which he was not ready or equipped.

Lily's words when she had stormed out of their apartment came back to haunt him. *I must have been out of my mind thinking I could live with a man who approaches marriage as if it's some kind of business contract and who doesn't want kids, ever!*

He took another deep breath but, even so, when he spoke his voice was raspy. "The baby's...all right?"

Ben said something short and flat. "You really didn't know. Well, that takes the cake. You're a security guru. You wrote the book on surveillance techniques and you produce software for half a dozen governments, and you don't know when your ex-girlfriend has your child? I thought you didn't want to know, because you don't want kids. Lily said enough about the sub—"

"Don't bring Lily into this." The response was automatic, because every thought was blasted away by the fact that Zara had given birth to his child.

The one outcome he had taken care to avoid, *except on one notable occasion*, had happened.

He was a father.

A final boarding call echoed down the phone.

"I've gotta go," Ben muttered. "Look, I'm sorry about breaking the news about Zara and the baby like this. The fact was, I thought you did know but were… you know, *avoiding* the whole issue." There was a rustling sound as if Ben was holding the phone awkwardly jammed to his ear as he surrendered his boarding pass. "Emily was fairly sure you didn't know. She seemed to think it was more that you lack emotional intelligence… whatever that means."

There was a feminine yelp in the background along with a further rustling noise as if Ben had jammed the phone against his chest to muffle the sound for a few seconds.

Ben's voice came back, loud and clear. "Anyway, I think we both know that trying to turn me into an executive wasn't working. I told you right from the start that the kind of locked-down life you lead isn't for me. I want to travel and do something with my fine arts degree. Anything but add up soulless numbers all day and stare at computer code, which, by the way, I will never understand. Don't try to find us. I'll send a postcard…eventually."

A click signaled the call had been terminated.

Damon slipped the phone back into the pocket of his sweatpants. There was no point in running after Ben now. The boarding calls meant that whatever flight Ben and Emily had booked, they would be airborne before he could pull the strings needed to either detain them or delay the flight. That was no doubt the reason Ben had rung just before the flight left. Damon guessed he was lucky that Ben, who had been kicking against Damon's authority for the past year, had called at all.

Feeling like an automaton, Damon went back over the conversation. Ben's crack about his lack of emotional intelligence grated. Apparently, he had missed two major cues in his life, Ben's utter lack of interest in Magnum Security and the fact that Damon had fathered a child, *despite Zara assuring him there was no chance of a pregnancy.*

He tried to remember the exact words Zara had used immediately after they'd had crazy, passionate, unprotected sex. She had dragged on a robe and escaped to the bathroom, pausing to send him an irritatingly neutral smile, before assuring him that he had no need to worry.

He had taken that to mean Zara had taken care of contraception. But now he knew it could also have meant that his assistant, in her usual brisk, efficient way, had been stating her intention to take full responsibility if there was a pregnancy.

Cold water splashed his ankles and Damon became aware that the tide had advanced and water was now surging around his shoes. Still absorbed with his thoughts, he strolled up the beach and headed for his house. Perched on a headland, the large multilevel house seemed to grow from the dark cliffs, stark and spare and a little forbidding. Built of stone, it reminded him of the medieval fortress Tyler had owned on the Mediterranean island of Medinos and which Damon had spent his adolescence exploring.

Fatherhood. The realization sank in a little deeper.

Damon turned to stare across the water in the direction of Auckland's cityscape, the first glimmer of evening lights visible in the distance. Somewhere across the water existed a child who, in a profound, unassailable way, belonged to him.

Just beyond the breaking waves a sleek gannet arrowed into the water, then surfaced with a silvery fish in its beak. Damon drew in a lungful of cold air as he struggled with imperatives that were as opposite as black and white. He had long ago decided that fatherhood was not for him, but fate had intervened and he was caught and held as fast as the small, flapping fish. He could not turn his back on his child.

The sun was sinking fast, the last burnished glow infusing the clear winter air with rose and gold. The sea breeze had dropped, leaving the water glassily smooth.

He did not understand why Zara had chosen to cut him out of his child's life, but that would soon change. In the methodical way of his mind, Damon began to formulate a plan to meet with Zara and discover what he could about the child. Although the practical to-do list seemed cold and antiseptic when he considered exactly what it meant—confronting his ex-lover about the child they had made together. And he knew exactly when that had happened—the first time they had made love.

As Damon climbed the steep cliff path to his house, memories flickered, vivid and irresistible.

Torrential rain pounding down as he held his jacket over Zara's head to shelter her as he dropped her home after a late business dinner. He shook out the wet jacket in the dimness of her porch. She laughed as she swept soaked hair back from her forehead. With her dark hair gleaming with moisture, her cheeks flushed, suddenly she was quite startlingly beautiful.

There was a moment when he bent his head, a split second before their mouths touched, when she could have stepped away and didn't. Instead, her breath hitched, her fingers closed on the lapels of his jacket and she lifted up on her toes for his kiss.

He caught the scent of her skin and desire closed around him like heated manacles. Sensation shuddered through him in waves as they kissed for long, spellbinding minutes. They made it to her bedroom, just.

He used a condom the first and even the second time, but in the hour before dawn, waking to Zara making slow, exquisite love to him, and caught in that strange halfway state between dream and reality, he did not.

The unprotected lovemaking had happened with blinding speed, over almost before he realized it, but that did not negate his responsibility. Zara's pregnancy had been his fault.

Damon climbed the steps to his house and paused in the shelter of the heavy stone portico, which protected the entryway from the wind. Peeling out of his wet shoes, he pushed open the heavy, ancient door made of thick oak and bands of iron that he had imported from Medinos and headed for his shower. After drying off, he pulled on soft, faded jeans with the fluid economy of movement he had learned during his years with the military in Afghanistan and the Middle East.

Not bothering with a shirt, Damon padded into his cavernous bedroom, found his laptop and keyed in the GPS program his firm used as a security measure for the company's top executives. He typed in his brother's phone number. Instantly a map materialized along with a tracking icon, which indicated that Ben was over the Pacific Ocean, just northeast of Auckland. It was somehow typical that Ben, with his utter disinterest in all things to do with Magnum Security, had been careless enough to forget that his phone could be tracked.

Damon checked the time then rang Walter, his head of security and one of his most trusted employees. Minutes later, Ben's flight details were confirmed. He was headed for the island of Medinos, and would, no doubt, be staying in the clifftop fortress Tyler had left to him and Ben jointly.

Retrieving his cell, he found the only number for Zara that he had, her employment agency. After a moment of hesitation, he dialed. In the past two months, ever since he had discovered that Zara had opened her own agency, apart from picking up his initial call, he had invariably found himself shunted through to her answering service. His jaw compressed when, as usual, the call went straight through to voice mail. He left a terse message and set the phone down on his bedside table.

Stepping out onto his balcony, he studied the gray clouds building overhead, blotting out the first scattering of stars. Ben had been right in pointing out the irony that Damon specialized in designing hardware and software to collect, unlock and decode information, and yet he could not unlock the mystery of the woman who had shared his bed and then attempted to disappear with all the skill of a master spy.

Cold droplets spattered Damon's broad shoulders as he turned from the darkening view, strolled through to the kitchen and lifted the lid on the casserole Walter's wife, Margot, had left for him. Not for the first time, he was keenly aware of the utter emptiness of his house.

For years he had been living in a kind of deep freeze. Just over a year ago, when Zara had strolled into his office in a beige jacket and skirt that on most women would have looked shapeless and boring, but on her had somehow looked sexy, the thaw had been instant and profound.

He had wanted her. If he was ruthlessly honest, that was also the reason he had reconnected with Zara again when he found out she had opened her own employment agency. To date, he had resisted what he'd come to view as a fatal attraction, but that was about to change. The knowledge that Zara had had his child had kicked away some invisible barrier. They were linked in the most primal, intimate way a man and woman could be linked and he was no longer prepared to tolerate the distance she seemed to prefer.

From now on, they were playing by his rules.

He had not forgotten Ben. As Ben's only close relative and the trustee of Ben's inheritance, Damon's course of action was clear. He needed to retrieve his brother before Ben did something completely irresponsible, like get married to a woman he had only known for a few weeks.

The retrieval of Ben, as luck would have it, dovetailed with Damon's need to gain access to his child. Zara Westlake stood at the center of both issues, which meant that, whether she liked it or not, she would have to meet with him face-to-face.

Out of the murk of the first two objectives, a third emerged. Despite Zara's betrayal, despite the grip the past still had on his life, he needed one more thing.

Zara Westlake back in his bed.

Two

A soft chime, indicating that a much-needed client had just opened the door of Zara's fledgling employment agency, diverted her attention from her four-month-old baby, Rosie. Thankfully, after a marathon effort to get Rosie to nap, her tiny daughter had finally drifted into a restless slumber.

Anxious to snag her client before he or she lost interest and decided to take their very valuable business elsewhere, Zara tiptoed out of the smallest interview room, which today doubled as Rosie's makeshift nursery. Makeshift, because normally, when Zara was working, Rosie was in day care. But, because Rosie had been a little off-color, the center hadn't wanted to take her, so Zara had planned to work from home while she kept an eye on her daughter. However, that arrangement had crashed and burned when her assistant, Molly, had called in sick at the last minute, meaning that Zara had been forced to bring Rosie to the office.

It wasn't until she had gently closed the door behind her that Zara realized she had left her high heels, which she had slipped out of while she had fed and changed Rosie, behind her desk. Added to that, her hair, once smoothed into an immaculate French pleat, was now disheveled from the playful grip of Rosie's fingers.

Pinning a smoothly professional smile on her face, she turned to her client. In that instant, the room seemed to whirl, reminding her of the last month of pregnancy when bouts of dizziness would hit out of the blue.

Disbelief froze her in place as Zara's gaze traveled from the rock-solid shape of a masculine jaw, with the hint of a five o'clock shadow, to the scar that sliced across one cheekbone, a fascinating counterpart to the damaged line of a once-aquiline nose. Her own jaw taut, she braced herself for the impact of the magnetic silvery gaze, which had always put her in mind of that of a very large, very focused wolf.

Her heart slammed against the wall of her chest. A complicated mix of panic, edged with another purely feminine reaction she refused to acknowledge.

He had found her.

Damon Smith.

Six foot two inches of scarred, muscular, reclusive billionaire standing in her tiny office, taking all the air, his sleek shoulders broad enough that they stretched the dark fabric of a very expensive black coat.

A stomach-churning anxiety kicked in as she wondered why he was here. Damon Smith had the kind of wealth and power that meant he did not have to leave his private island or his penthouse office unless he chose to do so. There was a small army of devoted, ex-military employees who had been with him

for years and who were ready and willing to do his
slightest bidding.

Damon turning up in her office was significant.

Cold air gusted, shaking the windows. Predictably,
her door, which had a malfunctioning catch, flung open.
Damon caught the door before it could bang against the
wall, his dark coat swirling like a mantle as he did so,
cloaking its owner in the shadows and secrets that permeated his life. Public secrets due to his work. Private
secrets, which she was privy to and wished she wasn't,
because they also scored *her* life.

He closed the door and tested it to make sure the
catch had engaged. His gaze, now distinctly irritable,
pinned her again. "You need to get that fixed."

"It's on my list."

Along with fixing the leaky tap in the tiny bathroom
and replacing some of the light fittings, which looked
like they had been salvaged from a Second World War
junk sale. Knowing her landlord, they probably had.

Keeping a neutral smile fixed firmly in place, Zara
girded herself to hold Damon's gaze with the equanim-
ity she had learned in an elite finishing school in Swit-
zerland, all paid for by her gorgeous, restless, jet-setting
supermodel mother, Petra Atrides, who had been known
in the fashion and media worlds as Petra Hunt. A practiced composure, which had been put to the test by the
paparazzi when Petra had plunged to her death along
with her new fiancé—Damon's uncle Tyler McCall.

Not that Damon knew any of that, which was the
way she wanted to keep it. There was no way Damon
would believe she had not known who he was when
she accepted the job as his personal assistant and then
practically flung herself into his bed. Not when he dis-

covered she was Petra Hunt's daughter *and* had given birth to his child.

The wind buffeted the front door again, the force of it actually making the lights flicker, but this time the door held.

Damon took in her small office in one sweeping glance. "So this is where you've been hiding out."

"What do you mean, 'hiding out'?"

Although the fact that she *had* been in hiding for the past thirteen months, hiding a pregnancy and now a baby, put an annoying blush on her cheeks.

Damon's expression was deceptively mild. "You haven't been answering your phone or returning calls, and the address you gave me over the phone a couple of months ago is incorrect. I've spent the past half hour walking the streets and questioning shop owners who had never heard of you. It wasn't until I went online and checked your social media site that I managed to get your real address."

Zara struggled to control another surge of heat to her cheeks. Weeks ago, when Damon had contacted her out of the blue, she hadn't meant to give him incorrect information. In a moment of panic, thinking that he had somehow found out about Rosie, the transposed figures had just tumbled out of her. But neither should he, a CEO, have been even remotely interested in the whereabouts of her office. When she had agreed to take on Magnum Security as a client, she had only done so because she had desperately needed the money and on the condition that all of her dealings were with Damon's dry-as-dust business manager, Howard Prosser. In theory she should never have had to deal with Damon, period.

She stiffened at the image of the extraordinarily

wealthy and private Damon Smith walking the streets
and questioning shop owners.

Hunting her.

A sharp little thrill shot down her spine. Instantly,
her jaw firmed. That was the kind of feminine reaction
toward Damon that she had never been able to afford,
because he was, literally, the one man she should not
want and could not have in her life.

Aside from being a link to a past she was determined
to leave behind, she had found out that Damon was
also the trustee of his uncle's estate. He had requested,
through his lawyers, that she, as Angel Atrides—her
name before she had legally changed it to Zara Westlake—sign a legal document relinquishing any claim
on Tyler's estate in exchange for a one-off, extremely
offensive cash offer.

Raw with grief, insulted and *hurt*, Zara had refused
the offer and had refused to sign the horrible legal
agreement. She had been sickened by the tactics of a
family who had obviously bought into the media hype
around her mother as a model who was past her prime
and who had inveigled her way into Tyler's über-rich,
normally sensible life. No doubt Damon believed that
Angel Atrides was just as trashy and opportunistic, and
that a chunk of cash and a legal agreement was a necessary insurance against her ever darkening his doorstep or, horror of horrors, trying to make a claim on
Tyler's fortune.

Once again, the calculated risk of accepting Magnum as a client made her heart pound. Her chest seized
on a sudden thought. Could Damon know about Rosie?

Last night he had left a message on her answering
service, a terse command to call him back. It was something she had deliberately left for Molly to attend to.

Summoning a smooth smile, and trying to control her racing pulse, Zara made it to the safe haven of her desk. "I'm sorry you had trouble finding me."

Feeling pinned by his gaze, she opened a drawer on the pretext that she wanted to check the address on her business cards. Although, she knew there was nothing wrong with her cards. Her mother might have been a creative, artistic personality who resisted being organized and hated dealing with numbers, but Zara was her polar opposite. A perfectionist and a details person, she preferred to lead, not follow, and she liked to get things right.

The flush on her cheeks seemed to grow more heated as she jerkily closed the drawer on her stack of perfectly aligned, perfectly correct business cards. "I'm sorry you somehow ended up with the wrong address."

Grim amusement flickered at the corners of Damon's mouth. "The number was reversed. But something tells me you already knew that."

Her chin jerked up. "What are you insinuating?"

Damon shrugged. "Thirteen months ago, you quit your job and disappeared. For the past couple of months, ever since I discovered you had opened up your own employment agency, apart from picking up my first call, you've consistently failed to return my calls—"

"You know I prefer to work via email. Besides, all the correspondence and contracts go through Howard."

He glanced around her office again, his gaze briefly settling on the door of the interview room where Rosie was sleeping. "Maybe the address you gave me was a genuine mistake."

But his tone told her he didn't believe that.

His gaze shifted thoughtfully back to the door of the

interview room and a sharp jolt of adrenaline made her heart pound.

She was suddenly certain that he *knew*.

A little feverishly, she straightened piles of paper that did not need straightening. The only way Damon could have found out about Rosie was through Emily, although her contact with Emily had been minimal, two interviews and a couple of phone updates. She was not even sure Emily was aware that Zara had a baby. Of course, there were other ways he could have pried into her life. Given that he was in the security and surveillance business and had once been some kind of Special Forces agent in the military, she was certain he could find out whatever he wanted.

Damon's gaze skimmed her neatly arranged office and Zara did her best to conceal her relief that he was no longer concentrated on the door to the interview room in which Rosie was sleeping. When it came to Damon, usually, she erred on the side of fighting, but today running was at the top of the list—with Rosie tucked invisibly under one arm so he would not uncover that particular guilty secret.

Shockingly, his gaze touched on hers before shifting and she realized he had noticed her hair. She took a calming breath and willed her heart rate to slow. There was nothing wrong with messy hair. It was a windy day. Her hair could have gotten disheveled when she'd gone out for coffee.

A weird part of her acknowledged that she had always known this could happen, that one day her most lucrative client, who also happened to be the father of her child, would walk into her office and she would have to deal with him face-to-face. But, not now, not today, when she was struggling from lack of sleep and with Rosie just feet away in the next room.

The last thing either of them needed was to be inescapably linked by Rosie. A small shudder went through Zara at the thought of the media attention that would erupt once it was found out that Petra Hunt's daughter, using a new identity, had had a child with Tyler McCall's nephew. They would come after her; they would come after Rosie. And Damon, apart from making it crystal clear that Zara was not welcome in his life, would hate that she had fooled him.

On cue, a small, snuffling sound came from the interview room. Zara's heart sped up. Lately, Rosie, who was usually a very good sleeper, was waking up after just a few minutes of restless slumber. A little desperately, she reached for a random file and slapped it down on the desk, trying to make enough noise that Damon would not hear Rosie. "So, now that you've found me, what can I do for you? Is there a problem with one of the employees I sent to you? Troy? Or Harold?"

Troy was young, just eighteen, with tattoos and a brow piercing, but he was bright and earnest. Zara had thought he would be perfect for Damon's IT team. Harold had been an older public servant who had failed to find a job through other employment agencies, owing to a rather unfortunate skin condition, and in desperation had come to Zara. She had found a place for him in Damon's accounts department.

Damon frowned slightly, as if he didn't know who either Troy or Harold were, then his face cleared. "They're fine, as far as I know. *This* is the problem."

He dropped the tabloid newspaper, which he had been carrying under one arm, on her desk. It was folded open at a tacky gossip columnist's page.

She drew a calming breath and forced herself to study a grainy black-and-white photo of Damon's younger brother, Ben, who had his arm flung around Emily's slim waist. The blaring caption, Magnum Security Heir's Hot Affair with Blonde Temp, practically leaped off the page.

Snatching up the paper, she skimmed the story—which was the stuff of her nightmares—with growing horror. Thankfully, the detail was minimal. To her relief, the name of her employment agency had not been mentioned...yet.

She took a closer look at the photograph. Details she had not noticed first off finally registered. Emily's hair seemed longer and curlier. Gone were the subtle makeup and low-key suits, the crisp blouses that had seemed to summarize Zara's star temp as sensible, trustworthy and professional. Emily looked younger and a touch bohemian. She certainly no longer looked like the poster girl for Westlake Employment Agency.

Zara quickly read the sketchy article. Of course, the journalist had painted Emily as a fortune-hunting employee and Ben as the kind of high-powered playboy businessman who was only interested in a quick fling and who would not be easily caught by a mere office girl.

Compassion for Emily mixed with a surge of outrage and a fierce desire to protect her protégé. Just because Emily had fallen for Ben and decided to make the best of herself did not make her a cheap, trashy opportunist. Zara had lost count of the times the papers had portrayed her mother as cheap and on the make, when the truth was that her mother had been so gorgeous she had literally had to fend off men. And yes, some of those men had been breathtakingly rich.

When Petra died, the behavior of the tabloids and women's magazines had worsened. They had smeared her reputation even more before turning their malicious spotlight on Zara. Although, luckily, Petra had always made sure Zara was hidden from the media, so their store of background information had been meager. Most of the photos they'd had were blurred shots of Zara as a child or as a plump teenager taken through telephoto lenses.

Horrified and frightened by the relentless pursuit of the media, Zara had ditched her degree and disappeared. Angel Atrides, the fictional spoiled party girl the media seemed intent on creating, had become the ordinary, invisible person she longed to be—Zara Westlake. Zara had been her paternal grandmother's name, Westlake her maternal grandmother's maiden name.

Her mother's cousin Phoebe Westlake, a sharp-edged accountant who was ill with leukemia, had provided the hideout Zara needed in the South Island city of Dunedin while she had painstakingly reinvented her life. Which had made it all the more frustrating when, almost three years later, with a new name and a degree in business management—in effect a new life—Phoebe's last act before she had died had been to secure Zara a job interview with the nephew of Tyler McCall.

Not that Zara had made *that* connection until after she had taken the job, because Damon's surname, Smith, was so neutral and ordinary that she hadn't suspected the link. To further muddy the waters, Damon was reclusive by nature, avoiding the media. It hadn't been until two weeks into her job and *after* she had made the mistake of sleeping with Damon, that he had handed her a takeover bid for Tyler McCall's electric company.

She had finally understood exactly who Damon was.

As much as she needed to sit down now, Zara remained standing. Once again, the desire to run was
uppermost, but she instantly dismissed that option. In
setting up her business after Rosie was born she had
made a stand. She was over running.

She was tired of giving up things that were important, like home and friendships and career choices,
and having to start fresh somewhere else. Having to
be someone else. If she ran now, she would have to give
up her cozy rented cottage, which was just a twenty-
minute commute from her office. She would have to
abandon her business, which she loved with passion,
because, finally, all of her study and hard work had paid
off and she had something of substance that was *hers*.
Plus, if she walked away now she would be deeply in
debt, with no way to repay it.

The thought of defaulting on her business loan made
her stomach tighten. It was a sharp reminder of exactly
why she had buckled and taken on Damon as a client in
the first place. It had been a huge risk, but if she hadn't,
she would have gone under. Damon, against all odds,
was her most lucrative client and had taken on a stag-
gering number of personnel, most of them temps, which
meant she continued to accrue fees.

Her jaw firmed. Right now, she could not cope with
another debt. It had taken her years to pay off her mother's funeral expenses. However, not running meant she
might have to face the press, and probably sooner rather
than later.

The way she saw it, her only viable option was damage control. Luckily, due to her current line of work,
she had become quite skilled at it. Refolding the paper
so she no longer had to look at the damaging article or
the gleeful smile of the gossip columnist, and utterly

relieved that the situation with Ben and Emily was Damon's reason for seeking her out, she directed a brisk glance at him. "When did they leave?"

"Last night, on a scheduled flight. Which is why the tabloids got hold of the story."

If it had been the firm's private jet, the press wouldn't have gotten a look in, but Damon would have been notified. Damon had been caught by surprise, which meant Ben had kept his plans secret. That being the case, it was entirely possible, given that Zara hadn't known about the relationship, that Damon had not, either.

Light glimmered at the end of a very long, very dark tunnel. Damon had clearly bought into the tabloid story, but there were other constructions that could apply to Ben and Emily leaving the country together—constructions that did not place the blame on either Emily or Westlake Employment.

Mind working quickly, Zara examined and discarded a number of options, finally settling on attack as the best form of defense. "It's highly irregular that Ben has taken Emily out of the country." She lifted her chin, but even so, in her bare feet, her gaze was only just level with Damon's throat. She tried not to be fascinated by a very interesting pulse along the side of his jaw. "When might I expect my temp to be returned?"

Damon's brows jerked together. "Emily was not kidnapped."

Surreptitiously, Zara felt around with her toes for her shoes. "I didn't say *kidnapped*, exactly."

Damon crossed his arms over his chest, which only served to make him seem even larger and more ticked off. "You're implying that she has been coerced in some way. Since Emily, at twenty-six, is older than Ben by a good six years, I doubt any coercion was involved."

The age twenty-six hit an unexpected nerve. It was the same age she had been when she'd had the wild, silly affair with Damon. Heat surged into her cheeks. It was hard to believe it had been little more than a year ago. So much had happened it felt like centuries had passed. "You're right, at twenty-six, she should have known better."

Zara only wished she had.

Damon's gaze clashed with hers. Zara dragged her gaze free, but not before her fiery irritation was replaced by other, more disturbing sensations coiling low in the pit of her stomach.

Upset and annoyed at the intense, too-familiar awareness that had hit her out of left field, as if they were still connected—*still lovers*—in desperation, Zara recommenced the search for her shoes. She finally located them in the shadowed recesses beneath her desk. Relieved to have a distraction, she bent down and snatched them up. Unlike her suit, which was black and neatly tailored, the shoes were a tad subversive, a gorgeous sea blue that unashamedly matched her eyes.

On the subject of eyes, she thought grimly, *note to self, never look into Damon's eyes for too long.* Apparently, despite dismissing him from her life and putting a great deal of effort into forgetting about him completely, even one second was too long.

With an effort of will, Zara smoothed out her expression, but there was another tiny issue that was bugging her. "And Emily being older than Ben by several years would, of course, make her the predatory one." She could not forget that the paparazzi had nicknamed Petra, who had been several years older than Tyler, "the Huntress." As if Petra had been cold and calculating, and had deliberately set out to ensnare a rich lover, when Zara knew that it had been Tyler who had pursued Petra.

Damon frowned. "I wasn't trying to imply that Emily was predatory because she's older—"

"Good, because we both know Ben is something of a party animal."

Damon seemed briefly riveted by the shoes, and she realized she was brandishing them in front of her like a weapon. Taking a deep breath, she placed the shoes on the floor and methodically slipped them on. The heels gave her an extra inch and half, which wasn't nearly enough.

Damon's gaze clashed with hers again, the hard edge tempered by something she had never seen before, something new, an intent curiosity, as if he was logging the changes in her and taking stock in a completely masculine way.

She suppressed her automatic panic that Damon would somehow equate her extra curves with motherhood. She had to keep reminding herself that Damon's focus was on rescuing Ben from Emily; he didn't know Zara had had his child. In any case, the obvious explanation for her more rounded shape was a whole lot simpler, that she had just put on a little weight.

Damon's expression shuttered. "You know very well that I meant Ben couldn't take a woman like Emily anywhere she didn't want to go."

In the midst of what was for Zara a stressful encounter, Damon's flat statement informed her that he knew exactly what she was trying to achieve with her line of reasoning. It was also a reminder of just why she had fallen for him in the first place. Most people, quite rightly, viewed him as cold and formidable, even dangerous. But that had not been Zara's experience. As

an employer she had found him to be demanding but
utterly straightforward. Far from being intimidated,
she had found that, on a purely feminine level, she had
liked his air of command and the knowledge that, in a
company full of alpha males, Damon was the scariest,
most alpha of them all.

Grudgingly, she conceded Damon's point that Emily
was not the type to be coerced. "Even so, this is out of
character for her. If she had wanted to take time off, she
would have emailed me or left a message."

Although the instant Zara said the words she remembered that she had seen an email from Emily but
hadn't opened it because she'd been so busy with Rosie
and walk-in clients.

Damon extracted his cell from his pocket, flicked the
screen with his thumb, then placed the phone down on
her desk so she could see Emily's email. "Her resignation is there in black and white."

Shocked, Zara flipped her laptop open and scrolled
down her inbox to confirm that she had received almost
exactly the same message. Hers, however, was peppered
with apologies and assurances that Emily would ring
once they got to Medinos.

Medinos. Zara tensed even further.

The island was exotic and beautiful and was popu-
larly styled as the Mediterranean isle of romance. It had
also been Zara's home as a child while her father, Angelo Atrides, the last *conte* of the once-aristocratic but
now-impoverished Atrides line, had been alive. But in
Zara's experience, since Angelo's death when she was
barely seven years old, the only thing that had come
out of Medinos was trouble. "I don't know why Emily
would run off with Ben. They're total opposites."

Ben, though ridiculously handsome, was too young

for Emily and a little spoiled. He hadn't been born with a silver spoon in his mouth; it had been platinum.

While Zara had been reading, Damon had been pacing around her office, examining her walls with their job-notice boards and career displays, reminding her of nothing so much as a large wolf on the prowl. "It would seem Emily's decided to take a break from work with Ben—"

"You think this is just a holiday?" Damon's tone was laced with disbelief.

Still upset at the physicality of her reaction to Damon, a reaction that should have been as dead as a doornail by now, Zara snatched up the newspaper and stared at the grainy photo. "What else could you call it? I don't see an engagement ring, so they're not eloping—"

Damon's gaze pinned her. "Damn right. Ben will not be marrying Emily."

The flat denial, which somehow implied that Emily was not good enough to marry Ben, flicked Zara on the raw. "Ben should be so lucky. Emily is smart and mature. Apart from this...*error* of judgment, she's an exemplary personal assistant."

"If there's been an error of judgment, then that also applies to Ben."

Zara slapped the newspaper back down on the desk. "Why does it always come back to that? You know, people can simply fall in love. When my father died, it took my mother years to find—" She stopped, appalled by what she had almost given away.

There was a moment of vibrating silence. "What do you mean by 'Why does it always come back to that?'"

Relieved that Damon had bypassed her comment about her mother, Zara blurted out her thoughts. "Isn't that what rich men automatically think? That women are attracted by their wealth?"

She cringed the moment the words were out, because she didn't actually believe that about all wealthy men.

Damon's gaze pinned her. "Is that what you believed about me?"

Three

The soft, flat question made her chest go tight and her heart pound. Damon zeroing in on their short, secretive fling was disorienting when a moment ago they had been firmly focused on Ben and Emily.

Zara found herself once more staring at the pulse throbbing along the side of Damon's jaw as she desperately tried to find a neutral way out of a conversation that had careered out of control.

She took a deep breath and decided on the truth. After all, what did it matter now? "Yes."

A curious satisfaction registered in Damon's gaze. "So that's why you didn't want a relationship. You thought I would think you were after my money."

It was only part of the truth.

The whole of it was that if Damon ever found out her real identity, he wouldn't just think she was after his money, he would be certain of it. Although, the irony was that, from the first moment she had met him, she couldn't have cared less about his wealth.

When she had walked into the interview with Damon, his remote gaze had connected with hers and for a split second she'd had a weird premonition that everything was about to change. She could not explain exactly what the phenomenon was, just that for her, at least, it had been instant, visceral and electric. Like a piece of flotsam caught in a powerful current, she had allowed herself to be swept along and had accepted the job. Two weeks later, she had ended up in Damon's bed.

Determined to redirect the conversation back to the situation with Emily and Ben, and hustle Damon out of the door before Rosie woke up, Zara briskly stepped around her desk and busied herself tidying piles of pamphlets that did not need tidying. "I'm sorry for the inconvenience of Emily taking an unplanned leave of absence—"

"Along with my little brother," Damon said drily.

With effort, Zara controlled her temper. She tended to see things from another angle entirely. It was a matter of record that the men in Damon's family were extremely good at seduction. Damon's uncle Tyler had swept Zara's mother off her feet; Damon had gotten Zara into bed in a matter of days. And now it seemed clear that Ben—who had routinely shambled into work around ten o'clock, taken long lunches and drifted away by four—had seduced poor Emily!

Zara moved on to another shelf of pamphlets, which was much nearer the front door, hoping Damon would take the hint. "As far as I'm concerned, Emily is outstandingly qualified and my best temp, and Ben has enticed her away. If anyone needs protection, it's Emily."

Damon gave Zara an incredulous look.

She checked her watch as if she was in a hurry to be somewhere. She had gotten seriously distracted by the Emily/Ben situation, but now she needed to wrap up the issue and get Damon out of her office before Rosie woke up. "I investigated Emily thoroughly before placing her on the books—she's perfectly trustworthy."

"Emily Harris is, but Emily Woodhouse-Harris isn't."

Zara froze as Damon slipped a folded sheet of paper out of his coat pocket and handed it to her. She stared at what was obviously a photocopy of a newspaper cutting depicting a more youthful Emily, the daughter of a disgraced financier who had lost all of his money, and that of the pension fund he had founded, in a financial crash. In the shot, Emily was dressed for the beach in a bikini and filmy sarong, and she was clinging to the arm of a prominent playboy businessman. One who, from the caption, had apparently dumped her in favor of marrying a socialite with her fortune intact.

Zara's jaw tightened. Her motto for Westlake Employment Agency was Reliable, High Quality, Vetted Office Staff, Privacy and Discretion Guaranteed. In this case, the reliability part of the motto hadn't held. Neither had the privacy or the discretion.

However, the tacky little article, far from making Zara feel disappointed in Emily, only made her feel even more fiercely protective of an employee who reminded her an awful lot of herself. *Even down to the way Emily had lost everything and had been forced to invent a new life.* She knew exactly how Emily was going to feel when she saw the piece.

She set the incriminating article down on her desk. "You had Emily *investigated.*"

Damon's expression grew impatient. "I waited for you to call back. When you didn't, I made some calls of my own. As it turns out, I should have done it a whole lot earlier."

"Choosing to use one half of a double-barreled surname, and a previous relationship do not make Emily a bad risk!"

"Maybe not, but before Vitalis, Emily was involved with another wealthy businessman."

Now that she knew Emily's full name, the whole embarrassing scandal was coming back to her, which made her feel even sorrier for Emily. "From memory, the Woodhouse-Harrises moved in wealthy circles, so, of course, Emily would meet wealthy men."

"The relationships wouldn't be such a problem if Emily hadn't tried to conceal her past."

"Maybe she had good reasons for doing so."

Damon crossed his arms over his chest. "Such as?"

Zara's chin came up. She felt she was fighting on two fronts, for Emily and for herself. "For a start, it can't have been much fun having the media hounding her."

"Granted."

The curtness of his reply seemed to emphasize that the bottom line for Damon was Emily's so-called deception. "Emily happens to be very good at her job."

"I'm not disputing that, just her motives in seeking employment with wealthy men."

That touched a nerve, guiltily reminding Zara that if Damon found out her true identity, he would ascribe the same kind of gold-digging motivation to her. She doubted he would believe that it had been Zara's well-connected aunt who had set up the job interview and set her up by placing her back in Damon's orbit in the hope that she might score another cash offer. Or that

Zara had zero interest in that money! "So you still think all Emily wanted was a wealthy husband?"

His expression cooled. "Or a lover. It's not exactly an uncommon motive."

His flat statement once again dredged up the stark memory of the legal letter she had received from Damon's lawyers. They'd offered to pay her off so she would not go to the press, attempt to contact his family or get her sticky fingers on the family inheritance. *As if.*

Zara could feel her blood pressure shooting through the roof. Before that moment, she had been able to separate Damon from the contents of that insulting letter, even though she knew he was the one who had authorized it. But now she realized how naive she had been. Damon's contempt for her and Petra was not so different from his ruthless assessment of Emily.

"There are women who don't give a hoot about your family's money, and Emily is one of them. She is not predatory."

A faint rustling sound from the interview room, as if Rosie was struggling out of her cozy blanket, sent a fresh surge of adrenaline shooting through Zara's veins. Damon's cool gaze fixed on the door, reminding her that not only did he possess exceptional eyesight, but that his hearing was no doubt excellent, as well. Attributes that, along with an uncanny sixth sense had, apparently, made him some kind of superspy during his time in the Special Forces. She needed to get Damon out of her office, now.

She forced a professional smile and apologized, which was more difficult than she expected. Bleakly, she realized she was still surprisingly angry with Damon. Although, she didn't know quite why that should be, since she was the one who had left Damon and not the other way around. Plus, she was *over* him, and had been for months.

She directed another breezy smile in Damon's general direction. As much as she thought Ben was at fault, it was clear the responsibility for the employment part of this disaster belonged with her. Damon's firm paid her to supply Magnum with the temping services they required, so it was up to her to fulfill the contract. She needed to find someone else to fill Emily's position, and fast, before Magnum took their business elsewhere.

"As luck would have it, I've got a temp on the books who might do to replace Emily. She's a little older, but extremely efficient—"

"No."

Zara blinked and plowed on. "Harriet has a long work record and an extremely good skill set—"

"I don't want Harriet," he said in a flat, cool voice. "I want you."

A pang of heat shot clear to Zara's toes, despite the fact that she knew Damon could only be referring to his need for an assistant. Even so, memories flickered, vivid and earthy, drawing every muscle of her body tight. She swallowed against a coiling tension that should not exist and desperately willed her body to return to normal. "Why?"

Damon's darkened gaze locked with hers for a piercing moment, and the reason she'd succumbed to a wild, irresponsible fling with him when she had known it was a huge mistake to sleep with the boss was suddenly crystal clear: chemistry. It shimmered in the air and ran through her veins like liquid fire, the pressure of it banding her chest, making it hard to breathe. For some unknown reason Damon had wanted her and, against all common sense, she had wanted him too.

Damon frowned and dragged lean fingers through his hair and she received the indelible impression that for a long, stretched-out moment he had actually forgotten what he was going to say. "Uh, the McCall takeover. Before you disappeared, you did a lot of the groundwork—"

She stiffened at the mention of the McCall takeover. McCall Electrical being the company that had belonged to Tyler McCall. If there was ever a project she did not want to work on, it would be that one!

"I didn't disappear—I resigned without notice." *Then* she had disappeared. She'd had to get out of town quickly, because she had known that if she had tried to have a normal, aboveboard relationship with Damon, the press would have become interested in her. Even though they had no clue what Angel Atrides looked like, it would only have been a matter of time before her true identity was uncovered, then all the careful work she had done to invent a normal life and career would have been for nothing.

"Resignation?" he muttered in a low growl. "You sent a text."

Warmth rose in her cheeks. "But I did resign."

She knew she shouldn't belabor the point, but a combination of her anxiety over Damon walking into her office and her extreme physical response to him were having a bad effect on her. She couldn't seem to stop arguing with him, which was counterproductive. She needed to concentrate on getting rid of him before Rosie woke up.

Swallowing the exhilarating desire to argue some more, she reached for calm. "I agree that texting was not the ideal way to finish." It had just been necessary at the time, because she had not wanted Damon to have her private email address. Email addresses opened too many online doors, some of which led back to her old life, and she knew how adept Damon was at utilizing those sorts of opportunities.

Damon's thoughtful gaze seemed to burn right through her. "Whatever. Before you *left* without any notice or forwarding address, you did the groundwork for the McCall takeover. Despite a hitch in the proceedings, I'm now on the point of closing the deal, so I would prefer to have someone who knows their way around the issues."

Zara had the sudden, suffocating sense of being entangled in a sticky web from which she could not escape. "I had thought you would have completed that months ago."

"There's been an unexpected complication, a missing block of voters' shares that could jeopardize the takeover. And I've had…other things that have needed attention."

A picture of the gorgeous blonde he'd been dating lately, heiress to a media empire, Caroline Grant, flashed into Zara's mind. That image was instantly followed by a snapshot of the reed-slim redhead he had started seeing on a regular basis not long after Zara had left. Another hot dart of anger unsettled her further.

She did not want to admit that the anger could be linked with the fact that Damon had started dating less than a month after she left his bed. Wining and dining beautiful women while she had been hiding out in her aunt's country cottage, feeling exhausted and nauseous in the first trimester of her pregnancy. Because, if she was angry, that meant Damon was still important to her, or worse, that she was jealous.

Another small sound drew Damon's attention back to the door of the interview room. Zara's heart rate increased another notch. Rosie was definitely awake.

The vibration of a cell, thankfully, distracted Damon. Despite her clear need to get rid of Damon fast, a sudden intense curiosity manifested itself as he extracted the phone from his coat pocket and checked the screen.

Jaw taut, she watched as he slipped the phone back into his pocket. She wondered if the call had been from Caroline Grant, and suddenly her mind was made up.

"No. Working for you is out of the question, I have—"

"I realize you have a business to run," Damon cut in smoothly. "But I only need you for three weeks, four at most, until the negotiations are completed. And you do have a part-time assistant who could fill in for you."

Damon offered a fee that was so generous it would cover her agency costs for the next year. More, she would finally be able to afford to fly to Medinos to check out a mysterious safe-deposit box she had recently discovered her mother had obtained not long before she died.

But, as tempting as the money was, as much as she needed it, she could not risk being that close to Damon. As it was, she was kicking herself that she had allowed financial desperation to hold sway when she had accepted him as a client.

"I'm sorry. I can't work for you."

Walking briskly to her front door, she yanked it open. She had to get Damon out of her office before he discovered Rosie. He would take one look at her coal-black hair and eyes that were changing by the day to look eerily like his and would instantly know she was his daughter.

Cold, damp air flowed in, making Zara shiver, but instead of taking the hint and walking through the door, Damon paused and she made the fatal mistake of looking into his eyes.

Long, tense seconds later, Damon's gaze dropped to her mouth and the heady tension she had so far failed to control tightened another notch.

"Damn," he muttered, "I promised myself I wasn't going to do this."

Zara froze as he cupped her jaw, unwillingly riveted by the tingling heat that radiated out from that one point of contact, the unbearably familiar masculine scents of soap and skin. Despite the cold air, she could feel herself growing warmer by the second. Damon's touch was featherlight; all she needed to do was step away, so why couldn't she do that one simple thing?

It was a bad time to discover that, despite everything that had happened, the heady excitement that had been her downfall a year ago was still just as potent, just as seductive.

It shouldn't be, she thought a little desperately. She had changed; she had moved on. When she did decide to allow a man back into her life it would not be because of an off-the-register sexual attraction. This time she would choose carefully. She needed steady and reliable, not—

Damon's mouth slanted across hers and any idea that the day was cold was blasted away by a torrent of heat. Her heart pounded so hard she found it difficult to breathe and her legs suddenly felt as limp as noodles.

This was why she had made "the mistake," she thought dimly. Her palms slid up over Damon's chest; her fingers convulsively gripped the lapels of his coat, as a familiar, guilty pleasure flooded her. Damon's hands settled at her waist, molding her more firmly against him and she found herself responding with an automatic, mindless pleasure, lifting up on her toes as she pressed into the kiss, clutching at his shoulders as if she couldn't get enough of him.

It was moth-to-the-flame stuff, irresistible and utterly dangerous, because it was abruptly clear to her that Damon was nothing short of an intoxicating addiction. When he was in the room she couldn't think; worse, she didn't want to think. As emancipated and independent as she was, as determined as she was to run her life in a practical, logical way, she had never been able to resist him.

Long, drugging seconds later Damon lifted his head. "Before I go, I have one more question."

A thin, high cry pierced the air. Zara's stomach sank. With a convulsive movement, she released her grip on Damon's coat.

Damon's gaze turned wintry. "Question answered."

With a sense of fatalism, undergirded by the sudden wrenching suspicion that Damon had known all along that there was a baby, Zara watched as he reached the door to the interview room in two gliding strides and pushed the door open wide.

Four

Damon stared at the baby in the bassinet.

He thought he had been prepared for this moment, but the reality of the tiny baby literally flipped his world upside down in the space of a moment.

The first thing he noticed about the child, *his child*, was the color of her sleep suit. Pink.

The tension banding his chest increased exponentially. Not only did he have a baby, he had a daughter.

"What's her name?" His voice came out more roughly than he cared for, but then it wasn't every day he discovered he was a father.

Emotion, painful and inchoate, seemed to burst through some interior barrier. With it came a torrent of memories. Memories that should have faded, but hadn't: his father's voice late at night, the muffled sounds that meant his mother was being hit and was trying to stay quiet so he wouldn't know. Later, when he was older, the breathless pain of broken ribs, the harsh chemical scents of the hospital emergency room.

Once, a memory of reckless fury bursting through him when his father had attacked Damon's mother, who had been pregnant with Ben at the time. Ten years old, but big for his age, Damon had hit out and caught Guy Smith by surprise. He could still remember the rage behind that punch, the hot rush of satisfaction that had poured through him when his father had gone down.

Fatherhood, he thought bleakly. It was something he had consciously avoided, just as he avoided emotional relationships in general. As a child he had learned that the kind of intense out-of-control love most people seemed to wish for was neither a practical nor a safe basis for any relationship. Although, looking at the tiny baby whose gaze had latched onto his with single-minded intensity as she sucked on one small fist, he registered that you could not prove that by him. The first night he had spent with Zara had been characterized by a distinct lack of control.

He noted the fact that Zara was hovering at the door. "She's mine."

"Yes."

"And you didn't tell me, because...?"

Her gaze met his squarely before falling away. "It's... complicated." Her gaze homed in on his again, brows jerked together in a frown. "How did you find out? Let me guess... Emily?"

"Ben. When he phoned from the airport, he let it slip." Damon's jaw tightened. "He thought I already knew—"

"But if you'd known, we would have had this conversation a long time ago."

Damon tensed against the waft of a familiar flowery perfume as Zara brushed by him and slung a piece of muslin over one shoulder, presumably in case of spills. Picking the baby up with unconsciously graceful movements, she cuddled the infant close, Zara's expression softening in a way that briefly riveted him and, out of nowhere, desire kicked. Jaw tight, he registered the stubborn, visceral need to reclaim Zara, which should have evaporated in the instant he had uncovered the baby and her deception, and yet it hadn't.

In a moment of self-knowledge, he noted that it was tied to the fact that Zara was now the mother of his child and therefore qualified for his protection and support. As strong and independent as Zara seemed, he could no more abandon her and the baby than he had been able to step away from his own mother when she had been the victim of his father's abusive nature.

Added to that, as much as he had tried to intellectualize the process, the fact that Zara had given birth to his child had tipped some internal balance. He had felt the change in the instant that Ben had told him there was a baby. The primitive, testosterone-fueled desire that had gripped him to claim not just his child, but Zara too.

He watched as Zara rubbed the baby's back and he waited for more unwelcome memories of his childhood to surface and douse a need he didn't want. The memories didn't come. Probably, he thought bleakly, because his only memories of a baby in the family were of Ben. And by the time Ben was born their father had been dead and buried.

Damon began noticing other things in the room. A desk, which held what looked like Zara's handbag and, beside it, a newspaper and a small pile of mail. There were also a couple of chairs, and a large bag in one corner that seemed jam-packed full of baby things. Feeling suddenly overwarm, he shrugged out of his coat and dropped it over the back of a chair.

"Were you ever going to tell me?"

Her gaze flashed to his as, one-handed, she rummaged through the baby bag and extracted an insulated container holding a bottle of what he guessed was baby formula. "I didn't think, given that I was just an employee and that we'd had an office affair, that you would want to be tied to me by a chil—"

"It wasn't an affair."

"It was temporary."

Damon frowned at her clipped reply. He was still processing the fact that there really was a baby, but he was clear on one point. "Temporary or not doesn't change a thing. She's my child. I had a right to know."

And in the saying of it, he felt a further internal shift, the forging of a link that was irrevocable. It quietly but absolutely changed everything.

Zara's expression was taut as she settled the baby in her lap and coaxed her to accept the bottle. "You don't want children—you made no secret about that. I came across a magazine article where your wife claimed the reason your marriage broke up was that you didn't want children. She wasn't exactly reticent about the subject."

Damon frowned, irritated, despite the fact that for once the media was accurate. "That was true enough. Lily and I had an...arrangement—"

"As I remember it, so did we. A short-term liaison, no strings." She sent him the kind of crisp, business-like glance that assured him everything was settled.

Unfortunately, the slick managerial technique—

straight out of Business Troubleshooting 101—only increased the fascination that had gripped Damon from the very first time he had met Zara. Over the years he had become used to being pursued by beautiful, successful women. With Zara, the opposite had proven to be true. And despite the clear evidence that she wanted him, she still seemed intent on avoiding him.

He should have been pleased. It was permission to step back, to keep his emotional involvement to a minimum, to simply be a biological father with legal access. No messy emotion or fallout when it all came apart.

The problem was, he thought grimly, that just minutes ago, Zara hadn't just let him kiss her, she had kissed him back. Despite walking out on him a year ago, she still wanted him. The mix of attraction and avoidance had an interesting but frustrating effect, fueling his need to have her back.

With every minute that passed, the desire to understand why Zara had run when she still clearly wanted him intensified. She had said she didn't want him to think she was after his money, and that she knew he didn't want children. Both were valid reasons, *if* their physical attraction had cooled off. But clearly it hadn't, which left him with a question mark.

"What's her name?"

The front door chime sounded.

Distracted, Zara peered past him into the office. "Rosamund, Rosie for short." She looked briefly torn. "Will you hold her while she finishes her bottle?"

A split second later, Zara was close enough that he could smell the flowery scent of her hair and other scents: the sourness of the milk spill on the muslin over her shoulder, the soft sweetness of baby powder.

"Hold her so her head is supported on your arm."

Damon froze as he found himself awkwardly cradling his daughter.

Zara handed him the bottle of formula, her expression both anxious and imperious. "Don't hold her so loosely. Closer, like this…"

She readjusted his hold so Rosie was cradled closer against his chest, her head resting comfortably in the crook of his arm. "And tilt the bottle—like this—so she doesn't gulp air."

Seconds later, Zara stepped out into the main office, closing the door firmly behind her.

Fumbling with the soft, warm bundle that wriggled and moved, Damon took the chair Zara had vacated and touched the nipple of the bottle to Rosie's lips. His anxiety that he was doing it all wrong evaporated almost instantly as Rosie's small hands clamped either side of the bottle and she began to drain what was left of the milk. After a minute or so the nipple popped out of her mouth, signaling that she was done. She stared at him unblinkingly, then put her fist into her mouth.

Gently, he attempted to lift her fist away and succeeded long enough that he caught a pearly flash against the redness of her gum before she was once again sucking on her fist. Feeling out of his depth, Damon let her have her way. If it was her fist that made her happy, who was he to argue?

Setting the bottle down on the desk, he eased himself into a more comfortable position and simply looked at the tiny warm creature in his arms. Something about Rosie informed him that even if she hadn't been wearing pink, he would have known she was a girl. It wasn't just that her skin was like porcelain and her features delicate—he guessed all babies shared those in common. And it wasn't the shock of silky dark hair that already showed a trace of curl, just like her mother's. Rather it was an indefinable, faintly imperious quality that announced her femininity, a quality her mother had in spades.

He dragged at his tie, loosening it. Rosie's gaze followed his action before she once more returned to a study of his face as if she was intent on imprinting his features. Caught in the net of his daughter's gaze, a profound sense of recognition riveted Damon. If there had been any doubt that he was Rosie's father, those doubts would have been nixed in that moment. Zara's eyes were a deep sapphire blue; Rosie's were already lightening to the unusual silvery gray that had run in his family for generations.

She had his eyes.

Something weird happened in the region of Damon's chest. He reached out a lean finger to touch a silky wisp of hair. Petal-soft fingers closed around his finger with surprising strength.

Rosie stared into his eyes, her gaze direct and fearless and, suddenly, she was her mother's daughter. Pale, delicate skin flushed and for a moment he thought she would cry. Instead her mouth curved in a gummy smile and he logged the moment that he fell utterly and completely under his daughter's spell.

"This complicates things," he muttered. "I'm not fit to be anyone's dad."

Rosie made a cute cooing sound. He tried to free his finger from her fierce grip, then was completely fascinated when she refused to let go.

"Babies have surprising strength." Zara's quiet voice broke his intense focus on his daughter.

He watched as she picked up the length of muslin,

which had fallen to the floor, and briskly tucked it away in the baby bag, the movement jerky. "What's wrong?"

"Nothing! At least I hope it's nothing. But that was not the normal type of client that strolls in off the street. She was too well dressed, too pushy and she seemed more interested in the fact that you were seen walking in here than in applying for a job. I'm pretty sure she was a reporter of some kind."

Damon frowned. Normally the press didn't bother him too much. But that was because he usually made damn sure he wasn't in the public eye. For the past few months, however, he'd had an uncomfortable amount of exposure, because his current date, Caroline, championed a number of charities and had insisted on dragging him along to some high-profile events. As a result, he'd had one reporter in particular dogging his footsteps, trying to snag some kind of exclusive on his personal life.

"Was she blonde, thin, with red-rimmed glasses?"

Zara looked up from jamming the empty bottle into the baby bag, her expression arrested. "You *know* her?"

"Not exactly. She's a friend of Caroline's. She usually covers charity events."

"Caroline?" Zara zipped the bag closed with unnecessary force. "That would be your current girlfriend, which would make Red Glasses what? A gossip columnist?"

Now distinctly irritated, Damon rose to his feet. The motion seemed to distract Rosie, because she finally let go of his finger. "If we're talking about the same person, then her name's Vanessa Gardiner. She freelances for the tabloids and a couple of women's magazines."

He knew that because he had seen her parked outside his apartment a couple of times and just last week she had followed him to an exclusive restaurant where he'd had a client lunch. The intrusion had ticked him off to the point that he had tasked Walter, his head of security, with calling her off. Apparently, the tactic hadn't worked.

"So, she followed you here, to *my* employment agency? Why on earth would she want to do that?"

Damon worked to release the sudden tension in his jaw. Lately, it felt like he'd landed in the middle of a soap opera. At times like this, he missed the simplicity of the life in the military he had been forced to relinquish when he took over the family business. Chain of command was clear-cut and logical, unlike personal relationships.

"A few days ago, at an awards dinner, Caroline accused me of seeing someone else. Unfortunately, Gardiner must have been close enough to pick up on the conversation."

Zara straightened, her eyes shooting blue fire. "And are you seeing someone else?"

Damon got the sudden, arresting notion that if he'd said yes to Zara's snapped-out question she would have done something interestingly violent, like throw something at him. An odd, warm glow spread through him. "I'm not exactly in the habit of dating two women at the same time. Besides, you know my work schedule."

She blinked as if she was still having trouble controlling her emotions. "So this reporter is stalking you, trying to find evidence that there's another woman and she ends up in *my* office, where there's not only another woman, but a baby, as well!" Zara drew a deep breath. "Just what I need in my life right now."

Dragging a trailing tendril of hair behind one ear, she began to pace, even though there was very little room for pacing. "You should have called me before showing up—"

"I did. You didn't return my call."

Zara stared at him, frustrated. "What I don't get is why you want to be involved with Rosie or with me! From all accounts, it didn't take you long to get over me. Within a month you were dating that redhead. What was her name? Janet, Jessica—"

"Jemima."

She glared at him. "Whatever. Now you're dating Caroline and her little reporter friend is following you."

The silence in the small room stretched out, fraught and intense. Somewhere in the distance a car horn honked. The gusting wind was now laced by rain, which pattered on a barred window. It was an odd moment to discover one salient fact that somehow changed everything: Zara had been jealous of Jemima. And if Damon didn't miss his guess, she was jealous of Caroline.

Out of nowhere, his pulse rate lifted. Dealing with Zara was like trying to get information from a sphinx on lockdown. In normal conversation she was guarded and controlled. The only chink in her armor was that she hadn't yet learned to control her emotions or her body language.

Just minutes ago, she had kissed him. The memory of it still made every muscle in his body tighten. Now her eyes were shooting fire and she was making no bones about the fact that she didn't like it that he dated other women. Against all the odds, Zara's unguarded response settled something in him, a question that had remained unanswered for the past year. He didn't know why she had left him, but he was now certain it had not been because she didn't want him.

Feeling oddly buoyed, he cradled a now-sleepy Rosie

a little closer and walked the few paces to the window, which looked out over a service lane. The rain had gotten heavier and the temperature in the room had dropped a couple of degrees. He made a mental note to ensure Zara and Rosie had adequate heating. "So, when did you discover you were pregnant?"

"A few days before I left."

That explained a few things: Zara had had a sick day when she had not seemed to be ill; her suddenly crammed schedule when, from the time they had started sleeping together, they had seldom spent a night apart.

His jaw tightened as memories he thought he had jettisoned came crowding back. He had to keep reminding himself that their relationship, such as it was, had lasted barely four weeks.

"I thought something had happened to you."

Until he had gone to her apartment and discovered that Zara had systematically packed up and left town. A quick word with the manager of the building had supplied the information that Zara had given notice some days before, which indicated the move had been carefully planned. "You could have talked to me. We could have worked something out."

Zara sent him a cool glance, left the room and returned almost immediately with the newspaper he had brought. She held it so that Ben and Emily's picture and the insulting headline were clearly visible. "Like this?"

"I'm not Ben."

"No, you're way more newsworthy. The media would have cut me to shreds. They would have made my life a misery." She tossed the newspaper into the trash can to one side of the desk.

Damon's gaze narrowed at the extremity of her reaction to the kind of publicity that was literally a five-minute wonder. He adjusted his hold on Rosie. "I could have arranged financial support."

Zara's head came up. "Money. Why did I know that it would come back to that? Do you always use money to solve your 'problems'?" She sketched quotation marks in the air.

He frowned at her reaction. "Not always. Sometimes a conversation works."

The phone ringing out in the office broke a tension that was suddenly thick enough to cut. There was an audible click as the call went through to the answering service.

"News flash," she said curtly. "With regard to your money, I don't want it. That's why I'm in business—I like to earn my own way."

Her glance was laced with defiance. With the flush on her cheeks and glossy tendrils of hair curling around her cheekbones, he couldn't help thinking that despite the buttoned-down suit and the attempt to tame her hair, Zara looked exotic and tempestuous.

Her flat statement underlined the certainty that had grown in him as he had cradled Rosie. He had thought that if there really was a child he would be able to control what he felt, that he could preserve his distance, but that idea had crashed and burned the second Rosie smiled at him.

One gummy smile and suddenly he had a whole new priority list.

He still intended to retrieve Ben ASAP, but, for the moment, Rosie and the attraction that was still very much alive between him and Zara had taken precedence over Ben and Emily's departure.

The implications were dizzying. After years of managing all his relationships, he was faced with two relationships that were distinctly out of his control. He should be drawing back, looking for ways to lessen his involvement and neutralize his dangerous emotions. The only trouble was, this time he didn't want to pull back. After years of being out in the cold, he couldn't seem to resist the warmth.

Damon glanced down at Rosie, who had dropped off to sleep in his arms with a relaxed abandon that was mesmerizing. Her cheeks were delicately flushed, her lashes dark, silky crescents against her skin. For a moment, he was transfixed by the phenomenon, which had at its heart the absolute trust a child gave to a parent. The kind of trust he had never thought would be given to him, but which now seemed vital.

He felt the moment of decision, a quiet settling into place of a plan that, less than an hour ago, would have been out of the question. A plan that would include both Rosie and Zara in his life.

The risk of attempting such a thing registered, but the concept of that risk was almost instantly swamped by a surge of possessiveness.

There was no reason he couldn't successfully incorporate Zara and Rosie into his life. But he had to be careful. Zara had walked away from him once before, disappearing almost without trace; he could not afford for that to happen again. This time he would move more slowly and the way forward seemed clear.

"Okay, let's talk business. Now that Emily's gone, I need a PA."

The wariness disappeared from Zara's expression with fascinating speed as she shifted into business mode. "I have a couple more possibilities on the books," she said smoothly. "A retired accountant who is looking for part-time work—although I'm sure he'd be happy to fill in for Emily for a couple of weeks. And a researcher who will probably be perfect—"

"Like I said before," Damon said flatly. "I don't want the temps on your books. We're out of time and you've worked on the takeover. I want you."

Shock reverberated through Zara at the flat demand of the last three words.

Even though Damon had couched the barely concealed demand in business terms, for a sharp, visceral moment Zara still registered that he wanted *her*. Not good.

She took a deep breath, which she suddenly desperately needed. The chemistry thing was happening again. Her heart was beating too fast and her skin felt oddly sensitive, her breasts taut. In certain places there was a distressing, tingling heat that was all too familiar…

She crossed her arms over her chest and tried to get a grip on herself. Because this was the same craziness that had gotten her into trouble in the first place. "I'm not available."

"If you're worried about this office, I'll compensate you for the cost of increasing Molly's hours, or even employing someone to replace you while you work for me. I'm also happy to pay for childcare. In fact, *all* of Rosie's childcare."

He glanced around the small room, which normally Zara barely registered, but she was noticing it now. Aside from Rosie's clutter, there was just the cheap desk and two chairs. Even the carpet, which was gray and threadbare in places, highlighted the fact that she had run out of money when it came to this room. The small decor budget she'd allowed herself had all been expended on the front office, because first impressions counted.

Damon's gaze pinned her. "This isn't charity—it's a business proposition."

Zara drew a swift breath. Damon's offer shouldn't have flicked her on the raw, but it did, since the last time Damon had offered her money it had been so she would go away for good. Not that he knew that!

"Like I said before, I really don't want your money."

"But you need it."

Shock jerked through her at the flat certainty in his voice, as if he knew just how financially stretched she was. Panic gripped her, making it hard to breathe. "You've been investigating me."

She didn't know why she hadn't thought of that before. Damon was in the surveillance business after all and she had read enough about Magnum to know that the company included a range of complementary businesses, one of them an actual detective agency.

Damon's gaze narrowed. "Believe it or not, I don't make a practice of investigating the women I sleep with. I like to think I can step away from the paranoia of the security business and have something approaching a normal life outside work hours. The reason I know you need the money is that you agreed to take Magnum Security on as a client. Given your reluctance to even take a phone call from me, it was fairly easy to conclude that you needed the money."

Zara drew a deep breath and tried to calm down. She had always known that if Damon decided to put her life under a microscope, he would unravel her secrets fairly quickly. Logically, the fact that he hadn't turned up at her door until now meant that he hadn't. Even so...

"It's still got to be no when it comes to money," she said stiffly. "I can manage."

Damon frowned. "Whether you want my money or not, the second I declare my paternity and apply to pay child support, you'll receive it, anyway."

The words *declare paternity* and *child support* stopped Zara in her tracks. Damon declaring his paternity was a legal process, which would inevitably result in Rosie's birth certificate being updated to include his name. Then that document would be supplied to Damon. When Damon looked at the birth certificate he would see Zara's name change and that her mother had been Petra Atrides, aka Petra Hunt.

If that wasn't bad enough, when the tax agency assessed his income and began making her mandatory child support payments from his bank account, he would hate her even more. Originally, he had tried to get rid of Zara, aka Angel, with one cash payment; now he would be stuck with years of payments. And because Damon earned a great deal, those payments would be substantial.

Zara tried to think, but she felt like she was caught in a whirlwind. Now that he had discovered Rosie, those legal processes would happen. There was nothing she could do to stop them. The only thing she could do was angle for time while she tried to figure out how to tell Damon the truth about herself without forever damaging his relationship with Rosie. And how to make the money problem go away.

Suddenly the interview room seemed claustrophobically small. In need of air and a few seconds' respite so she could *think*, Zara opened the door and peered out into her office. It was empty, and thanks to the rain, the street outside was fairly deserted.

The reporter seemed to have disappeared. Although, Zara didn't think she had seen the last of Vanessa Gardiner. She had stared at Zara as if she was a hound dog on the scent. Zara had gotten the distinct impression that Vanessa knew Zara used to work for Damon and now she was busily putting two and two together. That meant Vanessa would be back, and if she saw Zara with Rosie, the game would be up.

Zara tried to shake the horribly familiar hunted feeling—the same feeling she'd experienced when the press had tracked her after Petra's death—but it wouldn't go away. Whether she was right or wrong, her instincts told her she needed to be absent from Westlake Employment for a while.

Right now, her only option seemed to be to work for Damon. It felt a little like jumping out of the frying pan into the fire, but it was a fact that Damon worked in a hermetically sealed, high-security environment, fourteen stories up. Even the underground parking area was private and secure. To all intents and purposes, unless Gardiner found out where Zara lived, she would have seemed to have disappeared off the face of the planet.

Turning back, she met Damon's gaze squarely. "I could work for you, but on the condition that I'll need to bring Rosie with me. If that reporter tracked you here and thinks we might be involved, then there's no way I'm risking having her find out about Rosie or tracking her to her day care center."

"Not a problem. If you want an alternative center, I have a friend who owns a childcare franchise."

He mentioned the name of an exclusive franchise that was way out of her price range. The only problem was, she didn't think any center was safe, at least for the moment. And the way the tabloids had jumped on the

story about Ben and Emily was just a dress rehearsal
for the way they would behave when they discovered
Zara had given birth to Damon's child.

"I just don't want to risk the press finding out Rosie
is yours until we've had time to…settle things."

Suddenly, needing to have her daughter close, Zara
held out her arms and was inordinately relieved when
Damon instantly handed Rosie over. Unfortunately, in
the process, Zara had to get closer to Damon than she
liked. His arms brushed hers and his breath washed over
one cheek. The intimacy of the contact sent another one
of those sharp little pangs through her.

Damon shrugged out of his jacket, which had a small
milky spill on it and picked up a container of baby wipes
that resided on the desk. "Can I use one of these?"

She nodded and tried not to watch as Damon perched
on the edge of the desk and dabbed at the stain. Suddenly, he seemed too large and too male for the tiny
office, with the breadth of his shoulders stretching the
cut of his jacket and the bronze color of his skin glowing through the white cotton of his shirt.

Feeling edgy and unsettled and still whirling from
the decisions she'd had to make, Zara placed Rosie on
one shoulder and gently rubbed her back, encouraging
her daughter to stay asleep. Anything but dwell on the
relaxed intimacy of Damon cleaning the stain from his
jacket with Rosie's wipes—the kind of small, fascinating action that went with couplehood, or families.

He looked up, catching her off guard. "Rosie's teething, by the way. When she put her fist in her mouth her
gums were red and I saw a glimpse of white."

Instantly distracted, Zara lowered Rosie into the bassinet. Gently, she examined her mouth and was stunned to
see a tiny glimmer of white edging through Rosie's gum.

Three months was very early for teething, although Zara had learned from another young mother whose baby had been born with tiny "milk teeth" that anything could happen. "You're right, it must have just come through. No wonder she's had trouble sleeping." She shot Damon a faintly chagrined look. "How did you know?"

"My ex-wife's sister had twins. They both teethed early."

Zara could feel herself stiffening at his easy mention of his ex-wife, Lily. Shortly after Zara had discovered who Damon really was, two weeks into her tempestuous six weeks with him, she had searched online for snippets about his gorgeous, blonde and seemingly perfect ex-wife. Lily had since married again to an extremely wealthy banker.

Lily and Damon had seemed to have a poster-perfect marriage, which had ended in a quick and quiet divorce a few years ago. Logically, Zara knew that all the talk about perfection had to be untrue, since Lily and Damon had divorced, but Zara's mood had plummeted, anyway. It had underlined her decision to leave without telling Damon she was pregnant. If Damon had not been satisfied with Lily, how on earth could he ever contemplate a real relationship with Zara?

Damon shrugged back into his jacket. Zara was caught and held by the way his shirt briefly stretched across his muscled chest, and the flood of intimate memories that sight evoked, most of which had to do with breathless heat and naked skin. Predictably, his gaze caught hers in that moment, but this time she managed to quickly look away, although she couldn't do a thing about the warmth that seared her cheeks.

A split second later, he closed the distance between

them as he came to look down at Rosie. Zara was caught and held by the softness of his expression. It was a softness she had only ever seen in flashes, usually for the elderly or the very young.

"I'll let Howard know you're taking the job."

Her heart jolted at the singular clarity of Damon's gaze, the silvery irises with their dark striations, the thick, silky fringe of lashes. For a long, breathless moment her mind went completely blank. "Just so we're clear, I'll work for you for the time it takes to complete the McCall takeover, on the condition that your relationship to Rosie is kept secret until after the deal is completed."

Damon's incisive, wintry gaze settled on hers for an uncomfortable period of time, reminding her that when it came to deception she was a desperate amateur, while he had a formidable skill set. In terms of her deception she was suddenly profoundly aware that the clock was ticking.

He shot the cuff of his jacket and checked his watch, as if he needed to be somewhere. "Agreed. I've no more wish that the press get wind of this than you. I won't let on that Rosie is mine until the takeover is completed, and until after we've settled the custody arrangements."

Custody. Another crazy jolt to her heart. Implications she hadn't thought of flooded her, such as the fact that Rosie now had two parents instead of one. Rosie was no longer solely Zara's. She was so used to having her soft, sweet daughter all to herself, of being a cozy, self-sufficient family of two, that it was hard to consider the changes that were coming.

She was quite sure Damon would never try to take Rosie from her. She was equally certain that he would be entirely reasonable in terms of custody. Even so,

the notion of sharing Rosie shook Zara, underlining
that her cut-and-dried, controllable life had just swung
wildly off course.

Added to that, with the inescapable link of Rosie
binding Zara to Damon, she no longer had the option
of running and hiding. She would once more have to
face the world as Petra Hunt's daughter.

The last woman in the world Damon would wish to
be the mother of his child.

Five

Damon strolled down the windswept road in the direction of his Jeep Cherokee. His phone vibrated again. He ignored it, just like he'd ignored the last call, then grimaced as he saw his security chief camped out by Damon's Jeep, phone to his ear.

Walter, a retired assault specialist in the Special Forces, terminated his call. "You could have answered. I was worried. The whole office is in an uproar—"

"Can't see why." Damon found his car keys and unlocked the Jeep. "I was only gone for a couple of hours."

Walter tapped his watch. "Four hours. You missed two appointments, but don't worry, Howard rescheduled. He's more of a blunt instrument than a personal assistant, but he managed to quiet old man Sanderson down. Didn't have much success with Caroline though. Think you've got a bit of work to do there."

Damon went still. "You let Howard talk to Caroline?" Howard Prosser was another ex-army employee—an

accountant and steely-eyed auditor who had routinely
struck fear into entire military bases. Conversation was
an art form that Howard had never mastered. Normally,
he happily remained locked in his office and preferred
communicating via email.

"It was more a succession of grunts than actual
speech." Walter looked reflective. "I think he likes her."

Damon could feel a familiar frustration kicking in.
Caroline Grant, the daughter of a real estate magnate,
was elegant, beautiful and intelligent. She epitomized
the qualities of the kind of woman he wanted to be attracted to, but unfortunately, that was where it ended.
There was a vital component missing. Ever since his
marriage to Lily had quietly imploded, Damon had become acutely aware of what that component was. As
perfect as she was, he did not truly want Caroline.

The situation reminded him of his marriage. On the
surface everything looked perfect, but there was a lack
of spontaneity, of *warmth* that ruled out real intimacy.
The problem was that Caroline, and almost every other
woman he had dated aside from Zara, was just a little
too much like him, more interested in a cool, carefully
negotiated partnership than in flinging caution to the
wind and plunging into a fiery, risky liaison.

He tensed as a vivid image of Zara, wrapping her
arms around his neck and lifting up on her toes to kiss
him, momentarily blanked his mind and made every
cell in his body tighten. The honking of a car as it
braked behind a delivery truck dragged him back to
the chilly gray present and the conversation with Walter.

"Uh, what did Caroline say?"

Walter reached into his pocket. "She left you a note."

Damon took and opened the note. A ticket fluttered
to the pavement. He skimmed the neat, slanted writing,

which was heavily indented into the page, as if Caroline had pressed quite hard with the pen as she wrote. The message was succinct. Since he had missed their discussion about his promise of support for her latest charity over lunch last week and canceled their lunch date today, she had taken the liberty of signing him up for the gala evening she had arranged that evening. He could pick her up at six, sharp.

Walter scooped up the ticket and handed it to him. "A ticket to a gala ball. You hate gala balls."

With passion. Damon slipped the ticket into his wallet.

Walter's brows jerked together. "I hope you're not getting maneuvered into anything serious here."

A grim smile quirked one corner of Damon's mouth. Walter had been around for his marriage breakup and was somewhat protective. "Don't worry. I've got a feeling Caroline and I are strictly short-term."

Caroline needed an escort for tonight, but from the brevity of the note and the depth of the indentations, even piercing the page on the final period, whatever it was they had shared was over.

"All I can say," Walter muttered, "is that this city lifestyle is a far cry from Afghanistan."

"You hated Afghanistan."

"Margot hated Afghanistan," Walter corrected. "If I wanted to save my marriage, something had to go. Turns out it was the job. By the way, pretty sure I saw Vanessa Gardiner driving away just as I got here."

Damon's gaze narrowed as he automatically skimmed the flow of traffic. "She tried to fool Zara into thinking she needed a job."

Walter's eyebrows shot up. "I'll bet that went well."

Damon climbed behind the wheel and nosed into

traffic. He hadn't told Zara, but he was pretty sure it was Caroline who had manipulated the reporter into doing a little digging. She had become increasingly suspicious that there was another woman. For him, the suspicion spelled the end to a relationship that had grown increasingly irritating.

He was aware of Walter following close behind. Walter and Margot were longtime friends. There was nothing flashy or luxe about them. They had three kids, all grown now, and they lived a comfortable but low-key life. However, ordinary or not, they possessed something that had eluded Damon—a relationship that had lasted through thick and thin, characterized by warmth, loyalty and family values.

The fact that he was a father hit him anew.

He braked as traffic ahead slowed. He was still struggling to come to grips with the surge of possessiveness that had hit him out of left field for Rosie *and* Zara, and which was now driving a whole bunch of decisions that, twenty-four hours ago, would not have been viable.

Zara was making no bones about wanting to preserve her distance, which should have pleased him. After all, her reaction dovetailed with his own preference for avoiding emotional entanglements. Instead, contrarily, Zara's determination to remain independent had only served to aggravate and annoy him even more for one salient reason: he still wanted her.

His tactics in forcing Zara to work for him had been blunt and crude, but the situation was nonnegotiable. He was a father and that changed everything. He didn't just want to be a weekend visitor; he wanted Rosie in his life.

And, against all the odds, that was the way he was beginning to think about Zara too.

The lights changed. He accelerated into the inner city and took the ramp down into the parking garage beneath the gleaming office block that contained his offices and a penthouse apartment.

Damon held the private elevator for Walter, who had driven in directly behind him.

Walter grunted his thanks. As the elevator shot upward, Walter stared blandly at the floor numbers as they flashed. "What are you going to do about the baby?"

With a sense of resignation, Damon met Walter's gaze. He tried to tell himself that if his head of security couldn't find out that kind of information he would have been disappointed. "You've spoken to Ben."

"First thing when he landed. He's worried about you."

The elevator doors glided open. Damon checked his watch as he stepped into the foyer of Magnum Security. By his calculation, Ben and Emily would have landed a couple of hours ago, right about when Damon had been walking the streets, looking for Zara's office.

Walter waited until they were in the privacy of his office before he fired his next question. "Don't tell me you're going to marry her."

Damon shrugged out of his coat and hung it on the hook behind the door. "With a child in the mix, maybe it's the logical solution."

Walter gave him the kind of polite stare that said he wasn't buying that for an instant. "There are other solutions."

Damon had thought of them all. He could simply arrange access, offer financial assistance and step out of the picture, job done.

The problem was, he thought broodingly, that Zara

had kissed him. And it hadn't been just a kiss. There had been a fierceness to it that had riveted him.

"The baby changes things."

Walter frowned. "I don't see why you would even consider marriage. Zara's not exactly your usual type."

Damon's brows jerked together. "My usual type?"

Walter looked uncomfortable. "Classy, thin, *blonde*—"

"Instead of brunette, curvy, in charge." Despite the raft of problems involved with even attempting to have a relationship with Zara, Damon found himself grinning. "Favorite word, *no*."

There was a heavy silence. "So there's nothing I can say?"

"Relax, I'm not proposing a normal marriage." *With its inherent emotional instability.* "I'm talking about a marriage of convenience."

Walter's expression turned dour. "Seems to me I've heard those words before."

Right before Damon had married Lily. And there was his dilemma.

If a marriage of convenience hadn't worked with someone as sweet and straightforward as Lily, he was going to have his work cut out convincing a complicated career woman like Zara that it was the ideal solution.

On the plus side, he thought grimly, there would be no issues about whether or not to have children, because there was already a baby. Then there was the sex.

The thought of having Zara back in his bed made every muscle in his body lock up. He was abruptly aware of just how sexy and gorgeous Zara was, and that he had left her alone for over a year. In that time, he had to assume the only reason she hadn't gotten involved with another man had been because she was pregnant, then dealing with a new baby.

Damon stared out his window, barely noticing the bustling marina below or the grey, scudding clouds. He felt like a sleeper waking up. Just over a year ago, he had convinced himself he needed to walk away from Zara, but in doing so he had left her alone and available. Now he was acutely aware that if he didn't lay claim to Zara ASAP, it was only a matter of time before some other man did.

And that was happening over his dead body.

Zara opened the door of her tiny rented house in Mount Eden, which had become her haven in the last few months, and carried Rosie, who was sleeping peacefully after the car ride, through to her room. Frowning a little at the damp chill of the house, Zara laid Rosie down in her cot and tucked a warm quilt around her before turning on the wall heater and tiptoeing out.

She walked back out to the garage, shivering in the chill of the evening as she retrieved her handbag from the car. Hooking the strap over one shoulder, she hefted the bulging baby bag, which was now mostly filled with dirty things that needed laundering and bottles that needed to be washed out. Locking the car, she walked back into the house, awkwardly flicking on lights as she went.

The comforting scent of the chicken casserole she had put into the slow cooker that morning made her mouth water and her stomach rumble. After Damon's disruptive visit, she'd been too unsettled to eat more than a few bites of the sandwich she had packed. Until that moment, she hadn't realized just how hungry she was.

With a sigh of relief, she dropped the bags onto a couch. As she straightened, she caught a disorienting flash of her reflection in the mirror over an antique

drinks cabinet that had once belonged to her aunt. Apart
from her hair wisping around her face and the color
in her cheeks, she didn't look a lot different from that
morning. The problem was she *felt* different, off balance and distinctly unsettled, as if a low-grade electric
current was shimmering through her veins, making her
heart beat faster and putting her subtly on edge.

And she knew exactly why that was. In the space
of a few hours, everything had changed. Emily had
run off with Ben; Damon had discovered Rosie; Zara
was back working for Damon; that darned reporter had
found her…and Zara had kissed Damon.

A sharp pang of awareness zapped through her at
the memory of the heated, out-of-control kiss. She had
tried to convince herself that it had been an experi-
ment, that in kissing Damon she could somehow exor-
cise the craziness of their past attraction and put him
firmly in his place: in the past. But the truth was, aside
from acknowledging her own unwilling attraction to
Damon, she had been blindsided by the fierceness of
her own need and utterly seduced by the fact that *he*
still wanted her.

Frowning at her instant and unwanted reaction just
to the memory, Zara turned on the heater in the sitting
room, then walked through to the kitchen. She lifted
the lid on the slow cooker. The rich fragrance of the
chicken filled her tiny kitchen. She switched the cooker
off so that by the time she was ready to eat, the food
would have cooled a little. She put water in the kettle,
and when it boiled and the tea was made, she wrapped
her fingers around the mug and sipped, enjoying the
comfort and the warmth and the automatic cue to wind
down and relax.

Her cell chimed. She carried the tea out to the sitting room, set it down on the coffee table and fished her phone out of her bag. She picked up the call, then stiffened as she registered an unfamiliar number.

The low timbre of Damon's voice made her clench her stomach.

"How did you get this number?"

"I needed to access some of Emily's email correspondence. I found your number listed in her contacts."

Zara's stomach sank. She should have seen this coming. Since Emily had actually resigned, of course Damon would have to retrieve correspondence and files from her computer, along with contact information.

"I'm sending a car for you and Rosie in the morning—"

"I don't need you to send a car. I have a car."

"That's hardly practical since you'll have to find parking and carry Rosie and all of her baby gear through the streets."

Zara stiffened. The fact that Damon now had a legitimate stake in Rosie's life was suddenly real and she couldn't help feeling a certain resistance to the idea. "It's not a problem—I can put Rosie in a front pack. She's light, and the bag isn't much heavier than—"

"This is purely a practical solution, designed to make things easier for you."

She tensed at the low, curt timbre of his voice. When she had first gone to work for Damon, before she had known exactly who he was, he had made a lot of things easier and much more enjoyable for her. Gorgeous working lunches, a car and driver for office errands or when she'd had to work late. There had even been a clothing allowance, which, of course, she had not spent on clothes but had put aside for a deposit on a house. And the problem was, that generosity hadn't been just for her. He had been generous to everyone, no matter their position in the firm. Working for Damon, and falling for him, had been heaven—until she had discovered he was Tyler McCall's nephew.

Zara forced herself to loosen her grip on the phone. She could not allow herself to dwell on the past or become emotional about things she could not change. It had been a stressful day; tomorrow would be even worse.

All she knew was that she had to lay down some ground rules, fast. She could not afford to be seduced by Damon's openhanded generosity. Especially since, once he knew who she was, he would regret ever employing her. He would regret sleeping with her.

"Thanks, but no thanks. I don't need you, or anyone, to make things easier for me."

There was a small silence. "I thought you wanted to keep Rosie under wraps. If you park somewhere in town and walk to the building, that won't be possible."

Her stomach sank. "I hadn't thought about that." She stared bleakly into space and tried to think. She hated to admit it, but Damon was right. Entering Damon's office building lugging a baby bag and carrying Rosie was too big a risk. "Okay."

There was a brief silence. "The car will be outside your house at eight thirty."

"I suppose you also know where I live?"

"Don't make it sound creepy. Emily didn't have that information, but there was mail on the desk in the interview room where Rosie was sleeping. Since the street address was different to your agency address, it didn't take a genius to figure out that was where you lived."

Her fingers tightened on the phone. In the panic of Damon discovering Rosie, she had completely forgotten that she had left some personal mail on the desk. At the time it had seemed an innocuous thing to do, because she hadn't imagined anyone but herself entering that particular interview room. And, somehow, over the past year she had forgotten what Damon had done for a living, that beneath the designer suit and white linen shirt were the kinds of scars that did not come from a tame city existence. That, as effective as he was in the boardroom, he had another far more formidable skill set.

A feminine voice, somewhere in the background, shattered the last illusory remnants of intimacy. Damon coolly requested that Zara give him a minute.

Zara knew she shouldn't continue to listen, that she should allow Damon a measure of privacy, but she couldn't help straining to pick up snatches of the muffled conversation and the name *Caroline*.

Zara jerked the phone from her ear. That would be Damon's beautiful, wealthy, current girlfriend.

The kind of woman who moved in Damon's circles and who the tabloids and magazines and social media forums uniformly pronounced had the perfect profile to be the next Mrs. Smith.

Zara's cheeks burned with a sudden bone-deep embarrassment as she remembered the way she had kissed Damon that morning. She had completely forgotten that he was dating Caroline.

Out of nowhere, gloom settled over her, which was annoying. She should be happy that Damon had moved on so quickly. It put the fling they had shared in perspective.

Suddenly done with the conversation and just a little panicked by her own response to Damon, she terminated the call. Her behavior was abrupt and rude, cutting Damon off midspeech, but she didn't care. Setting the phone down on the coffee table, Zara paced to the window and stared out at the cold, rain-spattered night. She felt horribly off balance, one minute vibrating with anger at Damon, the next with anger at herself for responding to him. The loss of control was worrying. She couldn't help thinking that the last time she'd lost control of her emotions, she had gotten pregnant.

Her stomach churned hollowly, reminding her that she still hadn't eaten, which was probably why she felt so emotional and vulnerable. She was suffering from a blood sugar low.

Walking to the kitchen, she ladled some of the casserole into a bowl, grabbed a fork, returned to the sitting room and curled up on the sofa. After saying grace, she turned on her small TV and ate the chicken. Despite her hunger, she barely tasted it. She even had trouble concentrating on her favorite show, which was all about couples buying their dream homes. It had an irresistible appeal for Zara, because ever since she and Petra had lost their pretty villa on Medinos, she'd longed for a home, something that wasn't possible with Petra's jet-setting lifestyle.

For most of the year, she had been away at boarding school. During vacations, Petra would fly Zara to some exotic location, often someone else's house, or a holiday villa Petra had rented for the summer.

Very occasionally, Zara had stayed with her aunt Phoebe, which she had actually adored because Phoebe's house had become the closest thing she'd had to a home. She had loved the "sameness" of Phoebe's old Victorian villa, even if it had involved heavy furniture and walls of dusty books. She had loved having the same room every time, and the same narrow single bed with the squeaky spring. Even the scents of the garden and the fragrant meadow beyond had somehow spelled home.

The show came to an end. Still tense and unsettled, Zara switched the TV off and sat for long minutes just enjoying the sound of rain pattering on the roof and the cozy ticking of the heater. Sounds that should have relaxed her, but which barely registered. Because beneath the anger and the nervy tension was a thread of awareness, a feminine response to Damon, that shouldn't have been there.

Thoroughly annoyed with herself, she carried her bowl and fork back to the kitchen and rinsed them. If she was going to get through these next few weeks, she needed to get her head straight. It was a chance to sort out the future in a way that was acceptable to them both. A chance to earn money that would help her achieve the dream of her own home. A chance to afford the trip to Medinos to retrieve her mother's safe-deposit box.

Zara stopped, a damp tea towel in her hand, as the possibility of a future with some measure of financial security opened up. She did not want to be all about money, but with Rosie in the picture, she had to be.

The safe-deposit box could change everything for her and Rosie.

Zara had discovered that there was a safe-deposit box when her cousin Lena had given her a packet of letters that had been stored in Aunt Phoebe's house. Phoebe had died several months ago, but it hadn't been until recently that Lena, who lived in Australia, had been able to clean out the house and put it up for sale. When she'd cleaned out her mother's desk, she'd found the letters Zara's mother had sent to Phoebe over the years.

One evening, a couple of weeks ago, Zara had finally read through them. The hairs at the back of her neck had stood on end when she had read the final letter her mother had written, which mentioned that she had decided to get a safe-deposit box after a string of burglaries near the apartment she had rented. When Phoebe received the letter, she had been hospitalized, so, understandably, she had never mentioned the possibility to Zara.

After learning of the box, Zara had searched through her mother's effects, which she had stored in her spare room. She had finally found a small tagged key with the address of her mother's bank on Medinos.

Her knees wobbly, Zara had sat on the edge of her bed, staring at the key, a tingle electrifying her spine. Petra had always said she would look after Zara, that she had an investment plan. Zara had taken that to mean that her mother had invested with some financial institution or had deposits at her bank, but nothing of the sort had ever come to light.

Petra had, at times, made a great deal of money and she had also possessed some expensive pieces of jewelry that had vanished. Petra could have sold the jewelry to supplement her income as her career tailed off. However, a safe-deposit box suggested otherwise.

With any luck, there might be items of sufficient value to put a deposit down on a house. It was also possible that Zara's Atrides grandmother's jewelry, which had been missing from Petra's personal things, might also be in the box.

Zara did not know if the Atrides jewelry was valuable or not. The important thing was that pieces had been handed down the family line. They were her last tangible link to her father's family, aside from the name itself and a defunct title, both of which she did not use.

The safe-deposit box could be an Aladdin's cave of jewelry that would restore her grandmother's pieces to her, with the addition of enough soulless diamonds to fund a house. Then again, it could contain a disappointing array of trinkets that would not cover the cost of the airfare.

When she completed this temping job with Damon, she would finally be in a position to find out.

She finished drying the dishes, then divided up the remaining casserole, which was enough to make several meals, into containers. Once they were labeled and dated, she stacked them in her small freezer, then moved on to sorting through Rosie's bag, disposing of rubbish and putting soiled things into the laundry. Zara finished by washing Rosie's bottles and repacking the bag with formula, fresh diapers and the one hundred other things a baby seemed to need.

Feeling much calmer and more in control, Zara quickly showered and changed into leggings and a soft T-shirt. Shivering at the chill in her bedroom, she also pulled on a thick sweater.

Combing her hair out and leaving it to dry naturally, she padded back to the kitchen. She caught a glimpse of her reflection in the window over the bench. Not for the first time she was confronted by the fact that, with her dark hair and curvy figure, she was starkly different from the elegant blondes Damon seemed attracted to.

Caroline was a case in point. She was classically beautiful and stylish, a virtual carbon copy of Damon's ex-wife, Lily. The similarities reaffirmed that Zara was the exact opposite of the kind of woman he clearly preferred.

Which begged the question, why had he slept with her in the first place?

Feeling annoyed with herself for falling into the trap of comparing herself with other women who had nothing whatsoever to do with her life—unless one of them became Rosie's stepmother, and she didn't want to think about that—Zara found her laptop. Sitting down on the couch, she flipped it open. Usually she checked in with a few friends on social media or read a downloaded book until she felt sleepy, but on impulse, she typed Caroline's name into a popular search engine.

A huge selection of hits appeared. At the top of the list was a video feed of a charity dinner that had been posted less than thirty minutes before.

Stomach tight, knowing she shouldn't do it but unable to resist, she hit the play button. Her screen filled with an image of Caroline in a sexy pale peach gown with a plunging neckline and a slit that revealed one slender, perfectly tanned leg. According to the commentary, normally, Caroline preferred her blonde hair up, but tonight she had opted for a more natural look, and had styled her hair smooth and straight so that it flowed silkily around her shoulders. The reason? Her soon-to-be fiancé, Damon Smith.

Zara stabbed the pause button, but she was too late. The screen froze on a shot of Caroline, one arm coiled around a dark sleeve as Damon, looking broodingly masculine in a tux, half turned to end up center shot.

Her chest tight and burning with an emotion she did not want to label, Zara wondered if she was actually going to be sick.

Suddenly, the dilemma of accepting a lift to work, even with the risk of a nosy reporter, was decided. She would rather die than get into one of Damon's fabulous, glossy company cars. If Damon's driver was parked outside her house at eight thirty, then he would have a wasted trip, because she would be gone by eight.

She dragged in one breath, then another. Dimly, she registered a piece of knowledge that she had avoided for some time through the simple tactic of refusing to think about it, period.

She was jealous of Caroline. And there was nothing either gentle or half-hearted about the emotion, which pulsed through Zara in fiery waves. She had been jealous for months, ever since she had read on a social media site that Damon had started dating the blonde.

Jumping to her feet, Zara began to pace. Just seconds ago, she had felt tired, maybe even a little depressed. Now restless energy hummed through her.

Damon was going to marry Caroline.

How could he? When he had just found out he had fathered a child? *Their* child.

Clearly, Rosie did not mean as much to him as he had implied today. Although, unpalatably, it wasn't Damon's relationship with his daughter that was upsetting her so badly. It was his utter lack of a relationship with *her*.

The reason she was jealous of Caroline was blazingly simple. It had been staring her in the face for weeks, but she had been too intent on burying her head, and her emotions, in the sand.

She still wanted Damon.

Six

Zara ended up at one end of her tiny sitting room, staring at the rain streaming down her window. Feeling like an automaton, she jerked the curtains together, closing out the night.

Blankly, she forced herself to face the fact that Damon and Caroline were soon to be engaged. And why not? They had been dating for months. It should not have come as a shock.

But it had, she thought grimly, especially after the kiss they'd shared.

Numbly, she moved to the small set of French doors that opened out onto a drenched patio and yanked a second set of curtains closed. The fact was, the kiss had stirred up feelings she had thought she had suppressed, making her feel intimately, possessively connected with Damon, as if he was still her lover. And now Caroline had taken him.

The reality was that Damon had never been hers.

Neither of them had ever committed to anything more than a brief, secretive fling, and that fling had been more than a year ago.

But they had a baby together. That meant something.

Surely Damon could have taken some time to reassess. She took a deep breath and let it out slowly as she tried to rationalize the emotions that kept hitting her out of left field. Maybe she felt so shocked because, for the past year, even though she had left Damon, in a sense he had still been hers because, until Caroline, he had only dated sporadically.

Jemima had only lasted three weeks. Zara knew, because she had checked.

As she sat down, her knee brushed the mouse pad of her laptop, jolting it. The screen saver dissolved and she found herself once more looking at the happy couple.

If Damon was getting married, that meant Caroline would become Rosie's stepmother. Somehow that thought made her feel even more miserable.

If she was brutally honest, it was the knowledge that while Damon had been happy to sleep with her on the quiet, he clearly wanted marriage with the kind of woman who moved in his own social circle. Just seeing Caroline and Damon together ignited the same kind of deep, tender hurt Zara had experienced when she had left him and realized that, as formidably equipped as he was to find her, he had not cared enough to do so.

An unpleasant thought struck her. If Damon was planning on remarrying, it made all the sense in the world to clean out any skeletons in the cupboard. She and Rosie were a substantial skeleton.

Zara found herself back on her feet and pacing. Just seconds ago, she had felt chilled and more than a little

sorry for herself. Now heat flamed through her, flushing her cheeks and making her heart pound.

It was no wonder Damon had left his sealed penthouse office and prowled the streets to find her. No
wonder he was suddenly so keen to keep her close, even
down to offering her a job and dangling a huge fee!
Locked in his high-security office with all his ex-army
cronies there to help him keep an eye on her—that was
the definition of keeping her and Rosie, his two shady
secrets, under wraps.

Zara tried to calm down. She had been feeling guilty
about keeping Rosie a secret. She had even been feeling guilty about *who* she was, Petra's daughter, as if she
had to apologize for her very existence.

But she wasn't the only one with secrets. She did not
imagine that Caroline would be very happy to find out
Damon had recently become a father.

Burning with indignation at Damon's double-deal-
ing sneakiness and suddenly sick to death of living in
the shadows and trying to be invisible—of feeling that
she had committed some terrible crime just because she
had slept with Damon a few times—she snatched up her
phone. Unlocking it, she hit Redial on Damon's number. The second Damon picked up, Zara froze, caught
in the kind of panicked state that usually had no part
in her carefully organized life.

"Zara?" Damon's deep, curt voice sent adrenaline
zinging through her veins.

Her throat seized up. A fraught second later, she disconnected the call.

Horrified that she'd lost control to the point that she
had actually called Damon to find out whether he really was marrying Caroline—as if she had a right to
ask that question—Zara placed the cell on the coffee

table. She needed to pull herself together, to get back to the crisp, businesslike state of mind that had been her go-to with all things Damon over the past few weeks.

The phone chimed, almost stopping her heart. Damon's number glowed on the screen.

She stared at the cell as if it was a bomb about to explode, then kicked herself for not answering when a message popped up, informing her she had a new voice mail. With a sense of inevitability, she picked up the phone. Damon's message was edged with impatience. He wanted to know if Rosie was okay. He finished with the command that she call him.

When hell freezes over.

She should never have called him in the first place. With a jerky movement she did what she should have done just minutes ago—she turned the phone off altogether.

Still feeling crazily on edge, she looked in on Rosie, who had finally fallen into a deep sleep. Softly closing the door, Zara padded to the laundry and put on a load of clothes to wash, then did her last job of the night, which was preparing a bottle for Rosie's night feeding. As she tightened the screw lid on the bottle, the chime of her doorbell made her hand jerk.

Her first thought was that it was Damon, but she dismissed that possibility, because he was at the charity ball with the love of his life, Caroline. She glanced at the oven clock, disoriented to see that it was only nine thirty. It felt a whole lot later, probably because it had gotten dark so early.

Frowning, she put the bottle in the fridge and walked through the hall. Her front security light was on, illuminating the porch. Through the frosted glass side panels of the door she could make out a tall masculine figure, wearing a dark suit.

Adrenaline pumped. It *was* Damon.

Keeping the chain on, she opened the door a few inches.

Damon's gaze pinned hers. "You didn't call me back. What's wrong?"

The cool directness of his gaze paired with the five o'clock shadow decorating his jaw gave Damon a remote edge that made her spine tighten. "Nothing's wrong." She tried for a neutral smile. "It was a mistake."

His cool gaze seemed to laser right through her. "Is it Rosie? I thought she might be sick."

"Rosie's fine. She's asleep." Despite knowing she shouldn't, but too furious not to, Zara took the chain off the hook and opened the door wide enough that she could look past Damon to where his car was parked. She wanted to know if Caroline was with him. Frustratingly, because the windows of his car were tinted, she couldn't see a thing. He could have half a dozen women in the car for all she knew.

A little impatiently, Damon's gaze recaptured hers. "Now that I'm here, we should talk. I think we need to get clear on a couple of things."

Such as his impending marriage to a woman who was perfect for him, and the fact that Zara and Rosie had the potential to ruin those plans.

Zara gave the sleek black car at her gate a last probing glare. "It's late. Can't we do this some other time?"

Damon gave her a look of disbelief. "It's only just past nine thirty."

Zara stared at Damon's jaw. Now that she was aware of the scary chinks in her armor when it came to him, she was determined to avoid eye contact where possible. The last thing she needed was for him to know how much he affected her. "I usually go to bed early, because I have to get up for Rosie in the night."

He leaned one shoulder against her porch wall and crossed his arms over her chest. "Okay, let's talk here."

"Can't we discuss whatever it is you want to talk about at work?"

"We could, but I thought you were concerned about keeping our relationship and Rosie under wraps."

Her gaze snapped to his, which was a problem because then she had trouble ripping it away. "We don't have a relationship."

His expression was infuriatingly calm. "But we do have a daughter."

And suddenly the gloves were off. "And I guess, at this point, keeping *our relationship* and Rosie under wraps suits you just fine, doesn't it?"

His brows jerked together. "Would you care to explain that?"

Bright light, intense enough to make her wince, washed across Zara's front lawn and lit up her porch. Her next-door neighbor's security lights had just come on. That meant that Edna Cross, who lived alone and seemed to be unusually inquisitive about every move Zara made, had no doubt logged that she had a visitor. Edna was the secretary of the local neighborhood watch group, and so was also likely now to be out with her flashlight and possibly even a digital camera. Any conversation on Zara's porch could no longer be considered private.

Damon stared in the direction of the high-powered light. His gaze narrowed. "There's someone standing on the other side of your hedge."

"My neighbor Edna Cross. She's head of the local neighborhood watch."

"That would explain the military-grade spotlights."

Ignoring the dryness of his voice and feeling embattled, Zara opened the door a little wider. She didn't
want Damon in her house, but he clearly wasn't going
to leave anytime soon and what she had to say needed
to be said in private. "You had better come in."

With a last glance in the direction of Edna's silhouette,
Damon stepped into Zara's hall, dwarfing it and making the space feel distinctly claustrophobic. Zara closed
the door and, out of sheer habit, locked it, although the
second she did so, it occurred to her that the one person
she didn't want in her house was already inside.

As she turned, she realized Damon was waiting for
her. She noticed that his tie was dragged loose, the top
button of his white shirt was undone and his hair was
disheveled as if he'd run his fingers through it repeat-
edly. All of it made him look even more sexily gorgeous.
A pang of heat shot through her, making her clench her
stomach. She could not believe she was turned-on, even
in a marginal way when she was still so angry. Grimly,
she reminded herself that it was far more likely that it
was Caroline who had run her fingers through his hair.

Suddenly self-conscious about her leggings, the old
sweater that dragged past her thighs and the fact that
beneath all the soft layers she wasn't wearing a bra,
Zara led the way to her sitting room.

Damon padded straight to the window that looked
over Edna's property, pulled back the curtain and looked
out. He lifted a hand. Seconds later, the glaring security
lights flicked off. Amazing. Usually, if Edna felt im-
pelled to investigate at night, the place was lit up like
a landing strip for a good hour. In his blunt, masculine
way, Damon had dealt with Edna by summarily checking her out and dismissing her.

He closed the curtains. "She's persistent."

Amusement invested his tone with an intimacy that spun Zara back to evenings spent together in his apartment watching movies and eating gourmet takeout. As he turned from the window, the easy humor was replaced by a flicker of masculine awareness that informed her that if she thought he hadn't noticed she wasn't wearing a bra, she was wrong.

Folding her arms across her chest, Zara indicated that Damon should have a seat. Unfortunately, he chose the seat she had been sitting in and her laptop was still sitting on the coffee table.

Panic gripped her. She couldn't remember whether she'd closed the video clip about Damon and Caroline, or not. In her rush to grab the laptop, all while avoiding getting too close to Damon, she brushed the mouse pad again and the screen saver dissolved.

Damon's gaze settled on the screen a split second before she snapped the laptop closed.

His expression answered the question. No, she had not closed down the video.

Cheeks burning, she found her briefcase, which was on a sideboard, and stowed the offending laptop away. When she turned, Damon was no longer seated, but prowling her small sitting room. He came to a stop in front of a small oil of a Medinian ancestor, one of the few family pieces left from her Atrides past. As he studied the gloomy picture, she felt a crazy sense of relief that, in keeping with her new identity and her new life, she had made it a rule not to have any family photos on show. Those were all kept in albums in a drawer in her room.

Plastering a bright smile on her face, she decided to grab the bull by the horns.

"I hear congratulations are in order."

Damon seemed to go very still. "What for, exactly?"

"Your engagement to Caroline Grant." Despite every effort at control, she couldn't quite keep the husky note from her voice. "No mystery now as to why you were so keen that I should come and work for you *and* bring Rosie along."

There was an odd moment of silence. "I'm guessing that would be because you think I don't want Caro to find out that you've given birth to my child."

Caro. A red mist seemed to form in front of her eyes. Zara could feel her precarious hold on her temper slipping. "I don't think—I know. I can see why we never had a chance, quite apart from the fact that Caroline's *blonde*."

Two steps and Damon had covered the distance between them. "As I recall, you were the one who laid down the ground rules for the time we spent together."

Zara flushed guiltily at the reminder that she'd had very good reasons for limiting their involvement. "Ground rules that suited you."

His brows jerked together. "Why, exactly, did they suit me?"

Zara met his gaze squarely. "Because I'm not your type."

"Which is…?"

"Blonde. Your wife was blonde. Caroline is blonde."

Damon pinched his nose, which made her even more furious, so she listed another three blonde socialites from the past. Even the names made her feel slightly crazy: Jenna, Hayley, *Tiffany.* They were all pretty, flirty names, nothing like Zara, which sounded somehow heftier. "It's all over the media that you like blondes. And not just blondes. You like a certain type of blonde. Basically, slim, elegant and rich. I'm not any of those—"

"Therefore, I couldn't possibly want you."

She drew a rapid breath and tried to calm down, but she couldn't seem to stop hemorrhaging the disappointment and anger she'd bottled up for over a year. At some point she must have taken a half step closer to Damon, close enough to feel the heat radiating off his body, smell the faint, enticing scents of soap and cologne.

She jabbed a finger at his chest. "Couldn't have said it better myself. Maybe if I had dyed my hair blonde or bought a wig, we would have had a chance at a real relationship." She delivered the kicker. "I don't even know why you slept with me in the first place."

His fingers closed around her upper arms. "That would be because I wanted you," he growled.

Shock reverberated through her at the statement. Both palms were flattened on his chest. She could feel the steady pound of his heart, feel the heat blasting off him. She could have pulled back, stepped free, because his hold was loose but, crazily, it was the last thing she wanted to do.

Something had happened to her in the last hour or so; it was as if all the emotions she had suppressed had burst free and, like a Pandora's box, she couldn't put them back in. And if that wasn't enough, being held close to Damon, having his complete, undivided attention even though they were arguing, filled her with an intoxicating elation.

She glared at him. "Wanted, as in past tense."

In answer, he fitted her close enough against him that she could feel his clear arousal. "Does this feel like past tense?"

She drew an impeded breath and tried to think, which was difficult when tingling heat was pouring through her and all she wanted to do was drown in the

intense sensations. Damon bent his head and bit down
gently on the sensitive lobe of one ear. A white-hot pang
of heat lanced through her.

His jaw brushed her cheek, sending a sensual shiver
through her. With a breathless effort, she resisted the
urge to sag against him, even though her bones had
turned to water. "You can't kiss me. You're engaged."

Irritation registered in Damon's gaze. "There's no
engagement. As a matter of fact, Caroline and I are
finished."

"Because of Rosie?"

"Rosie is part of it."

Damon lifted his head before she could ask if the rest
of the reason was that he thought he now had some kind
of responsibility toward them both. Afraid that she was
pushing him away with her questioning, Zara's fingers
gripped the lapels of his jacket, keeping him close. Minutes ago, she had been furious with Damon and determined to keep him at a distance but, in the space of a
few seconds, somehow everything had changed. She
took a deep breath, then finally asked the question that
had tormented her ever since she had found Damon on
her porch. "So... Caroline's not in your car?"

Damon gave her a look of disbelief. "Why would
she be in my car?"

Relief and pleasure cascaded through Zara. He really
wasn't going to marry Caroline, after all. The media had
made up the story, and didn't Zara know how that went?

In some distant corner of her mind she knew she
should be reacting differently; she shouldn't feel so happy
and so relieved that Caroline was out of the picture.

Damon's expression was curiously intent. "What
would you have done if Caroline had been in the car?"

Emotion surged through Zara. A list of scenarios

flashed through her mind, all of which involved getting Caroline *out* of the car.

Damon grinned. "Thought so." He dropped his hands to her hips and pulled her closer still but, frustratingly, he didn't kiss her. Zara finally realized that he was waiting for her to make the next move.

Her mouth dry, her heart pounding—the memory of the kiss they'd shared that morning emboldening her—she lifted up on her toes, looped her arms around his neck and kissed him A split second later his arms came around her, locking her tight against him, as if he had missed her, as if he wanted her just as badly as she wanted him, as if he truly needed her close.

Ridiculous tears burned beneath her lids as she gave in to the simple pleasure of soaking up the heat and comfort of being back in Damon's arms. A comfort that she had tried to forget but which, against the odds, she still desperately needed.

He released his hold for the moment it took to shrug out of his jacket and toss it over the back of a chair. Another slow, drugging kiss, then she found herself slowly, irresistibly propelled backward into the narrow hall, which led to the bedrooms.

Damon lifted his head. In the deep shadows of the hall the narrow band of light that flowed out from the sitting room glanced across mouthwatering cheekbones and the rock-solid line of his jaw, turning his gray gaze molten. "This room?"

Dimly, Zara logged another opportunity to call a halt, to throw cold water on a passionate interlude she should already be regretting. Somehow, they had gone from zero to out-of-control passion in the space of minutes. The problem was, she had been so upset at the thought that Damon was engaged, then so relieved when he wasn't, that her rules for dealing with him had dissolved. She had become someone she barely recognized—fiercely possessive and determined to reclaim him, even if only for one night.

By pure luck Damon had chosen her room. She caught a glimpse of her bed with its rich red coverlet and pretty cushions, the deep blue drapes and the jewel-bright Medinian rug at the foot of her bed. The lush riot of color was very different from the restrained image she was so careful to project through the rest of the house, and in the way she dressed. She was suddenly unbearably conscious of her vulnerability in inviting Damon into a room that was an intimate and unashamed expression of herself.

But for the first time in years she didn't feel like apologizing for loving the flamboyant colors and rich fabrics of her childhood, for being Angel Atrides. With him, right now, she felt bold and passionate, and she knew exactly what she wanted.

"Yes."

Lifting up on her toes, she kissed Damon on the mouth, tangled her fingers with his and drew him into the room. Three steps and she felt the soft quilt of her bed brush the backs of her legs. Another kiss and she had managed to undo most of the buttons on Damon's shirt.

With an impatient movement, Damon completed the job and shrugged out of the shirt, revealing tanned and sleekly powerful shoulders, a broad chest and washboard abs.

She caught the quick gleam of his teeth. "Time this went."

His hands settled on her waist then swept upward, peeling her sweater and T-shirt up and over her head.

The chill of the air was instantly replaced by the hot shock of skin-on-skin as he pulled her close.

Feeling a little vulnerable, because it had been more than a year since they had made love, Zara buried her face in the curve of Damon's throat and allowed herself to be swamped by his masculine heat and scent. It occurred to her that being held in Damon's arms made her feel oddly like she had come home. She stiffened at the thought.

"What's wrong?"

With relief, she decided that the familiar timbre of Damon's voice provided the explanation for what she was really feeling. Not homecoming, but familiarity.

"Nothing. Absolutely nothing."

This time the hungry pressure of the kiss made her head swim.

Long seconds later, Damon cupped her breasts then bent and took one nipple into his mouth. Her breath came in as sensation coiled and burned for long aching moments then, with shocking abruptness, splintered.

Damon said something short and flat. A split second later she found herself lifted and deposited onto the bed. The cool softness of the quilt beneath her overheated skin was subtly shocking, but not as much as the disorienting fact that Damon had barely touched her and she had climaxed.

When he began peeling her leggings and panties down her legs, she automatically lifted her hips then felt hopelessly shy because her body wasn't as toned and sleek as it had been before she'd had Rosie. The chill of the air made her shiver, which was a convenient excuse to wriggle under the coverlet, dragging it high as Damon stripped off his pants.

When he straightened, she caught her breath at how

beautiful he was with the murky half light turning his skin to bronze and making the trace of scars that criss-crossed his chest seem beautiful in a completely masculine way.

Damon retrieved something from his pants pocket, a condom. She watched as he sheathed himself and the blunt awareness of what they were about to do hit home. Somehow, in the space of one day, they had gone from cool, businesslike distance to passionate lovemaking. The knowledge should have made her feel disoriented and angsty, instead, for the first time in a year, she felt oddly settled and, for want of a better word, happy.

She wasn't yet ready to examine exactly what it was she still felt for Damon. For now, all she wanted was to forget the heartache and loneliness of the past year and simply *feel*. For this one night it was enough that Damon was hers.

Damon joined her in the bed, flipping the coverlet aside as he did so. Zara surreptitiously attempted to drag the sheet over her breasts, but he stymied her plan by pulling her close so that she was half-sprawled against his chest.

Pleasure cascaded through her at the blazing heat of his body, the clean, faintly musky scent of his skin and the automatic, sensual way they fitted together, almost as if more than a year hadn't passed since they had last made love.

"Don't cover yourself," he said quietly. "You're beautiful."

She cupped his jaw, enjoying the faintly abrasive feel of his five o'clock shadow. "It's been a while."

He stopped in the process of trailing his fingers from the small of her back to the curve of her bottom. "No one else?"

She tried to muster up some indignation, but with the slow, enticing stroke of his hands it was hard to concentrate. "Why would there be anyone else? I was pregnant, then having a baby. There was barely time to breathe."

An entirely masculine brand of satisfaction registered in his gaze. "My baby."

He rolled, taking her beneath him. The fiery, seductive heat of Damon's weight pressing her down into the bed made it incredibly difficult to marshal her thoughts. And why would she want to think?

As much as she might deny it, this was what she had missed so much and still craved. The plain fact was that she had never gotten over the attraction that had hit her the very first time she had walked into his office. It was the reason she had slept with Damon in the first place, the reason she had let him back into her life. It was probably also the reason why there had been no other man in her life.

Zara went still inside as a thought she had resolutely suppressed over the last year once again surfaced.

Could she be in love with Damon?

She desperately dismissed the sudden tension that gripped her, because loving Damon was a worst-case scenario...*unless he fell in love with her.*

Suddenly, intensely curious about how he felt, she cupped his face. "Would it have mattered if there was someone else?"

"You were pregnant with my child."

The answer was flat and unequivocal, and sent a sharp thrill through her. Despite being a modern woman, she couldn't help but adore that Damon was possessive of her, even if it was only because she had borne his child. And his response was proof that he felt something genuine, even if only sexual desire.

Although, in her heart of hearts, she didn't want just the desire, she thought fiercely.

She was very much afraid that she *was* falling for Damon, despite all the reasons they should never be in the same room together, let alone in the same bed.

But perhaps making love could create a bond that would hold. And maybe, just maybe, that bond would be strong enough to survive the revelation of her past.

Dipping his head, Damon kissed her. Feeling suddenly acutely vulnerable, Zara gripped his shoulders, arching against the blunt pressure of penetration as he slowly, carefully entered her. When they were fully joined, Damon stopped, his darkened gaze locking with hers.

"Are you sure this is all right? It's not so long since the birth."

With the aching heat of him deep inside her, it was difficult to think. "It's been four months." And before that, nine months. In total it had been thirteen long months since they had last made love. She inhaled at the sensations that gripped her, some familiar, some even more intense than she remembered.

"I'll take it easy."

In answer, she pressed closer still. An agonizing second later, Damon began to move. The heated, stirring pleasure that, lately, had only been a part of her dreams, wound tight, pressing all the air from her lungs until it finally peaked, splintering into the night.

Seven

Damon stirred, awakened by the heavy drumming of rain on the roof and the first stirrings of arousal as Zara trailed her hand down his abdomen. The silky curtain of her hair brushed across his chest as she bent and kissed him slowly and deliberately on the mouth. Her hand slid lower, found him and gently squeezed.

He held on to his control, just. "The last time this happened, I seem to remember we got pregnant."

She waved the foil packet of a condom at him.

"Resourceful."

Long minutes later, Zara collapsed on his chest and he rolled, taking her with him so that they lay sprawled together. The rain had stopped and the wind had dropped, making the night seem almost unnaturally still and quiet.

After long minutes, she readjusted her position, so that her head was snuggled into the curve of his shoulder and neck. One hand trailed over his jaw.

"Do you know why we made love?" she murmured sleepily.

Damon stiffened at the question. "Why?"

Zara yawned. "Can't resist you. It's fate, kismet. Last thing either of us need."

There was a curious, vibrating silence following the slightly slurred pronouncement. But the tension, Damon realized after a few seconds, was his and his alone. Zara didn't require an answer because she had fallen asleep.

She couldn't resist him.

Unbidden, warmth and forbidden delight unfolded in Damon. That was a first, he thought ruefully. But then there had never been anything calculated or pragmatic about making love with Zara. It had always been spontaneous. This time they had actually made it to a bed.

He didn't know about either fate or kismet. He preferred to operate with cool, hard facts. If Zara couldn't resist him, then that dovetailed nicely with his plans for the future…and the undeniable fact that he was having a whole lot of trouble resisting her too.

The next time Damon awoke it was to a small, unfamiliar sound.

Rosie was awake.

He noted the time on the digital clock on the bedside table: three thirty. If he didn't miss his guess, because Rosie was so young, she needed feeding in the night. Carefully disentangling himself from Zara, he found his pants and quickly pulled them on. As he did so, he found himself automatically mulling over Zara's declaration that she couldn't resist him.

Fierce satisfaction filled him at that fact, even though desire itself was uncomfortably akin to the kind of dangerous, unstable emotions he was careful to avoid. If they were going to continue—and now that he had gotten Zara back in his bed, he fully intended they would—he needed to find a way to control the relationship.

Grimly, he noted that the hot, out-of-control sex could have been because he hadn't made love in a year, ever since Zara had left his bed. That fact, in itself, was disturbing.

He had dated a number of beautiful, interesting women. Caroline was a case in point. Any man with red blood cells in his veins would have wanted her, and yet he had not even been vaguely interested in taking her to bed.

Because he had not been able to stop thinking about Zara.

And there was his problem, the same kind of obsessive behavior that had dogged his father, his uncle Tyler and now Ben. The kind of behavior Damon had sworn off all of his adult life and which experience had taught him he could not afford.

Not bothering with a shirt, he stepped out into the hall. It wasn't difficult to find where Rosie slept, since there was only one other bedroom in the cottage.

When he opened the door, it squeaked. Cursing beneath his breath, he checked on Zara, who still seemed to be sleeping deeply, before going to Rosie. The baby waved her arms at him so he picked her up and propped her on one bare shoulder, figuring that was the easiest and most stable way to hold her if he was going to attempt to feed her.

Grabbing a small shawl that was folded over the end of her cot, he draped that across her back in case she got cold, and made his way to the small kitchen. He closed the door, which also squeaked, before switching on the

light. Absently, he noted that was two doors that needed
oil on their hinges.

He immediately saw that the baby bag sat on the
bench. Although he figured that Zara probably had a
bottle already prepared in the fridge since she must do
regular night feeds.

He opened the door and saw it straight off. Guessing it needed to be warmed, he ran the bottle under
hot water for a minute or two. When it was done, he
checked the temperature of the milk. He seemed to remember, after visiting friends who had a baby, that the
milk needed to be lukewarm, so he tested it by shaking
a little onto the back of his hand.

"Seems good to go."

Rosie, who had half twisted around on his shoulder
to check what he was doing, made a cooing sound, patted him on the jaw and smiled, flashing the clean edge
of one pearly tooth.

Damon was momentarily transfixed by the sight
of his daughter's first tooth, his chest swelling with a
raw hit of emotion. If he had planned on being distant
and disconnected from his daughter, that idea had just
crashed and burned.

Opening the kitchen door just enough to allow a
sliver of light to flow into the sitting room, he sat in an
armchair and attempted to resettle Rosie in the crook
of his arm, all while juggling the bottle. But if he had
thought Rosie would allow herself to be carefully repositioned while there was a full bottle of milk tanta-
lizingly within reach, he was wrong. She wriggled and
squirmed, her gaze zeroing in on the bottle. The instant it got close enough, strong small hands wrapped
around the neck and almost wrenched the formula from
his grasp.

She drained the milk in sixty seconds flat, spat out the nipple, then with imperiousness attempted to fling the empty bottle away. Damon found himself grinning as he fielded the bottle, placed it on the coffee table and rose to his feet with his daughter in his arms. When he had noticed Rosie's eyes the previous day, he had seen himself, but right now she was *definitely* her mother's daughter.

In that moment he understood how people became so centered on their children that they married when they'd sworn off marriage, and made career U-turns that were detrimental to success. The answer was simple: their priorities changed because they were besotted by the baby.

Rosie's face screwed up, her pale skin flushing. For a heart-stopping moment he thought she was going to cry. He seemed to remember that after Rosie had been fed the previous day, Zara had put her over her shoulder to burp her, so he figured he should do that next.

After circling the small room a couple of times and carefully rubbing her small back, Rosie made a hiccuping sound and spit up on his shoulder. Feeling ridiculously proud that Rosie had burped right on cue, he headed back to the kitchen, found a paper towel and cleaned around her mouth, before blotting the milk from his shoulder.

After disposing of the paper towel in the trash can he found beneath the counter, he carried his daughter back to the sitting room.

"So, what do we do now?"

Rosie patted his jaw again, as if she was fascinated by the roughness of his five o'clock shadow and, at that point, Damon noted a certain sogginess at her rear end.

"Problem solved. We change your diaper."

Rosie made a small crowing sound, as if that was a hilarious idea, so he returned to the kitchen and did a brief search through the baby bag, finding disposable diapers and baby wipes. Walking through to the sitting room, he carefully laid Rosie down on the carpet. Five minutes later, he had the dirty diaper off and the clean diaper fitted. Feeling a sense of achievement, he bagged up the dirty diaper and soiled wipes and placed them in the trash. After washing his hands, he collected a now-sleepy Rosie and carried her back to her room and tucked her into her crib.

After watching her for long minutes to make sure she really had fallen asleep, he walked back to the bedroom. It was four thirty; an hour had passed while he'd fed and changed Rosie. In that time, Zara hadn't moved and still seemed soundly asleep. With effort, he curbed the instinct to get back into bed with her. If he did that, he wouldn't be able to resist making love to her again, which would be counterproductive, given that his first priority had to be control.

Collecting his shirt and shoes, he walked back to the sitting room and finished dressing. He shrugged into his jacket and checked that he had his cell before he let himself out of the house. As he walked down the steps, the next-door neighbor's obnoxiously bright security lights came on.

Damon frowned. If Zara and Rosie were going to stay in the cottage, he would ensure that the motion sensors for those security lights were repositioned so they would no longer be triggered by movement on Zara's property. But, now that he knew Zara was the mother of his child, *now that Zara was back in his bed*, he did not intend for her and Rosie to remain in a suburban cottage with minimal security.

The solution he had arrived at the previous day settled in more firmly.

It was logical, practical and would cut through a whole lot of red tape. It also had the added advantage of nixing dangerously unstable emotions and dampening any media hype.

A marriage of convenience.

Zara's alarm pulled her out of sleep at six thirty.

She groped for the clock. The low buzz ceased and she stared at the numbers that glowed in the pitch dark of early dawn, amazed at the time. By some miracle, Rosie had slept through the night.

Bracing herself, she switched on the bedside lamp. Gold light flooded her room, making her blink and pushing home the reality that she was alone in the bed. Although she had known Damon was gone the second she had reached across the cold expanse of the bed to get to the alarm.

Heated memories cascaded through her, making her blush. Jackknifing, she sat up. Cold air raised gooseflesh on her skin. Shivering, she dragged the quilt up around her chin, because, of course, she was naked, having spent the night making love to Damon. Claiming him physically.

Another memory took center stage. In the moments before she had fallen asleep, she had blurted out something about not being able to resist Damon.

Another wave of embarrassed heat burned through her. She could vaguely remember the silence after she had made her pronouncement, the stiffening of his shoulder beneath her head—probably because he didn't find her irresistible—then nothing more because she had dropped into a deep, dreamless sleep.

Feeling mortified at the way she had exposed a very private weakness, she pushed the thick feather duvet aside and scrambled out of bed. The icy chill of the marble-smooth, polished wood floor struck through her bare feet as she toed on her slippers and quickly wrapped herself in the thick fluffy robe that was hooked on the back of her door.

She shouldn't feel embarrassed, she thought a little desperately. But it was hard to blot out the fact that Damon hadn't responded to her declaration.

Opening her bedroom door, she glanced down the hall and through the sitting room to the kitchen. She tensed when she realized she was looking for Damon on the off chance he was sitting on the couch doing business on his phone or in the kitchen making breakfast.

Of course, Damon wasn't here. His side of the bed had been stone cold; he had been gone for hours. Her mood plummeted even further. He had probably left at a run not long after she had gone to sleep.

She opened Rosie's door. Rosie was still fast asleep. Gently, so as not to wake her, she checked her diaper, which seemed inordinately dry. Frowning, Zara walked through to the kitchen and saw the night feed bottle, which had been rinsed and was sitting on the kitchen counter. A quick check of the trash can confirmed there was also a diaper wrapped in a plastic bag sitting on top.

Clearly, Damon had not left as quickly as she had thought. She closed the cupboard door. The last thing she would have expected was for Damon to feed and change Rosie, but that was exactly what had happened.

Moving on automatic, she put hot water on to boil for tea. She made herself a piece of toast, smeared it with butter and the fig-and-ginger jam she'd made with fruit from the fig tree in the backyard, then prepared a morning feeding for Rosie.

She took a half-hearted bite of the toast, barely tasting it. She guessed she should be happy that Damon was interested in forming a relationship with Rosie, since it was less than a day since he had found out he was a father. But she couldn't help thinking that Damon's interest in her, Zara, was depressingly linked with his focus on his daughter and that any idea that she and Damon could remain lovers was majorly flawed.

First, Damon had shown up at her house not for her, but because he had thought Rosie was ill. Second, yes, he had made love to Zara, but that had probably happened because she had literally thrown herself at him.

Another even more horrifying thought froze her in place. Damon was probably under the impression that since she'd had his baby, and now had managed to get him back into her bed, that she was angling for marriage.

She groaned inwardly and ate some more toast. It was no wonder he had left in the night without waking her. He had come for Rosie's sake and Zara had not only seduced him, but made the silly mistake of revealing how much she wanted him.

Given that Damon had never once said he wanted to be in a committed relationship with her, even when they were first sleeping together, the odds that he did now were bleak. Damon's true motivation in showing up at her house was his caring for Rosie.

Wiping crumbs from her fingers, she carried her plate to the sink and washed and dried it. As she was putting the plate away a brief flash of the kiss they'd shared in her office stopped her in her tracks. She did not know if Damon had known about Rosie at that point, but she had been clear on the fact that he had wanted her.

Closing the cupboard door, she straightened. It was also a fact that Damon had walked back into her life weeks *before* he had known about Rosie. And he hadn't just walked back in, he had pushed his way back into her life, insistently forging a business link and employing people she knew for a fact he did not need. That all pointed to the fact that Damon's desire for her was genuine and persistent.

Feeling suddenly cheered, she wrapped chilled fingers around her gently steaming mug of tea and sipped. There was hope. She just had to hold her nerve and look for the right opportunity to tell him who she was, in such a way that he wouldn't despise her.

Feeling buoyed, she checked on Rosie, who was still sleeping soundly. Zara quickly showered, dried off and wrapped herself in the robe while she searched out something to wear.

Dressing wasn't normally a problem, but today she felt the feminine need to dress for attractiveness as well as for business. Unfortunately, most of her suits were quite plain and, owing to the fact that she had lost a little weight, were becoming a little loose and shapeless.

Happy that her figure had improved, but annoyed at the wardrobe dilemma, she flicked through the closet. Her fingers lingered on an outfit she had worn before she had gotten pregnant.

She pulled out the blue dress and the fitted black jacket that went with it. It was a deceptively simple but gorgeous outfit she hadn't been able to fit into since her pregnancy.

The dress was also soft and warm and extremely comfortable, but would it fit? She held the blue dress against her and stared into the full-length mirror, which was hung on the inside of her closet door. The sapphire blue did great things for her skin, giving it a honey glow and making her eyes look brighter and her hair more lustrous. The dress also had a V neckline, which showed the merest shadow of cleavage, but wasn't too blatant.

After slipping into clean underwear, she pulled on the dress, which—happily—was made of a stretchy, bouclé material. Her figure was still more rounded than it had once been, and her waist wasn't as narrow, but the dress was unexpectedly forgiving. To her surprise the jacket also fitted, cinching in neatly at her waist.

She studied her reflection, her breath momentarily suspended. With her hair still knotted on top of her head from her shower, and dark tendrils clinging to her neck, she looked businesslike, but subtly, classily sexy.

With quick movements, she brushed out her hair and coiled it up into a loose knot, then applied smoky makeup to her eyes and a layer of pink gloss to her mouth.

She had just fitted blue-and-silver earrings to her lobes when Rosie woke up and began crowing happily to herself. Checking her watch and groaning because she was fast running out of time if she wanted to leave early, Zara hurried into Rosie's room.

Rosie stopped crying the instant she spotted her mother, held out her small arms and smiled her wide, gummy smile, which now contained one tiny, gleaming half tooth.

Warmth and a fierce, tender love suffused Zara as she lifted her daughter out of her crib and cuddled her close. Rosie's soft, sweet baby scent rose to Zara's nostrils and the anxious fears around being in a relationship with Damon, if that was even possible, drifted away.

In moments like these, *everything* was worth it—
the months of worry and uncertainty, the solitary birth
without anyone to support her except her midwife. The
effort and frustration of learning all the things a mother
needed to know without her own mother to show her.

Half an hour later, after feeding and changing Rosie
and dressing her in a cute pink playsuit, Zara finally
got Rosie back to sleep in her fleece-lined car seat.
She draped a warm fluffy blanket around her daughter and settled a cute pink beanie on her head so she
would stay cozily asleep. Then Zara carried the car seat
out to the hall.

After propping Rosie's portable crib beside the car
seat, Zara rinsed out the used bottle and put it into the
dishwasher. She checked her watch. Shock reverberated
through her when she saw that it was eight o'clock. If
she wanted to avoid Damon's driver and keep her independence, she needed to leave, *now*.

Moving quickly, she found a pair of black boots that
would go perfectly with the dress and slipped them on.
She zipped the baby bag closed and set it in the hallway, then found her handbag and cell. As she looped
the strap of her handbag over one shoulder, the sound
of a car made her stiffen. She peered through the narrow glass panes of her front door just in time to see a
gleaming black car glide to a halt outside her front gate.

Her heart thumped once, hard. She was too late;
Damon had second-guessed her and sent the car early.

Eight

Feeling distinctly outmaneuvered, Zara tried to check out the driver, but the windows of the car were too darkly tinted.

Another pump of adrenaline made her stomach churn as she noted the kind of car Damon had sent. She had hoped for a taxi, and had been resigned to a company car, but the glossy curves of a long, low sports car did not bode well. It looked like the car Damon had been driving last night. A split second later, Damon climbed out from behind the wheel.

Feeling suddenly vulnerable, she opened the door a split second before Damon could knock and tried not to notice how broodingly masculine he looked in a dark suit teamed with a black V-neck T-shirt. A pair of dark glasses added a remote edge that seemed to negate the intimate things they had done in bed just hours ago.

Movement off to the right caught her eye. Her heart sank when she saw Edna, who, if Zara wasn't mistaken, was in the process of noting Damon's license plate and the make and model of his car.

"I thought you were sending a driver."

"I'm the driver." Damon's glittering gaze swept over her, making her feel acutely conscious of how sexy the blue dress was and the fact that, from his height, he could probably see more than just the hint of cleavage she had noted in the mirror. "I thought we should spend some time together before we go into the office."

Desperate to control the sudden warmth in her cheeks, Zara switched her attention back to Edna, who was now taking down details about Damon himself. No doubt height, weight, hair color and any other distinguishing features.

Although she wouldn't find any of those unless she managed to get Damon naked.

"What do you mean, 'spend some time together'?"

"There's a little café along the waterfront. It's quiet. The coffee's good, and we could walk on the beach, if you want."

In public? A small shudder went through her at the thought that they could get snapped together by a reporter. If that happened, her quiet life of anonymity, and the chance she needed to tell Damon who she was before the media spoiled everything, would be gone. "I don't think that's a good idea."

"We need to talk about Rosie and I'd prefer a more private setting than the office."

Zara noticed a bright blue hatchback driving slowly down the street, as if the driver was searching for an address. The hatchback glided past. Maybe she was being paranoid, but after what had happened yesterday, she could not help the crawling suspicion that the driver was a reporter, in which case, the sooner they left the better.

"A walk on the beach is not a good idea right now," she said hurriedly. "Rosie's sleeping." And if that had been a reporter, they could be followed to the beach. "We should go straight to the office."

Damon lifted a brow. "The sooner you start working, the sooner you can finish up and leave?"

Zara picked up the baby bag and portable crib and handed them to Damon, before collecting Rosie, who was still sound asleep in the car seat. Zara set the car seat down on the step and locked the front door. By the time she'd returned the key to her bag, Damon was back and had picked up the car seat.

Zara hurried after Damon, stepped outside her front gate and stopped dead. Last night when she had seen Damon's car, it had been dark, but now, in the full light of day she realized Damon was driving the same car he'd had when they had been dating.

The very last time they had made love, before she had disappeared, had been in *that* car. Memories she had ruthlessly suppressed unfolded. Her acute emotionalism at being pregnant with Damon's child coupled with her need to be with him just one last time, to store up memories. The awful feeling of emptiness when she had thought she would never see him again.

The car flashed and beeped as Damon unlocked it. "What's wrong?"

Zara quickly smoothed out her expression. Note to self, she thought grimly, if she wanted to conceal her emotions, she needed to get a pair of dark glasses herself.

"Nothing," she said brightly.

She slipped into the front passenger seat while Damon strapped Rosie into the rear. As Damon slid behind the wheel of the Audi, Zara fastened her seat belt, then turned to check on the baby. She noticed a second safety seat, which Damon had installed in the back. A much nicer, more expensive seat than the basic model she had bought.

Suddenly, any notion that Rosie could be just a novelty for Damon evaporated. He must have gone shopping for the seat the previous afternoon. If he had gone to the trouble of buying a car seat, then that meant he was serious about fatherhood.

As Damon pulled away from the curb, Zara sank back into the luxurious seat. "I don't mind accepting a lift today, but in the future, I would prefer to take my own car to work."

Damon braked for a traffic light before accelerating through an intersection and joining the flow of cars heading for the central city. "If you want to drive your car to work, you can have Ben's parking space."

She glared at Damon. "You could have let me use that today!"

His gaze, still frustratingly masked by the dark glasses, connected with hers. "I didn't want to risk you not turning up for work."

"I agreed to work for you. I honor my agreements."

Damon stopped for another light, this one in the busy hub of downtown. "You walked out on me a year ago."

She dragged her gaze from the taut cut of Damon's cheekbones, the clean line of his jaw. Her heart was pounding again, but this time for an entirely different reason. It suddenly occurred to her that no employer manipulated and then personally drove an employee to work because they couldn't risk them not showing up. Certainly not a billionaire like Damon.

And he had refused to accept just any assistant;

Damon had wanted *her*. He wanted her in his bed *and* at his work.

She was abruptly certain that whatever Damon was feeling, it wasn't just sexual attraction.

Her mood soared. Suddenly, Damon wanting her *as a person*, maybe even falling for her, seemed… possible.

Minutes later, using a key card to gain entrance, dim shadow swamped the car as Damon took the ramp down into the underground garage of his building. Zara's stomach did a nervous flip at the sheer familiarity of the garage as Damon removed his sunglasses, killed the engine and exited the Audi.

Before he could walk around the front of the car and help her out, Zara hurriedly unfastened her seat belt, collected her handbag and swung the door of the sleek, low car wide.

As she exited the car and straightened, she found herself close enough to Damon that when she inhaled she caught the clean scent of his skin, the utterly familiar tang of his cologne. In the dimness of the garage the impact of his gaze made her breath catch in her throat. Yesterday she would have kept her manner neutral and breezed past him, but today was a new world.

Hooking the strap of her bag over her shoulder, she allowed Damon to close the door with a *thunk*. Before she could lose her nerve, she met his gaze. "Thanks for being so understanding about Rosie. The last thing I wanted was for you to feel trapped into fatherhood." And trapped into a relationship with her.

Balancing herself by resting one palm on his shoulder, she lifted up on her toes to kiss him on the cheek.

Damon cupped her neck, stopping her from stepping back. The heat of his palm burned into her skin as, slowly and deliberately, he bent his head and kissed her on the mouth.

Long seconds later, her legs feeling as limp as noodles, she stumbled back a half step. It occurred to her that while the garage was a secure one, it did still service a number of clients.

"Maybe we shouldn't kiss in public," she said a little breathlessly. As soon as she said the words she realized that Damon would pick up on the clear implication that he could continue to kiss her in private.

Surprise and a glint of masculine satisfaction registered in his gaze as he caught her close and kissed her again. The kind of kiss shared by couples who were not just lovers, but who were in a real relationship. Couples who liked one another. The very nature of it filled Zara with hope because she was certain that in the past few minutes they had turned some kind of corner.

As he released her, Zara noticed a blue-suited janitor and froze. As quiet as their conversation had been, in the cavernous garage it had echoed. From his frozen posture, the janitor had heard every word.

Zara's breath froze in her throat as he disappeared from sight behind a large concrete pillar. For a split second she tried to buy into the fantasy that maybe the janitor hadn't heard. And if he had, who would he tell, anyway?

Potentially everyone.

Now thoroughly rattled, the warm sense of togetherness with Damon splintered, Zara freed Rosie from her car seat and lifted her out. As she straightened, in her hurry, the back of her head caught the frame of the Audi's door, which was lower than that of her own car. She winced and straightened. As she did so, her bag, which she'd hooked over her shoulder, flopped to the ground, sending items scattering.

Damon steadied her. "Babe, are you all right?"

Muttering that she was fine, Zara clutched Rosie's warm, soft little body securely against her own and rubbed at the sore patch.

Babe. The surprise of the endearment was so distracting that Zara forgot she'd dropped her handbag and stepped back. Something crunched beneath her heel.

Her mood plummeted even further. That would be her phone. A little awkwardly, she retrieved it. A cracked screen, and the insides were undoubtedly mashed too. It would be a miracle if it ever worked again.

Before she could pick up any other items, Damon collected the keys and compact that had scattered, dropped them into her bag and handed the bag to her. Seconds later, he collected Rosie's things, locked the car and indicated the elevator. "If you're worried about the phone, don't be. I was giving you a company phone in any case."

Zara walked into the familiar private elevator. As Damon joined her, the feeling of disorientation that she was actually returning to work for Damon intensified.

The first person Zara saw as she stepped into the foyer was Howard Prosser, Damon's office manager. Howard's look of surprise that Zara was holding a baby informed her that Damon had been true to his word. If he hadn't confided the fact that Rosie was his child to Howard, then he hadn't told anyone.

Zara adjusted her grip on Rosie, who was becoming restless, and tried to look as if her relationship with Damon was as casual and incidental as Howard clearly thought it to be.

Damon glanced at a file Howard handed him. "Zara's just filling in for a few days, until the McCall takeover is complete."

Howard looked distinctly grumpy. "That's not likely to happen unless you track down whoever has that block of missing voting shares."

Damon's palm briefly cupped her elbow as he urged her toward the door to her old office. The small, proprietorial touch sent a small thrill of awareness through her.

"A rival firm's been buying shares," he explained as he set the baby bag and portable crib down behind the desk. "That wouldn't be a problem except that ten percent of the voting shares are held by an anonymous shareholder, something that should never have happened. The net result is we've been having difficulty securing a majority of the stock."

Zara set her handbag down beside the desk. "Why shouldn't the shares be held by an anonymous shareholder? Surely that happens all the time."

"Not with voting shares. And these were Tyler's personal shares. By rights they should have remained in the family, since they guaranteed the majority vote. At some point, and for some reason I can't fathom, he must have sold them. We'd buy them back but, unfortunately, there's no record of the transaction."

Zara shifted Rosie from one arm to another and became immediately aware that the baby needed a diaper change. As she rummaged in the baby bag for a changing pad and a diaper, Rosie wriggled and craned around and sent Damon a smile that was literally blinding. She held out her arms as if she had already recognized that Damon was her daddy.

Damon lifted a brow. "May I?"

"She needs a diaper change."

"If that's supposed to frighten me, you're failing."

"Because you're already an old hand at it, having changed her diaper last night."

Damon's gaze caught hers. "I figured you could use the sleep."

Zara's cheeks burned as she considered exactly why she had needed the sleep and, with an odd reluctance, because up until now Rosie had been solely hers, she allowed Damon to take his daughter. As he balanced Rosie against one broad shoulder, his hand cradling her head, Zara experienced a curious sinking feeling in the pit of her stomach. She should look away, she thought a little desperately, except that she couldn't. There was something about Damon cradling Rosie that was utterly mesmerizing.

With effort, she dragged her gaze from the too-fascinating juxtaposition of Rosie's cute pink beanie and the tough line of Damon's jaw and concentrated on laying the changing pad out on the desk. While Damon was dealing with the dirty diaper, she found baby wipes, ointment and a plastic bag.

When Rosie was freshly changed, Damon picked her up as if she was a fragile piece of porcelain, hugged her close for a few seconds, then handed her back to Zara. "By the way, I've received confirmation that Ben and Emily are on Medinos, staying at a house we own there. I've arranged to fly out in the company jet and talk to Ben."

Sudden crashing disappointment hit Zara. A trip to Medinos and back meant Damon would be away for the best part of four days. When she didn't know how much time they had before the media discovered Damon had a daughter, four days was an eternity.

"Can't you just talk to Ben on the phone?"

"He would have to answer his phone for that to happen." Damon walked to the windows and stared out at the view as if he was mulling something over. When he turned, the morning light threw his face into shadow. "Since it'll be a working trip," he said quietly, "I want you and Rosie to come with me."

As shocking as the idea of flying overseas anywhere with Damon was, the idea of going to Medinos irresistibly appealed. For one thing, because she'd been absent for so long it wasn't likely that she'd be recognized. And the trip could prove a lifeline because it would buy her more time with Damon away from the Auckland reporters. It would also allow her to check out her mother's safe-deposit box. Added to that, traveling in the Magnum company jet would cost her nothing.

A cautious sense of relief gripped her. Could it be, after so much had gone wrong with her life, that her luck had finally turned? "Okay."

Damon didn't try to hide his disbelief. "You agree?"

"Either way I'll still be working, and at least it'll stop that nosy reporter from sniffing around." Zara struggled to keep her expression bland when what she really wanted to do was give in to the relief and either grin or cry. She checked her watch and saw it was time for Rosie's feeding. She grabbed at the excuse to do something, anything, that would distract her from revealing to Damon just how important it was for her to get to Medinos.

Frowning, Damon perched on one corner of the desk as she made a production of finding the insulated container that held Rosie's bottle.

"There's just one glitch—we'll need to get Rosie a passport. Walter can probably pull some strings and get one in a day or—"

"Rosie already has a passport." Zara could feel her cheeks burning as she directed what she hoped was a matter-of-fact smile in Damon's direction. As if it wasn't

at all unusual for a four-month-old baby to have a passport. As if they hadn't been planning to go to Medinos
all along. "When do we leave?"

There was a small silence during which the sounds
of the office registered: a phone ringing, the low burr
of Howard's voice, the tapping of a keyboard.

Damon checked his watch, his expression oddly
grim. "The only holdup would have been getting Rosie
a passport. Since you've taken care of that already, I'll
call the flight crew. We leave this afternoon."

Nine

An hour later Damon gave up on his efforts to call Ben, who had clearly turned his phone off, or more probably thrown it into the deep blue Mediterranean Sea.

He paced to the enormous glass doors that stretched the length of one entire wall in his office. The heavy cloud from last night had gone and the day was clear and dry, the sun sparkling on the harbor and gleaming off the glossy, expensive yachts tied up in the viaduct. But the view, spectacular as it was, barely impinged on his thoughts. At this point, even Ben was the least of his problems.

Zara had gotten Rosie a passport.

There was no point doing that unless Zara had intended to leave the country with Rosie. Disappearing from sight again as she had tried to do just over a year ago.

Broodingly, he considered that maybe Zara had only

wanted to take a vacation? The problem with that scenario was that he knew Zara didn't have that kind of money. Walter had made a few discreet inquiries, so Damon knew that in financial terms, Zara was struggling to keep her head above water. The fact was, *he* had been propping up her finances for months, by hiring people he didn't need.

If Zara couldn't afford a holiday there was only one scenario left, she had been planning on leaving the country with Rosie and, in the process, *leaving him.*

But why start a new business if she was planning on emigrating? None of it made sense.

With sudden decision, he walked through to Walter's office. "I need you to run a security check on Zara."

Walter looked up from a thick legal pad on which he was making notes. "Didn't we do that last year?"

"Not in depth." Since Zara was fresh out of college, he had just asked for a standard check, which was relatively superficial, establishing whether or not there were any criminal convictions or debt issues that might compromise business loyalties, checking that qualifications and references were authentic. Since Zara had just graduated with an honors degree, and had been referred by a business acquaintance, an in-depth check had seemed like overkill.

"What exactly are you worried about?" Walter's gaze narrowed. "The baby's not yours."

"Rosie's mine."

Walter gave him a bland look. "Knew it as soon as I saw her."

Despite his irritation, Damon had to stop himself from grinning. "That obvious?"

"'Fraid so." Walter shook his head. "At least the baby

explains why Zara left. Although it still doesn't really add up."

Damon's brows jerked together. "Explain."

"Disclosure. It's big with women."

Damon waited for more; when it didn't come he kept a grip on his irritation. "Walter, you're going to have to use more words."

Walter sat back in his chair. "Margot made me join this group for men who have difficulty communicating—"

"I thought Margot liked the strong, silent type."

Walter gave him a stony look. "Do you want to hear this or not? According to the group facilitator, women actually like to talk about their emotional lives. It's called disclosure. Darned irritating and a waste of time if you ask me, but Margot has got some bee in her bonnet because, *apparently*, I don't discl—"

"Let's take it back to Zara."

Walter blinked as if he'd just returned from a dark place. "Okay. Simple equation. Zara was in love with you, so, being a woman, she should have told you about the pregnancy."

Damon's chest locked up. He felt like he'd just been kicked by a mule. "What makes you think Zara was in love with me?"

Walter gave him an "are you serious?" look. "Zara has all the raw materials of a sergeant major or a general. She could organize a war. So, it figures, why else would she let down her guard and sleep with you if she wasn't, you know, *in love*?"

Damon's jaw tightened on a complex surge of emotions—heat, raw possessiveness, unaccountable relief. An hour ago, any idea that Zara was in love with him would have had him warily backing off. But that was before she had calmly admitted that she already had a passport for Rosie. The passport was a game changer because it signaled that Zara and Rosie were leaving, and he did not want that to happen.

"So why do you think, if Zara was in love with me, that she didn't 'disclose' the pregnancy?"

Walter looked reflective. "Zara's a decisive woman. Maybe she just got tired of you." He nodded his head. "Yep, that's a pretty clear-cut reason for leaving."

Damon restrained his irritation with difficulty. He could see why Margot had sent Walter to counseling. "She didn't get tired of me."

Walter drummed his fingers on the desk. "I guess, since she's back."

Damon's jaw tightened. *And* she still wanted him. "Which is why I need that security check. ASAP."

Given Walter's summation of Zara's character, which was startlingly accurate, Zara's contention that she had left him because she didn't think he would want her in his wealthy, successful life now seemed both wimpy and implausible.

There had to be another reason.

That meant she was hiding something. Something important.

Several frantic hours later, Zara boarded Damon's private jet, carrying Rosie. A uniformed steward followed, carrying the baby bag and all of Zara's and Rosie's luggage.

Since Zara had only ever worked for Damon for a few weeks, she had never seen the jet, which was unashamedly luxurious, with spacious cabin seating and a well-appointed bathroom and sleeping cabin at the rear.

Damon stepped into the cabin, instantly dwarfing the

compact space. His cool gaze briefly connected with hers, leaving her feeling oddly confused, because the warmth of that morning seemed to have disappeared. He tossed his jacket over the back of a leather seat and chatted with the steward, whose name was Mark.

Predictably, Mark was an older man with a lean, muscled physique and a somewhat grizzled face marred by what looked like a serious burn scar on one side. She had no doubt whatsoever that this was another of Damon's ex-soldiers.

As Zara tried to settle Rosie, enough that she could put the baby down to sleep in the portable crib Damon had sent ahead, the door to the flight deck popped open. Zara expected another ex-army type would have the job of pilot. Instead, a stunning blonde wearing a crisp flight uniform stepped into the cabin.

Zara continued to rock Rosie on her shoulder as the blonde introduced herself as Buffy McNamara, the pilot. Buffy lifted a hand at Damon, her polite smile transforming into a sparkling grin. Her casual "Hey, Damon" made Zara tense up inside.

Rosie chose that moment to spit up on Zara's shoulder. Feeling distracted and out of sorts, Zara searched for some baby wipes.

When Damon didn't end the conversation with Buffy, but showed every evidence of enjoying the exchange, even down to calling her Mac—the first part of her surname, and obviously some kind of extra special pet name—Zara's tension coalesced into annoyance. She was busy trying to untie Rosie's bib. What she really wanted to do was frog-march *Mac* back to the flight deck and tell her to stay there.

Jaw taut, Zara located a laundry bag and jammed the soiled bib inside it. She knew what the problem was.

She was jealous, horribly jealous, although she could not afford to let Damon know that.

Damon took the seat next to her and dragged at his tie. "Is there something wrong?"

Zara found herself snared in the net of his gaze. Adrenaline zinged through her and her heart sped up. She took a deep breath and attempted a smile. "Rosie's just a little unsettled, that's all."

At that moment Buffy strolled by on her way back to the flight deck. She paused by Damon's seat and beamed at Rosie. "Cute baby. If you need help settling her, Mark can give you a hand. In fact, you could think about moving her into the bedroom at the rear—it's quieter there and she might sleep better."

And no doubt with Rosie tidily out of sight and out of Damon's sleek, high-powered executive space, the flight would go more smoothly for the boss.

Zara fought another unreasoning spurt of annoyance. Buffy couldn't know that Rosie was Damon's daughter because they'd agreed to keep that a secret for now. "Thanks, that's a good idea, but I think Rosie will be happier here in the cabin with me."

When Buffy strode through the door of the flight deck Zara glimpsed the copilot, who *was* an older military type, just before the door closed.

Damon, his gaze tinged with amusement, offered to take Rosie. Feeling embattled, Zara handed over the baby and Rosie settled like a lamb on his shoulder.

Mark, who was busy stowing bags, looked bemused. "Hidden talents, Damon?"

"Looks like." Damon patted Rosie on the back, but he scarcely needed to because she had already fallen asleep.

Minutes later, Damon lowered Rosie into the crib and

tucked a cotton blanket around her. Zara busied herself zipping the baby bag closed before stowing it beneath the seat closest to the crib. She searched through her handbag and found her phone so she could check and see if Molly, who had agreed to work full-time in the agency until Zara got back, had sent her any last-minute texts. There were none, which was a relief—

"You should come and sit down."

The low timbre of Damon's voice made her tense. She took a deep breath and tried to calm down, but despite the good talking-to she had given herself, she was still terminally annoyed at the way he had flirted with Buffy. The kind of conversation that underlined the fact that despite Rosie, despite them sleeping together *again*, she had absolutely no claim on Damon at all.

Slipping her phone back into her handbag, she took her seat and snapped open the magazine she had bought for the flight and found herself staring at a page filled with photographs of women dressed for glamorous occasions. Caroline Grant was center stage, wearing the exact same dress she had worn to the charity gala she had attended with Damon.

Zara stuffed the magazine into her bag.

"You don't have to be jealous of Mac," Damon said quietly.

Zara fastened her seat belt with a crisp click. "I'm not jealous," she muttered, keeping her voice equally low, so that Mark, who was seated at the rear of the cabin, couldn't hear. "Although I guess Buffy *is* blonde, and you do seem to have this thing for blondes."

"You're not blonde."

The jet picked up speed before leaving the ground.

Zara's stomach tightened automatically as they gained height.

"And neither am I your date." She made the mistake of turning her head and was instantly ensnared by the molten silver of Damon's gaze.

"You were last night."

Heat flooded her along with a raft of memories she had been working hard to suppress and which now, literally, welded her to the seat.

"Mac is the wife of a friend. She was in the air force, part of the crew attached to our Special Forces group. She married one of the team, Brendan McNamara, which is why she goes by the nickname Mac."

Relief surged through Zara, making her feel a little shaky and ridiculously happy. Happy that Buffy/Mac was just a friend, but even happier that Damon had been considerate enough to reassure Zara. It seemed to signal another positive turn in their relationship.

"I wasn't going to do this right now," Damon murmured with an odd flatness to his voice, "but now that we're in the air and you can't walk out on me, I have a proposition for you."

Zara tensed. "A proposition?"

"As in marriage. We have a daughter. We're good together. It won't be a marriage in the usual sense, but I think what we have is workable."

Not a marriage in the usual sense... Workable.

Zara wondered if she'd just time warped back to the nineteenth century. "Let me get this right. You're proposing a marriage—with sex—on the basis that we have a child?"

She drew a deep breath. The conditions he was offering were businesslike but more than a little hurtful. In a blinding moment of clarity she understood why. It was because a 'workable' marriage of convenience was the absolute opposite of what she wanted.

Because somehow, despite everything, she had fallen in love with Damon.

For a split second her heart seemed to stop in her chest. When it started up again, it pounded so hard she could barely breathe.

"I think you know by now that I'd like to, but I... need some time."

Because there was no way she could agree to an engagement, no matter how much she longed to. Not until he knew who she really was.

And once he knew that, he probably wouldn't want to marry her.

Ten

When Zara exited Damon's private jet, it was night. She didn't think she would be recognizable as Petra Hunt's daughter on Medinos, since it had been years since she was last here, but even so, she took precautions.

As she stepped onto the tarmac outside the terminal, she fished in her handbag and pulled out the white ball cap she had bought before boarding the flight. She had bought it expressly because it matched her white linen shirt and she could pull the bill of the cap down low over her forehead so the upper half of her face was shaded.

They stepped into the terminal and waited to clear customs. Zara relaxed a little when she noticed groups of tired tourists, a couple of people with high-visibility vests and uniformed officials, but no one resembling either a journalist or photographer.

She sent Damon a brilliant smile and tried not to notice how gorgeous and natural he looked with Rosie over his shoulder. She glanced anxiously around for their luggage. "Mark's taking a long time with the suitcases."

Damon gave her an odd look. "It's only been fifteen minutes."

Just then Mark appeared, trundling some kind of prehistoric cart with all the luggage from the flight, including that of the flight crew, who would be staying on the island until Damon and Zara were ready to fly back.

Despite the fact that it was night, it seemed to have gotten even steamier. She wiggled her toes in her white sneakers, which had been perfectly comfortable on the flight, but which were now hot and sticky.

Damon glanced at her hat as they collected their luggage. "Aren't you hot in that cap?"

Beneath the cap she was pretty sure her hair was already wet and plastered to her scalp. That was the second reason she wasn't taking it off. "It's not that hot."

"It's got to be over ninety degrees."

"I like the cap."

Damon lifted a hand to his mouth. It could have been an innocent gesture, but as Zara wheeled her case to the customs line she was pretty sure Damon had the nerve to think something about her cap was amusing. She sucked in a lungful of damp, warm air, feeling irritated because she longed to fling the blasted thing off. Her hair was already thick; the cap just added an extra sweltering layer. She caught Damon's gaze on her again as he joined her and this time she was sure he was laughing.

"I guess Rosie's going to be just like this."

"Just like *what*?"

"Frustrating. Cute."

There was a moment of vibrating silence during

which Zara found it increasingly difficult to breathe. The moment was broken as the line moved forward to the customs desk. Zara dragged the hat off and quickly tried to finger comb her hair, which did feel horribly flattened and damp. The cooling relief was only momentary because a pair of dark, vaguely familiar eyes met hers. She froze like a deer caught in the headlights. Jorge—the son of her mother's gardener, Aldo—who now clearly worked for airport customs, was looking at her as if he had seen a ghost.

Before he could open his mouth and say the only name he had ever known her by—*Angel*—she shook her head. His eyes widened perceptibly, but he seemed to get the message, because his gaze swiveled to Damon.

Groaning, she kept her head down, and Jorge whisked her through customs so quickly she barely had time to look around and log the changes. The last time she had been on Medinos, the airport had been on the small side and lacking in amenities. Now it was considerably larger and more complicated, with a sophisticated set of duty-free shops attached.

Half an hour later, they arrived at the hotel, an old but sumptuous building that looked like it had once been a palace of some sort, with gorgeous tiled floors, jewel-like water features and lavish displays of white roses and trailing star jasmine.

The suite Damon had booked was on the sixth floor. It was was breathtakingly luxurious, with three bedrooms, two reception rooms, a study and a fully equipped kitchen.

Feeling a little off balance that Damon had booked a multiroomed suite rather than two separate suites, as if they were already a family, Zara stowed Rosie's things in one of the rooms. When the bellhop had gone, and

Rosie was tucked into bed, Damon opened the French doors that led out onto a stone balcony. He threaded his fingers with hers, sending a sharp pulse of awareness through her as he pulled her outside.

As distracted as she was by Damon standing beside her, muscular and relaxed in a white T-shirt and jeans, as problematic as being on Medinos was, Zara couldn't help but drink in the view.

The stars were out, along with a silver half-moon. Whitewashed buildings, bleached by moonlight, with their dark, terra-cotta tiled roofs, tumbled down to the bay below. In the distance, she could make out the promontory, with its cluster of villas that used to be home.

Out of nowhere, her throat closed up. She hadn't realized how much she had missed Medinos, missed having a place to truly call home. Added to that, since her mother had died, she hadn't been able to afford to come back. This would be her first opportunity to visit Petra's grave.

"It's...beautiful."

Damon plucked the cap from her head and tossed it over the balcony.

Utterly surprised, Zara yelped. She had no time to grab for the cap; all she could do was watch as it sailed down to the gardens below.

Damon tugged at her fingers, coaxing her in close. "That's better." His fingers tangled in her hair. "Your hair is too gorgeous to hide. Never wear that cap again."

Terminally annoyed, because she *needed* that cap, Zara's palms landed on his chest. Although, as annoyed as she was, a renegade part of her loved that he had pulled her close and didn't want to push him away. "That hat was *mine*."

His expression turned rueful. "I suppose you'll just go out and buy another one."

"I don't need to—I've got a spare in my suitcase."

He shrugged and released her. "Okay, wear it if you want. Just not around me."

In the instant he let her go, contrarily, she didn't want to be free. Taking the half step needed to bring her close again, she wound her arms around his neck in a loose hold.

She was aware that she was playing with fire, but she couldn't resist. Something had changed with Damon, and she couldn't put her finger on quite what it was, except that he seemed suddenly extremely confident of her.

"I'm interested. What else am I not allowed to wear around you?"

"Clothing. Of any sort."

With a grin, Damon swept her into his arms and carried her to a sumptuous master bedroom. He tumbled her onto the very large bed, which looked like it had been made for an entire family.

A little breathlessly, Zara watched as Damon peeled out of his shirt and pants. Lit by the golden glow of a single lamp, she decided that with his broad shoulders and olive-toned skin, the black hair and tough jaw, he looked remarkably like one of the Templar knights depicted in a Medinian oil painting she had once seen.

He came down on the bed beside her and propped himself on one elbow. He ran one finger down her throat to the first button of her shirt, popping it open. "Now you."

Her breath dammed in her throat at his playful streak, which was new and unexpectedly precious because it seemed to signal the kind of intimacy she hadn't

dared hope for. She climbed from the bed and began to
undress, but when she got down to her bra and panties
her nerve gave out, and she clambered back onto the
vast bed, making up for her sudden shyness by straddling him.

Damon pulled her so that she sprawled across his
chest. "That's it?"

She cupped his jaw, the clean scent of his skin making her clench her stomach. "Uh-huh. I'm not *that* experienced at this."

Damon went oddly still. "What, exactly, are you saying?"

She frowned because when they had first made love
she had expected him to *know*. When he hadn't mentioned anything, she had kept the knowledge to herself
because the relationship was so new and she hadn't
wanted him to think she was trying to tie him to her.

Before she could actually say it, he muttered something short and flat beneath his breath. "You were a
virgin."

She traced the line of his mouth with the pad of her
thumb and tried to make light of it She hadn't consciously set out to stay a virgin; she had just never met
anyone she actually wanted to make love with until
Damon. Petra's death and the problems with the media
hadn't helped. Zara had basically retreated into her shell
and stayed there.

She shrugged. "It doesn't matter now. But I'm glad
that you know." Then, even if the worst happened and
he hated her for being Petra's daughter, he would at least
know that the tabloids had lied about her.

He caught her fingers in his and pulled them to his
lips. "I'm sorry I missed that moment, babe. But I'm
glad you've only ever been mine."

Babe. Happiness seemed to expand inside her as he rolled so that she was beneath him. But despite the heat that shimmered through her, despite the coiling tension that was already making it hard to breathe, let alone think, a tiny thought niggled. "What about you?"

Damon had dispensed with her bra, now he cupped her breasts, his palms faintly abrasive against her tender skin. His thumbs swept across her nipples, making it difficult to concentrate on what was, suddenly, a very important question.

His gaze captured hers. "What do you mean, what about me?"

She drew in a sharp breath as he took the nipple of one breast into his mouth. "I mean, Caroline."

Damon moved and she lifted her hips to assist him as he peeled down her panties. "Remember that reporter who came to your office?"

Zara drew in a sharp breath as Damon parted her legs with his thigh. She tried to think, but with his muscular weight now pressing her down into the mattress, her normally excellent memory had deserted her. "Um… Red Glasses."

Damon grinned and rewarded her with a kiss, which sent a ridiculously happy glow through her.

"Vanessa Gardiner. She was a friend of Caroline's. Why do you think Caroline put a reporter on my tail?"

Zara tried to gather her thoughts, but with the enticing pressure between her legs and the heated ache low in her belly, it was difficult to think of anything but how long it was going to take Damon to actually start making love to her. "I give up."

Damon's darkened gaze pinned her. "Caroline wanted to know who I was sleeping with."

Understanding finally dawned. "Because you weren't

sleeping with her." She swallowed, feeling suddenly, unexpectedly teary. "That means—"

"I haven't slept with anyone else."

Feeling just the tiniest bit fierce and possessive, she
coiled her arms around his neck and pulled him close,
relieved when he finally began entering her. When he
was fully sheathed, she wrapped her legs around his
hips, trying to pull him closer still.

She thought she had already felt everything she was
going to feel with Damon, that nothing could be more
intense and more meaningful than the lovemaking they
had already shared. But as they began making slow, exquisite love to each other she discovered she had been
wrong.

The knowledge that he had been celibate for the last
thirteen months changed things. It made the deep, last-
ing love she craved with Damon seem possible. As she
kissed him back, touched him back, with every breath,
suddenly the night was alive with emotions that shimmered and burned, melded and entwined...

Zara awoke to sun streaming through the French
doors and Rosie patting her cheek. A little startled that
she had slept so late and that Damon had taken charge
of Rosie, Zara shifted up in the bed, pulling the linen
sheets around her breasts as she cuddled her daughter.

Damon looked gorgeous in light jeans and a white
T-shirt, his phone to one ear. He terminated the call,
bent down and kissed her on the mouth.

"Stay in bed and rest. I'm driving out to the house
to talk to Ben. Rosie's had her breakfast, so if you like,
I can take her with me. I'll only be a couple of hours at
most, and Mark ordered a car with tinted windows and
a car seat, so she'll be safe *and* incognito."

Zara watched, a faint lump in her throat, as Damon strapped on the front pack and neatly fitted a gurgling Rosie into the cushioned frame. He seemed to be an expert at the fatherhood thing already. But she was all too aware after Damon's revelation and the fact that they seemed poised on the brink of a real relationship that the bubble of happiness she was presently living in could burst at any moment.

She needed to tell Damon the truth today.

Zara showered and dressed in an ice-blue dress that made the most of her tan. Humming beneath her breath, she sat at the exquisite antique dressing table to do her hair. As she coiled the heavy, glossy strands into a knot on top of her head and began sliding in pins, she couldn't help noticing that she looked *different*. She had heard women speak of glowing when they were in love. She was glowing. Her eyes were alight, her skin radiant, her mouth softly curved.

She applied minimal makeup, fitted earrings and did a final check of her appearance. She had a floppy-brimmed hat to wear, but at the last minute decided she was over the hat idea. She dragged a pair of large sunglasses out of her handbag instead. *Good!* With the sunglasses hiding her eyes and her cheekbones, she barely recognized herself.

She checked her watch. Damon wouldn't be long. If she was going to visit Petra's grave, see her mother's lawyer, then go to the bank to see what, exactly, Petra had stashed in the safe-deposit box—if anything—she needed to hurry.

She bought an armful of pretty flowers from a street vendor, then took a taxi to the local cemetery, which was situated on the windblown side of a hill overlooking the sea. Finding Petra's grave was easy, because she was buried near the ancient stone chapel, right beside Zara's father. Chest tight, her throat locked, Zara gently laid the flowers down. She hadn't quite known how she was going to feel, but there was a wild beauty about the hillside and the stone cross of the chapel etched against blue sky, a curious sense of peace and closure.

A few minutes later, the taxi delivered her to the address on the last letter she had received from her mother's legal firm. The white limestone building was situated on one of the steep, narrow streets that were a feature of Medinos.

She stepped out of the glaring heat of the sun into the inky well of shade offered by the foyer. She stopped by the front desk, and the receptionist, who was on a call, put the phone down. Before she could show Zara to Takis's office, a plump, balding man with a rumpled suit stepped out of a door.

The receptionist spoke in rapid Medinian. Zara heard her own name and realized she was looking at her mother's lawyer.

Takis stared at her for a long moment. "You do not look like your mother."

Tell me about it. "Nevertheless, I am Petra Hunt's daughter."

He held his door open with discernible reluctance. Jaw set, Zara walked into the small, rather messy office.

"Please, take a seat. What can I do for you?"

"I would like to view my mother's file."

"You know she signed the prenuptial—"

"I'm not worried about that." She attempted a smooth smile. "It's the offer by the McCall estate that I'm really interested in."

Takis frowned. "I don't understand. I sent you a copy—"

"I burned it."

There was a moment of taut silence. Takis walked to a wall of files, searched for what seemed an age before pulling out a folder. The chair behind his desk squeaked as he sat down. He flipped open the file, turned it around and pushed it across the desk toward her.

Zara skimmed the document, turned a page and froze. Damon's signature seemed to leap off the page. When she had originally received the offer, she hadn't paid much attention to the signature. Since then, a part of her had hoped it hadn't been Damon who had signed it, that it actually had been some faceless lawyer.

"May I have a copy of this?"

Minutes later, still feeling numb because Damon had been the architect of that horrible offer after all, Zara strolled down the steep street and into the bustling center of Medinos. The midday heat poured down as she crossed at a busy intersection, thronged with holiday-makers, but she barely noticed the swarms of brightly colored tourists.

Feeling suddenly thirsty, she stopped at a small café and bought one of Medinos's signature drinks, an enticing cordial of plum and lemon poured over shaved ice that quickly dissolved in the heat.

The bank her mother had used was easy enough to find. An entirely new tension hummed through her as she took in the high-vaulted ceilings, plaster frescoes and elegant marble floor. A pretty bank clerk directed her to an office that opened off the reception area. A trim, darkly suited clerk checked Zara's ID and the copy of Petra's will she had brought with her before escorting her down an echoing corridor. He entered a code into a thoroughly modern keypad and waited for her to precede him into another room.

A guard seated at a desk asked to see her key. He took note of the number and disappeared into an adjacent room. Seconds later, he appeared with a key, then opened a steel door into the vault and indicated she follow him. Zara watched as he unlocked a steel compartment and pulled out a long, narrow steel box, which he laid on a small table. Nodding politely, he withdrew, leaving her in privacy to unlock the box.

Out of nowhere, her heart began to pound.

When her mother had died, Zara had been thousands of miles away and had not had the funds to get back for the funeral. A model friend of her mother's had packed up Petra's things and freighted them to Zara. Opening those boxes and sorting through her mother's clothes and personal effects had been the only ritual left to her. That was possibly why she was now unbearably aware that the last time this safe-deposit box had been opened, it had been by her mother.

Petra had stood in this same sterile room while she placed whatever it was that she had held most precious in the narrow steel box. Emotion swelled in Zara's chest—a sudden, powerful sense of connection with the mother she had lost, emotions she had avoided because losing Petra had cut the ground from under her. Despite their differences they had always been a pair—two against the world.

Taking a deep breath, she inserted the key, turned it and opened the box. She instantly recognized the faded leather cases that held Atrides family jewelry; she had seen them often enough as a child. After lifting them out, she opened them, emotion swelling as she looked at the pretty collection of French brooches and pendants, the huge old-fashioned cameo her great-grandmother had worn with a black bombazine dress.

Her fingers brushed against a small black velvet bag. She loosened the cord and emptied the contents into the palm of her hand. Not jewelry as she had expected, but a glittering cascade of diamonds; single stones of varying sizes, all of them glowing with an expensive fire.

Once, over a glass of wine, Petra had alluded to her *life savings*. She hadn't said what the savings were exactly. Zara had thought she was talking about money, but the amount in Petra's bank accounts had been too small to qualify as savings of any sort. Now she knew that her mother had been referring to this cache of diamonds, her hedge against the hard times that would come when her looks faded.

Heart thumping, she poured the diamonds into the pouch like so much liquid fire and carefully retied the cord. Her mother hadn't lived long enough to need the money the diamonds would bring. But Zara was certain Petra would love it that her *savings* would be put to good use, and not just for a deposit on a house—she would buy the whole thing.

The final items in the box were a plain white envelope, a solitaire engagement ring, a gold wedding ring worn thin over the years and a silver cross that she recognized as once belonging to her father.

Zara's throat closed up as she extracted the jewelry that had been the intimate, personal belongings of her parents. She had wondered what had happened to her mother's rings, which Petra was usually never without. She had assumed they had been lost in the accident somehow, or maybe misplaced by the people who had sorted through Petra's things.

Frowning, Zara opened the last item, the envelope, and extracted a sheaf of what looked like certificates. Her heart seemed to stop in her chest as the name *Mc-*

Call Electrical jumped out at her. Stunned, Zara flipped through a sheaf of numbered shares in McCall Electrical. Voting shares, the shares Damon had been chasing for the past year or so and which had blocked his takeover bid of the company. Shares that Tyler must have gifted to Petra and which now, technically, belonged to Zara.

With careful precision, because her fingers were shaking, she placed the certificates on the table. From her work on the McCall deal, Zara knew they represented a 10 percent chunk of McCall Electrical, which meant they were worth tens of millions of dollars.

Suddenly, her aunt Phoebe's motives in placing Zara at Damon's business made an even more horrible kind of sense. Her aunt must have known about the existence of the shares and their value. She had obviously hoped that if Zara got to know Damon before she found out about the shares, that she wouldn't reject them as she'd rejected the cash offer by Damon.

"Sorry, Phoebe," Zara muttered beneath her breath. "You should have known you were wasting your time. I wouldn't touch these with a barge pole."

As far as she was concerned, they belonged to Damon and Ben; she wanted no part of them. She stared at the shares, feeling suddenly utterly panicked. It was bad enough that she had to explain her true identity to Damon; having to explain the shares was too much.

First off, if she gave the shares back to Damon, he would know that her mother had had them, which would confirm his opinion of Petra and make him doubly suspicious of Zara. Second, she was almost certain that Damon would view her gesture as calculated. He was a billionaire and had already proposed marriage, so financially she would not need the shares. Whichever way she looked at it, giving the shares back to Damon herself could mean he would no longer want marriage with her, and she could not risk that.

She would have to find a way to get them back to Damon so that he would never know she'd had them all along.

Last night she had seen a glimmer of what the future could hold for them. She couldn't bear it if he rejected her outright. She loved him, and she wanted him to love her. With the shares in her possession, more than ever, she needed to pick the right time to tell him. Although, she was beginning to wonder if such a moment existed.

Hating even to touch shares that she would rather die than accept, Zara shoved them back into the envelope. As she did so, she noticed a slip of paper. It was a note written from Tyler to Petra in a clean, slanting hand. In essence it said that because Petra had insisted on a prenuptial agreement and refused to share in his wealth and assets, he insisted she accept the shares, which were an engagement present.

Knees feeling wobbly, Zara sat down. Her spine and scalp were tingling, all the fine hairs at her nape raised, her chest tight. The words Tyler had written were straightforward and businesslike, but Tyler giving Petra stock in his firm could mean only one thing, just as Petra taking off the wedding rings Zara's father had given her could mean only one thing.

They had been deeply in love.

Zara's fingers closed automatically over the thin wedding band and the pretty solitaire diamond. Petra had loved Zara's father to the point that no man had ever lived up to him. Even after his death, she had worn his rings and had never consented to wearing anyone else's jewelry. Zara had known that, because as a child, worrying about who might replace her father, she had come to realize that as long as Petra wore her wedding ring, there would be no replacement. Every time Petra had visited her at school, or taken her away on holiday, the first thing Zara had done was check her mother's left hand. Despite all the speculative media reports about who Petra was dating, if she was still wearing her wedding rings, that meant their small family of two was still intact.

Zara reread the note Tyler had written, and this time she noticed the date. Two days before Petra and Tyler had died.

Petra had been engaged. Her relationship had been real and valid. The shares proved that.

The shares.

Zara felt like flinging them somewhere, *burning them*, but she couldn't do either thing. She was caught between a rock and a hard place, because Damon needed the shares to gain control of McCall Electrical.

Feverishly, she tossed Tyler's note onto the table while she examined the envelope itself. It was plain and white, with no writing on it. Good. She would find a way to have the shares delivered to Damon, maybe pay someone to drop them off at the concierge desk. It had to be someone she trusted, yet who couldn't be connected to her.

Feeling like a cat on hot bricks—elated because the diamonds represented the financial security she and Rosie desperately needed, and utterly stressed at finding the missing McCall shares—she gathered everything from the table and shoved it all into her bag.

She had hoped she would recover some family jewelry today, and she had; what she hadn't expected was for the past to rush back at her like a freight train. A past she had to explain to Damon so he wouldn't end up hating her.

Above all, she didn't want him to think the reason she was so attracted to him had anything to do with his money. It wasn't true and it would never be true. What she wanted was what she had always wanted, to be loved and cherished for herself.

Pushing to her feet, she hooked the strap of her bag over her shoulder and checked her watch. Anxiety made her stomach hollow when she saw how much time had passed. Almost an hour, although it had felt like a lot less.

After handing in her key because she wouldn't be needing the box again, she made a beeline back to the main foyer of the bank. As she stepped out onto the pavement, the glare of the afternoon sun had her rummaging for her sunglasses. Sliding them onto the bridge of her nose, she hailed a cab. Relieved when the cab veered toward her, she slid into the back seat and gave the cabbie the hotel's address, suddenly anxious to get back to Rosie.

Five minutes later, the cab stopped at the hotel entrance. After paying the fare, Zara stepped into the foyer. She stopped dead when she saw Emily, who was sitting in one of the leather chairs, watching the entrance and clearly waiting for her.

"What's wrong?"

Emily dragged Zara toward the most secluded couch, positioned beneath a lush indoor palm right next to the elevators. "Damon's talking to Ben." Her face crumpled. "At first I thought Damon was okay with Ben and I being together, then Walter called, and everything changed. We had to come here because the cell phone coverage is practically nonexistent out on the coast and Walter had emailed some kind of report—"

"An investigative report."

Emily's face went white. "I think so, because Ben knows about Daniel now."

Zara took the seat next to Emily. "Daniel? I thought his name was Jason."

Emily flushed. "I guessed by now you would know too. Daniel was before Jason. He was a business partner of my father's. My father wanted me to marry him. I liked him quite a lot—I even thought I might be in love with him—so I agreed, but then I met Jason."

"So you pulled out of the marriage."

She shrugged. "I fell for Jason. He could have been a pauper for all I cared."

"But he wasn't. He was even richer, so it made you look like you were chasing a bigger catch."

Emily looked miserable. "I thought I'd made the right choice until Jason dumped me. Unfortunately, when it happened some columnist wrote a snarky piece about it, accusing me of bed-hopping and chasing a rich husband. I felt so humiliated, I left my job in my father's business—"

"Changed your name and came to work for me."

Emily flushed. "You seem so calm about this. I thought you'd be steaming mad. I thought you'd hate me." She grimaced. "Just like Ben will. I'm pretty sure Walter will have dug up that horrible article."

Abruptly, the fear that had been sawing at Zara ever since she'd discovered the shares died and was replaced by an odd sense of calm. If Walter had investigated Emily, then he would be investigating her, which meant she was out of time. She grimly wondered if Damon had also received a security report about her.

The last few days, her life had been tipped upside down and spun around and, quite frankly, she was over the stress of it. She was a good person. She loved her daughter and she loved Damon and she wanted to share her life with him. But if he preferred security reports and the rubbish the media invented over her word, then she was out of options.

A painful flush suffused Emily's face. "Damon's very protective of Ben. I can understand why he would want to warn him off—"

"Ben's an adult," she said crisply. "He doesn't need his older brother interfering in something that is none of his business."

Emily looked startled. "I thought you'd be furious, which is why I wanted to catch you before you spoke to Damon. It was bad enough that I walked out on my job—" She fumbled in her handbag, found a tissue and blew her nose. "I've made a real mess of things. I don't even know if Ben will ever let me explain—"

The elevator doors opened. Ben strode out, his face pale, his expression taut. His gaze zeroed in on Emily.

"You're still here," he muttered. "Thank goodness. I thought you would have run a mile."

Emily jumped to her feet. "Why would I run?"

"Because my family's so messed up. Why would you want to be a part of us? I've just heard it all. My father was a crazy, violent drunk and a womanizer who squandered the family fortune on mistresses. I was born after he died, so I never knew him, but Damon did, and he's literally got the scars to prove it. That's why he's so…overprotective. He doesn't want me falling into the same pit of snakes." Ben grinned lopsidedly.

Emily looked devastated. "He thinks I'm a pit of snakes?"

Ben instantly clasped her upper arms and pulled her close, his expression anxious. "Baby, that came out all wrong. The pit of snakes is the out-of-control, addictive behavior Damon thinks runs in the family line, not you."

"Phew," Emily said, with the glimmer of a watery smile. "For a moment there I thought Damon must hate me."

"Damon doesn't hate anyone. He just doesn't want me to get hurt."

Emily stiffened. "And do *you* think I'll hurt you?"

"Only if you leave me."

"I wasn't intending to leave. Why would I? I love you."

Relief washed over Ben's face. "Ditto. I don't care about your past relationships, and the truth is I've hardly been an altar boy myself, if you know what I mean. If you're happy with me, that's all I want to know."

Emily threw Zara a radiant glance as Ben hurried her out of the hotel. "Sorry about the job, Zara, but it looks like I'm definitely not coming back!"

Zara watched as Ben settled Emily into a low-slung sports car, which was parked just across the road. Feeling a little stunned by what Ben had revealed about Damon's past, Zara made a beeline toward the elevators.

Damon having a father who had driven the family broke with his spending on mistresses neatly explained his attitude toward Petra, and to Angel Atrides. It also made sense of his attempt to pay her off and get her to sign that insulting "go away" agreement. Ben had also mentioned scars, and that their father had been violent. She had always thought Damon's scars had been earned in battle, but some of them must have been inflicted by his father.

Slowly, quietly, the pieces of the puzzle fell into place and her heart squeezed tight at what Damon must have endured as a child. She was beginning to understand why he had such an issue with trust.

As the elevator whizzed upward, her stomach tensed. Emily's expression had glowed; she had gotten her happy ending. An ending Zara now very much doubted would be hers.

When she stepped into the suite, Rosie, who was lying on a rug on the floor playing with a rattle, crowed, flung the toy aside and held her arms out to Zara. A rush of pure maternal love brought tears to Zara's eyes. It might not be possible that she could ever have the true, adult love she needed from Damon, but she had her daughter.

Zara carried her handbag, with all of its incriminating evidence, into Rosie's room and stashed it in a dark corner. She walked back out to the sitting room and scooped Rosie up, needing the comfort of her child in her arms.

Damon strolled out of the adjoining study, a cell in his hand. Zara decided to take the bull by the horns. "I saw Emily and Ben in the lobby. Luckily, Ben had the maturity to see beyond Emily's past to what a nice person she is."

Damon dropped the phone into his back pocket. "I agree that Emily is nice," he said mildly. "But if she had been up-front about her past to begin with, there wouldn't have been a problem."

"Maybe Emily had some very good reasons for keeping her life, and her name, private."

"Most people don't deal with it by changing their name."

Zara stared at Damon for a long moment, wondering if there was a double meaning to his words because he knew she had changed her name. Rosie, who had slumped into a contented doze almost as soon as Zara had picked her up, stirred, as if even in sleep she could sense the uncomfortable currents. "You say that as if she did it to deliberately deceive Ben, when all she wanted was to escape the press and keep her privacy."

Damon frowned. "The press were not exactly hounding Emily. As I recall, it was one gossip columnist."

"Just one? Then Emily can't have been that notorious." Afraid that she would lose her temper and reveal too much, Zara walked through to Rosie's room, placed her in her crib and covered her with a light cotton blanket. She drew a deep breath and discovered that her hands were shaking. The one ray of hope was that, given that they were still talking about Emily, maybe Damon hadn't yet received a report about her.

When she walked out to the sitting room, Damon's gaze was wary. "What have I done now?"

He was standing at a set of French doors that opened out onto a sun-drenched patio. With his arms crossed over his chest, making his shoulders seem even broader, he looked brooding, utterly masculine and more than a little dangerous.

Zara got straight to the point. "Emily said you got Walter to dig into her past."

"Ben's my brother. He's in love with a woman who, at some point, changed her name." He shrugged. "Of course, I got Walter to do a little digging—"

"I suppose you think Emily's not good enough for Ben?"

Damon's brows jerked together. "These days what I think doesn't really impact Ben."

But it impacted Zara! "Okay, then, *you* don't think Emily's good enough."

Damon reached her in two strides. Linking his fingers with hers, he pulled her close, which was disorienting when she was still bracing herself for the fact that he had received some kind of damning report on her.

"Forget Emily," he muttered. "I had hoped we might be doing something else right about now."

The bell to the suite buzzed. Damon swore softly. "Talk about bad timing."

He opened the door to a waiter, who wheeled in a cart with a bottle of champagne on ice and two glasses. Damon tipped the waiter and closed the door behind him before wheeling the cart off to one side.

His expression was rueful. "I was supposed to give you something before that happened."

He fished a velvet box out of his pocket and flipped the lid. For a split second she thought he had an engagement ring, then she saw a pair of gorgeous diamond earrings.

For a moment she battled disappointment, then the sheer relief that Damon still wanted to give her a gift, and the sheer beauty of the earrings, took over.

Despite his contention that he wanted to keep things on a businesslike footing, he had obviously been thinking about her and wanting to please her, even down to doing something romantic like ordering champagne. A lump formed in her throat as it occurred to her that, even though everything seemed to be happening in reverse—as in having sex and a baby!—Damon was now courting her.

"You don't have to give me jewelry—"

"After last night, I wanted you to have something."

Understanding dawned. Last night she had told him that she had only ever been his.

Fingers shaking slightly, she picked up the gorgeous earrings, walked over to the mirror and inserted them in her lobes. She had been about to say that she couldn't accept them, but now she didn't want to let them go because she was certain they were a genuine gift of love, even if Damon didn't realize it.

"They're…beautiful."

Damon came up behind her and pulled her back against the warmth of his chest. "You're beautiful."

He turned her around in his arms and kissed her. Zara wound her arms around his neck and kissed him back, happiness shimmering through her as she wallowed in the sheer warmth and comfort of being back in Damon's arms, but the moment was bittersweet. As wonderful as it was to just be with Damon, to let her imagination run riot and pretend that they were both in love, it was a fact that they were on borrowed time.

And she had the sudden premonition that if she didn't make love to Damon now, she never would again.

A little feverishly, she began undoing the buttons of his shirt.

Damon lifted his head, his gaze heated. "Now?"

For an answer, she kissed him again and dragged at more buttons. Damon's shirt dropped to the floor. This time he pulled her close and kissed her. Long drugging seconds later her dress followed suit and she found herself propelled in the direction of the bedroom.

Damon kicked the bedroom door closed behind them as they stepped through. By the time they reached the bed, Damon had stepped out of his pants and her bra was gone. There was a momentary pause while Damon sheathed himself with a condom then they were lying tangled together on the sun-drenched bed.

She felt the glide of Damon's fingers as he peeled her panties down her legs. Desire shivered and burned as he came down between her thighs. With one smooth thrust he was inside her and they were deeply, perfectly linked.

Damon's gaze locked with hers and his fierce tenderness struck her to the heart. For a split second, she felt the utter rightness of being together, that he truly belonged to her and she to him.

She clasped his shoulders as they began to move, tears blinding her at the sheer intimacy of what they were doing. She felt as if she was finally, truly getting to know Damon and at the same time saying goodbye.

Eleven

Damon woke to small noises signaling that Rosie was awake. Carefully, so as not to disturb Zara, he disentangled himself, slid from the bed and pulled on his jeans. Walking into Rosie's room, he found her cuddle rug, which was lying on the floor, then looked around for her favorite toy, a rattle, which had also ended up on the floor. As he picked up the rattle, he noticed Zara's white leather handbag, which was lying at a drunken angle between an armchair and the wall with her phone precariously balanced on top. Probably in a rush to put Rosie in the crib, she had simply dumped the lot.

He handed the rattle to Rosie, who instantly started to chew on it, then retrieved Zara's phone. As he did so, the bag, which seemed stuffed full, slumped to one side. A number of items spilled out on the floor, among them a black velvet bag that scattered brilliant crystals.

Jaw tight, Damon stooped to gather up gems that burned with the fiery, unmistakable glitter of diamonds.

He was no expert, but given the size, number and weight of the stones, he was looking at a small fortune. He tipped the stones back into the velvet bag and placed it in Zara's handbag. As he did so, he noticed a thick envelope, which had also fallen out of the bag. The envelope was plain, but the contents, which had partly slid out of the envelope, looked gut-wrenchingly familiar. He picked up the envelope, already knowing what he was going to find. Even so, his stomach contracted when he pulled out the sheaf of old-fashioned and utterly familiar share certificates.

The missing McCall shares.

Why would Zara have the shares in her possession? How had she gotten hold of them?

The only answer that made sense was that Zara was somehow connected with Tyler. Because the voting shares were supposed to be held only by family members, he had considered the possibility that Tyler had given them to Petra, then on Petra's death they had ended up in Angel's hands. But the shares had never appeared on the market, so he had scrapped that idea.

It suddenly occurred to him that Zara was the same age as Petra's daughter, Angel Atrides. It was a leap—a big one. She looked nothing like Petra, but the more he thought about it, the more the facts fitted. It explained why Zara was so sensitive about any contact with the press, and why she had been so protective of Emily changing her name.

He had a sudden flash of Zara's bedroom, which had been decorated in a distinctly Medinian way and suddenly he was sure.

Zara Westlake was Angel Atrides.

It was there in the mystery about Zara's *nondisclosure*, the fact that she had gotten passports for her and Rosie, and had been surprisingly willing to come to Medinos. If he didn't miss his guess, Petra had stored the diamonds and the share certificates at some bank, and Zara had needed to come to Medinos personally to retrieve them.

Keeping hold of the envelope, Damon rose to his feet. He felt as if the scales had fallen from his eyes. He had been bedazzled, incapable of operating with his usual methodical precision.

A little grimly, he wondered if this was how Tyler had felt when he had fallen for Petra and handed over the shares of a business that had been his life's work. A company he had built up with clever innovation and long hours of hard work. A company he had always maintained would remain in the family.

A soft buzzing distracted Damon. He retrieved his phone from the back pocket of his jeans. Walter's text advised Damon that the report on Zara was in his inbox and he needed to read it before he did something stupid.

Too late. Damon walked to the study and used his laptop to read the confirmation that Zara Westlake was Angel Atrides.

Picking up the envelope that contained the shares, he walked back to the bedroom as Zara's eyes flickered open.

The words Ben had spoken over the phone just before he had flown away with Emily came back to haunt Damon. He lacked *emotional intelligence*.

He had no argument with that summation. He had ignored his usual caution and allowed himself to be conned by Petra's daughter.

It had all been a sham from the first moment.

He dropped the envelope on the pillow. Some of the shares slipped out, fanning across the tangled sheet. He saw the comprehension in Zara's gaze and the cold in his stomach seemed to settle a little deeper.

"How did you get hold of the shares?"

Zara jackknifed, clutching the sheet around her breasts. "You searched my bag?"

"I didn't search anything. I went in to check on Rosie. I noticed you'd left your phone on top of your bag. When I picked it up your bag fell over and a few things you obviously didn't want me to see fell out."

"It's not what you think." She averted her gaze from the certificates. "They were in a safe-deposit box at my mother's bank."

"Which was why you wanted to come to Medinos."

"I didn't know the stock certificates were there!"

"What about the diamonds?"

"Not those, either! I came because I wanted to find out what was in the box. I had hoped my Atrides family jewelry would be there, and it was."

"Atrides, as in Angel Atrides."

Her gaze turned fierce. "That's right. I changed my name for practical reasons—"

"Like Emily."

"I did it to escape the media. Not that I would expect you to understand that!"

"And the small fortune in diamonds didn't really matter?"

"Actually, *yes*, it does, because right now Rosie and I need the money. To be honest, I was *glad* there were diamonds."

"Not that you need the diamonds, with the shares being worth a small fortune."

Her face went white. "I told you I didn't know the

certificates were there. I didn't know any of it was there!"

Damon's jaw tightened. "Just like you didn't know when you slept with me that I was Tyler's nephew?"

"You think I slept with you and got pregnant, *deliberately*?" Zara clambered from the bed and dragged on one of the hotel robes, belting it tight. "You're wrong about my mother, and you're wrong about me! My aunt Phoebe pulled some strings to help get me the job. And, yes, *she* had an agenda, but she didn't let me in on it! If I had known which Smith you were, I wouldn't have taken the job—I wouldn't have touched you with a barge pole—"

"I can't believe you didn't know who I was."

"Your name is Smith. Do you know how many people have that surname? The firm is Magnum Security, which I had never heard of before. It wasn't until I started working on the McCall takeover that it finally clicked that you were *that* Smith."

Damon dragged lean fingers through his hair. He couldn't believe how much he wanted to believe her. "Maybe if the shares weren't involved—"

"Tyler gave those shares to my mother because he *loved* her."

"And you have proof of this?" Damon couldn't keep the sardonic twist from his mouth. Although there was no humor in a situation that took him straight back to his childhood and his father's penchant for lavishing expensive gifts on his mistresses.

Zara shot him a fiery glance. "You think you have all the facts, but you don't. My mother wouldn't agree to marry Tyler without a prenup, because she didn't want his money. Tyler agreed, but in return, he insisted she take shares in his company. I can prove it. There was a note from Tyler in the safe-deposit box."

Damon's expression was utterly neutral. "Sounds like true love."

"It was. My mother took off her wedding rings. If you had known her at all, you would have known what that meant, because she adored my father and grieved him for years. Until she met Tyler she never took off her rings. But you didn't know Petra, just like you don't know me."

Damon followed Zara as she marched into Rosie's room, found her bag, carried it out to the sitting room and feverishly searched through it. When she couldn't find what she was looking for she began emptying items onto the coffee table. After a few minutes, she quietly repacked her bag.

"No note?"

Frustration brimmed in her gaze. "I must have left it in the vault. Although you won't believe that because you think I'm lying."

He frowned. "I didn't say that."

"I've told you what happened," she said flatly, "but I don't think you want the truth. You'd rather see me as flawed and dishonorable, because if you were convinced that I was genuine, then that might demand some kind of genuine response from you, and that's something you don't want to give. What happened a year ago is a case in point. I left and you didn't come after me."

"I did," he said quietly. "And I found you, but I left before you saw me."

Her expression was oddly stricken. "That's even worse."

Zara marched back to the bedroom, gathered up the shares and shoved them back into their envelope. She remembered the earrings Damon had given her and which she was still wearing! Fingers shaking, she fumbled the earrings out of her lobes, located the box they had come in, then placed the jewelry box on the coffee table with the shares.

"The shares are yours—I don't want them. You can have the earrings back, as well. Consider yourself freed."

Silence seemed to stretch between them, hollow and unbridgeable.

Damon's phone buzzed. Turning on his heel, he walked back into the study and closed the door.

Moving on automatic pilot, Zara made it to the bathroom and locked the door behind her. Feeling sick to her stomach, she stared blankly at her reflection in the lavish mirror, which occupied most of one wall. Taking a deep, slow breath that hurt because her chest was tight with misery, she noted that, with her hair a wild tangle around her face and the robe gaping slightly over her breasts, she looked lush and wanton. The complete opposite of the woman she knew herself to be.

Although, Damon could not seem to see *her*.

Suddenly unable to bear looking at herself, she dropped the robe on the floor and stepped beneath the shower. She winced as cool water struck her skin. As the water gradually warmed, her numbness faded and the decision she knew she had to make settled into place.

She had to leave. Now.

She could not afford to argue with Damon anymore. If she did, she would end up begging, and she absolutely did not want to beg.

She loved him, but it was clear that Damon did not love her. Not even close. The death knell had been when he admitted that a year ago he had found her and *then walked away*.

If he had truly wanted her, he would have pursued her back then, and he would be fighting for her now, just like Ben had fought for Emily. But Damon was clearly more interested in pushing her out of his life than holding on to her.

She didn't blame him for being angry or distrustful, because she had hardly engendered his trust. She should have told Damon who she was a long time ago. She had been guilty of cowardice, guilty of running away, but it was also a fact that some things had just happened.

Their relationship had been fatally flawed from the beginning, but it had resulted in Rosie, who was gorgeous and lovable and who Zara could never regret having. To Zara's mind there was nothing that was not forgivable between her and Damon. The problem was that Damon did not trust in love. And the very strength she had found so attractive in him had ended up finishing them.

Minutes later, dried and with the robe once more belted around her middle, she opened the door and listened. Reassured by the silence that pervaded the suite that Damon had left, she walked quickly to the bedroom. A quick peek at Rosie told her that she had fallen back to sleep.

Zara dressed quickly in cotton jeans, a camisole and an airy white shirt. Leaving her hair loose, she used minimal makeup and slipped on comfortable sandals.

Her stomach churned as she quickly packed, but she knew it was the right thing to do. She could not stay with a man who felt contempt for her, no matter how wrong she knew his attitude to be.

She checked the bedside clock. Barely fifteen min-

utes had passed since she had stepped out of the shower.
She didn't know how much time she had before Damon
came back to the suite. All she knew was that after
their horrible confrontation, she couldn't bear to see
him again.

In her haste, she emptied an entire drawer into her
suitcase, not bothering to fold or be neat. She remembered to grab her toiletries from the bathroom, shoving
them into a plastic bag so nothing would leak.

She collected Rosie's bag and stuffed in clothes,
bottles, baby formula and diapers. After making up a
bottle, she zipped the bag closed with difficulty and deposited it, along with the folded front pack, in the tray
below the baby stroller. After letting the backrest of
the stroller down so that it formed a bed, Zara gingerly
deposited Rosie in the stroller and tucked her cotton
blanket around her. Rosie blinked sleepily.

Relieved, Zara checked the bedroom and the sitting
room. She would not be able to take all of Rosie's equipment with her; the portable crib and the bedding that
went with it would have to stay behind.

Zara wheeled her suitcase to the door and collected
her handbag. She stopped dead when she checked inside to make sure she had her sunglasses and noticed
the bag of diamonds jumbled in among the Atrides jewelry cases. No doubt Damon had thought all the wrong
things about her when he had seen them, along with
the share certificates.

Tucking the jewelry cases and the diamonds in the
bottom of her suitcase, she looped the strap of her handbag over one shoulder, wheeled her suitcase out into
the hall, then wheeled the stroller out. She tensed as
she walked toward the elevator, pushing the stroller
with one hand and wheeling the suitcase along behind

her with the other. She didn't know where Damon had gone, but she was aware that he could return at any time. She punched the call button for the elevator. When the doors slid open to reveal an empty car, she breathed a sigh of relief.

She pushed the stroller in and turned it around and managed to drag the suitcase in beside her just before the doors closed. She pushed the ground floor button, then slid sunglasses onto the bridge of her nose.

As she struggled out of the elevator, she automatically scanned the foyer. There was a group of tourists checking out, their luggage attended by two bellhops. A couple sat in the sleek lounge area and, across an expanse of marble floor, the café and bar was filled with tourists enjoying the thick aromatic local coffee. Heart still beating too rapidly, Zara made a beeline for the door.

When the concierge started toward her, a frown on his face, she fell back into the training she had received at her finishing school and politely smiled as she shook her head. Dismissed, the concierge retreated and, with a weakening sense of relief, she made it through the doors to the first taxi.

She tipped the driver double what she expected to pay for the fare after he folded up the stroller and stowed it in the trunk, and asked him to drive her to the law firm. The driver waited for her while she took Rosie into the office. Fifteen minutes later, Zara exited the building with a baby who was now distinctly unhappy, but she had the document she needed, signed and witnessed by the receptionist.

Sliding into the back seat of the taxi, she rummaged in the baby bag and found the bottle of formula she had prepared. Popping it into Rosie's mouth, she asked the taxi driver to take her back to the hotel, but to park down a side street where she could walk through the hotel café to the foyer. That way she could get into the hotel without the exposure of parking at the front entrance.

With no alternative but to take Rosie with her, she asked the driver to wait once more, tipping him to make sure he didn't drive off with her luggage. Jamming the almost empty bottle back into the baby bag, she exited the taxi and walked into the hotel through the busy café, pausing before the open expanse of the foyer, just in case by some chance Damon might be walking through.

When the coast seemed clear, she walked briskly to the concierge's desk and asked that the document be delivered to Damon's suite.

Damon walked into the vault of the third and final bank on Medinos. He'd had to call in some favors, but he'd managed to get access to the vaults, long enough to check if there was anything that resembled the handwritten note Zara had claimed his uncle had written. Maybe it was a wild-goose chase, but despite the odds against finding a note, he couldn't forget the stark expression on Zara's face when he had tossed the shares on the bed or the raw hurt when he'd accused her. The report Walter had sent him had been just as conflicting, confirming her identity, and also confirming that—aside from the change of name—Zara was everything she claimed to be.

The first two banks had been dead ends, and he had literally turned those rooms over; this was his last chance to find the note, if it existed.

The clerk accompanied him into the vault and waited

while he did a quick search of the room. The small trash can was empty. He was just about to leave when a corner of white caught his eye. A piece of paper had slipped down between the wall and the stainless steel desk used for opening safe-deposit boxes.

He fished out the piece of notepaper and went still inside, all the hairs at his nape lifting. He would recognize Tyler's firm, slanted writing anywhere.

He read the brief note, then read it again. He tried to breathe, but his chest had closed up. Zara had been telling the truth.

And he had made a mistake, the biggest mistake of his life.

He suddenly became aware of how much time had passed. He checked his watch, thanked the clerk, then left the bank.

It took him ten minutes to reach the hotel, but he had the odd feeling that it was ten minutes too long. As he stepped into the lobby, the concierge stopped him and handed him an envelope.

Impatient to reach the suite, Damon opened the envelope as he stepped out of the elevator. He instantly recognized a copy of the letter he had instructed his lawyers to send to Zara's lawyer years before, which, if she had signed it, would have meant she relinquished any claim to the estate.

The fact that Zara had not gotten her lawyer to draft a new letter, but had obtained a copy of the old one he had originally sent to her, conveyed a message he couldn't ignore. Years ago, he had assumed Zara had refused to sign because she had wanted to keep him dangling and her options open, so she could sue for more money later on. Now he knew that her reasoning had been the exact opposite. She hadn't signed or corresponded with him because she quite simply hadn't wanted *anything* from him.

Her signature and the date seemed to jump out at him. It had been signed that afternoon, less than an hour ago, with an initialed condition that Zara would not accept the payment offered on signing or any family share certificates or payment of any kind, ever.

He unlocked the door to the suite and stepped inside and the sense of cold seemed to grow more acute, because he instantly knew that the suite was empty. He quickly searched the rooms, but Zara and Rosie were gone, and he only had himself to blame.

He had accused Zara of being deceitful and manipulative, had seen her as a pretty gold digger looking for the good life, just like her mother. Now he knew how wrong he'd been.

Raw with grief over Tyler's death, he now realized he had jumped to conclusions and bought into the media hype, but it was a fact that Tyler had been no fool when it came to judging character. He'd had zero tolerance for superficial relationships or fortune hunters, and yet he had fallen for Petra, to the point of asking her to marry him.

The fact that Petra had insisted on the prenup, then Tyler had countered by gifting Petra a 10 percent stake in the company he had loved said it all. Damon had been wrong about Petra. And at a gut level he knew he had been utterly wrong about Zara.

Too late to remember that one of the things that had attracted him to Zara had been her fierce independence, her desire to forge her own way and not lean on anyone, least of all him.

Damon found the number for the airport while he took the elevator to the underground garage. After a short conversation, during which he managed to establish that there were flights leaving for London and Dubai in the next hour, Damon terminated the call. He found his car and accelerated out into the street.

Zara's taxi was stalled in traffic.

She spoke in rapid Medinian to the driver, but he simply gesticulated. A truck had overturned on the road; they were going nowhere. Maybe in a few minutes.

Craning around, she checked the traffic lined up behind, trying to see if she could spot Damon's glossy black car. She was almost certain she had glimpsed it as she and Rosie had slipped out of the hotel, which meant he would have received the document she'd left for him and knew they had gone.

A car honked; they inched forward. Long minutes later, they idled past the overturned vegetable truck, moving at a snail's pace. She asked the driver to go faster. He gave her a blank look in the rearview mirror.

A wad of Medinian notes solved the problem. Minutes later, the taxi was zooming toward the airport at breakneck speed. The cluttered streets of Medinos finally gave way to hilly countryside dotted with goats and ancient olive groves. Lush vineyards lined with vines that were festooned with leaves and dripping with ripe black grapes signaled that the airport, situated on a plateau in the midst of the most fertile land on Medinos, was near.

Zara's phone chimed and her heart almost stopped in her chest. She checked who was calling—Damon.

She turned the phone off and held on for dear life as the taxi careened into a space outside the departures gate. After muttering her thanks and shoving more money at the driver, she scrambled out and put Rosie in the stroller. Looping her handbag over one shoulder, she grabbed her suitcase with her spare hand and headed for the desk.

She checked the overhead computer. There was a flight leaving for London in forty minutes. She pressured the attendant behind the counter to let her get on the flight, but was flatly refused. Zara checked the screen; the next flight out was an hour and twenty minutes away.

Just when she was about to give up, she saw Jorge. She called out to him, and he turned, his expression comical.

He grinned and shook his head. "So you're not too famous to talk to me today."

He held up a tabloid paper and she almost died on the spot. There was a blurry picture of her and Damon kissing in the underground garage. The janitor hadn't just overheard them, he had snapped them as well, then sold the story.

She stared at the grainy photo, her mind working quickly. She hated the notoriety of it, but for once she was going to use it. She stared at Jorge. "Now you see why I have to get off Medinos. Can you help me?"

Twenty minutes later, and after paying an exorbitant amount for tickets, she and Rosie were personally escorted to their seats. Zara had had to buy first-class seats, but for once the money hadn't mattered, and first class had fitted with her celebrity-on-the-run-from-the-paparazzi plea.

A few minutes after that, the flight taxied out, but instead of taking off, it wheeled to a halt. Apparently, there were birds on the runway. Zara's stomach hollowed out. She was beginning to wonder if they would ever get off the ground.

Twelve

Damon terminated his latest attempt to call Zara when he arrived at the airport terminal. Like every other call had, it would go straight to voice mail. He had already left a message and Zara hadn't replied, so there was no sense leaving another.

He parked and headed for departures. The flight to London was already on the tarmac waiting to depart, but the Dubai flight had yet to board. He skimmed the passengers massed in the lounge. Zara wasn't there, so she must have boarded the first flight out, which was London bound.

He called Walter. He needed confirmation of which flight Zara had taken. Walter had connections in the aviation world. If anyone could get the information, quickly, he could.

Walter called him back a few minutes later and confirmed that Zara and Rosie were on the London flight.

Jaw tight, Damon watched as the jet began moving down the runway, picking up speed. A few seconds later it was in the air. Taking out his phone again, he called Mac. He had already asked her to fuel the jet and get ready to fly, but he was aware that they would have to queue.

It took an hour to file the flight plan, another hour to get a takeoff slot. When they were finally in the air, Damon opened up the file on his laptop and read through Walter's report in detail.

Zara was Petra's daughter and, yes, there were a few wild media stories about her, but on close inspection, there wasn't a lot of substance to any of them. He studied the few photos that were included and shook his head. There was a photo of a child who was recognizably Zara, cute in plaits, and a blurred snapshot of a teenager with dark hair who could be anyone. Finally, he stared incredulously at an article entitled Angel Parties Hard. It was an article supposedly about Angel Atrides, but the photograph depicted a long-haired bottle blonde who was a complete stranger.

Grimly, Damon read on. The claims that she slept around were outright lies. He knew that for a fact because Zara had only ever slept with him. Claims that she was a fortune hunter looking for a rich husband were similarly flawed, because she had clearly never been a party girl, or dated anyone who actually had a fortune, except himself, and she'd had no compunction about ditching him.

Walter hadn't just dug for information, he had mined.

After Petra's death, Zara had been saddled with Petra's funeral expenses. Damon knew she could have taken the easy way out and accepted his money, but instead, as a student, she had paid off her mother's funeral expenses in tiny increments until the debt was cleared.

Those were not the actions of a woman who was looking for some man to bankroll her lifestyle. She hadn't *had* a lifestyle. What she'd had were debts and worry, then a child to care for—his child—and a determination to make her own way. *Without him.*

Zara had no credit cards and almost no debt, just the mortgage on her business. Somehow, in this modern day and age, she managed to make all of her purchases with cash. From what Damon could glean, despite the Swiss finishing school and the jet-setting mother, Zara only bought what she could afford, and that was mostly necessities. No designer clothing or shoes, and definitely no jewelry. That meant the diamonds were exactly what she had claimed.

Security and stability.

The final nail in the coffin was the information he already knew, but which he had stubbornly ignored. When Zara had become pregnant and could have demanded money from him, she had determinedly made her own way.

Her business was a case in point. Zara had gotten her business degree, worked and saved, gotten a loan, then opened her own business. She had accepted him as a client only because she had needed the cash flow. Then she had insisted on dealing only with Howard, making it clear that she didn't want Damon to step any further into her life.

Closing the file, Damon checked the time. They wouldn't land for several hours. He needed to sleep, but first he needed to figure out how he was going to win back Zara when he had done his level best to drive her away.

When they landed at Heathrow, it was only to find that Zara and Rosie had caught a last-minute connection to Los Angeles.

Mac yawned. "What do we do now?"

Damon noted Zara's arrival time in LA. He didn't know if she would take a connecting flight from there, or choose to stop over. What mattered was that she appeared to be heading home.

"We get some dinner, get some sleep and then go home."

Zara paid the taxi driver, who obligingly wheeled her luggage through her front gate while Zara carried Rosie.

Rosie was not happy. She had been fractious on the red-eye flight from LA to Auckland, which had taken thirteen long, horrible hours. Her lashes were spiky from crying and her cheeks were red. Zara suspected that she was cutting another tooth, which was, literally, the last straw.

Blinking against the brilliance of the morning sun, when her body clock wanted it to be night, she unlocked the front door and carried Rosie through to her room and settled her in her crib.

Feeling dizzy with exhaustion, she trudged back out to the porch to claim her luggage, only to be buttonholed by Edna Cross, who was waiting on the step with a woman's magazine. "It says in here that you're the daughter of that famous supermodel—"

"Petra Hunt. She was my mother."

Edna blinked. "That explains why that blonde reporter was hanging around. I called the police on her."

The sun seemed to shine a little brighter. "Vanessa Gardiner. Way to go, Mrs. Cross."

"If she comes back, I can slap a harassment charge on her if you like."

"Will that work?"

"Probably not, but it'll make her life difficult."

Zara's chest suddenly felt a little tight. "Thank you, Mrs. Cross."

"You can call me Edna. Just being neighborly. If there's anything else you need, let me know."

Zara watched as Edna ambled back to her house. Across the road another neighbor—old Mr. Harris, who was out washing his car—paused and lifted a hand. It was a strange moment to feel that, finally, she belonged somewhere.

After depositing her bags in the sitting room and opening up a few windows to air out the house, she called Molly to see how she was coping. Apparently, owing to the media attention, they'd had an influx of new clients and there was a long list of new job applicants to screen. The magazine article, and a number of tabloid follow-ups, all of which Molly assured her she had hated, had done wonders for business. She'd had to take on one of their temps to cope with the increased workload and Harriet was proving to be a real gem.

Molly paused. "Are you really Angel Atrides and a *contessa*?"

Zara smothered a yawn. Now that she was home, tiredness was closing in. All she wanted to do was sleep. "Yes and yes. But the *contessa* thing is a bit like the sheikh taxi driver who just dropped me off. Without an estate and a huge bank account, it doesn't actually mean anything."

"Hmm. Harriet thinks it's an asset. She's had a lot of experience with public relations and thinks it could provide an important point of difference for the agency.

Not to mention an opportunity to harness the media attention in a good way."

After a brief discussion, Zara decided that with Harriet in the mix, she could take a few days off and disappear from sight until the media furor died down. Molly instantly offered Zara the use of a family beach house on Auckland's west coast.

Even though she was exhausted, Zara decided to leave straightaway. They were already packed and even though Rosie was still out of sorts, at least if they went for a drive in the car, she might fall asleep.

Two hours later, with Rosie bathed, changed and fed, all of her luggage transferred to the car and enough groceries to last a few days, Zara drove until she found the small cottage, which was situated on a windswept cliff overlooking a wild stretch of coastline. She found the key, which was sitting beneath a flowerpot, unlocked the door and began ferrying bags inside.

Rosie, thankfully, had fallen into a deep slumber, so Zara gently transferred her from her car seat to a portable crib she had managed to borrow from a friend.

The sun was sliding into the sea by the time she made herself a sandwich and a cup of tea for dinner and collapsed into a faded armchair. She woke hours later to find that she had fallen dead asleep in the chair and was now freezing cold. She blinked at the noise that had woken her and realized it was her phone.

Retrieving the cell from the kitchen table, she checked the screen. Her heart slammed hard against her chest. Damon had tried to call her for about the twentieth time.

She stared at her voice mail, which also registered a message from Damon. What she really needed to do was throw the whole phone, which belonged to Magnum Security, away.

Switching on a light, she checked on Rosie who was warmly cuddled up beneath thick blankets and searched out a sweater and a warm pair of socks for herself. She checked her watch as she filled a kettle with water so she could make a hot drink and was shocked to see it was only ten o'clock. She was about to turn the kettle on when she thought she heard a noise. Frowning, she listened hard. There was a road not far from the cottage, which led to a popular beach suburb, so there was traffic, but this didn't sound like a car.

Another sound, this one more distinct, made her stiffen. Suddenly wondering if a reporter had tracked her here and was even now sneaking up to the window to snap a photo of her, she grabbed the kettle, which was full of cold water. Instead of walking out the front door and being an instant target for anyone with a camera, she padded out the back door and walked quietly around the small cottage.

A low sound behind her spun her around. Damon's gaze locked with hers, but it was too late to stop the flight of the kettle which, out of sheer fright, she'd flung in the direction of the sound.

He caught the kettle, but water sprayed, drenching his dark jersey and jeans. "Remind me to put you on one of my security teams." He wiped water from his face. "No, cancel that. Walter said you should be running a war. I'm in complete agreement. You can run the teams."

Zara rubbed her arms against the biting cold and tried to ignore the fact that even dripping wet and probably just as tired as she, Damon looked certifiably gorgeous. "What are you doing here?"

"Looking for you."

"Why?"

"I found the note from Tyler. It was in the bank, like you said."

Her heart pounded at that, but she refused to let herself hope. "So you believed *Tyler*."

Turning on her heel, she walked back into the house, but despite every effort to be indifferent to Damon her pulse was hammering and she was hopelessly aware of him. A little desperately she wondered what it took to get rid of the zing of attraction, or the crazy, heady feeling of hope springing to life again.

If she let herself hope, she thought ruthlessly, she would only set herself up to be hurt again and she was over being hurt.

She flicked on lights, illuminating the tiny rooms with their jumble of mismatched furniture, the miniature kitchen that fitted two or three people at the most. When Damon stepped into the kitchen, the room seemed to shrink even more.

He put the kettle on the bench. "I'm sorry I frightened you. I thought I heard someone around the back."

"That would be me!"

"As it turned out."

Okay, so he had been protecting her. She tried not to feel happy about that as she filled the kettle with water again and put it on to boil. Feeling crazily nervous to have Damon so close, in her personal space when she never thought he would be again, she busied herself finding a towel.

In the meantime, Damon had peeled out of his jersey, which was soaked, and hung it over the back of a chair. Zara tried not to notice his bronzed biceps, or the way the T-shirt clung across his chest. She concentrated, instead, on making tea. After he had blotted the worst of the moisture from his T-shirt, Damon tossed the damp towel over the back of another chair.

She poured tea and handed him a mug. His gaze caught hers. "You were right. I didn't believe you, and for the reason you said. I have difficulty with...trust."

Leaning against the bench, he began to talk about his childhood, the words at first hard and slow, then flowing more smoothly. Ben had given Zara a brief outline of how Damon's life had gone, but he had barely scratched the surface. By the time Damon had finished, the tea had gone cold.

Zara set her mug down. "But growing up, you must have realized your parents' marriage was...dysfunctional."

He set his mug down, the drink untasted. "Maybe, but I wasn't exactly brought up under normal circumstances even after they died. Tyler was the closest thing Ben and I had to a real father—"

"And he was a confirmed bachelor until he met my mother."

"Then there was my stint in the army. I'm not making excuses. I'm just trying to explain why I've been so resistant to a real relationship."

Her head came up. For a long, vibrating moment she thought she'd heard wrong. "What do you mean by a real relationship?"

He caught the fingers of one hand and drew her close. "I mean you and me and a second chance."

"Why? Because of Rosie?"

He pulled her closer still. "You know it's not about Rosie. I love her, she's my daughter and finding her jolted me. But it was falling for you and losing you that made me realize how empty my life was. I've been trying to control my relationships but that approach never worked. Lily hit it right on the button. If I refused to risk myself and go out on a limb for someone else, I couldn't expect to be in a relationship."

"Which explains why you walked away from me when you found me in Dunedin over a year ago!"

His gaze locked with hers. "I didn't say I wasn't stubborn. But, when you came back to town, it didn't take me long to track you down. And once I did, I tried to stay close. Why do you think I kept employing your temps?"

She tried not to drown in the molten heat of his gaze. "I did wonder." She suddenly remembered the question that had gnawed at her earlier. "By the way, how *did* you find me this time?"

"GPS. You've got a company phone."

She tried to breathe, but it seemed to be getting awfully hot and close in the tiny kitchen. "I was thinking of throwing the SIM card away."

He grinned. "Why do you think I got here so fast?"

He reached into his pocket and she caught the glint of something shiny. Her heart slammed hard in her chest. At first she thought he was returning the earrings to her, but she was wrong. It was an engagement ring.

Suddenly all the vulnerabilities that had gone with loving Damon surged back. If they were going to do this, she couldn't bear it if it all fell apart again.

Damon went down on one knee, with difficulty, because the space between the kitchen counter and the small table was so cramped. One shoulder bumped against a shelf of pots, sending a lid spinning onto the tiled floor. When Zara stepped back to allow him more room, a chair crashed to the floor. The noise woke Rosie, who began to make cute sounds in her room. It was bedlam and it was the most romantic thing that had ever happened.

Damon gripped her hand. "I don't want to lose you again. I've loved you from the first moment you stepped into that interview room. The problem was, you made me feel too much and I had gotten used to closing down and looking for reasons not to trust. I'm sorry, babe—I didn't mean to hurt you. I just didn't have the courage to admit that I needed you. When you walked out on me this time, I knew that I loved you. It was too late, but I finally understood exactly what I wanted. You, Rosie and the home we can make together, if only you'll trust *me*."

Damon grasped her left hand. "Will you marry me, for better or worse, for richer or poorer?"

The vows of the marriage service made Zara's throat close up so that when she spoke her voice was husky. "That's all I ever wanted. I just hadn't thought it was possible."

But as Damon slid the engagement ring onto the third finger of her left hand, and rose up to kiss her—knocking his mug of tea into the sink—she suddenly realized that it was more than possible.

Two people truly, honestly in love, and their baby.

It was real and just a little chaotic, and she knew it was going to be *perfect*.

* * * * *

MIRACLE ON
KAIMOTU ISLAND

MARION LENNOX

To the men and women of Christchurch
—and to one amazing paramedic.
Rosie, you're awesome.

PROLOGUE

No one knew how old Squid Davies was. The locals of Kaimotu could hardly remember the time he'd given up his fishing licence, much less when he'd been a lad.

Now his constant place was perched on the oil drums behind the wharf, where the wind couldn't douse a man's pipe, where the sun hit his sea-leathered face and where he could see every boat that went in and out of Kaimotu harbour. From here he could tell anyone who listened what he knew—and he did know.

'She'll be a grand day at sea today, boys,' he'd say, and the locals would set their sights on the furthest fishing grounds, or 'She'll be blowing a gale by midnight,' and who needed the official forecasters? Kaimotu's fishermen knew better than to argue. They brought their boats in by dusk.

But now...

'She's going to be bigger'n that one that hit when my dad's dad was a boy,' Squid intoned in a voice of doom. 'I know what my grandpa said, and it's here now. Pohutukawa trees are flowering for the second time. Mutton birds won't leave their chicks. They should be long gone by now, leaving the chicks to follow, but they won't leave 'em. And then there's waves hitting the shore on Beck's Beach. They don't come in from the north in April—it's not natural. I tell you, the earth moved in 1886 and this'll be bigger.'

It had to be nonsense, the locals told themselves nervously. There'd been one earth tremor two weeks back, enough to crack a bit of plaster, break some crockery, but the seismologists on the mainland, with all the finest technology at their disposal, said a tremor was all there was to it. If ever there was a sizeable earthquake it'd be on the mainland, on the fault line, through New Zealand's South Island, not here, on an island two hundred miles from New Zealand's northern most tip.

But: 'There's rings round the moon, and even the oyster-catchers are keeping inland,' Squid intoned, and the locals tried to laugh it off but didn't quite manage it. The few remaining summer tourists made weak excuses to depart, and the island's new doctor, who was into omens in a big way, decided she didn't want to live on Kaimotu after all.

'Will you cut it out?' Ben McMahon, Kaimotu's only remaining doctor, squared off with Squid in exasperation. 'You've lost us a decent doctor. You're spooking the tourists and locals alike. Go back to weather forecasting.'

'I'm only saying what I'm feelin',' Squid said morosely, staring ominously out at the horizon. 'The big 'un's coming. Nothing surer.'

CHAPTER ONE

PREDICTIONS OF EARTHQUAKES. Hysteria. One lone doctor. Dr Ben McMahon was busy at the best of times and now there weren't enough hours in the day to see everyone who wanted to be seen. His clinic was chaos.

There was, though, another doctor on the island, even though she'd declared she was no longer practising medicine. Up until now Ben had let Ginny be, but Squid's doomsday forecasting meant he needed her.

Again?

The last time Ben McMahon had asked anything of Guinevere Koestrel he'd been down on one knee, as serious as a seventeen-year-old boy could be, pouring his teenage heart out to the woman he adored.

And why wouldn't he adore her? She'd been his friend since she was eight, ever since Ginny's parents had bought the beautiful island vineyard as their hobby/holiday farm and Ben's mother had become Ginny's part-time nanny. They'd wandered the island together, fished, swum, surfed, fought, defended each other to the death—been best friends.

But that last summer hormones had suddenly popped up everywhere. On the night of his ill-advised proposal Ginny had been wearing a fabulous gown, bought by her wealthy parents for the island's annual New Year's Eve Ball. He'd

been wearing an ill-fitting suit borrowed from a neighbour.
Her appearance had stunned him.

But social differences were dumb, he'd told himself. Suddenly it had seemed vital to his seventeen-year-old self that
they stay together for ever.

Surely she could change her plans to study medicine in
Sydney, he told her. He planned to be a doctor, too. There
was a great medical course in Auckland and he'd won a
scholarship. If he worked nights he could manage it, and
surely Ginny could join him.

But the seventeen-year-old Ginny had smiled—quite
kindly—and told him he was nuts. Her life was in Sydney.
The tiny New Zealand island of Kaimotu was simply a place
where she and her parents came to play. Besides, she had no
intention of marrying a man who called her Carrots.

That had been twelve years ago. Ben had long since put
the humiliation of adolescent love behind him, but now there
was a more important question. Ginny had been back on the
island for six months now. She'd signalled in no uncertain
terms that she wanted privacy but Ginny Koestrel was a doctor and a doctor was what the island needed. Now. Which
was why, even though looking at her brought back all sorts
of emotions he'd thought he'd long suppressed, he was asking yet again.

'Ginny, I need you.'

But the answer would be the same—he knew it. Ginny
was surrounded by grapevines, armed with a spray gun,
and she was looking at him like he was an irritating interruption to her work.

'I'm sorry, Ben, but I have no intention of working as a
doctor again. I have no intention of coming near your clinic.
Meanwhile, if these vines aren't sprayed I risk black rot. If
you don't mind…'

She squirted her spray gun at the nearest vine. She wasn't

good. She sprayed too high and lost half the mist to the breeze.

Ben lifted the spray pack from her back, aimed the gun at the base of the vine and watched the spray drift up through the foliage.

'Vaccination is one of my many medical skills,' he told her, settling a little, telling himself weird emotions were simply a reaction to shared history, nothing to do with now. They both watched as the spray settled where it should, as emotions settled where they should. 'There's a good vine, that didn't hurt at all, did it?' he said, adopting his very best professional tone. 'If you grow good grapes next year, the nice doctor will give you some yummy compost.' He grinned at the astounded Ginny. 'That's the way you should treat 'em, Carrots. Didn't they teach you anything in your fancy medical school?'

Ginny flushed. 'Cut it out, Ben, and don't you dare call me Carrots. In case you haven't noticed, it's auburn.' She hauled her flaming curls tighter into the elastic band, and glowered.

'Ginny, then.'

'And not Ginny either. And I'm a farmer, not a doctor.'

'I don't actually care who you are,' Ben said, deciding he needed to be serious if he was to have a chance of persuading her. 'You have a medical degree, and I'm desperate. It's taken me twelve months to find a family doctor to fill old Dr Reg's place. Dr Catherine Bolt seemed eminently sensible, but she's lived up to her name. One minor earth tremor and she's bolted back to the mainland.'

'You're kidding.'

'I'm not kidding.' He raked his hand through his hair, remembering how relieved he'd been when the middle-aged Catherine had arrived and how appalled he'd felt when she'd left. He really was alone.

'Every New Zealander has felt earth tremors,' he told Ginny. 'We're not known as the shaky isles for nothing. But you know Squid's set himself up as Forecaster of Doom. With no scientific evidence at all he's been droning on about double flowers of the pohutukawa tree and strange tides and weird bird behaviour and every portent of catastrophe he can think of. There's something about a shrivelled fisherman with a blackened pipe and a voice of doom that gets the natives twitchy. 'As well as losing us our doctor, I now have half the islanders demanding a year's supply of medication so they can see out the apocalypse.'

She smiled, but faintly. 'So you want me on hand for the end of the world?'

'There's no scientific evidence that we're heading for a major earthquake,' he said with dangerous calm. 'But we do have hysteria. Ginny, help me, please.'

'I'm sorry, Ben, but no.'

'Why on earth did you do medicine if you won't practise?'

'That's my business.'

He stared at her in baffled silence. She was a different woman from the one he'd proposed to twelve years ago, he thought. Well, of course she would be. His mother had outlined a sketchy history she'd winkled out of the returning Ginny, a marriage ending in tragedy, but...but...

For some reason he found himself looking at the elastic band. Elastic band? A Koestrel?

Ginny's parents were the epitome of power and wealth. Her father was a prominent Sydney neurosurgeon and her mother's sole purpose was to play society matron. Twice a year they spent a month on the island, in the vineyard they'd bought—no doubt as a tax deduction—flying in their friends, having fabulous parties.

The last time he'd seen Ginny she'd been slim, beautiful, but also vibrant with life. She'd been bouncy, glowing, aching to start medicine, aching to start life. Ready to thump him if he still called her Carrots.

In the years since that youthful proposal he'd realised how wise she'd been not to hurl herself into marriage at seventeen. He'd forgiven her—nobly, he decided—and he'd moved on, but in the back of his mind she'd stayed bouncy, vibrant and glowing. Her mother had carefully maintained her fabulous exterior and he'd expected Ginny to do the same.

She hadn't. The Ginny he was facing now wore elastic bands. Worse, she looked…grim. Flat.

Old? She couldn't be thirty, and yet… How much had the death of a loved one taken out of her?

Did such a death destroy life?

'Ginny—'

'No,' she snapped. 'I've come back to work the vineyard, and that's all.'

'The harvest is long over.'

'I don't care. I'm spraying for…something, whatever Henry told me I had to spray for. When I finish spraying I need to gear up for pruning. Henry's decided to retire and I need to learn. I'm sorry, Ben, but I'm no longer a doctor. I'm a winemaker. Good luck with finding someone who can help you.'

And then she paused. A car was turning into the driveway. A rental car.

It must be Sydney friends, Ben thought, come over on the ferry, but Ginny wasn't dressed for receiving guests. She was wearing jeans, an ancient windcheater, no make-up and she had mud smeared on her nose. A Koestler welcoming guests looking like a farmhand? No and no and no.

'Now what?' she said tightly, and she took the spray pack from Ben and turned to another vine. 'Have you brought reinforcements? Don't you know I have work to do?'

'This isn't anyone to do with me,' Ben said, and watched

who was climbing out of Kaimotu's most prestigious hire car. The guy looked like a businessman, he thought, and a successful one at that. He was sleek, fortyish, wearing an expensive suit and an expression of disdain as he glanced around at the slightly neglected vineyard. The man opened the trunk and tossed out a holdall. Then he opened the back car door—and tugged out a child.

She was a little girl, four or five years old. She almost fell as her feet hit the ground, but the man righted her as if she was a thing, not a person.

'Guinevere Koestrel?' he called, and headed towards them, tugging the child beside him. 'I'm Richard Harris, from Harris, Styne and Wilkes, partners in law from Sydney. You were expecting me? Or you were expecting the child?'

There was a long silence while Ginny simply stared, dumbstruck, at the incongruous couple approaching.

'I…I guess,' she managed at last. 'But not yet.'

The lawyer was tugging the child closer and as he did…

Down's syndrome, Ben thought. The markers were obvious. The little girl was beautifully dressed, her neat black hair was cropped into a smart little cut, there was a cute hair ribbon perched on top—but nothing could distract from the Down's features.

He glanced back at Ginny, and he saw every vestige of colour had drained from her face. Instinctively he put out a hand to steady her and she grabbed it, as desperately as if she'd been drowning.

'I didn't expect…' she said. 'I thought…this wouldn't happen for months. The legal processes…'

'Our client was prepared to pay whatever was needed to free her to go to Europe,' the man said, clipped and formal. 'We sent you emails. We received no response and we had no phone contact. Our client left the country last Friday, giving us no choice but to bring her. We had a nanny accompany us to New Zealand but the girl gets seasick and refused to come on the ferry.'

He gazed down at the child, and at the look on his face Ben wondered how much leverage had been applied to make such a man do a job like this. A lot, he was sure.

'I don't…I don't check emails any more,' Ginny managed, and the lawyer looked at her as if she was a sandwich short of a picnic. A woman who didn't check emails? His expression said she must be as disabled as the child beside him.

But… 'No matter,' he said, making a hasty recovery. 'My only fear was that I wouldn't find you, but now you're here this is the official handover. According to the documents we mailed to you last month, you've accepted responsibility for her. Her mother's left for Europe. Her instructions were to deliver her to you and here she is.'

And he propelled her forward, pushing her away from him, a little girl in a pretty pink dress, with pink sandals and an expression that said she didn't have one idea of what was happening to her.

If she weren't a Down's child, she'd be sobbing, Ben thought, but he knew enough about the syndrome to know sobbing was a last resort. But still…

'Oh, my…' Ginny said faintly, and Ben's hold on her tightened still further. He'd seen patients in shock before, and Ginny was showing every symptom.

'Ginny, what is this? What's going on?'

Ginny gave herself a shake, as if trying to rid herself of a nightmare. She, too, was staring down at the child. 'I… This is…'

She stopped and looked helplessly towards the lawyer and then at the little girl beside him. 'Tell him,' she said weakly. 'Please…tell Ben.'

And the lawyer was happy to comply. He was obviously

wanting a businesslike response and it looked like he'd decided Ben was the most likely to give it.

'This is Barbara Carmody,' the man said, clipped and efficient, not even looking at the little girl as he introduced her. 'The child's the result of an extra-marital affair between my client and Dr Koestrel's late husband. Her mother raised her with her other two children but unfortunately her husband has finally discovered that the child isn't his. He's rejected her. The marriage has failed and Mrs Carmody has left for Europe.'

'Her parents have deserted her?' Ben said incredulously.

'There are provisions for her care,' the lawyer said smoothly. 'Dr Koestrel's late husband left funds in his will for this eventuality, and there are institutions that will take her. On Mrs Carmody's instructions we contacted Dr Koestrel for the release of those funds but instead of releasing money she's agreed to take on her care. So here she is. The paperwork's all in her suitcase. If you need to contact her mother, do it through us—the address is with her papers. If you could sign the included documents and forward them to our office I'd appreciate it. If you'll excuse me, I don't wish to miss the return ferry. Good afternoon.'

And he turned back towards the car.

The little girl didn't move. Neither did Ginny.

The man was about to walk away and leave the child behind.

No.

Ben strode to the car, slammed closed the car door the lawyer was attempting to open then set himself between lawyer and car while Ginny stood in stunned, white-faced silence.

The little girl didn't move. She didn't look at the lawyer. She didn't look at anyone.

'Abandoning a child's a criminal offence,' Ben said, quite

mildly, looking from the little girl to Ginny and back again. Ginny was staring at the child as if she was seeing a ghost.

'There must be formal proceedings...'

'I'll miss my ferry,' the man said. 'Dr Koestrel has signed the most important documents. Additional paperwork can be sent later.'

'You can't dump a child because you'll miss your ferry,' Ben said, and folded his arms, settling back, not understanding what was going on but prepared to be belligerent until he did.

'Dr Koestrel's agreed to take her. I'm not dumping anyone.'

'So...what did you say? Barbara's the result of an affair between some woman and...Ginny's late husband? Ginny, can you explain?'

'W-wait,' Ginny managed. She looked helplessly at the little girl and then something seemed to firm. Shock receded a little, just a little. She took a deep breath and reached out and took the little girl's hand.

She led her to the edge of the vines, where a veggie garden was loaded with the remains of a rich autumn harvest. Lying beside the garden was a hose. She turned it on and a stream of water shot out.

'Barbara,' she said, crouching with water squirting out of the hose. 'Can you give my tomatoes a drink while we talk? Can you do that for us?

The little girl looked at the hose, at the enticing stream of water. She gave the merest hint of a smile. Whatever had been happening in this child's life in the last few days, Ben thought, she needed time out and somehow Ginny had a sense of how to give it to her.

'Yes,' the girl said, and Ginny smiled and handed over the hose then faced Ben and the lawyer again.

'James...died six months ago,' she managed. 'Of non-

Hodgkin's lymphoma.' Then she stopped again and stared across at the little girl fiercely watering tomatoes. She looked like she could find no words.

'So tell me about this child.' Ben still had his arms folded. The guy in the suit with his professional detachment in the face of such a situation was making him feel ill, but he glanced at Ginny again and knew he needed to keep hold of his temper. He needed facts. 'What's her full name?'

'I told you...Barbara Louise Carmody. Everything's in the case. All her paperwork. Get out of my way, please,' the lawyer snapped. 'I'm leaving.'

'Ginny...' Ben said urgently, but Ginny wasn't looking at him. Or at the lawyer. She was staring at the tiny, dark-eyed girl.

'This...this little girl broke my heart,' she whispered, and Ben suddenly figured it out. Or the bones of it. Her husband had fathered a child with someone else. She'd faced her husband's death, and now she was coping with betrayal as well as loss.

How could anyone expect her to accept this child? he wondered incredulously. How could she even bear to look at her? But she'd reacted to her with instinctive protectiveness. At such an age, with Down's, with a hose in her hand and plants to water, the hurtful words around the little girl would disappear.

But...*she'd said she'd take her. Indefinitely?*

'Do you have her medical records in her luggage?' Ginny asked, in a cold, dead voice.

'Of course,' the lawyer said smoothly. 'I told you. Everything's there.'

'Did you know she's Down's?' Ben demanded, and Ginny nodded.

'Yes, I did. I'm sorry, I should be more prepared. This is fine.' She took a deep breath, visibly hauling herself together. 'You can go,' she told the lawyer. 'You're right, the documentation can happen later. Thank you for bringing her to me. I regret I didn't receive the emails but I'd still rather have her here now than have her spend time in an institution.'

Then she stooped down and took the little girl's hands in hers, hose and all, and she met that long, serious gaze full on as the water sprayed sideways. And Ben saw the re-emergence of the Ginny he knew, the Ginny who faced challenges head on, his brave, funny Ginny who faced down the world.

'I was married to your...to your father,' she said. 'That means I'm your stepmum. If it's okay with you, Barbara, I'll look after you now. You can live with me. I need help watering all my plants. I need help doing all sorts of things. We might even have fun together. I'd like that and I hope you'll like it, too.'

CHAPTER TWO

THERE WAS NOTHING else Ben could think of to say. The lawyer climbed into his rental car and drove away. The car disappeared below the ridge, and the sound faded to nothing.

There was a long, long silence. Somewhere a plover was
calling to its mate. The sea was a glistening backdrop, the
soft hush-hush of the surf a whisper on the warm sea breeze.

Ginny's world had been fragmented and was now float-
ing in pieces, Ben thought.

He thought of her blank refusal to practise medicine. He
thought of the unknown husband's death. He thought of her
accepting the responsibility for a child not hers, and he knew
that fragmentation hadn't happened today. It was the result
of past history he knew little about.

He'd hardly talked to her for years. He knew nothing of
what had happened to her in the interim except the bare
bones she'd told his mother when she'd returned to the island, but now she was kneeling beside the tomatoes, holding Barbara, looking bereft, and he felt his heart twist as…
as Ginny had made his heart twist all those years before.

But now wasn't the time for emotion. He flipped open
the child's suitcase and searched, fast. If the medical and
legal stuff wasn't there he could still stop the lawyer from
leaving the island.

But it was all there, a neat file detailing medical history, family history, lawyer's contacts, even contacts for the pre-school she'd been going to.

She might not have been loved but she'd been cared for, Ben thought grimly.

How could a family simply desert her?

'She has Mosaic Down's,' he said out loud, skimming through the medical history, and Ginny closed her eyes. She'd know what that meant, though. Mosaic Downs meant the faulty division of chromosomes had happened after fertilisation, meaning every cell wasn't necessarily affected.

But it was still bad. Barbara had the distinct look of Down's. Who knew what organs were affected?

Taking on a child was huge, Ben thought. Taking on a Down's child...

Barbara had gone back to watering. She was totally occupied in directing the hose. They could talk.

They needed to talk.

'Ginny, are you serious?' he said urgently. 'I can still stop him.'

'And then what'll happen?' She shook herself. 'No. I'm sorry. I'm not handling this well. I did know this was coming. I did agree to this, even if it's happened sooner than I thought. I *will* look after her.'

'No one can ask that of you,' Ben said, and Ginny met his gaze head on. There was a long silence and then she gave a decisive nod, a gesture he remembered.

'No,' she said. 'They can't, but I will. Veronica and James did exactly what they wanted. Their selfishness was boundless but there's no way this little one should suffer. James's death set me free, and Barbara should be free as well, not stuck in some institution for the disabled.' She managed to smile at the little girl—but then she felt silent again.

She was overwhelmed, Ben thought, and rightly so. Her world had just been turned on its head.

And Barbara? She was totally silent. She didn't look upset, though. She simply stood patiently watering, waiting for what came next.

Down's syndrome…

A man could mount arguments, Ben thought, for giving the whole human race Down's. Yes, it took Down's kids longer to learn things. Down's kids seldom reached average intellectual milestones, but, on the other hand, the Down's patients he had were friendly, selfless and desired little more than for those around them to be happy.

He walked forward and crouched beside Barbara. Ginny seemed almost incapable of speech. Maybe she'd said what she needed to say, and it was as if she didn't know where to go from here.

'Hi,' Ben said to the little girl. 'I'm Dr Ben.'

If he was right about this little one being well cared for, physically at least, then she'd be accustomed to doctors, he thought. Strange places would be associated with medical tests. Using the term 'doctor' might make this situation less strange.

And he was right. The little girl turned her gaze to him, but not to him personally. To his top pocket.

The arc of water went wild and no one cared.

'Jelly bean?' she said hopefully, and he grinned because some things were universal. Doctors' bribes.

'Jelly baby,' he said, and fished a yellow jelly baby from a packet in his shirt pocket. She took it gravely and then continued gazing at him—assessing him for more?

'Do you like jelly babies, Barbara?' he asked, and she frowned.

'Not…not Barbara,' she whispered.

'You're not Barbara?'

'Not Barbara,' she said, suddenly distressed. She looked down at her pink dress, dropped the hose and grabbed a button and pulled, as if trying to see it, as if trying to reassure herself it was still there. 'Button.'

'Button?' Ben repeated, and the little girl's face reacted as if a light had been turned on.

'Button,' she said in huge satisfaction, and Ben thought someone, somewhere—a nanny perhaps—had decided that Barbara was far too formal for this little girl, and Button it was.

'Your name is Button,' Ginny whispered, and Ben saw a wash of anger pass over her face. Real anger. Anger at her late husband and the unknown Veronica? He watched as she fought it down and tried for calm. 'Button, your mum's sent you to me so I can look after you. Maybe watering these tomatoes can wait. Would you like to come inside and have a glass of lemonade?'

'Yes,' Button said, and Ginny smiled. And then she looked uncertain.

'I have nothing,' she faltered. 'I really wasn't expecting her until next month. I don't know...'

'Tell you what,' Ben said, rising and dusting dirt from his knees. What was happening here was dramatic but he still had imperatives. Those imperatives had seen him take time out to try and persuade Ginny to be a doctor. That was a no go, especially now, but he still had at least twenty patients to see before he called it a day.

'You take Button inside and give her lemonade, then go through her suitcase and see what she has. When you have it sorted, bring her down to the clinic. I can give Button a good once-over—make sure everything's okay...'

'I can do that.'

'So you can,' he said. 'You're a doctor. Okay, forget the once-over. But our clinic nurse, Abby, has a five-year-old and she's a mum. If you don't need a doctor, you might need a mum to tell you all the things you're likely to need, to lend you any equipment you don't have. I have a child seat in the back of my Jeep—I use the Jeep for occasional patient transport. I'll leave it with you so you can bring Button down. I'll have Abby organise you another—the hire car place has seats they loan out.'

'I... Thank you.'

He hesitated, and once again he felt the surge of emotion he thought he'd long forgotten. Which was crazy. One long-ago love affair should make no difference to how he reacted to this woman now. 'Ginny, is this okay?' he demanded, trying to sound professionally caring—instead of personally caring. 'Are you sure you don't want me to ring Bob—he's the local cop—and have him drag the lawyer from the ferry?'

She looked at him then, really looked at him, and it was as if somehow what she saw gave her strength.

'No. I'm okay,' she said. 'I need to be. I don't have a choice and neither does Button. Thank you for your help, but we'll be fine.'

'You will bring her to the clinic?'

She hesitated. 'Yes,' she conceded at last.

'Big of you.'

She gave a faint smile. 'Sorry. I guess I'm not up for awards for good manners right now. But I am grateful. I'll come to the clinic when I need to. Thank you, Ben, and goodbye.'

She watched him go and she felt...desolate.

Desolate was how she'd been feeling for six months now. Or more.

Once upon a time her life had been under control. She was the indulged only daughter of wealthy, influential people. She was clever and she was sure of herself.

There'd been a tiny hiccup in her life when as a teenager

she'd thought she'd fallen in love with Ben McMahon, but even then she'd been enough in control to figure it out, to bow to her parents' dictates.

Sure, she'd thought Ben was gorgeous, but he was one of twelve kids, the son of the nanny her parents had hired to take care of her whenever they had been on the island. At seventeen she'd long outgrown the need for a nanny but she and Ben had stayed friends.

He had been her holiday romance, welcoming her with joy whenever her parents had come to the island, being her friend, sharing her first kiss, but he had been an escape from the real world, not a part of it.

His proposal that last year when they'd both finished school had been a shock, questioning whether her worlds could merge, and she'd known they couldn't. Her father had spelled that out in no uncertain terms.

Real life was the ambition her parents had instilled in her. Real life had been the circle she'd moved in in her prestigious girls' school.

Real life had become medicine, study, still the elite social life she'd shared with her parents' circle, then James, marriage, moving up the professional scale...

But even before James had been diagnosed with non-Hodgkin's lymphoma she'd known something had been dreadfully wrong. Or maybe she'd always known something had been wrong, she conceded. It was just that it had taken more courage than she'd had to admit it.

Then her father had died, dramatically, of a heart attack. She'd watched her mother, dry eyed at the funeral, already gathering the trappings of rich widow about her.

The night of the funeral James had had to go out. 'Work,' he'd said, and had kissed her perfunctorily. 'Go to bed, babe, and have a good cry. Cry and get over it.'

Like her mother, she hadn't cried either.

She'd thought that night… She'd known but she hadn't wanted to face it. If she worked hard enough, she didn't have to face it.

'Lemonade or raspberry cordial?' she asked Button. She sat her at the kitchen table and put lemonade in front of her and also the red cordial. Button looked at them both gravely and finally decided on red. Huge decision. Her relief at having made it almost made Ginny smile.

Almost.

She found herself remembering the day of James's funeral. It had been the end of a truly appalling time, when she'd fought with every ounce of her medical knowledge to keep him and yet nothing could hold him. He'd been angry for his entire illness, angry at his body for betraying him, at the medical profession that couldn't save him, but mostly at Ginny, who was healthy when he wasn't.

'—you, Florence Nightingale.' The crude swearing was the last thing he'd said to her, and she'd stood at his graveside and felt sick and cold and empty.

And then she'd grown aware of Veronica. Veronica was the wife of James's boss. She'd walked up to Ginny, ostensibly to hug her, but as she'd hugged, she'd whispered.

'You didn't lose him. You never had him in the first place. You and my husband were just the stage props for our life. What we had was fun, fantasy, everything life should be.'

And then Veronica's assumed face was back on, her wife-of-James's-boss mantle, and Ginny thought maybe she'd imagined it.

But then she'd read James's will.

'To my daughter, Barbara, to be held in trust by my wife, Guinevere, to be used at her discretion if Barbara's true parentage is ever discovered.'

She remembered a late-night conversation the week before James had died. She'd thought he was rambling.

'The kid. He thinks it's his. If he finds out…I'll do the right thing. Bloody kid should be in a home anyway. Do the right thing for me, babe. I know you will—you always do the right thing. Stupid cow.'

Was this just more? she thought, pouring a second glass for the obviously thirsty little girl. Guinevere doing the right thing. Guinevere being a stupid cow?

'I'm not Guinevere, I'm Ginny,' she said aloud, and her voice startled her, but she knew she was right.

Taking Button wasn't doing something for James or for Veronica or for anyone, she told herself. This was purely between *her* and Button.

They'd move on, together.

'Ginny,' Button said now, trying the name out for size, and Ginny sat at the table beside this tiny girl and tried to figure it out.

Ginny and Button.

Two of a kind? Two people thrown out of their worlds?

Only she hadn't been thrown. She'd walked away from medicine and she'd walked away from Sydney.

Her father had left her the vineyard. It had been a no-brainer to come here.

And Ben…

Was Ben the reason she'd come back here?

So many thoughts…

Ben's huge family. Twelve kids. She remembered the day her mother had dropped her off, aged all of eight. 'This woman's looking after you today, Guinevere,' she'd told her. 'Your father and I are playing golf. Be good.'

She'd got a hug from Ben's mother, a huge welcoming beam. 'Come on in, sweetheart, welcome to our muddle.'

She'd walked into the crowded jumble that had been their home and Ben had been at the stove, lifting the lid on pop-corn just as it popped.

Kernels were going everywhere, there were shouts of laughter and derision, the dogs were going nuts, the place was chaos. And eight-year-old Ben was smiling at her.

'Ever made popcorn? Want to give it a go? Reckon the dog's got this lot. And then I'll take you taddying.'

'Taddying?'

'Looking for tadpoles,' he'd said, and his eight-year-old eyes had gleamed with mischief. 'You're a real city slicker, aren't you?'

And despite what happened next—or maybe because of it—they'd been pretty much best friends from that moment.

She hadn't come back for Ben; she knew she hadn't, but maybe that was part of the pull that had brought her back to the island. Uncomplicated acceptance. Here she could lick her wounds in private. Figure out where she'd go from here.

Grow grapes?

With Button.

'We need to make you a bedroom,' she told Button, and the little girl's face grew suddenly grave.

'I want Monkey in my bedroom,' she said.

Monkey? Uh-oh.

She flipped open the little girl's suitcase. It was neatly packed—dresses, pyjamas, knickers, socks, shoes, coats. There was a file containing medical records and a small box labelled 'Medications'. She flipped this open and was relieved to find nothing more sinister than asthma medication.

But no monkey.

She remembered her mother's scorn from years ago as she'd belligerently packed her beloved Barny Bear to bring to the island.

'Leave that grubby thing at home, Guinevere. You have far nicer toys.'

'I want Monkey,' Button whispered again, and Ginny looked at her desolate little face and thought Button couldn't have fought as she had. Despite her mother's disgust, Ginny had brought Barny, and she'd loved him until he'd finally, tragically been chewed to bits by one of Ben's family's puppies.

But fighting for a soft toy wouldn't be in Button's skill range, she thought, and then she realised that's what she'd taken on from this moment. Fighting on Button's behalf.

She tried to remember now the sensations she'd felt when she'd received the lawyer's initial documents laying out why Button was being deserted by the people who'd cared for her. Rage? Disgust? Empathy?

This was a child no one wanted.

Taking her in had seemed like a good idea, even noble. Veronica and James had acted without morality. She'd make up for it, somehow.

Alone?

She was glad Ben had been here when Button had arrived. She sort of wanted him here now. He'd know how to cope with a missing Monkey.

Or not. Don't be a wimp, she told herself. You can do this. And then she thought, You don't have a choice.

But…he had offered to help.

'I guess you left Monkey at home,' she told Button, because there was no other explanation but the truth. 'I might be able to find someone who'll send him to us, but for now… let's have lunch and then we'll go down to Dr Ben's clinic. I don't have any monkeys here, but Dr Ben might know someone who does.'

Ben had told her the clinic would be busy but she'd had no concept of just how busy. There were people queued up through the waiting room and into the corridor beyond.

Plague? Ginny thought, but none of the people here looked

really ill. There were a few people looking wan amongst
them but most looked in rude health.

She'd led Button into the reception area, but she took one
look and tugged Button backwards. But as she did, an inner
door swung open. Ben appeared, followed by a harassed-
looking nurse.

Ben-the-doctor.

She'd seen him a couple of times since she'd returned to
the island. She'd met him once in the main street where he'd
greeted her with pleasure and she'd been calmly, deliberately
pleasant. But dismissive. She'd returned to the island to get
some peace, to learn about vineyards, but to treat the place
as her parents had treated it—an escape. She'd had no intention of being sucked into island life.

Then this afternoon he'd asked her to help him—and then
he'd helped her. She'd been incredibly grateful that he'd been
there to face down the lawyer on her behalf.

But now he was facing, what, twenty patients, with one
harried-looking nurse helping.

He looked competent, though, she thought, and then she
thought, no, he looked more than competent.

At seventeen they'd shared their first kiss after a day's
truly excellent surfing, and there had been a reason she'd
thought she'd fallen in love with him. He'd been her best
friend but he had been an awesome surfer, he'd been kind
and…cute?

There was no way she'd describe Ben as cute now. Twelve
years had filled out that lanky frame, had turned boy into
man, and the man he'd become…

He was tall, lean, ripped. He had sun-bleached brown hair
and sea-blue eyes. Did he still surf? He looked a bit weathered, so maybe he did. He was wearing chinos, a shirt and
a tie, but the shirtsleeves were rolled up and the tie was a

bit askew, as if he'd been working hard and was expecting more work to come.

He'd taken time out today to visit her. That was why the queue had built up, she thought, and then she thought taking time out must have been an act of desperation. He'd made himself later still in an attempt to get the help he desperately needed.

He was surrounded by need. He looked harassed to the point of exhaustion.

'Ginny,' he said flatly as he saw her, and then managed a smile. 'Hi, Button.' He sighed. 'Ginny, I need to spend some time with you and Button—I reckon she does need that check-up—but as you can see, I'm under pressure. Do you think you could come back in an hour or so? I hadn't expected you so soon.'

An hour or so. She looked around the waiting room and thought…an hour or so?

She knew this island. There was a solid fishing community, and there were always tourists, but there was also a fair proportion of retirees, escapees from the rat race of the mainland, so there were thus many elderly residents.

What was the bet that Ben would have half a dozen house calls lined up after clinic? she thought, and glanced at his face, saw the tension and knew she was right.

'Can I help?' she said, almost before she knew she intended to say it.

His face stilled. 'You said…'

'For this afternoon only,' she said flatly. 'But you helped me with Button.' As if that explained everything—which it didn't. 'If there's someone who could care for Button…'

'You're sure?' Ben's face stilled with surprise, but before she could speak he shook his head. 'Stupid, stupid, stupid. The lady's made the offer in front of witnesses.' And before she could speak again he'd knelt by Button. 'Button, do you like making chocolate cake?'

'Yes,' Button said, a response he was starting to expect. She was puzzled but game.

'This is Nurse Abby,' Ben said, motioning to the nurse beside him. 'Abby's little boy is making chocolate cupcakes with my sister, Hannah, right now. We have a kitchen right next door. When they're finished they'll decorate them with chocolate buttons and then walk down to the beach to have fish and chips for tea. Would you like to do that?'

'Yes,' she said again, and Ginny thought, God bless Down's kids, with their friendly, unquestioning outlook on the world. If Button had been a normal four-year-old, she'd no doubt be a ball of tension right now, and who'd blame her? But Down's kids tended to accept the world as they found it.

She would get her Monkey back for her, she thought fiercely, and she picked Button up and gave her a hug.

'You're such a good girl,' she said, and Button gave a pleased smile.

'I'm a good girl,' she said, and beamed, and Abby took her hand and led her out to where chocolate cupcakes were waiting and Ginny was left looking at Ben, while twenty-odd islanders looked on.

'Everyone, this is…' Ben hesitated. 'Dr Ginny Koestrel?'

'Yes,' she said, and turned to the room at large. She had no doubt what the islanders thought of her parents but she'd never changed her name and she had no intention of starting now.

'Many of you know my parents owned Red Fire Winery. You'll know Henry Stubbs—he's been looking after it for us, but he hasn't been well so I've come home to run it. But Ben's right, I'm a doctor. I'm an Australian and for this afternoon I'm here to help.' She took a deep breath, seeing myriad questions building.

Okay, she thought, if she was going to be a source of gossip, why not use it to advantage?

'Ben says many of you are just here for prescriptions,' she said. 'If you're happy to have an Aussie doctor, I can see you—we can get you all home earlier that way. I'll need to get scripts signed by Dr Ben because I don't have New Zealand accreditation yet, but I can check your records, make sure there are no problems, write the scripts and then Dr Ben can sign them in between seeing patients who need to see him for other reasons. Is that okay with everyone?'

It was. First, Ben's face cleared with relief and she knew she was right in thinking he had house calls lined up afterwards. Second, every face in the waiting room was looking at her with avid interest. Guinevere Koestrel, daughter of the millionaires who'd swanned around the island, splashing money around, but now not looking like a millionaire at all. She'd been on the island for months but she'd kept herself to herself. Now suddenly she was in the clinic with a little girl.

She knew there'd have been gossip circulating about her since her arrival. Here was a chance for that gossip to be confirmed in person. She could practically see patients who'd come with minor ailments swapping to the prescription-only side of the queue. She glanced at Ben and saw him grin and knew he was thinking exactly the same.

'Excellent plan, Dr Koestrel,' he said. He motioned to the door beside the one he'd just come out of. 'That's our second consulting suite. I'm sorry we don't have time for a tour. You want to go in there and make yourself comfortable? There's software on the computer that'll show pharmacy lists. I'll have Abby come in and show you around. She can do your patient histories, guide you through. Thank you very much,' he said. 'And you don't need to explain about Henry. Henry's here.'

He turned to an elderly man in the corner, and she realised with a shock that it was her farm manager.

Henry had been caretaker for her parents' vineyard for ever. It had been Henry's phone call—'Sorry, miss, but my arthritis is getting bad and you need to think about replacing me'—that had fed the impulse to return, but when she'd come he hadn't let her help. He'd simply wanted to be gone.

'I'm right, miss,' he'd said, clearing out the caretaker's residence and ignoring her protests that she'd like him to stay. 'I've got me own place. I'm done with Koestrels.'

Her parents had a lot to answer for, she thought savagely, realising how shabby the caretaker's residence had become, how badly the old man had been treated, and then she thought maybe she had a lot to answer for, too. At seventeen she'd been as sure of her place in the world as her parents—and just as oblivious of Henry's.

'This means I can see you next, Henry,' Ben said gently. 'We have Dr Ginny here now and suddenly life is a lot easier for all of us.'

She'd said that her help was for this afternoon only, but she had to stay.

Ben had no doubt she'd come to the clinic under pressure, but the fact that she'd seen the workload he was facing and had reacted was a good sign. Wasn't it?

It had to be. He had a qualified doctor working in the room next door and there was no way he was letting her go.

Even if it was Ginny Koestrel.

Especially if it was Ginny Koestrel?

See, there was a direction he didn't want his thoughts to take. She was simply a medical degree on legs, he told himself. She was a way to keep the islanders safe. Except she was Ginny.

He remembered the first time she'd come to the island.

Her parents had bought the vineyard when he'd been eight and they'd arrived that first summer with a houseful of guests. They'd been there to have fun, and they hadn't wanted to be bothered with their small daughter.

So they'd employed his mum and he'd been at the kitchen window when her parents had dropped her off. She'd been wearing a white pleated skirt and a pretty pink cardigan, her bright red hair had been arranged into two pretty pigtails tied with matching pink ribbon, and she'd stood on the front lawn—or what the McMahons loosely termed front lawn—looking lost.

She was the daughter of rich summer visitors. He and his siblings had been prepared to scorn her. Their mum had taken in a few odd kids to earn extra money.

Mostly they had been nice to them, but he could remember his sister, Jacinta, saying scornfully, 'Well, we don't have to be nice to *her*. She can't be a millionaire and have friends like us, even if we offered.'

Jacinta had taken one look at the pleated skirt and pink cardigan and tilted her nose and taken off.

But Ben was the closest to her in age. 'Be nice to Guinevere,' his mother had told him. He'd shown her how to make popcorn—and then he'd shown her how to catch tadpoles. White pleated skirt and all.

Yeah, well, he'd got into trouble over that but it had been worth it. They'd caught tadpoles, they'd spent the summer watching them turn into frogs and by the time they'd released them the day before she'd returned to Sydney, they'd been inseparable.

One stupid hormonal summer at the end of it had interfered with the memory, but she was still Ginny at heart, he thought. She'd be able to teach Button to catch tadpoles.

Um…Henry. Henry was sitting beside him, waiting to talk about his indigestion.

'She's better'n her parents,' Henry said dubiously, and they both knew who he was talking about.

'She'd want to be. Her parents were horrors.'

'She wanted me to stay at the homestead,' he went on. 'For life, like. She wanted to fix the manager's house up. That was a nice gesture.'

'So why didn't you?'

'I have me dad's cottage out on the headland,' Henry said. 'It'll do me. And when I'm there I can forget about boss and employee. I can forget about rich and poor. Like you did when she were a kid.'

Until reality had taken over, Ben thought. Until he'd suggested their lives could collide.

Henry was right. Keep the worlds separate. He'd learned that at the age of seventeen and he wasn't going to forget it.

Think of her as rich.

Think of her as a woman who'd just been landed with a little girl called Button, a little girl who'd present all sorts of challenges and who she hadn't had to take. Think of Ginny's face when the lawyer had talked of dumping Button in an institution…

Think of Henry's indigestion.

'Have you been sticking only to the anti-inflammatories I've been prescribing?' he asked suspiciously. Henry had had hassles before when he'd topped up his prescription meds with over-the-counter pills.

'Course I have,' Henry said virtuously

Ben looked at him and thought, You're lying through your teeth. It was very tempting to pop another pill when you had pain, and he'd had trouble making Henry understand the difference between paracetamol—which was okay to take if you had a stomach ulcer—and ibuprofen—which wasn't.

Ginny…

No. Henry's stomach problems were right here, right now. That was what he had to think of.

He didn't need—or want—to think about Ginny Koestrel as any more than a colleague. A colleague and nothing more.

CHAPTER THREE

GINNY WORKED THROUGH until six. It was easy enough work, sifting through patient histories, checking that their requests for medication made sense, writing scripts, sending them out for Ben to countersign, but she was aware as she did it that this was the first step on a slippery slope into island life.

The islanders were fearful of an earthquake—sort of. Squid was preaching doom so they were taking precautions—buying candles, stocking the pantry, getting a decent supply of any medication they needed—but as Ginny worked she realised they weren't overwhelmingly afraid.

Earth tremors had been part of this country's history for ever. The islanders weren't so worried that they'd put aside the fact that Guinevere Koestler was treating them. This was Ginny, whose parents had swanned around the island for years and whose parents had treated islanders merely as a source of labour.

She hadn't been back since she'd been seventeen. Once she'd gone to medical school she'd found excuses not to accompany her parents on their summer vacations—to be honest, she'd found her parents' attitude increasingly distasteful. And then there had been this thing with Ben—so the islands were seeing her now for the first time as a grown-up Koestler.

The island grapevine was notorious. Every islander would

know by now that she'd been landed with a child, and every islander wanted to know more.

She fended off queries as best she could but even so, every consultation took three times longer than it should have and by the time she was done she was tired and worried about Button.

Button?

Where was she headed? She'd spent the last six months building herself a cocoon of isolation. One afternoon and it had been shattered.

She needed to rebuild, fast.

She took the last script out to the desk and Ben was waiting for her.

'All done,' she said. 'Mrs Grayson's cortisone ointment is the last.' She handed over the script she'd just written. 'This'll keep that eczema at bay until Christmas.'

He grinned and greeted Olive Grayson with wry good humour, signed the script and watched the lady depart.

The waiting room was empty. The receptionist was gone. There was no one but Ben.

'Button...' she started, and headed towards the kitchenette, but Ben put a hand on her shoulder and stopped her.

It shouldn't feel like this, she thought, suddenly breathless. Ben touching her?

For heaven's sake, she wasn't seventeen any more. Once upon a time she'd thought she was in love with this man. It had been adolescent nonsense and there was no reason for her hormones to go into overdrive now.

'I hope you don't mind but I sent her home with our nurse, Abby,' he said.

'You...what?'

'Abby's a single mum and the tremors happening when she can't be with her son are doing her head in. So my mum's taking a hand. Abby will be having dinner with us, so I sug-

gested she and Hannah—my sister—take both kids back to
our place. They'll have put them to bed, and dinner's waiting for us. Mum says there's plenty. I have a few house calls
to make but they can wait until after dinner if you'd like to
join us.'

'You…'

'I know, I'm an overbearing, manipulating toad,' he said,
smiling. 'I've manipulated you into working for us this af-
ternoon and now I've manipulated you into a dinner date.
But it's not actually a dinner date in the romantic sense.
It's Mum, Dad, whichever of my siblings are home tonight,
Abby, Button and you. It's hardly candlelit seduction.'

She smiled back, but only just. This was exactly what
she didn't want, being drawn into island life. She wanted to
work on her vineyard. She wanted to forget about being a
doctor. She wanted…

Nothing. She wanted nothing, nothing and nothing.

'Why not medicine?' Ben said softly, watching her face,
and she thought almost hysterically that he always had been
able to read her thoughts.

'What…what do you mean?'

'I mean I did some research when I heard you were back
on the island. You've got yourself a fine medical degree.
And yet…'

'And yet my husband died of cancer,' she said flatly, almost defiantly

'And there was nothing you could do? You blame yourself or your medicine? Is that it?'

'This is not your business.'

'But you walked away.'

'Leave it, Ben. I changed direction. I can't let the vineyard go to ruin.'

'We need a doctor here more than we need wine.'

'And I need wine more than I need medicine. Now, if you don't mind…I'll collect Button and go home.'

'My mum will be hurt if you don't stop and eat.'

She would be, too.

She'd popped in to see Ailsa when she'd arrived back at the island—of course she had. Ben's mum had always been lovely to her, drawing her into the family, making her time on the island so much better than if she'd been left with the normally sullen adolescent childminders her parents had usually hired on the mainland.

But she'd explained things to Ailsa.

'I need time to myself—to come to terms with my husband's death.' To come to terms with her husband's betrayal? His anger? His totally unjustified blame? 'I'm done with relationships, medicine, pressure. I need to be alone.'

'Of course you do, dear,' Ailsa had said, and had hugged her. 'But don't stay solitary too long. There's no better cure than hugs, and hugs are what you'll get when you come to this house. And if I know our kids and our friends, it won't only be me who'll be doing the hugging.'

Nothing had changed, she thought. This island was a time warp, the escape her parents had always treated it as.

She wanted this island but she didn't want the closeness that went with it. For six months she'd held herself aloof but now…

'Irish stew and parsley dumplings,' Ben said, grinning and putting on a nice, seductive face. His left eyebrow rose and he chuckled at her expression. 'Who needs candlelight and champagne when there's dumplings?' He held out his hands. 'Mum says it's your favourite.'

She'd remembered. Ailsa had remembered!

'And the kids are already sorting toys for Button,' he said, and tugged her toward the door. 'Come on home, Ginny.'

Home.

She didn't want to go. Every sense was screaming at her to go back to the vineyard.

But Button was asleep at Ailsa's. Ailsa had made parsley dumplings.

Ben was holding her hands and smiling at her.

What was a woman to do? A woman seemed to have no choice at all.

'Fine,' she said.

'That doesn't sound gracious,' he said, but still he smiled.

She caught herself. She was sounding like a brat.

'I'm sorry. It's very generous...'

'It's you who's generous,' he said gently. 'If you hadn't helped I wouldn't be getting any dinner, and Mum knows that as well as I do. So thank you, Ginny, and don't feel as if by coming you're beholden. Or even that you're somehow putting your feet into quicksand. You can draw back. You can go back to your vineyard and your solitude but not before you've eaten some of Mum's Irish stew.'

There were eight people around Ailsa's kitchen table, and the kids were asleep on the squishy living-room settee just through the door. The children were still in sight of the table. They were still part of the family.

It had always been thus, Ginny thought. Not only had Ailsa and her long-suffering Doug produced twelve children, but their house expanded to fit all comers. Doug worked on one of the island's fishing trawlers. He spent long times away at sea and when he was home he seemed content to sit by the fire, puffing an empty pipe.

'I know you smoke it at sea, but not in the house, not with the children,' Ailsa had decreed, and Doug didn't mind. He regarded his brood and Ailsa's strays with bemused approval and the house was the warmer for his presence.

Eight was a small tableful for these two, but the kids were

mostly grown now, setting up their own places. Ben was the third of twelve but only the three youngest were home to-night. Becky, Sam and Hannah were fourteen, fifteen and seventeen respectively, and they greeted Abby with warmth and shoved up to make room for her.

Abby, the nurse who'd worked with her that afternoon, was already there. The nurse had impressed Ginny today, not only with her people skills but with her warmth. She looked at home at the table, as if Ben often had her here.

Abby and Ben? A question started.

Ben was helping his mother ladle dumplings onto plates. Doug hardly said a word—it was up to the kids to do the entertaining, and they did.

'It's lovely to see you again,' seventeen-year-old Hannah said, a bit pink with teenage self-consciousness as she said it. 'We missed you when you went.'

'Ginny was Ben's girlfriend,' fourteen-year-old Becky told Abby, with no teenage self-consciousness at all. 'I'm too young to remember but everyone says they were all kissy-kissy. And then Ginny went away and Ben broke his heart.'

'Becky!' her family said, almost as one, and she flushed.

'Well, he did. Maureen said he did.'

Ginny remembered Maureen. Maureen was the oldest of the McMahon tribe, self-assertive and bossy. She'd come to see Ginny on the last night Ginny had been on the island, all those years ago.

'You could have been kind. Ben's so upset. You could say you'll write. Something like that.'

How to say that she couldn't bear to write? That even at seventeen all she'd wanted to do had been to fling herself into Ben's arms and stay? That she'd talked to her parents about the possibility of university in Auckland but she hadn't been able to divorce the request from the way she'd felt about Ben, and her parents had laid down an ultimatum.

'You're being ridiculous. The boy has no hope of making it through medicine—twelve kids—they're dirt poor. Cut it off now, Guinevere, if you want to be kind, otherwise you'll simply distract him from trying. You're going to university in Sydney and if there's any more nonsense, we'll send you to your aunt in London.'

The boy has no hope of making it through medicine. You'll simply distract him from trying.

The phrases had stung but even at seventeen she had been able to see the truth in them.

Ben had wanted so much to be a doctor. He'd dreamed of it, ached for it. Since he'd been fifteen he'd worked on the docks after school, unloading fish and cleaning them for sale. It was a filthy, hard job, and every cent of what he'd earned had gone to his doctor training fund.

You'll simply distract him from trying.

And then her father had issued another ultimatum, this one even worse.

Okay. If she couldn't study in Auckland... If she couldn't be with him...

She'd made a decision then and there, a Joan of Arc martyrdom, an adolescent burning for a cause. She'd renounce him and prove her parents wrong. She'd tell him not to write, to forget her, to focus purely on his career. Then, when they were both qualified doctors, she'd come again, appear out of the mist, probably wearing something white and floaty, and the orchestra would play and...and...

She found herself smiling, and everyone at the table was looking at her oddly. Even Ben.

'Sorry,' she said. 'I was just remembering how romantic it was. Our first love. I hope your heart wasn't broken for long, Ben.'

He grinned. 'For months,' he said.

'I thought you started going out with Daphne Harcourt

that same summer,' Hannah retorted. 'Now, *they* were kissy kissy. And then there was that painted one you brought home from uni.'

'And Jessica Crosby with the weird leggings and piercings,' Becky volunteered. 'She was hot. And now Mum thinks Abby—'

'Enough,' Doug said, breaking in abruptly. 'Leave the lad alone.'

They subsided as everyone always did when Doug spoke, and why wouldn't you subside when Ailsa's Irish stew was in front of you? But Ginny couldn't help thinking…thinking…

So Ben hadn't carried a flame for her. That was good, wasn't it? Yeah, it was, for of course at seventeen she hadn't carried a torch for him all that long either. She'd immersed herself in university life, she'd had a couple of very nice boyfriends, and then she'd met James.

He'd been older than her, his parents had moved in her parents' circle and he'd already been a qualified surgeon. She'd been thrilled when he'd noticed her, even more thrilled when he'd proposed.

And that same naivety that had had her dreaming of returning to Kaimotu in clouds of white mist with orchestra backing had then propelled her into a marriage that had been a disaster.

'Ginny,' Ben said gently, and she looked up and met his gaze. He looked concerned. Drat, he'd always been able to read her face and it was disconcerting. 'Are you okay? Did we work you too hard?'

'Would you like to stay here the night, with the little one?' Ailsa asked. 'Ben says you've been dropped into parenthood and it's hard. She's sound asleep now. She'll be right here.'

It was so tempting. She could step back into the McMahons' protection, she thought, as she'd stepped into it all those years ago.

Its warmth enfolded her. This family...

And then she glanced at Abby, who was looking fiercely down at her dinner plate, and she thought, What am I messing with? If there was something between these two, the kids talking of past loves must really hurt.

Joan of Arc syndrome again? Move aside, Ginny?

It wasn't dumb, though, she thought. There were no white mists and orchestras in the background now, just hard reality that had been drummed into her ever since she'd made her wedding vows.

'Thank you but no,' she managed. 'It's a lovely offer but Button and I will be fine.'

'I've put together a wee pack of toys for her,' Ailsa said. 'She likes Ben's old stuffed turtle, Shuffles.'

She flashed a glance at Ben at that, and then looked away fast. Noble doctor donating his Shuffles... It was dumb but why did that tug her heartstrings?

'Thank...thank you.'

'If there's anything else we can do...'

'I can babysit,' Hannah said. 'I'm supposed to be at uni but I copped glandular fever and missed the first two months of the semester. We figured it was best if I took the next two months off as well and start again at mid-year. So if you want to help Ben at the clinic I can keep helping out with Button. I...I do it for money,' she said, a trifle self-consciously. 'I mean...I'm sort of saving to be a doctor, too.'

'We'd love some help,' Ben said. 'Wouldn't we, Abby?'

'And you know, Ginny, it might help Button settle,' Ailsa said softly. 'She'll find it strange just the two of you. Ben seems to think she's been used to babysitters, so maybe stretching the care might help her adjust. Hannah looks after Abby's little boy, Jack, after school. The little ones played really well tonight. It might help you, too, and as Ben says, we need all the medical help we can get.'

They were all looking at her. The pressure...the pressure...

'No,' she said, and seven lots of eyebrows went up.

'Whoops, sorry,' she said, realising how petty her 'no' had sounded. 'It's just...'

'It's very fast,' Ailsa said, and came round the table to give her a hug. 'Ginny, we all know your husband died and we're very sorry. We should give you space. It's just...we know how hard Ben's pushed.'

'When I'm qualified, I can help,' Hannah said, and Ginny glanced at the girl and saw how much she meant it.

They all wanted to help—and she could.

'I'm sorry,' she managed. 'It's just...I can't.'

'Then you can't,' Ailsa said solidly, and glared at Ben. 'If she can't then she can't, so don't ask it of her. Ben, I know Ginny and I know she's been through a bad time. You're not to nag and you're to leave her alone until she's ready. Thank her very much for this afternoon and let her be.'

'Thank you very much for this afternoon,' Ben said gravely, and then he smiled at her.

It was the smile she remembered. It was the smile that had twisted her seventeen-year-old heart.

It was a white-mists-and-orchestra smile.

Enough.

She focussed on her dumplings and the talk started up again, cheerful banter as there always was around this table. As she'd always remembered.

People didn't look at her at this table. They didn't focus on her manners, they didn't demand she join in politely, they simply...were.

She glanced up and Ben was still watching her. His smile was faintly quizzical.

He wouldn't push. This whole community wouldn't push. They'd settle for what she was prepared to give.

How mean was it of her not to help?

She...couldn't.

'Call yourself a doctor... Stupid cow, you can't even give an injection without shaking...'

It wasn't true. She'd been okay until James...until James...

'Call yourself a doctor...'

'It's okay, Ginny,' Ben said gently. 'No pressure.'

She flushed and tried to look at him and couldn't. She'd been a doctor that afternoon, she told herself fiercely. Why couldn't she keep going?

Because Button needed her, she thought, and there was almost relief in the thought. In one day she'd become a stepmother. It was scary territory, but not as scary as stepping back into...life?

The chatter was starting up again around the table. No pressure.

This family was full of friends, she thought ruefully, and maybe...maybe that was what she needed. She could accept friendship.

Without giving anything in return?

It had to wait, she thought. If she said yes... If she got her New Zealand registration, she'd be expected to be a real doctor again.

'Call yourself a doctor...'

'No pressure at all,' Ailsa said gently beside her. 'The island can wait. Your friends can wait. We can all wait until you're ready.'

She smiled at Ginny, a warm, maternal smile.

Friends, Ginny thought, and tried to smile back. Friends felt...good.

So much for isolation, she decided as she tried to join in the cheerful banter around the table, but at least she'd left the white mists and orchestras behind her.

* * *

Ben walked her out to the car. He helped her buckle the sleeping Button into her newly acquired child seat, and then stood back and looked at her in the moonlight.

'We tried to blackmail you,' he said softly. 'The lawyer and then me. I'm sorry.'

'I... You didn't.'

'I manipulated you into helping this afternoon.'

'I did that all by myself.'

'Sort of,' he said wryly. 'I know how conscience works. Mrs Guttering met me in the supermarket last week and started complaining about her toe. Before I knew it she had her boots off and I was inspecting her ingrown toenail between the ice cream and frozen peas. How do you say no? I haven't learned yet.'

'And yet I have,' she said, trying to smile, trying to keep it light, as he had, and he put a hand out to cup her chin.

She flinched and moved back and he frowned.

'Ginny, it's okay. Saying no is your right.'

'Th-thank you.'

The lights were on inside. The kids were still around the table. Someone had turned the telly on and laughter sounded out through the window.

Kids. Home.

She glanced away from Ben, who was looking at her in concern. She looked into the car at Button and something inside her firmed. Button. Her stepdaughter.

Out of all of this mess—one true thing. She would focus on Button. Nothing else.

'You want her,' Ben said on a note of discovery, and she nodded, mutely.

What had she let herself in for? she thought, but she knew she wanted it. The moment she'd seen that clause in James's will...

When she and James had married, a baby had been high on her list of priorities, but James hadn't been keen. 'Let's put it on hold, babe, until our careers are established. The biological clock doesn't start winding down until thirty-five. We have years.'

But for Ginny, in a marriage that had been increasingly isolating, a baby had seemed a huge thing, something to love, something to hold, a reason to get up in the morning.

As medicine wasn't?

It should be, she thought. There'd never been a time when she hadn't thought she'd be a doctor. Her parents had expected it of her. She'd expected it of herself and she'd enjoyed her training.

She'd loved her first year as an intern, working in Accident and Emergency, helping people in the raw, but it had never been enough.

'Of course you'll specialise.' That had been her father, and James, too, of course, plus the increasingly ambitious circle of friends they'd moved in. 'You'd never just want to be a family doctor. You're far too good for that, Ginny.'

She was clever. She'd passed the exams. She'd been well on the way to qualifying in anaesthetics when James had got sick.

And after that life had been a blur—James's incredulity and anger that he of all people could be struck down, James searching for more and more interventionist cures, the medical fraternity around them fighting to the end.

'I should have frozen some sperm,' James had told her once, but she'd known he hadn't meant it—he'd never considered it. The idea that he was going to die had been inconceivable.

She'd watched as medical technology had taken her husband over, as he'd fought, fought, fought. She'd watched and experienced his fury. At the end he'd died undergoing yet another procedure, another intervention.

She remembered standing by his bedside at the end, thinking she would have liked to bring him here to this island, to have him die without tubes and interventions, to lie on the veranda and look out to sea...

James would have thought that was crazy.

'Can you tell me why you've decided to give up medicine?' Ben asked, and she shrugged.

'It couldn't save James.'

'Is that what you hoped? That you could save everyone?'

'No.'

'Then...'

'There was too much medicine,' she said flatly. 'Too much medicine and not enough love. I'm over it.'

'I'm sorry,' he said, as the silence stretched out and she stared out at the moonlight to the sea beyond—the sea was never far away on this island—and tried to figure where her life could go from here.

'We will find another doctor,' he said gently. 'This need is short term.'

'Are you still saying I should help?'

'I don't see why you can't. You were great today.'

'I need to look after Button.'

'That's not why you're refusing. You know it's not.'

'I don't need to give you any other reason.'

She looked into the back seat again, at the little girl curled into the child seat, sucking one thumb and hugging Ben's disreputable Shuffles with her spare arm. Ailsa and Abby had presented her with a dozen soft toys, from glossy teddies to pretty dolls, and Button had considered with care and gone straight for Ben's frayed turtle with one eye missing.

She looked like James, a little, and the thought was strange and unsettling, but even as she thought it Button wriggled further into her car seat and sighed and she thought, no, she looked like Button. She looked like herself and she'd go forward with no shadows at all. Please.

Ben was smiling a little, watching her watch Button hugging Shuffles. 'Mum never throws anything out.'

'You'd never have let her throw Shuffles out?' she asked incredulously, and amazingly he grinned, tension easing.

'Maybe not. Actually not. Over my dead body not.'

'Yet you let Button have him.'

'Button will love him as Shuffles needs to be loved,' he said, and then he looked at her—he really looked at her. 'Will you love her?' he said, and she stared at Button for a long, long moment and then gave a sharp, decisive nod.

'Yes.'

'And if her parents reclaim her?'

'They won't.'

'If they do?'

'Then I'll cope,' she said. 'Everyone copes. You know that. Like us thinking we were in love when we were seventeen. You move on.'

'Button needs a greater commitment than we were prepared to give,' he said, and she flushed.

'You think I don't know that?'

He gazed at her gravely, reading her face, seeing...what? How vulnerable she felt? How alone? How terrified to be landed with a little girl she knew nothing about?

Kids with Down's had medical problems to contend with, as well as learning difficulties. Heart problems, breathing problems, infections that turned nasty fast...

She'd cope. Out of all the mess that had been her relationship with James—his betrayal, his fury that she be the one to survive, his death—this little one was what was left.

James's death hadn't left her desolate but it had left her...

empty. Medicine was no longer a passion. Nothing was a passion.

If she could love this child...

But nothing else, she told herself fiercely. Nothing and no one else. She'd seen how fickle love was. Her parents' relationship had been a farce. James's professed love had been a lie, leading to bleakness and heartbreak. And even Ben... He'd said he loved her at seventeen but he'd found someone else that same summer.

'You moved on, too,' he said mildly, which brought her up with a jolt.

'Don't do that.'

'I don't know how not to,' he said obtusely, but she knew what he meant. That was the problem. She'd always guessed what he was going to say before he said it and it worked both ways.

'Then don't look at me,' she snapped, and then caught herself. 'Sorry. I didn't mean...'

'I know what you mean.

'Ben...'

He smiled wryly and held up his hands in surrender. 'Okay, I'm mentally closing my eyes here. Tomorrow afternoon, then? One o'clock?'

'No.'

'Ginny...'

'No!' She hesitated, feeling bad. Feeling trapped. 'In an emergency...'

'Isn't a host of panicked islanders an emergency?'

'Tell the islanders Squid has something obtuse like delusional encephalitis. Lock him in your quarantine ward until he starts prophesying untold riches instead of earthquakes.'

He grinned at that. 'It'd need back-up medical opinion to confine him. You'll sign the certificate?'

She smiled as well, but only faintly.

'I can't sign,' she said gently. 'I don't have New Zealand registration and I don't intend to get it.'

'Not if…?'

'No.'

He gazed at her for a long, long moment, reading her face, and she shifted from foot to foot under his gaze. He knew her too well, this man, and she didn't like it.

'Ginny, if I'd known you were having such an appalling time…' he said at last.

'I wasn't. Don't.'

'I should have written.'

'I told you not to.'

'And I listened,' he said obtusely. 'How dumb was that?' He shrugged. 'Well, you're home now. There's no need for letters, but I won't pressure you. I'll cope. Meanwhile, just see if you can open up a little. Let the island cure you.'

'I'm not broken. I've just…grown up, that's all.'

'Haven't we all,' he said, and his voice was suddenly deathly serious. 'Even Button. Cuddle her lots, Guinevere Koestrel, because growing up is hard to do.'

It was a night to think about but Ginny didn't think. She didn't think because she was so tired that by the time she hit the pillow her eyes closed all by themselves, and when she woke up a little hand was brushing through her hair, gently examining her.

It was morning and she was a mother.

She'd taken Button with her into her parents' big bed, fearful that the little girl would wake up and be afraid, but she didn't seem afraid.

She was playing with Ginny's hair and Ginny lay and let the sensations run through her, a tiny girl, unafraid, sleeping beside her, totally dependent on her, bemused by her mass of red curls.

She hadn't had a haircut since James had died—she hadn't been bothered—but now she thought she wouldn't. James had liked it cropped, but Ben...

She'd had long hair when Ben had known her. Ben had liked it long.

Ben...

It was strange, she thought. She'd been such good friends with Ben, but she'd barely thought of him for years.

She didn't want to think of him now. The sensations he engendered scared her. She'd fought so hard to be self-contained, and in one day...

It wasn't his fault she'd been landed with Button, she told herself, but she knew the sensations that scared her most had nothing to do with Button.

Button...Button was here and now. Button was her one true thing.

She found a brush and they took turns brushing each other's hair, a simple enough task but one Button found entrancing. Ginny enjoyed it, too, but she didn't enjoy it enough to stop thinking about Ben. To stop feeling guilty that she'd refused to help.

If she'd agreed... She wasn't sure about Australian doctors working in New Zealand but she suspected there'd be no problem. She might even be able to do more than write scripts.

She'd thought she wasn't missing medicine but yesterday, watching the diverse group of islanders come through her door, she'd thought...

She'd thought...

Maybe she shouldn't think, she told herself. The thing to do was just whatever came next. It was her turn to brush Button's hair.

She brushed and it felt good. Making Button smile felt good. Sharing her home with this little girl felt....right.

She thought of last night, of Ailsa's table, and she thought homes were meant to hold more than one.

Button was winding her curls around her fingers. 'Red,' she said in satisfaction.

'Carrots,' she said, and Button considered—and then giggled.

'Carrots.'

Family, Ginny thought, and then suddenly found herself thinking of Abby, Ben's clinical nurse.

She seemed lovely. She was a single mum and a competent nurse. She worked beside Ben, and his parents obviously cared for her.

Good. Great, she told herself. It was lovely that he had a lady who was so obviously right for him.

Wasn't it?

Of course it was, she told herself harshly, and then it was her turn to brush so she needed to focus on something that wasn't Ben and Abby.

For there was no need to think of anything past Button and the vineyard.

No need at all.

Ben woke early and thought about Ginny. He should think about Abby, he told himself. His family had been matchmaking with every ounce of coercion they could manage. Abby was lovely. She was haunted a bit by her past but she was a gorgeous woman and a true friend.

As Ginny had been a friend?

See, there was the problem. One hot day in his eighteenth year Ben had stopped thinking of Ginny as a friend. They'd been surfing. It had been a sweltering day so there'd been no need for wetsuits. They'd waited, lying at the back of the swell for the perfect wave, and when it had come they'd caught it together.

They'd surfed in side by side, the perfect curve, power, beauty, translucent blue all around them.

The wave had sunk to nothing in the shallows and they'd sunk as well, rolling off their boards to lie in the shallows.

Her long, lithe body had touched his. Skin against skin...

He'd kissed her and he'd known he would never forget that kiss. It had him still wanting to touch her after all these years. Still unable to keep his hands away from her.

What he felt for Abby was friendship, pure and simple. But Ginny... Seeing her today, spending time with her, watching her care for Button...

Yeah, the hormones were still there.

Hormones, however, could be controlled. Must be controlled.

'There should be pills,' he told himself, and then thought there probably were.

Anti-love potions?

Except he didn't need them. It was true he'd got over his adolescent lust. He'd had other girlfriends, moved on.

Out of sight, out of mind? Definitely. He'd had a few very nice girlfriends. Nothing serious, but fun.

The problem was that Ginny wasn't out of sight now and the physical attraction had slammed straight back...

But the class thing still held true. He remembered that final night, in his shabby suit, Ginny dressed as if she'd just come off the Paris catwalks, and he remembered her gentle smile.

Impossible.

Yeah, so class, social standing had been important then, he told himself. Not so much now.

But then there were her ghosts. Big ones, he thought. A guy who'd betrayed her? A past that made her want to give up medicine? He didn't know it all. He could only guess.

If he wanted her...

What was he about, still wanting her?

He didn't, he told himself. This was nostalgia speaking, surely.

'Get over it,' he told himself harshly. 'She's rich, independent and wants nothing to do with you. She doesn't want to be a doctor any more and she can surely afford to do what she likes. It's her call. Leave her alone. One haunted society doctor who doesn't want to be a doctor at all—no and no and no.'

The week wore on.

Down on the docks, Squid's doomsday forebodings were increasing rather than fading.

'She'll be a big one. I'm telling you, she'll be a big one.'

Ben thought longingly of Ginny's suggestion of quarantine and locks and keys and thought he could almost justify it.

But despite Squid's doom-mongering, the islanders were calming down. They were growing accustomed to his prophecy; starting to laugh about it. The urgent medical need faded.

He received a couple of applications for doctors to take Catherine's place, but neither of them was prepared to come to the island for an interview. What sort of commitment was that? he thought, trying to figure out how he could find time to take the ferry to Auckland and interview them.

Maybe Ginny could help.

Maybe he couldn't ask her.

A couple of days after their dinner, she booked Button into the clinic, brought her in and together he and Ginny gave the little girl a complete medical assessment. That was weird, a mixture of personal and medical. It made him feel…

Like he didn't want to feel.

'You haven't changed your mind?' he asked, labelling

blood samples to send to the mainland for path. testing. He was…they both were…a bit concerned about Button's heart. Heart conditions were common in Down's kids. He thought he could hear a murmur. There was nothing about a murmur in her medical records but Ginny thought she could hear one, too.

'Button needs me,' she said simply, and it was true, but it worked both ways, he thought. He could see how much she cared for the little girl already.

He looked at them both, Button playing happily with Shuffles, calmly accepting his ministrations, seemingly unperturbed that her life had been turned upside down—and he looked at Ginny's pale, strained face.

'Maybe you need Button more than she needs you,' he said gently.

'No.'

'I won't go there, then,' he said equitably, and lifted Button from the examination couch and popped her on the floor. Ginny took her hand and backed away—almost as if she was afraid of him.

'I'll let you know when the results come through,' he said.

'Thank you.'

'Ginny…'

'Thank you,' she said again, and it was like a shield. Patient thanking doctor.

Nothing personal at all.

Once in the car she could block out the personal. Once out of sight of Ben.

She kind of liked taking Button home. No, more than liked. She was trying to hold back, aware at any minute that Veronica or Veronica's husband could change their mind and want her again, but Button was a little girl who was easy to love, and she found her heart twisting at the thought of her being discarded.

She might even fight for her, she thought. What rights did a stepmother have?

Maybe none, she thought, but there was a real possibility she'd be taking care of Button for life—and right now Button was filling a void. Button needed her and she intended to do the best job she could.

Which meant she was justified in refusing to help Ben, she decided, and squashed guilt to the back of her mind. One of her girlfriends had once told her, 'Don't have kids, Ginny. The moment you do, every single thing is your fault. No matter what you do, you feel guilty.'

So she was just like other mothers, she decided, and thought she should ring Ben up and tell him.

Or not.

Focus on Button. And the vineyard? She wasn't actually very good at growing grapes. She should find someone to replace Henry. She didn't actually have a clue what she was doing.

But, then, so what if she missed a harvest? she decided. The world had enough wine and she didn't need the money. Henry popped in to see her and worried about it on her behalf, but she calmed him.

'Next year, when I'm more organised, I'll hire staff and do it properly. I should have done it this year but neither of us was organised. And you're not well. Thank you for dropping by, but I'll manage. Did Ben…? Did Dr McMahon give you something that'll help?'

'He wants me to go to the mainland and have a gas-gastroscopy or something. Damned fool idea. You want me to teach you about—?'

'No,' she said gently, thinking of the old man's grey face.

'Let's put this year's harvest behind us and move on next year.'

That was a great idea, she decided. She'd put the whole of the last year aside. She'd refuse to be haunted by shadows of the past.

She and Button could make themselves a life here. She watched Button water her beloved tomatoes—watering was Button's principal pleasure—and thought…she could almost be happy.

But happiness was a long-ago concept. Pre-James.

Happiness went right back to Ben—and there was the biggie.

But why was it unsettling her? Once upon a time she'd thought of him as her best friend. Friends instead of lovers? Why not again?

He wanted her to do more. She could, she conceded. Hannah could look after Button.

Working side by side with Ben?

Why did she keep remembering one hot day in the surf?

Why did the memory scare her stupid?

CHAPTER FOUR

RUNNING A SOLO practice was okay, was even feasible, except in emergencies.

With only ten beds, Kaimotu Hospital was not usually used for acute care. Acute-care cases were sent to the mainland, and now, with only one doctor, it was a case of deeming more cases acute.

With two doctors on the island they could cope with routine things like appendicitis, hernias, minor surgery, but with only one...well, the Hercules transport plane from the mainland got more of a workout.

The islanders hated it. They loathed being shipped to the mainland away from family and friends, but Ben had no choice. Until they found another doctor, this was the only way he could cope.

He did cope—until the night Henry's ulcer decided to perforate.

Why did medical emergencies happen in the small hours more often than not? Someone should write a thesis, Ben thought wearily, picking up the phone. His apartment was right by the hospital. He switched his phone through to the nurses' station while he slept, so he knew the nurse on call had overridden that switch. This call, therefore, meant he was needed.

'Ben?' It was Margy, the island's most senior nurse, and he knew the moment he heard her voice that he had trouble.

'Mmm?'

'Henry's on the phone. I'm putting you through now.'

'B-Ben?'

The old winemaker wasn't voluble at the best of times, but now his voice was scarcely a whisper.

'Yeah, Henry, it's me. Tell me what's wrong.'

'Me guts,' Henry whispered. 'Pain…been going on all night. Took them pills you gave me and then some more but nothing's stopping it and now…vomiting blood, Doc. Couple times. Lotta blood.'

To say his heart sank would be an understatement. He was already out of bed, reaching for his pants.

'You're at home? Up on the headland?'

'Y-yeah.'

'Okay, I want you to go back to bed and lie very still while I wake Max and Ella up,' he told him. Max and Ella were the nearest farmers to Henry's tiny cottage. 'They'll bring you down to the hospital. I reckon you might have bleeding from your stomach. It'll be quicker if they bring you here rather than me go there.'

Besides, he thought, he needed to set up Theatre. Call in nurses.

He needed to call on Ginny. Now.

'I might make a mess of their car,' Henry whispered, and Ben told Henry what he thought about messing up a car compared to getting him to hospital fast.

Then he rang Max and Ella and thanked God for good, solid farming neighbours who he knew would take no argument from Henry. There'd also be no tearing round corners on two wheels.

Then he rang Ginny.

* * *

Ginny was curled up in her parents' big bed, cuddling a
sleeping Button—and thinking about Ben.

Why did he keep her awake at night?

He didn't, she conceded. Everything kept her awake at
night.

Memories of James. Memories of blame.

*'You stupid cow, how the hell can you possibly know how
I feel? You're healthy—healthy!—and you stand there acting sorry for me, and you can't do a thing. Why can't you
get this damned syringe driver to work? How can you sleep
when I'm in pain?'*

The syringe driver *had* been working. It wasn't pain, she
thought. It was fear, and fury. He'd had twelve months of illness and he'd blamed her every moment of the way.

So what was she doing, lying in bed now and thinking of
another man? Thinking of another relationship?

She wasn't, she told herself fiercely. She was never going
there again. She was just…thinking about everything, as
she always did.

And then the phone rang.

She answered it before Button could wake up.

'Ginny?'

Ben's voice did things to her. It always had.

No.

'Ben?'

'Ginny, I need you. Henry has a ruptured stomach ulcer.
He's been bleeding for hours. There's no time to evacuate
him to the mainland. Mum and Hannah are on their way to
your place now to take care of Button. The minute they get
there I need you to come. Please.'

And that was that.

No choice.

She should say no, she thought desperately. She should tell him she'd made the decision not to practise medicine.

Not possible.

Henry.

'I'll come.'

'Ginny?'

'Yes?'

'How are you at anaesthetics?'

'That's what I am,' she said, and then corrected herself. 'That's what I was. An anaesthetist.'

There was a moment's stunned silence. Then... 'Praise be,' Ben said simply. 'I'll have everything ready. Let's see if we can pull off a miracle.'

Henry needed a miracle. He'd been bleeding for hours.

Ginny walked into Theatre, took one look and her heart sank. She'd seen enough patients who'd bled out to know she was looking at someone who was close.

Ben had already set up IV lines, saline, plasma.

'I've cross-matched,' he said as she walked through the door. 'Thank God he's O-positive. We have enough.'

There was no time for personal. That one glance at Henry had told her there was hardly time for anything.

She moved to the sink to scrub, her eyes roving around the small theatre as she washed. He had everything at the ready. A middle-aged nurse was setting up equipment—Margy? Abby was there, slashing away clothing.

Ben had Henry's hand.

'Ginny's here,' he told him, and Ginny wondered if the old man was conscious enough to take it in. 'Your Ginny.'

'My Ginny,' he whispered, and he reached out and touched her arm.

'I'm here for you,' she told him, stooping so she was sure he'd hear. 'I'm here for you, Henry. You know I'm a doctor.

I'm an anaesthetist and I'm about to give you a something to send you to sleep. We need to do something about that pain. Ben and I are planning on fixing you, Henry, so is it okay if you go to sleep now?'

'Yes,' Henry whispered. 'You and Ben...I always thought you'd be a pair. Who'd a thought... You and Ben...'

And he drifted into unconsciousness.

She was an anaesthetist. *Who'd a thought?* Henry's words echoed through Ben's head as he worked and it was like a mantra.

Who'd a thought? A trained anaesthetist, right here when he needed her most.

Ben had done his first part of surgery before he'd returned to the island. It had seemed sensible—this place was remote and bad things happened fast. He'd also spent an intense six months delivering babies, but if he'd tried to train in every specialty he'd never have got back to Kaimotu.

Catherine had had basic anaesthetic training, as had the old doctor she'd replaced. For cases needing higher skills they'd depended on phone links with specialists on the mainland. It hadn't been perfect but it had been the best they could do.

Now, as he watched Ginny gently reassure Henry, as he watched her check dosage, slip the anaesthetic into the IV line he'd set up, as he watched her seamlessly turn to the breathing apparatus, checking the drips as she went to make sure there was no blockage in the lines, he thought... He thought Henry might just have a chance.

Henry had deteriorated since Ben had phoned Ginny. By the time Ginny had walked into Theatre he'd thought he'd lose him. Now...

'Go,' Ginny said, with a tight, professional nod, and she

went back to monitoring breathing, checking flow, keeping this old man alive, while Ben...

Ben exposed and sutured an ulcer?

It sounded easy. It wasn't.

He was trained in surgery but he didn't do it every day. He operated but he took his time, but now there was no time to take.

He cut, searched, while Margy swabbed. There was so much blood! Trying to locate the source of the bleeding...

'One on each side,' Ginny snapped to the nurses and they rearranged themselves fast. Ben hadn't had time to think about it but the way they had been positioned only Margy had been able to swab, with Abby preparing equipment.

'I can do the handling as well,' Ginny said calmly. 'Get that wound clear for Dr McMahon. Fast and light. Move.'

They moved and all of a sudden Ben could see...

A massive ulcer, oozing blood from the stomach wall.

That Henry wasn't dead already was a miracle.

'Sutures,' he said, and they were in his hand. He glanced up—just a glance—in time to see that it was Ginny who was preparing the sutures. And monitoring breathing, oxygen saturation, plasma flow.

No time to think about that now. Stitch.

Somehow he pulled the thing together, carefully, carefully, always conscious that pulling too tight, too fast could extend the wound rather than seal it.

The blood flow was easing.

How fast was Ginny getting that plasma in?

He glanced up at her again for a fraction of a moment and got a tiny, almost imperceptible nod for his pains.

'Oxygen saturation ninety-three. We're holding,' she said. 'If you want to do a bit of pretty embroidery in there, I think we can hold the canvas steady.'

And she'd taken the tension out of the room, just like that.

He and both the nurses there had trained in large city hospitals. They'd worked in theatres where complex, fraught surgery took place and they knew the banter that went on between professionals at the top of their game.

Ginny's one comment had somehow turned this tiny island hospital into the equal of those huge theatres.

They had the skill to do this and they all knew it.

'Henry's dog's name's Banjo,' Margy offered. They were all still working, hard, fast, not letting anything slide, but that fractional lessening of tension had helped them all. 'We could tell him we've embroidered "Banjo" on his innards when he wakes up.'

'He'd need *some* mirror to see it,' Ben retorted, and went back to stitching, but he was smiling and he had it sealed now. That Henry had held on for this long…

'Oxygen level's rising,' Ginny said. 'That's the first point rise. We're aiming for full within half an hour, people. Margy, can you find me more plasma?'

And Margy could because suddenly there was only the need for one to swab. Ben was stitching the outer walls of the stomach closed then the layers of muscle, carefully, painstakingly. Ginny was still doing her hawk thing—the anaesthetist was the last person in the room to relax—but this was going to be okay.

But then… 'Hold,' Ginny said into the stillness. 'No, hold. No!'

No!

They'd been so close. So close but not close enough. Ben didn't need to see the monitors to interpret Ginny's message—he had it in full.

A drop in blood pressure. Ventricular fibrillation.

He was grabbing patches from Margy, thanking God that at least the bulk of the stitching was done, but not actually thanking God yet. Saying a few words in his direction, more like.

Or one word.

Please… To get so close and then lose him…

Please…

The adrenaline was pumping. If Ginny hadn't been here…

Please…

'Back,' Ginny snapped, as he had the patches in place, as he moved to flick a switch…

A jerk… Henry's body seemed to stiffen—and then the thin blue line started up again, up and down, a nice steady beat, as if it had just stopped for a wee nap and was starting again better than ever.

'Oh, my God,' Margy said, and started to cry.

Margy and Henry's daughter had been friends before they'd both moved to the mainland, Ben remembered. That was the problem with this island. Everyone knew everyone.

'Every man's death diminishes me.' How much more so on an island as small as Kaimotu?

'He… I think he'll be okay,' Ginny said, and Ben cast her an anxious glance as well. Henry had worked for her parents for ever. Did she consider him a friend? The tremor in her voice said that she did.

'We'll settle him and transfer,' Ben said, forcing his hands to be steady, forcing his own heartbeat to settle. 'I want him in Coronary Care in Auckland.'

'He won't want that,' Margy said.

'Then we transfer him while he doesn't have the strength to argue,' Ben said. 'I'm fond of this old guy, too, and he's getting the best, whether he likes it or not. Thank God for Ginny. Thank God for defibrillators. And thank God for specialist cardiac physicians and gastroenterologists on the mainland, because if we can keep him alive until morning, that's where he's going.'

* * *

It was an hour later when he finished up. Henry seemed to have settled. Margy had hauled in extra nursing staff so he could have constant obs all night. Ben had done as much as he could. It was too risky to transfer Henry to the mainland tonight but he'd organised it for first thing in the morning. With his apartment so close he was just through the wall if he was needed.

Enough.

He'd sent Ginny home half an hour ago, but he walked out into the moonlight, to walk the few hundred yards to the specially built doctors' quarters, and Ginny was sitting on the rail dividing the car park from the road beyond. Just sitting in the moonlight.

Waiting for him?

'Hey,' she said, and shoved up a little on the rail to make room for him.

'Hey, yourself,' he said, feeling…weird. 'Why aren't you at home?'

'You reckon I could sleep?'

'I reckon you should sleep. What you did was awesome.'

'You were pretty awesome yourself. I didn't know you were surgically trained.'

'And I didn't know you'd done anaesthesia.'

'Once we were friends,' she said softly into the night. 'We should have kept up. I should have written. I should have let you write. One stupid summer and it meant we cut our friendship off at the knees.'

'As I recall,' he said carefully, 'it was a very nice summer.'

'It was,' she said, and smiled. 'We had fun.'

'You were the best tadpole catcher I ever knew.'

'I'm going to teach Button,' she said, and he wanted to say he would help but it wasn't wise. He knew it wasn't wise. She was opening up a little just by being here, and he wouldn't push for the world.

Except…he needed to ask.

'Why did you give up medicine?' he asked into the stillness, and the night grew even more still.

'You know,' she said at last, 'that when the world gets crazy, when there are things around that are battering down in every direction, a tortoise retreats into his shell and stays there. I guess…that's what I've done.'

'Your shell being this island.'

'That's the one.'

'But medicine?'

'While James was dying… We tried everything and I mean everything. Every specialist, every treatment, every last scientific breakthrough. None of it helped.'

'You blame medicine?'

'No,' she said wearily. 'But I thought… My dad pushed and pushed me to do medicine and James pushed me to specialise, and when both of them were in trouble…Dad and then James…they both turned. They were so angry and there was nothing I could do. I used to go to bed at night and lie there and dream of being… I don't know…a filler-up of potholes. A gardener. A wine-maker. Something that made it not my fault.'

'It wasn't your fault your dad and James died.'

'No,' she said bleakly. 'But you try telling them that.'

'They're dead, Ginny.'

'Yes, but they're still on my shoulder. A daughter and a wife who didn't come up to standard.'

'That's nuts,' he said, and put a hand on her shoulder. He felt her stiffen.

'No,' she said.

'So you've rejected medicine because of them. You're rejecting friendship, too?'

There was a long silence while they both sat and stared out over the moonlit sea. He kept his hand where it was, gently on her shoulder, and he felt her make a huge—vast—effort to relax.

What had those guys done to her—her father and her husband? He thought back to the laughing, carefree girl who'd been his friend and he felt...

Yeah, well, there was no use going down that road. He couldn't slug dead people.

He wanted to pull her closer. It took an almost superhuman effort to keep it light, hold the illusion that this was friendship, nothing more.

'I'll come out eventually,' Ginny said at last. 'I can't stay in my shell for ever and Button will haul me out faster.'

'You'll go back to the mainland?'

'No!' It was a fierce exclamation.

'This island's not for hiding, Ginny,' he said softly. 'Life happens here as well.'

'Yes, but I can take Button tadpoling here.'

'She'll love it.' He hesitated but the urge was too great. 'Let me in a little,' he said. 'We used to be friends. I'm the second-best tadpoler on the island. We could...share.'

She stiffened again. 'Ben, I don't... I can't...'

'Share?'

'That's the one.' She rose, brushing away his touch. Her face was pale in the moonlight and he wondered again what those guys had done to her. Unbidden he felt his hands clench into fists. His beautiful Ginny...

'It's okay,' he made himself say, forcing the anger from his voice. 'Treat the island as a shell, then. You have Button in there with you, though, and I have a feeling she'll tug you out. And you came out tonight. Henry's alive because you came out, and you can't imagine how grateful I am.'

'It's me who should be grateful,' she said. 'Henry was my friend.'

'Henry *is* your friend.' And then, as she didn't reply, he pushed a little bit further.

'Ginny, no one on this island judged you because of who your parents were. You stayed here for ten summers and there are lots of islanders who'd call you their friend. My family almost considered you one of us. We're all still here, Ginny, waiting for you to emerge and be our friend again.'

'I can't.'

'No,' he said, and because he couldn't stop himself he touched her cheek, a feather touch, because the need to touch her was irresistible and she was so beautiful and fearful and needful.

So Ginny.

'You can't,' he said. 'But tonight you did.' And then, before he knew what he was going to do, before she could possibly know for he hadn't even realised he was about to do it himself, he stooped and kissed her, lightly, on the lips.

It had been a feather touch. He'd backed away before she'd even realised he'd done it, appalled with himself, putting space between them, moving away before she could react with the fear he knew was in her.

But he had to say it.

'We're all here, waiting,' he said into the darkness. 'We'll wait for as long as it takes. This island is as old as time itself and it has all the patience in the world.'

And as if on cue the world trembled.

It was the faintest of earth tremors, exactly the same as the tremors that had shaken this island since time immemorial.

A tiny grumble of discord from within.

Nothing to worry about? Surely not.

'Or maybe it's saying hurry up,' Ben said, and grinned, and Ginny managed a shaky smile.

'It'll have to wait.'

'Maybe the island's giving you a nudge. Like we gave you a nudge. You saved Henry tonight, Ginny, so there's a start. No pressure, love, but when you come out of your shell, we're all waiting.'

No pressure.

He watched as she put her fingers to the lips he'd just kissed. He watched as she watched him, as something fought within her.

What had her father and husband done to her?

'I...I need to go,' she faltered, and he didn't move towards her and God only knew the effort it cost him not to.

'Yes, you do.'

'Ben...'

'Don't say anything more,' he said softly. 'You've done brilliantly tonight. I love what you're doing with Button— we all do. One step at a time, our Ginny, that's all we ask.'

He tugged open the door of her car and watched as she climbed in.

He didn't touch her and it almost killed him.

'Goodnight, Ginny,' he said softly, and she didn't say a thing in reply.

He stood back as she did up her seat belt, as she started the engine, as she drove away, and he thought...

She looks haunted.

Not by him, he thought. She needed time.

He would give her time. Except for emergencies. Even knowing she was on the island, another doctor...

Who was he kidding? Even knowing she was on the island...his Ginny.

He would give her time. He had to.

She reached the vineyard. The lights were on inside the house. Ailsa and Hannah would be there, keeping watch over Button, waiting for her, anxious about Henry.

This island was like a cocoon, she thought, a warm, safe blanket that enveloped her and kept her safe from the real world.

Did she ever need to go back to the real world?

Kaimotu was time out, a holiday isle, a place of escape. She could make it real.

But if she did, would the world move in?

She thought back to her marriage. The fairy-tale. A big, gorgeous, clever man her parents had approved of, dating her, making love to her, making her feel like the princess in a fairy-tale. She could have her parents' life. She could have a happy-ever-after.

Yes, she'd had a childhood romance with Ben but that had been years before. She'd felt that what she'd found with James had been real, wonderful, a grown-up happy-ever-after.

And she'd stepped into James's world and realised that grown up wasn't fantasy. Not one little bit. Grown up was trying to meet expectations, climbing the career ladder, accepting scorn when you failed.

Grown up was realising that medicine couldn't save lives—that you could do nothing to help your father or your husband.

Grown up was learning to hate yourself as well as copping hate from those around you.

'I need a shrink,' she said out loud, and then closed her eyes, took a deep breath, stared up at the starlit sky and figured she didn't need a psychiatrist. She needed to move on. Move forward.

But not very much, and certainly not in the direction of Ben.

Ben had kissed her.

Ben was real.

No. He'd be just the same as all the other fantasies, she

told herself. She no longer trusted her judgement. She no longer trusted men who told her she was capable, beautiful, wonderful.

She no longer trusted.

'My job is to take care of Button and to make wine,' she told herself, and thought that actually she hadn't managed very well in the picking and processing department and there wouldn't be all that much Chardonnay coming out of the vineyard this season.

'It doesn't matter,' she said stubbornly. 'Button's the important thing.' Like Henry was important. She'd helped save Henry.

Yes, but for how long? He'd have another coronary, he'd arrest, he'd die and she'd feel…she'd feel…

'I'm not going to feel,' she said savagely into the dark. 'If Ben's desperate I'll help but nothing else. I will not be responsible for anything else but Button. It won't be my fault.'

'That's a cop-out and you know it,' she told herself, and she bit her lip and turned resolutely towards the house.

'I know it is,' she told herself. 'But it's all I'm capable of. And if Ben McMahon thinks he can change my mind just by kissing me… Pigs might fly, Ben McMahon, but you are not stuffing with my life.'

Sleep was nowhere. Ben lay in the dark and stared at the ceiling and all he could think about was that kiss.

He'd wanted her when he'd been seventeen, and he wanted her still. Crazy or not, his body was reacting to her as it had at seventeen.

He wanted her.

But while he wanted her as a woman, as the desire he'd felt all those years ago surged back to the surface, he needed her as a doctor. The skill she'd shown had knocked him sideways. He had to persuade her to join him; with her skills the island could have the medical service it deserved.

All sorts of possibilities had opened up as he'd watched her work. Islanders with cancer pain often needed to be transported to the mainland, at a time when they most wanted to stay here. He didn't have the skills to help them.

As an anaesthetist, Ginny had those skills.

So…was he messing with that need by making it personal? By letting his desire hold sway? He'd kissed her and she'd shied away like a frightened colt.

'So don't kiss her,' he said out loud, knowing that was easier said than done.

She'd been injured by the men in her life, he thought. She'd been injured by the arrogant bully he remembered her father being, and a husband who sounded like a bottom feeder. Ben wasn't seeing her as a victim, though. With her determination to keep Button, with the skill and humour she'd shown in Theatre tonight, he knew that underneath the battered armour there was still the lovely, feisty, carrot-haired girl he'd fallen in love with all those years ago.

'It was an adolescent crush,' he growled to the night. 'Get over it.'

But an adolescent crush wasn't what he was feeling. When his mouth had touched hers, a fire had reignited.

For her, too?

If it had, she wasn't letting on. Her armour might be battered but it was still intact, and if he wanted any chance at all of persuading her to work with him, he needed to respect it.

'So leave her be.'

'Except to ask her to work?' He was arguing out loud with himself.

'Yes,' he told himself. 'She worked that first afternoon because she saw desperate need. She worked tonight for the same reason. At the moment she's giving you back-up when you most need it. Respect that, give her space, give her time.'

'But the way you feel?'

'Get over it,' he said harshly. 'You're not seventeen any more. Go find yourself a lady who wants you.'

'And isn't that the whole trouble?' he groaned, and punched a pillow. This island was small, and any affair he had, even asking someone on a date, led to expectations and complications.

Like tonight. One kiss...

Expectations and complications?

'Leave it alone,' he growled, and punched the pillow once more then gave up and got up and went across to the hospital to check on Henry—who was sleeping soundly and didn't need his attention at all.

He went back to bed and finally he slept, but when he slept he dreamed of Ginny.

She was an adolescent crush who'd turned into the woman of his dreams. The idea was romantic nonsense, he told himself, even in his sleep.

And down on the harbour... It was five in the morning and almost every islander was asleep, but Squid Davies was wide awake and pacing.

'It's coming,' he muttered. 'The big one's coming. I feel it in my bones.' He grabbed a piece of paper and started to write.

'Just in case,' he muttered. 'I'll be prepared even if they're not.'

CHAPTER FIVE

BEN DIDN'T SEE Ginny for days.

Henry spent four days in hospital in Auckland and then was transferred back to the island. Ben heard from his mum that Ginny had tried to persuade the old man to come back to the vineyard and stay with her, but Henry wanted to go back to his ancient cottage on the headland. It was too far from anywhere, he thought. He wouldn't mind talking to Ginny about it.

'But Ginny's doing all she can,' Ailsa told him. 'She's visiting him twice a day. There's nothing more she can do. There's nothing more anyone can do.'

So he didn't have an exc—a reason to talk to her. But finally Button's cardiac results came through.

There'd been a query on Button's medical records, tests taken but not recorded. Her family doctor had noted that slight heart murmur, he'd sent her to a specialist but then she'd been brought to the island and the notes she'd brought hadn't contained results.

It had taken a week's perseverance on Ben's part to get them. Laws protecting a patient's privacy were a concern, especially when the patient was four years old, one parent had disappeared to Europe and the other wanted nothing to do with her. Ben had run out of professional ways of getting the results and had finally reverted to the personal. He'd rung

Veronica's husband, a man who blustered about not wanting anything to do with a child who wasn't his but at least didn't hang up on him.

'For now you're still legally Barbara's parent,' Ben had snapped at him. 'I'm now her doctor, Ginny's her acting guardian until the legalities are completed and we need full access to her medical records. Do you want her to die of heart failure because of your pride?'

The man had finally complied, and when Ben eventually received the results he swore.

There were problems. They'd have to be sorted. He and Ginny had to talk.

It was Monday, a gorgeous autumn day. Ben did a long morning's clinic then he needed to make some house calls, and Ginny's house was first.

He'd just reached the vineyard gate when the earth moved.

One moment Ginny was supervising Button eating her boiled egg and toast. The next moment she was on the floor and the world was crazy.

It was as if the whole house had been picked up and was being violently shaken. Walls became floor, floor became walls. Furniture was crashing everywhere.

She grabbed a chair but the chair slid sideways, crashed, rolled, tumbled.

Button!

She was screaming. Was Button screaming? The noise was unbelievable.

Somehow she grabbed the little girl as the chair she'd been sitting on crashed almost on top of her. She scooped her into her arms, and then the floor seemed to roll again.

The table. The table!

Drop and hold. Where had she heard that? In some long-ago safety lecture, maybe here in New Zealand when she'd been a child? New Zealand was known as the shaky isles for good reason.

There was another mantra. Get out of the house. Into the open.

But it was no use thinking that now, or trying to attempt it. This was like a wild, bucking, funfair ride, only there was nothing fun about this. Everything that wasn't nailed down was crashing around them.

She had Button cradled hard against her but she was struggling to hold her. She was fighting to stay on her knees.

The table... If she could get past these crazy chairs...

The table was big, solid, farmhouse wood. If she could get under...

Getting anywhere was impossible. Something sharp hit her head, and she thought, Drop further.

She dropped onto her side, ignoring the crunch of things breaking under her. Button was clinging to her, limpet-like, whimpering in terror, and Ginny could move where she wanted and she knew Button wouldn't let go.

Move where she wanted? That was a joke.

The table. She was three feet away. Roll. Roll!

The floor lurched again, tipping the other way, and under she went. She crashed into chair legs as she rolled but Button was with her, clinging so hard that Ginny had a hand free.

Grab.

She grabbed a table leg and clung.

She was under the table. The world was still rolling in great, fearsome waves, but the table and the floor beneath it were rolling with it and Ginny could hold and ride.

Thank God the house was single-storey, Ginny thought as she clung. And had an iron roof. No vast bank of heavy tiles.

Visions of knife-sharp iron flooded her mind but she

shoved them away. Just hold on. Use her body to protect Button and hold on.

Wait until the earth found a new level.

Ben was just about to turn into the gate when the road buckled.

As buckles went it was truly impressive. The coast road was long and flat, and he saw the buckle start half a mile ahead of him, rising with a massive, unbelievable heave of solid earth. It hurled towards him, a great, burrowing mound, trees swaying, bitumen cracking and falling away, coming, coming...

It must have been seconds only before the great buckling mound hit him but he had enough time to think about getting out of the car and then to change his mind and decide to stay in the car but veer away fast from trees, head for the grassy verge away from the sea, pull to a halt. Or almost pull to a halt for then it hit and the car rose in the air as if it had been thrown.

It wasn't just the one wave. It was a series of massive jolting, shaking heaves, as if the world was shifting and not knowing where to settle.

He gripped the steering-wheel and hung on. It was all he had to hold onto—the car was like a bucking bronco.

Oh, God, his island.

And stunningly, even while he was holding on for dear life, he felt himself switch into doctor mode. Earthquake. Casualties. This was major.

Squid had been right. Never doubt the sages, he thought, and then he stopped thinking because he had to hold tight and nothing else could matter.

The car rolled—it almost rolled right over—and then, unbelievably, it rolled back again, righting itself with a massive thump.

What sort of power…? What sort of damage…?

Tsunami.

The vision crashed into his mind with sickening dread. Earthquake, tsunami. Get to high land.

Not yet. He could do nothing yet but hold on.

His seat belt was holding him safe—sort of. He was fine, short of the cliff caving in and his car sliding into the sea…

Not a lot of use thinking that.

Hold on. There was nothing he could do until the rolling stopped.

But he was still thinking medicine.

Casualties. He hardly dared think but already he knew the islanders were in real trouble.

One doctor.

No, two. First things first. He'd grab Ginny.

Please, God, she was okay.

Don't go there. He glanced towards the house and saw it heave and shift on its foundations. Please, hold.

He'd get Ginny, take her back to the hospital, leave Button with his mother…

His parents. The kids.

Do not go there.

Plan instead. The earth was settling. Panic was turning to focus.

He'd call the mainland, get help organised. Maybe he could do it now.

He flicked his phone. He had a signal.

And then he didn't.

The telecommunications tower at the airport must have toppled.

No phone.

The authorities on the mainland would figure it out anyway, he thought grimly. A quake this size would show on every seismograph in the world.

He had two nurses on duty at the hospital, with six more on call. How many could get there?

Roads would be cut.

Roads... How...?

The car jerked and bucked and his grip on the wheel tightened.

Ginny, he thought. Please.

He stopped planning. He held on like grim death and he said the word over and over and over.

Please.

It went on and on and on. Just when she thought it had ended it started up again. She couldn't move—she daren't. Yes, the safest place was outside but to get there she'd have to negotiate her way through the house. There were massive exposed beams in the historic homestead. She was terrified of those beams and the table was midway between two of them so she was staying right where she was.

Button was amazingly calm. She clung and clung, and didn't say a word as they lay huddled under the massive table.

Weirdly, Ginny found herself singing, odd little nursery rhymes she'd heard from nannies as a child, and sometimes she heard Button add a word or two as well.

There was nothing and no one but the two of them and this table. The vineyard was miles from the nearest neighbour. The shaking went on.

She held Button, she clung to her table leg and she'd never felt so alone in her life.

One part of Ben was totally focussed on what was happening, seeing the cracks open in the road, watching parts of the cliff fall into the sea, watching Ginny's house buckle and sway.

One part of him was moving on, thinking tsunami warn-

ings, casualty centres, evacuation plans, emergency re-
sources.

The hospital was on high ground. It was weatherboard,
and watching Ginny's house he thought weatherboard was
the way to go.

But one of Ginny's chimneys had crashed.

Please…

Don't go there.

The ground was settling now, the massive undulations
passing. Any minute now he'd dare to get out of the car.

And go see if Ginny was safe.

The thought of her inside, near that crashed chimney,
made him feel ill.

But… It wasn't that he was especially worried about
Ginny, he told himself. It was just because she was here, now.
He'd watched her house heave—of course he was worried.

Plus she'd been part of his childhood. A friend.

But he knew there was more.

What were the levels of love?

It was hardly the time to think about that now. Finally the
world was ceasing to shake.

Maybe it was worst on this side of the island, he prayed.
Here the roads were buckled beyond using. Here huge trees
had crashed. Here Ginny's house…

Was still standing. He could see broken windows and
tumbled masonry. He thought suddenly of those massive
beams above the kitchen and the thought had him out of
the car and running before the earth had completely settled.

Ginny.

She should take Button out from under the table.

She was afraid to move.

The quake seemed to have passed. There were still tremors, but minor ones. She could venture out from under her table and make a run for outside.

She didn't want to. Here seemed the only safe place.

She stayed under her table and she held the silent Button and she hugged and hugged.

'It's okay, it's over,' she whispered, but she barely believed it.

'Ginny?'

The voice came from nowhere. No, it didn't, it came from the back veranda.

'Ben?' She could scarcely believe it. Ben! Here!

'Where are you?' he yelled.

'I-in the kitchen. Under the table. But the beams...'

She didn't finish. There was a series of crashes, like a bull moving through her living room, but maybe it was one desperate doctor hauling away the litter of damaged furniture blocking his path.

And then, unbelievably, he was under the table with her. He was gathering her—and Button—into his arms and he was holding them.

He held and held and her world changed yet again.

She'd thought it was over, but just as she pulled away a little, just as she relaxed and thought the world was settling, that Ben was here, that they were safe, another tremor hit.

It wasn't nearly as big as that first, vast wave, but it was big enough for Button to cling, for Ben to haul them both close again, for her to cling back.

And think again.

What she'd just thought.

Which was nonsense. Which was everything she'd vowed never to think again.

Safe in the arms of someone who loved her?

Life was a travesty, she thought as she clung, because she

still needed to cling, for Button's sake as well as her own. Button was cocooned between them, safe, protected by their bodies, a Button sandwich between her two protective adults.

Button needed Ben.

For now Ginny needed Ben—but just for now. Only for now, she told herself fiercely.

This was crazy. This was an earthquake, for heaven's sake, so why was she suddenly thinking of James, of a marriage that had made her glow, had made her think this was happy-ever-after, had made her believe in the fairy-tale?

Why was she thinking of the travesty that marriage had turned out to be? Of infidelity, of shattered trust. Of anger, more, of hatred, that she was the one to live. Of the knowledge that her judgement was appalling, that trust was stupid, that love was for the pages of fairy-tales.

'Ginny...'

'Mmm.' It seemed almost wrong to speak, as if somehow voices might stir the demons to shake some more.

'We need to get outside.'

'I think I like my table.'

'I like your table, too,' he said. 'But there's the little matter of beams above us. We can't depend on them falling straight if this gets any worse. We need to risk it. Button, we're going to run. We're going to wriggle out from under here, I'm going to carry you, because I'm stronger and faster than Ginny...'

'Ginny,' Button said, and clung tighter.

'I can see Shuffles,' Ben said, lightly now, making it seem almost conversational. 'He's right by the door on the floor. If you let me carry you, we'll rescue Shuffles and take him outside.

Button considered. There was silence while they let her make up her mind and then she gave a decisive nod.

She turned within their sandwich squeeze and transferred her hold to Ben.

'Get Shuffles,' she ordered. 'Go.'

'Yes, ma'am,' Ben said, and touched Ginny's face—just fleetingly, but she felt herself flinch.

He gave her a sharp, questioning glance but the time for questions wasn't now.

'Let's go,' he said, and hauled himself backwards from under the table, holding Button and Button holding him, and there was nothing left for Ginny to do but follow.

Outside was weird.

It was as if a giant hand had picked up and shaken the house, leaving its contents a vast, jumbled mess. Outside it almost looked normal.

The veranda steps had cracked and fallen sideways. The downpipes were hanging at crazy angles, windows were broken and a chimney had crumpled. Otherwise you might almost look at it and think nothing had happened.

'Old and weatherboard,' Ben said. They'd scrambled out of the house, moving fast in case another tremor hit, but now they were in the yard between house and stables, with no trees close, nothing but open ground. There was a deep crack running across the width of the yard, a foot wide, heaven knew how deep, but they were well clear of it.

'Wooden houses seem to stand up to quakes much better than brick,' Ben said. 'Thank God most of the island houses are wooden.'

He turned and stared towards the town and Ginny could see his mind turning to imperatives. Medical imperatives? Plus the fact that his parents and siblings were in the valley.

'Tsunami,' he said, and just as he said it a siren started, loud and screeching, blaring a warning. Even as a child here Ginny had learned what it meant.

What Ben had just said.

'It's too close,' she whispered.

'What?'

'I did a project at school. Tsunamis come when quakes happen out to sea. This one was so big...surely the fault's right under us.'

'Let's not bet our lives on it,' Ben said grimly. 'Get in the Jeep, now.'

'I can—'

'Get in the Jeep or I'll throw you in,' he said grimly, and he grabbed her hand with his free one—he was still cradling Button with the other—and ran across the yard.

Seconds later they were bucketing across the paddocks, heading up the steep valley incline. Fences were ignored—Ben simply steered his battered Jeep between the posts and crashed straight through.

Tsunami.

The word was enough to block out everything else. She held Button tightly—Ben had obviously decided he wasn't wasting precious seconds fastening her into her child seat—and stared down at the sea. Willing it to be okay.

Willing a wave not to come.

It didn't. They reached the ridge above the vineyard and stopped, then climbed from the Jeep and watched the sea while the siren still wailed across the island.

Ben produced field glasses from the Jeep and his expression grew more and more grim as he surveyed what he could of the island.

Ginny didn't ask to see. She didn't want to see. She held Button and she thought this was a hiatus. The last moment before reality.

She thought suddenly of the day she and James had gone to the hospital for him to get tests. They'd been practically sure but not...not prepared. Did anything prepare you for such a thing?

The tests were run. 'Come back at six and get the results,'

the oncologist had said, so they'd gone to the beach, swum, had a picnic, talked of everything under the sun until it was time to go back.

'If I'm okay we'll even have a baby,' she remembered James saying.

And she remembered thinking, Please, let this time not end.

Knowing that it would.

She was still watching the sea. Waiting for the world to end?

Ben was jabbing at his cell phone then turning his field glasses toward the island's small airport.

'The tower must be down,' he said, staring at the screen. 'I hoped it was just a glitch during the shake but every-thing's dead. We should be able to see the tower from here. There's no reception.'

Ginny hauled her phone out of her back jeans pocket and stared. No bars. Nothing.

'Oh, God,' she whispered.

'It'll be okay,' Ben said, and she saw the way he hauled himself under control. What lay before them might well be appalling. For him to be the only doctor... 'The guys on the fishing boats have radios that'll reach the mainland. A quake this big will be sensed from there. I'm guessing we'll get help fast.' His eyes roved over the island, noting signs of damage that from up here seemed small but she knew that once they got close it could spell calamity. 'Choppers can get here fast. An hour to scramble, two hours for the flight...'

'They'll come?'

'If they can't contact the hospital they'll come anyway. Hell, Ginny, I need to be there.' He winced as the siren kept on wailing and Ginny wondered whether if he wasn't sad-dled with Button and with her, he would have gone now, tsunami threat or not.

'If the coast road's out…we'll go overland as soon as the siren stops,' Ben said grimly, his field glasses sweeping slowly across the valley again. 'The coast road won't be safe. It'll be rough but the Jeep should do it.

'What…what's a few fences?' she said unsteadily, and Ben managed a smile.

'I hear the local landowner shoots trespassers on sight. Risks are everywhere.'

The local landowner would be her. She managed a smile back. 'You might be granted dispensation.'

'Dispensation. Wow!' And then his smile died. 'Ginny, will you help?'

'Of course I will.'

'No, *really* help,' he said. 'No holds barred. We'll need to leave Button with Hannah, as long as Hannah…' He broke off and went back to staring through his glasses and Ginny followed his line of sight and thought he'd be staring at an old wooden house in the middle of town that held his mum and dad and siblings.

'I think the hospital's intact. It's on high ground overlooking the harbour. It looks solid. I hope to hell our equipment's safe,' Ben said.

Ginny nodded. Ben needed to think of medical imperatives, she thought, or any imperatives rather than thinking about family, friends, for a quake of this magnitude had to mean casualties on a massive scale.

'Your family will be okay,' she said stoutly. 'Your house is as old and sturdy as mine, and your kitchen table's bigger. And I'm thinking your mum's the one who taught me about diving under it.'

'And Mum was preparing lamb roast for dinner tonight,' Ben managed. 'I hope she's taken the spuds under there with her. She should be peeling them now.'

She grinned, and then hugged him because she knew how

hard it had been to joke—and then she pulled away because there was no way she wanted him to think a hug meant anything but a hug.

'Ginny,' he said, and put a hand to her face, and for the life of her she couldn't stop herself flinching again.

Why did she flinch? Of all the stupid… Wasn't it about time she learned some control?

There was a moment's loaded pause, a silence broken only by the wail of the siren. For a long, long moment Ben gazed down at her, as if he was seeing right inside her.

'What did that *bastard* do to you?' he asked at last.

No. One minute they'd been talking earthquake, thinking earthquake, feeling earthquake, and the next…this?

She stared at him, stunned to stupefaction. She didn't want him to see. She didn't want anyone to see.

'I won't hurt you, Ginny,' Ben said gently, and he touched her face again. 'How can you think I will?'

She shook her head. This was crazy. There was no way she was answering that, here, now, or at any time.

She'd made a vow. Life on her terms, now and for ever.

As long as this shaking world permitted.

'Of course I'll help at the hospital,' she said, far too quickly.

'Good,' he said, and moved his field glasses on. But she knew he wouldn't be deflected. He knew her, this man, like no other person had ever known her—and the thought was terrifying.

She went back to hugging Button. Apart from the siren, it was incredibly peaceful. It was a gorgeous autumn afternoon. The sun was sinking low on the horizon and the grass underfoot was lush and green.

But there were cattle in the paddocks, and every beast had its head up. Because of the siren?

Um...no. Because the earth had just shifted and neither man nor beast knew what would happen next.

And then the siren stopped.

Ben's field glasses swung around until he found what he was looking for.

'We send the siren out from four points of the island,' he said slowly, thinking it through as he spoke. 'The sirens are set off from the seismology centre on the mainland. They're supposedly quake-proof and they get their signal via satellite. If they've stopped we can assume that boffins somewhere have decided there will be no tsunami. Thank God.'

'Thank God,' she repeated, and once again she got an odd look, the knowledge that he saw more than she wanted him to see. Earthquake or not, she knew now that there was a world of stuff between them, and she also knew it was stuff he'd hunt down until it was in the open.

'It's okay, Ginny,' he said gently. 'We can work side by side, I promise. This is professional only. We treat it as such. We go see what the damage is and how best we can start putting things back together again. And we put everything else aside until later.'

CHAPTER SIX

ON TOP OF everything else, she was fearful for her farm manager. Henry now lived on the headland beyond the vineyard, on his own.

'His place is so remote. Ben, we need to check…'

'We can't,' he said, as gently as he could manage. 'Henry's four miles that way overland, the coast road'll be cut and we'll have casualties coming into the hospital now. Ginny, I'm sorry, but triage says hospital first. We have to get to town.'

She knew he was right but it didn't make her feel better. Her car was a sedan, not capable of going cross-country. Ben's Jeep was their only mode of transport. They needed to travel together and there was only one direction they could head.

Henry was on his own and it made her feel ill. How many islanders were on their own?

They headed down the valley. It sounded simple. It wasn't.

Driving itself was straightforward enough. Ben had wire cutters in the Jeep, so if they came to a troublesome fence they simply cut the wires. The ground was scattered with newly torn furrows where the earth had been torn apart, but the Jeep was sturdy and Ben was competent.

Ginny thought they'd get back to the hospital fast, and then they crossed the next ridge and her nearest neighbours came into view. Caroline and Harold Barton. Caroline was sitting by a pile of rubble—a collapsed chimney—and she was sobbing.

'He went back in to try and get the cat,' she sobbed. 'I can't get the bricks off him. And the crazy thing is…' she motioned to a large ginger tom sunning himself obliviously on a pile of scattered firewood '…Hoover's fine. Oh, Harold…'

There was a moan from underneath the bricks and then an oath.

'Would you like to stop reporting on the bloody cat and get these bricks off me?' Harold's voice was healthily furious.

Ben lifted Button from the Jeep and handed her over to the sobbing lady.

'Button, this is Mrs Barton and she's crying because she's had a fright,' he said matter-of-factly. 'But now she's going to introduce you to her cat. Caroline, your job is to keep Button happy. Ginny, how are you at heaving bricks?'

'Fine,' Ginny said, knowing how desperate Ben was to get to the hospital but knowing they had no choice but to help the hapless Harold.

Ten minutes later they had him uncovered and, miraculously, his injuries were minor.

'Felt the bloody thing heave so I dived straight into the cavity itself,' he said. 'It could'a gone either way, on top of me or around me, so I was bloody lucky.'

He was, Ginny thought as Ben cleaned a gaping gash on his arm and pulled it together with steri-strips. It'd need stitching but stitching had to wait. The important thing to do now was stop the bleeding and move on.

Triage. The hospital. What was happening down in the town?

Bricks had fallen on Harold's leg as well. 'There's possibly a break,' Ben said, but Harold waved him away.

'Yeah, and you might be needed for something a bit more major than a possible ankle break. Caroline can put me on the tractor and we'll make our way down to town in our own good time. With the cat. With this ankle I'm not even going to be able to kick him so there's not a lot of choice. Get yourself down to those who need you, Doc.' And then he turned to Ginny. 'But thank God you came home when you did, girl. When you were a kid we always reckoned you belonged here. Seems we were right. You've come home just in time.'

They passed three more houses, with three more groups of frightened islanders. They crammed two women, three kids and two dogs into the back. There was nothing wrong with them except scratches and bruises, but they were all stranded and they wanted, desperately, to be in town with community support.

'I'm hoping someone's set up a refuge,' Ben said tightly to Ginny. 'I need to be there.'

He couldn't be there, though. At the next farmhouse they came to, an entire stone barn had collapsed. Once again they found a sobbing woman but there was no humour about this situation. One of the women distracted the kids while the rest grimly heaved stone. The elderly farmer must have been killed instantly.

They left old Donald Martin wrapped in a makeshift shroud, they tucked Flora into the front of the Jeep, and Flora sobbed all the way to the village—and hugged Button.

Button was amazing, Ginny thought. She was medicine all by herself. She even put her arms around this woman she'd never met before and cuddled her and said, 'Don't cry, lady, don't cry,' whereupon Flora sobbed harder and held her tighter. A normal four-year-old would have backed away in fear but Button just cuddled and held her as Ben pushed the loaded Jeep closer to town.

He was desperate, Ginny thought. The hospital, the whole

town was currently without a doctor. It was now almost five hours since the quake. They'd seen a couple of helicopters come in to land and Ben had relaxed a little bit—'Help must be coming from the mainland.'—but she could still see the tension lines on his face. Why wasn't he at the hospital?

If he hadn't been calling in on her... If he hadn't been bringing Button's test results...

'Ben, I'm so sorry,' she told him from the back seat, and Ben swivelled and gave her a hard stare before going back to concentrate on getting the Jeep across the next paddock.

'There's no fault,' he said grimly. 'Cut it out, Ginny, because I won't wear your guilt on top of everything else. I don't have time for it.'

And that put her in her place.

It was self-indulgent, she conceded, to think of guilt. She was crammed between two buxom women. She had kids draped over her knees.

Ben didn't have time to think about guilt, she thought, and then they entered the main street and neither did she.

The first things they saw were road cones. Orange witches' hats were stretched across the main street, forcing them to stop.

The light was fading but they could see the outlines of the buildings. They could see devastation.

Porches of old, heritage-style shopfronts had come crashing down. A car parked at the kerbside was half-buried under bricks and stones—and maybe it was more than one car, Ginny thought, gazing further along the road.

Right near where they'd been forced to stop, the front of Wilkinson's General Store had fallen away. So had the front of Miss Wilkinson's apartment upstairs. The elderly spinster's bedroom lay ripped open as if a can opener had zipped along the edge. Her bedroom, with chenille bedspread, her dressing gown hanging on the internal door, her teddy bears spread across the bed, was on view for all to see.

She'd be mortified, Ginny thought, appalled for the gentile old lady. And then she thought, Please, God, that she's safe enough to feel mortified.

There were no lights. At this time of day the streetlights should be flickering on, but instead the scene was descending into darkness.

A soldier was approaching them from the other side of the road block. A soldier?

Ben had the Jeep's window down, staring at this uniformed stranger in dismay. For heaven's sake, the man even had a gun!

'The main street's been declared a red zone,' the soldier stated. 'It's too dangerous to proceed. My orders are to keep everyone out.'

'I'm needed at the hospital on the other side of town,' Ben said with icy calm, and Ginny felt like reaching out from the back seat, touching him, reassuring him—but there was no reassurance to be had. 'I'm a doctor,' he said. 'I have people here who need treatment.'

'Sorry, sir, you still need to follow protocol,' the soldier said. 'You can pull the car to the side of the road—as far away from the rubble as you can, sir, and report to Incident Control Headquarters.'

'Incident Control Headquarters?' Ginny demanded, because Ben seemed almost speechless. She could see where his head was. Soldiers coming in and taking control of his island? 'Where exactly is Incident Control Headquarters?'

'Um…it's the tourist information centre,' the soldier said, unbending a little.

'Thank you,' Ben said tightly, and parked the Jeep, and he and Ginny ushered his tight little group of frightened citizens round the back of the shattered buildings towards the sounds and bustle and lights of…Incident Control Headquarters?

Here there were people everywhere. Floodlights lit the outside of what was normally tourist central. Serious men and women Ginny didn't recognise, wearing hard hats and bright orange overalls, were spilling in and out.

Ginny was clutching Button and holding Flora's hand with the hand she had spare. She was feeling ill. Ben was carrying two of the toddlers they'd brought down from the ridge, and he looked as grim as she felt.

It was almost five hours since the quake had hit, and what five hours ago had been a peaceful island setting had now been transformed. These people represented professional disaster management, she thought. They'd have been brought in by the choppers they'd seen.

Kaimotu Island must now be officially a disaster scene.

And then there was Abby, flying down the steps to meet them. Abby was also wearing orange overalls and a hard hat. A grim-faced man came behind her, obviously keeping her in sight, but Abby had eyes only for Ben.

'Ben—oh, thank God you're okay,' the nurse said. 'I've been so worried. Where have you been? We've been going out of our minds. Your mum—'

'She's okay?' Ben snapped, and Ginny had a further inkling of what he'd been going through. What he still was going through.

'She's fine,' Abby said hurriedly. 'As far as I know, all your family is okay. Doug's out with the searchers. Your house is intact and your mum and Hannah have set it up as a crèche.'

'Flora!' It was a cry from inside the hall. A group of ladies was dispensing sandwiches. One of these ladies darted forward and Ginny realised with relief that it was Daphne Hayward, Flora's sister.

And then she thought, irrelevantly, I know these people. I haven't been near this island for twelve years but I know them.

I'm one of them?

'Can you clear the entrance, please?' a soldier asked, and they all turned round and glared at him, Ginny, too, and Ginny thought incredulously, I'm an islander.

And then Ben lifted Button from her arms and she let her be lifted because it was the natural thing to do, to let Ben help her.

Ben. Her friend.

Her island, in trouble.

'Why aren't you at the hospital?' Ben was asking Abby as he hugged Button close. 'Who's in charge there?'

'Things are as under control as they can be,' Abby said, but her voice was tight and strained. Really tight and strained. 'We've had four choppers arrive containing emergency personnel, including two doctors. Margy's doing triage, and every nurse on the island's with her. One of the helicopters has already evacuated Percy Lockhart and Ivy Malone—both have serious crush injuries. One of the doctors is a surgeon. He's reducing a compound fracture now— Mary Richardson's arm. It's bad, Ben, it's really bad.'

Her voice faltered and she motioned to the grim-faced man behind her. 'This is Tom Kendrick. I... We know each other. He's with Search and Rescue from the mainland. We've been out. They wanted a nurse who knew people. I... I...'

The stranger behind Abby moved in closer, and Ginny saw his arm go round her waist. That was odd, she thought, but Ben was standing really close to Ginny, and she was sort of leaning against him. In fact, her own arm was suddenly round Ben. It was because she needed contact with Button, she told herself, but she knew it was more.

She wanted contact with Ben, and if Abby needed contact with this stranger…it sort of gave her permission to ask for contact herself.

But even as she thought it, she looked at Abby's face, she saw the lines of strain and fear—and suddenly she got it.

'Abby, where's Jack? Where's your son?'

'On…on the bus,' Abby whispered. 'We've just come back to get the chopper. Tom's organising a drop of blankets and food.'

'What the…?' Ben started.

'It's okay,' Tom reassured him, solid, professional, assured. 'We had a tense time for a while when we couldn't locate the school bus but we have it now. One of the fishing boats has seen it from the sea. It's trapped on the coast road round past the mines at the back of the island. There's been two landslips and the bus is trapped between them. As far as we know, they're all fine, but we're not going to be able to get them out until morning. Hence the airdrop. We'll drop a radio in as well.'

'So it'll be okay,' Abby said, still in that tight, strained voice, and Ginny wondered what else was wrong. But she had to move on. They all had to move on.

'They need you at the hospital,' Abby said, forcing her voice to sound almost normal. 'Here's Hannah— Ginny, is it okay if Button goes with her? You and Ginny are needed for medical stuff. Please, go fast. There are so many casualties. But Tom and I need to go now. We need this food drop done before it's completely dark. Tom, let's go.'

New Zealand was set up for earthquakes. Emergency services stood ready twenty-four hours a day. It had been years since there'd been a major quake but that didn't mean they'd relaxed.

The personnel who'd arrived were moving with clinical precision. As Ben and Ginny walked through the almost abandoned town, skirting damaged buildings, they saw teams moving silently from house to house, quickly checking, in some cases with dogs by their sides, making sure everyone was out and then doing lightning assessments of each building.

Using spray paint. Numbers. Colours or degrees of risk. Miss Wilkinson's general store came under the 'Do Not Approach Under Any Circumstances' heading and Ginny thought bleakly of those little pink teddies and a dignified old lady having to bunk down in the school hall tonight without her dressing gown and her pink friends.

Ben was holding her hand. Ginny hardly realised it, but when she did she didn't pull away.

This was too big to quibble. If Ben needed reassurance…

She even managed a slight smile at that. Who was she kidding? Her hold on his hand tightened and he gave her a reassuring smile in the dark.

'We'll get through this.'

'Oi!' It was a soldier, one of the many patrolling the streets. 'You guys need to get to the evacuation centre. That way. This street's not safe.'

'Doctors,' Ben said briefly. 'We need to be at the hospital.'

And all of a sudden they had a military escort and Ben held her hand tighter and it seemed even more…right that she held his. And held and held.

It was so silent, so dark—and then they rounded the bend and the hospital was in front of them and it wasn't dark at all.

Kaimotu Hospital was a small weatherboard hospital up on the headland, looking over the town. Once it had been a gracious old house overlooking the harbour. Over the years it had been extended, with a brand-new clinic at the rear, a doctor's apartment to the side, the rooms expanded to make a lovely ten-bed hospital with most rooms looking out over the veranda to the harbour beyond.

It had been expanded even more now. Some sort of camp hospital had been set up on the front lawns overlooking the sea. It was a vast canvas canopy, lit by floodlights on the outside and by vast battery-powered lanterns inside. A huge red generator was humming from the side of the tent, and the lights were on inside the hospital.

Ginny, who'd thought bleakly of dealing with casualties in third world conditions, felt herself relax. Just a little.

'Docs,' the soldier escorting them said briefly, as yet another soldier came forward to greet them. 'Two of 'em. You can use them?'

'Doctors?' A fresh-faced kid who looked about eighteen pushed aside the canvas door and looked at them. 'Real doctors?'

'Ben McMahon and Ginny Koestrel,' Ben said, and held his hand out in greeting. 'I'm a family doctor with surgical training and Ginny's an anaesthetist.'

'Whew.' The guy whistled. 'I'm Dave Marr, doc with New Zealand Search and Rescue. We have Lou Blewit here as well but I want to send her back with the next chopper. I have a guy with a crush injury to his chest—breathing compromised. He needs a thoracic surgeon. If you guys can help...'

He was dressed in green theatre garb. He might look young but he didn't sound young, Ginny thought. He sounded every inch a doctor, like he knew exactly what he was doing.

Thank God for emergency personnel. Thank God for helicopters. If she and Ben had been on their own...

'You guys swear you're doctors?' Dave said, his tired face breaking into a slight smile. 'You look like chimney sweeps to me. Was that what kept you?'

'Digging the odd person out,' Ben said. 'We got here as fast as we could.'

'Well, thank God for it,' Dave said bluntly. 'From now on…yeah, we need diggers but we need doctors more. I have a truckload of casualties coming in now. You ready to deal with them?'

'Yes,' they said in unison, and Dave grinned.

'Excellent. You guys use the theatre inside the hospital—that's what you're familiar with. I'll stay on triage out here—this is my territory. By the way, you might need to wash. We've set up a washroom over there—we've attached hoses to the garden tanks out back but use a bit more antiseptic than usual because Abby tells us the tank often holds the odd dead possum. We're working on a safe water supply now.'

He glanced up as a battered farm truck turned into the car park. 'Here's the next load,' he said. 'Let's go.'

For the next eight hours Ginny and Ben scarcely had time to breathe.

Luckily most of the injuries were minor, caused by flying debris and masonry. The most common presentation was lacerations. Most of the island homes were weatherboard with corrugated-iron roofs. If they'd been brick homes with slate or tile roofs, the injuries would have been more severe, but corrugated iron, crashing down in sheets, could slice to the bone. Added to that, people had crawled out of collapsed buildings, trying to get out as fast as they could, often unaware that they had been crawling over shattered glass and crockery.

The wounds were caked with dust, and they couldn't be stitched fast.

Some people needed to be transferred to the mainland. Some would need plastic surgery to stop scarring for a lifetime, but there was enough work to hold Ben and Ginny in Theatre, working as hard and fast as they could.

They worked side by side rather than together, seeing two

patients at a time. They shared a nurse—Prue, the youngest of the island's nurses—and they helped each other.

It was hardly best medical practice to operate on two patients in the one small theatre but it meant help was always on hand. If one of them got into trouble, Ben helped Ginny or Ginny helped Ben. Ben's surgical skills assisted Ginny, Ginny's anaesthetic skills assisted Ben...

And besides...

It settled her, Ginny thought as she worked through the night. The day had been terrifying. Just the fact that she had Ben six feet away, a solid, reassuring presence, helped her to focus.

There was no question that she was a doctor now. She'd walked away from medicine six months ago but now she was in medicine up to her neck.

And for the first time in years she felt grateful to be a doctor.

She'd helped Ben save Henry but she'd been almost resentful that she'd been hauled out of her reclusive shell. Here there was no resentment.

She liked being able to help. She loved having the necessary skills.

The knowledge was almost like a lightning bolt. She remembered the early days of training, working as an intern. She remembered the almost terrifying sensation of making a difference to people's lives. The dependence on colleagues. The gut-wrenching pain of loss and the mind-blowing feeling of success. She remembered heading to the pub after work with a group of colleagues to unwind, joking about the macabre, understanding each other, knowing she'd be working side by side with them the next day.

Like she was working side by side with Ben now.

It had all stopped when she'd met James. Her social life

had centred on him from that point on. She'd started specialist anaesthetic training.

She'd still worked in a team in Theatre but the atmosphere had subtly changed. She had become the girlfriend of a senior consultant and James had often stopped by, to watch, to give a little advice, to make sure everyone in the theatre knew she was his woman.

Why was she thinking of that now? She was cleaning slivers of glass from Bea Higgins's knees. Bea was seven years old, she'd been having a day off school when the quake had hit because she'd needed to go to the dentist, and had ended up crawling out of the Higgins's lean-to bathroom.

'And Mum says I still have to go to the dentist,' she said mournfully.

'Cheer up,' Ben said from the other side of the room. He was stitching an elderly farmer's arm—Craig Robb had been trying to get his pigs out of their sty when sheets of corrugated iron had fallen and slashed. Farmer, not pig. 'Doc Dunstan's front porch has collapsed,' he told Bea. 'You might not get a dentist appointment for months.'

'Cool.' Bea grinned happily as Ginny dressed her cuts and grazes. She'd hurt when the anaesthetic wore off, Ginny thought, but kids bounced back. For most of these kids this earthquake would end up being an adventure.

And for the rest of the island? The damage didn't seem massive. There'd been no tsunami. There hadn't been any reports of multiple deaths—three so far, and all of them elderly. Could the island get off so lightly?

But there might well be more casualties. There were still the islanders who lived in outlying areas, where searchers hadn't been able to reach. There was still a trapped school bus.

There was still Henry.

'Worry about what's in front of you right now,' Ben said.

She flashed a glance at him and thought again, He knows me as no one else does.

The thought was terrifying, yet she was suddenly no longer terrified. She was working side by side with him, and no matter what was happening in the outside world, she wasn't terrified at all.

All his attention should be on his island. All his focus should be on deaths, injuries, damage.

Instead, he was working alongside Ginny Koestrel and it felt…okay.

As a seventeen-year-old he'd thought he loved her. Love was a pretty big word—a word he reserved for his family. There'd been a few women since Ginny, but not one he'd applied the 'love' word to.

His mother had been suggesting he could get together with Abby. Abby was competent, a caring professional, pretty, smiley, a great mum to her little boy. 'Does the fact that she has a child stop you being interested?' his mother had asked him recently, and he'd laughed. It made not one whit of difference. He'd lived in a household of twelve kids. If he didn't like kids he'd have gone nuts long since.

So what had been stopping him? He and Abby had dated a couple of times—yeah, okay, just social functions like the hospital fundraiser where it was easier to have a partner—but they had still been dates.

There'd been friendship and laughter, but not a single spark.

And here was this woman, this stranger, really, as he hadn't seen her for twelve years, working alongside him. She was a different person from the one he'd thought he'd been in love with all those years ago, yet sparks were flying everywhere.

How could there be sparks when he was so tired?

How could he hear her talk softly to Bea and crane his
neck to hear, just to listen to her voice?

How could he get close? How could he brush away all the
wounds that had been inflicted on her—for he knew there
were deep wounds. How could he help her move on?

Move on towards him?

They ushered Craig and Bea out at the same time. Their two
patients were welcomed into the arms of their relieved rel-
atives, and there was a moment's peace while they waited
for Dave to direct them to the next need. The young nurse,
Prue, was almost dead on her feet. 'Go home,' Ben told her.
'You've done brilliantly.'

She left and Ben put his arms around Ginny and held her.

'So have you,' he said.

They stood at the entrance to the makeshift emergency
hospital, and for a moment all was silent.

He kissed her lightly on her hair. 'You're doing a fantastic
job, Dr Koestrel,' he told her. 'As a medical team, we rock.'

She didn't pull back. She was exhausted, she told herself
as he tugged her closer. It was okay to lean on him.

The queue outside had disappeared. Islanders were settling into the refuge centre or in some cases stubbornly returning to their homes. There'd still be myriad minor injuries
to treat, she thought, but Dave hadn't been waiting for them
when they'd emerged this time.

There was this moment to stand in this man's arms and
just…be.

It couldn't last. Of course it couldn't. A truck arrived and
a weary-looking Dave emerged from the back.

'I need you to see two more patients and then I'm standing us all down,' he said. 'I'm dealing with a suspected early
labour—I'll stay with her until the team arrives to evacuate
her. I think she'll settle but I'm taking no chances.'

'Who?' Ben asked.

'A tourist,' Dave told her. 'She was on a boat in the harbour when it hit.' He grinned. 'Which is something of a relief because the islanders want Ben first, Ginny as second best and me a poor last. But, as I said, it's easing. We have paramedics who'll stay on call for the rest of the night and I have another doctor flying in to take over from me. It's four now. If anything dire happens we'll call you out but you need to catch some sleep. The searchers will find more at first light so medically things will speed up again. Is there anywhere here you both can sleep?'

'My apartment's at the back of the hospital,' Ben said. 'If it's anything like the rest of the hospital it'll be unscathed. Ginny can stay with me.'

'I can give you a bed in a tent if that's not okay,' Dave told her, but Ginny shook her head, even though the tent might be more sensible.

But she didn't feel sensible. She was still leaning against Ben. She still wanted to lean against him.

But there were problems. She needed to focus on something other than this man's arms.

'Button…' she started.

'Whoops, I have a message about someone called Button,' Dave told her, looking rueful. 'One of the guys passed it on. The message is that Ailsa and Hannah said to tell you that Button and Shuffles are fast asleep and happy. They also said to tell you someone's left a basket of kittens with Ailsa because their laundry's collapsed and apparently Ailsa is a sucker for animals, so the message continues that Ailsa says Button would like a black one with a white nose. Button says she wants to call it Button, too.'

He grinned, pleased with himself for remembering the full gist of the message, and Ginny found herself smiling, too. It was exactly the kind of message she needed to hear.

She found herself sniffing and when Ben's arm tightened around her she didn't resist. How could she pull away?

Weirdly, her world, which had been shaken to the core years before, the day James had got his diagnosis, or even earlier, she thought, maybe even the day her father and James had taken her to dinner and hammered into her that she was a fool not to specialise, a fool to keep working in the emergency medicine she loved, seemed, on this day of all days, to be settling.

'You said…' she managed. 'You said…we have two more patients to see?'

'Minor problems,' Dave said. 'The searchers have just swept the wharf. Brian Grubb was trapped in the co-op storeroom when the door shifted on its hinges. He's cut his leg and needs an X-ray to eliminate a fracture to his ankle.

'We also have a Mr Squid Davies—a venerable old gentleman. The search dogs found him under a pile of cray pots and they've brought him in, protesting. He's had a bang on his head. I can't see any sign of concussion but he didn't have the strength to heave the pots off himself. He tells us he forecast the earthquake. He's busy telling all and sundry, "I told you so." Are you sure you can handle it?'

Squid and his end-of-the-world forecasting. Could she handle it?

She grinned at Ben and he grinned back.

'It'll be a pleasure to treat him,' Ben said, and his smile warmed places inside her she hadn't even known had been cold. 'We might even concede we should have listened.'

CHAPTER SEVEN

BEN TOOK ON Brian; Ginny took on Squid. Squid was brought in on a stretcher, but he was sitting bolt upright, his skinny legs dangling down on either side.

'I can walk, you fellas,' he was protesting. 'One hit on the head and you think you can treat me like a namby-pamby weakling.'

'Indulge us,' Ginny said, as the hefty paramedics transferred him smoothly to her examination couch. 'Come on, Mr Davies, lie down and let me see that bump on your head.'

'Since when have I been Mr Davies?' Squid demanded. 'I'm Squid. And you're the Koestrel girl. Bloody uppity parents. Folks say you turned out all right, though.'

'I think she's all right,' Ben said from the other side of the theatre. 'What about you guys?' he asked the paramedics. 'Do you think she's all right?'

There were grunts of agreement from the two burly paramedics, from Brian and from Squid himself, and Ginny thought, wow, she'd been in an earthquake, she'd spent half a day digging people out from under rubble, she'd been working as an emergency doctor for hours...and they thought...

'She's cute,' Squid decreed.

'Nah,' one of the paramedics said, eying her red hair with appreciation. 'It's politically incorrect to say cute. How about handsome? Handsome and flaming?'

'You've got rocks in your head, all of you,' Ginny said, as Ben chuckled. It was four in the morning. She felt punch-drunk. They all must be punch-drunk. 'Speaking of heads, lie down, Squid, while I check yours.'

'Won't,' said Squid.

'Lie down or I take over,' Ben growled, 'and we'll do the examination the hard way.'

'You and whose army?'

'Do you know how many soldiers we have outside? Lie down or we'll find a fat one to sit on you. Now.'

And there was enough seriousness in his tone to make Squid lie down.

Someone—Margy? —had been organised enough to find the islanders' health files and set them at hand. Ginny could see at a glance if there were any pre-conditions that could cause problems. She flicked through Squid's file fast while Ben started work on Brian. Ben knew each patient inside out; he didn't need their histories, but Ginny was wise enough to take care.

She flipped through Squid's history and did a double-take at his age. Ninety-seven.

Prostate cancer. Treatment refused. Check-ups every six months or so, mostly *or so*, because *regular* didn't seem to be in Squid's dictionary.

A major coronary event ten years ago.

Stents and bypass refused.

'There's nothing wrong with me but a bump on the head,' Squid said sourly. 'There I was, minding me own business, when, *whump*, every cray pot in the shed was on top of me. I warned 'em. Don't you stack 'em up there, I said, 'cos the big one's coming. Didn't I say the big one was coming, Doc?'

'You did,' Ben said wryly. 'I would have thought, though, with your premonition, you would have cleared out of the way of the cray pots.'

'I'm good but I'm not that good,' Squid retorted. He'd submitted as Ginny had injected local anaesthetic around the oozing gash across his forehead but he obviously wasn't worrying about his head. 'I was right, though. Wasn't I right, Doc? That German doc was right, too, heading for home. But you stayed here. And you, too, miss,' he said to Ginny. 'Did you listen? No.'

'Yeah, but I didn't get hit on the head with cray pots,' Ginny retorted. 'So I must have done something sensible. Squid, you have fish scales in this wound!'

'I was wearing me hat. There's always fish scales in that hat. Dunno where it is now; expect I'll have to go digging for it. Get 'em out for me, there's a lass, and make it neat. I don't want to lose me handsome exterior. Not but what I'm getting past it for the need for handsome,' he added, swivelling on the table to look thoughtfully at Ben. 'Not like you two. Not past it at all, not you two. At it like rabbits you were when you were kids. Going to take it up again now?'

'We were not,' Ginny retorted, 'at it like rabbits.' This night was spinning out of control. She was close to exhaustion, but also close to laughter. *At it like rabbits?*

'You woulda been if that gimlet-eyed mother of yours would have let you,' Squid retorted. 'But now you can. Got a littlie, now, though. Does that make a difference, Doc?' he demanded of Ben.

'That is not,' Ben said levelly, 'any of your business.'

'Island business is my business,' Squid said happily. The local anaesthetic was taking hold and any pain that might have interfered with his glorious I-told-you-so attitude was fading fast. 'That's why I warned you. The big 'un's coming. Did you listen? Not you. People are dead, Doc, 'cos they didn't listen.' He lay back, crossed his arms and his smile spread beatifically across his ancient face. 'Told you so. Told you so, told you so, told you so.'

'Ginny, could you give me a hand with Brian's X-ray?' Ben said, grinning across at Squid's obvious bliss. 'It'll take a couple of moments for that anaesthetic to work, and I'd rather not call any of the nurses back. Squid, I want you to lie still and keep quiet. We have patients resting just through the canvas.' Then, as Squid opened his mouth to protest, he put up a hand in a peremptory signal for him to stop.

'Squid,' he said sternly. 'Rest on your laurels. You said the big one was coming and it did. The whole island's in awe. Enough. Lie there and think about it, but while you're thinking, stay still. We're taking Brian next door for an X-ray and when we get back I don't want you to have moved an inch. Right?'

'R-right,' Squid said in a voice that told Ginny he wasn't quite as brave as he was pretending to be. He really was a very old man. He would have been scared.

She put a hand on his shoulder and gave it a gentle squeeze. 'This'll take no more than five minutes,' she told him. She'd checked his vital signs. She'd checked his pupils, his reactions. His bump on the head seemed to be just that, a bump on the head. 'You won't move, will you?'

'Not if you promise to keep looking after me,' Squid said, recovering, and Ginny smiled.

'I promise.'

'Then off you go, Brian, and let the lady photograph you,' Squid decreed. 'She's some lady, isn't she, Doc?

'I... Yes,' Ben said.

'Good call,' Squid said. 'I think I'm about to make another prediction. You want to hear it?'

'No,' Ginny and Ben said together, too fast, and they wheeled Brian out of the door towards X-Ray before Squid could say another word.

* * *

The X-ray took effort on both their parts. They were both needed to do the roll transfer that was part of their training. From there the X-ray went smoothly, confirming a greenstick fracture.

'I'll put a simple splint on it tonight,' Ben told Brian. 'We'll check it again tomorrow—it'll need a full cast but we'll wait until the swelling goes down.'

'Good luck,' Ginny said. Because she was feeling more and more like an islander, she gave the burly farmer a hug, then headed back to attend to Squid.

He was curled on his side, his back to the door.

'Sorry I've been so long,' she said cheerfully, and crossed the six steps to the examination couch.

But by the third step she knew something was amiss. Dreadfully amiss.

The stillness was wrong. She'd seen this.

Breathing was sometimes imperceptible but when it wasn't present, you knew.

She knew.

'Ben,' she called, in the tone she'd been taught long ago as a medical student. It was a tone that said, I don't intend to frighten any other patient but I want you here fast. Now.

She put a hand on Squid's leathery neck as she called, her fingers desperately searching for a pulse.

There wasn't one.

Ben was with her almost instantaneously, the door closed firmly between them and Brian.

They were alone in the room. Ben and Ginny and Squid.

Or Ben and Ginny.

'Oh, God, I shouldn't have left him.' Ginny was hauling the equipment trolley from the side of the room, fumbling for patches. No pulse… She didn't even have monitors set up. No IV lines. She hauled Squid's shirt open, ripping buttons.

She was barely aware that Ben was with her. Where was the laryngosope? She needed an endotracheal tube.

Panic was receding as technical need took over, and the knowledge that everything she needed was in reach. She put the patches on with lightning speed…

And Ben grabbed her hands.

'No,' he said.

What the…? She hauled back, confused. They had so little time before brain damage was irreversible. Did he want monitors? Proof? 'Ben, there's nothing—'

'Exactly,' he said, and his hands held hers in a grip that brooked no opposition. 'And that's the way he'd want it.'

'What do you mean? He's healthy. He was sitting up. It's only a bump on the head. Let me go!'

'No,' he said. 'Leave it.' And he held her for longer, while Squid's body settled more firmly into that awful stillness, while the time for recovery, for miracles, passed them by.

'Let me go.' She could hardly make herself coherent. 'Are you mad?'

'I'm not mad. Squid's ninety-seven, Ginny,' Ben said, and his voice was implacable. 'He's left clear instructions. You think he'd thank us for trying to resuscitate him?'

'He's well. It's just the shock.' She was still struggling but it was already too late. There'd been such a tiny window of opportunity. That Ben could stand there and stop her… That Ben could do nothing…

'He's your friend,' she hurled at him, and it was an accusation.

It was also true.

True for her as well?

When they'd been kids Squid had taught them to fish for flounder, to jag for the squid he'd taken his name from. He'd also shared the eternal supply of aniseed balls he'd always carried in his back pocket.

He was almost a part of the island itself. For Ginny... The thought that this was the end...

She gave one last despairing wrench and finally Ben set her free. But even as he did so, she knew it was too late. She knew it. She felt cold fury wash through her that she hadn't been allowed to fight. She wanted to hit out, hit something. Hit Ben?

'You know about medical DNRs,' Ben said, watching her, calmly questioning. Do Not Resuscitate. 'Squid signed one years ago.'

'But they're for people who have no chance,' she managed, thinking of a counsellor handing a form to James, 'Do Not Resuscitate', and James screwing it into a ball and hurling it back.

'That's for people whose life is worthless. I don't need it, dammit.'

Her father had acted the same way. He'd had three coronary occlusions, a cardiac arrest, pacemaker fitted, defibrillator, there was nothing more to be done, yet he'd never have dreamed of signing a form that said 'Do Not Resuscitate'.

Do not go gently into that good night.' Dylan Thomas's words had been her father and James's mantra, drilled into her with fury.

That anger was with her now. Not to be permitted to fight...

This was why she'd walked away from medicine, because she couldn't win. Because she wasn't good enough to win. To make a conscious decision not to win seemed appalling.

'Ginny, Squid is ninety-seven years old,' Ben said again, placing strong hands on her rigid shoulders. He must feel her anger but he was overriding it. 'He might look as if he's weathered to age for ever, but he's been failing for a long time. He has arthritis in almost every joint. He can't do the fishing he loves, and he's been getting closer and closer to needing nursing-home care. Add to that, from the moment the earth shook his face has been one vast smile. He was right, we were wrong. You don't think that's a good note to go out on?'

But how could death be a good note? 'We could have…'

'We could have for what, Ginny?' Ben said, still in that gentle yet forceful voice that said he saw things behind her distress and her anger. Things she didn't necessarily want him to see.

'You have to fight.' She could hardly speak. So many emotions were crowding in. James's words, flooding back…

You stupid cow, get the medication right, you know I need more. Damn what the oncologist says, give me more now!

'No,' Ben was saying. 'If we pulled Squid back now, what then? You know cardiac arrest knocks blood flow to the brain. You know the really old struggle to re-establish neural pathways. Ginny, he's left us at the moment of his greatest triumph and I for one wouldn't ask for anything better for such a grand old man.'

Anger was through and through her, but behind it was a fatigue that was almost overwhelming. It was like all the emotions that had built within her from the moment of James's death were here in this room, the armour she'd tried to place around herself shattering into a thousand pieces.

'I fight the battles I want to win,' Ben said. 'I wouldn't want to win this one.'

'You didn't want him to live?'

'I want everyone to live,' he said evenly, refusing to rise to the emotion she was hurling at him. 'But at ninety-seven I know where to stop. Ginny…'

'Don't Ginny me,' she whispered, and he touched her

face, to give pause to the hysteria she was so close to. She flinched and he stopped dead.

'Is that what happened?' he said. 'Did James hit you because you couldn't save his life?'

There was a moment's deathly silence. Okay, more than a moment, Ginny conceded. There was a whole string of moments, packed together, one after the other, leading to a place where she was terrified to go.

'No,' she said finally in a dead, cold voice, a voice she scarcely recognised as her own. She glanced at Squid, at the peace on the old man's face, and she knew Ben was right. She knew it. She had no reason to be angry with him.

There was a time to die and that Squid had died at his moment of greatest triumph... *A consummation devoutly to be wished?*

Maybe, but that was the problem, she thought. James and her father had seen death as defeat. It was why, afterwards, she'd walked away from medicine. To see death, time and time again...

'No,' she said, and then decided it was time to be honest. 'Okay, once. Towards the end. Don't think of me as a battered wife, though, Ben. I was no doormat. Yes, I put up with abuse when he was dying, but he was dying. The one time he slapped me I walked away for a week. Then I had a call from the hospital saying he'd had a bleed. I had no choice but to go back. James lashed out because I was living and he wasn't. There was nothing I could do but put up with it until it was done.'

He did touch her then, a feather touch on her cheek. 'You should never have put up with it. Dying gives no one the right to abuse another. That someone could hit you...'

'It's okay.'

'It's never okay.'

'Yet you say Squid's death is okay.'

'You equate death with violence? It's not the same thing, Ginny, and you know it. Not a peaceful, timely death at the end of a life well lived.'

There was another of those silences. The searchers had ceased for the night, ready to start again at daybreak. The stream of incoming patients had ended.

'Is this why you took Button?' Ben asked finally, heavily. 'Because you felt obligated? Like you felt obligated to return to James?'

'No.' She shook her head fiercely at that. 'No way. Do you really think of me as a wimp?'

'No, but—'

'I did go back to James because he was dying and there was no one else to care,' she said. 'But Button's no obligation. The way I see it, Button's the one true thing that's come out of this. Veronica and James can betray all they like, but to hurt Button... I'll love her and we'll make a new life for ourselves, without their shadows.'

'Good for you,' Ben said, a trifle unsteadily, and then he touched her face again. 'And this time you didn't even flinch. You're some woman, Ginny Koestrel.' He hesitated, glancing down at Squid.

'I'll organise this,' he told her. There'd be paperwork, formalities for Squid that had to be done and they had to be done now. Medical imperatives had to take over. 'You fix Brian's splint and then we need bed. We're both exhausted. Too much emotion. Too much work. Too much...everything.' His hands were on her shoulders again, but there was no force, only warmth and reassurance and friendship.

And something more?

'I...I do need to find Button,' she managed.

'Mum and Hanna have Button safe. They won't thank you for waking them, and you know they'll contact you in a heartbeat if Button needs you. My apartment's here. Stop fighting the world, Ginny. Squid's stopped fighting. It's time you stopped, too.'

It was four-thirty when Ben finally led Ginny into his apartment at the rear of the hospital. She was so tired she could barely stand. She should sleep in the search and rescue tents, she thought, or in the refuge centre or…or…

Or stop fighting. Stop thinking she had to fight.

'Bed,' Ben said. 'The bathroom's through that door. You want pyjamas, there're spares in the bureau, bottom drawer. They'll be big on you but they'll be comfy. There's a spare toothbrush in the bathroom cabinet.'

'You're ready for anything,' she murmured.

'I'm ready for any of my eleven siblings to land on my doorstep any time,' he said dryly. 'You try having brothers and sisters on an island as small as Kaimotu. *Ben, Mum'll have a fit if she sees me like this. Ben, I just need a bit of quiet. Ben, no one at home understands me.* This place doubles as the McMahon refuge centre.'

'You have lucky brothers and sisters,' she said wearily, and looked at the nice, big sofa in the sitting room. 'This'll do me nicely, as I suspect it does your siblings. Thank you, Ben. Goodnight.'

'You're using the bed.'

'I'm not taking your bed. There's no need. The way I feel, I'd sleep on stones.'

'Me, too,' he said, and then there was silence. A long silence.

Exhausted or not, things were changing. Twisting. It was like a void was opening, a siren was calling them in.

'I don't suppose,' Ben said, oh, so casually, 'that you'd like to share.'

'Ben…'

'No, okay, not an option,' he said hastily. 'I'd never sleep with a woman who expects a raised hand to be followed by a slap.'

'I know it wouldn't,' she said, astounded. 'I know it never would be.'

'And I'd never sleep with a woman who thought I might blame her for things that go wrong.'

That was a bigger statement. It was a statement to take her breath away.

Not all men were like James or like her father, the statement said.

Ben was her friend.

But Ben was standing in front of her now and she knew he was asking to be much more.

Sharing a bed...

More even than that.

'We do need to sleep,' she said uncertainly, but *more* was right in front of her, a huge, overwhelming impossibility that suddenly seemed possible.

To take a moment that had happened all those years ago—and take it forward?

Ben's hands were on her shoulders again—she was starting to get used to it. She was starting to get used to the feel of him. To the comfort of him. To security and to caring.

To love?

How could she possibly think that? How could she possibly fall in love again?

But right now fatigue was taking the edges off fear and caution and the knowledge that love could haul your life out of control and spin it into a crazy vortex of darkness. Right now there was only Ben, gently propelling her into his bedroom.

He proposed to sleep out here. Alone. Well, why not? He'd

asked to share and she'd reacted with fear. The moment she had, he'd backed away.

He'd never push. He respected her.

Did she want respect?

The feel of his hands...

The knowledge that his body was right here, right now...

The fact that this was Ben...

Things were twisting, changing. She was feeling like a caterpillar cocooned in her impenetrable skin, only suddenly the skin was bursting.

She wasn't sure what was inside.

She wasn't sure, but Ben was here, now. Her lovely Ben.

No matter what this night had held, no matter about her armour, no matter about all her vows, this man was a huge imperative overriding all else.

Instead of allowing him to twist her away, to propel her away, she twisted back, so she stood within his hold, so close she could feel his breath, so close she could feel his heartbeat.

'Ben,' she said, and she looked up at him and he looked down at her and she knew she didn't have to say a word. Everything that had to be said had been said.

'You know I love you,' he said, and the world held its breath.

Love?

'I always have,' he said conversationally. 'I may not always have been faithful...'

'Not? When I'd imagined you pining for years and years?' Somehow she managed to sound shocked, and somehow, amazingly, there was laughter in the room.

'No, but when you smacked Robbie Cartwright over the head with a wet chaff bag because he'd spilled my tadpoles and then went down on your hands and knees and scoured the mud until every last tadpole was saved...I fell in love with you then. Yes, Ginny Koestrel, there have been other women, as there have been other men for you, but our love was forged when we were eight years old and it seems it's there for life.'

'Ben...'

'And I'm not teasing,' he said softly, laughter fading. 'I have no idea why this emotion has surfaced again after all these years but it has, and if you'd care to share my bed...'

'But in the morning...'

'Can we worry about the morning in the morning?' he asked. 'Ginny, this is just for here, for now. It's been one hell of a day. Say no now and we'll sleep apart, but...'

'Yes,' she said. 'I'm saying yes.'

There was a moment's loaded pause. Maybe more than a moment. She looked up at him and he was so...solid. Here.

This man had been her friend for life. She'd walked away from him for all sorts of reasons, some of them right, some of them wrong, but now, for this night, he was offering her love and warmth and desire.

Love...

This wasn't a going-down-on-bended-knee love, she thought. This was a love born of friendship. She knew, she just knew, that taking what Ben was offering would never be used to hurt her, to hold her, to commit.

He wanted her in his bed now, in his arms, and there was no place she'd rather be.

'It's nearly five,' she whispered. 'We need to sleep.'

'So we do,' he said.

'So you'd best make love to me now,' she said, 'because there's no way I can sleep without it—except with drugs, and I don't hold with drugs when there's a very sensible alternative.'

'Is that what I am?' Amazingly laughter was suddenly all around them. 'A sensible alternative?'

'Yes,' she said, and she lifted her arms and wound them

around his neck and then she raised her face to be kissed. 'My Ben,' she said. 'My prescription tranquilliser.'

'If you think I'm your tranquilliser,' Ben said, sweeping her into his arms and carrying her toward the bed, without so much as a hint of asking permission, 'then you have another think coming. Tranquilliser indeed. Is that what you really need, Dr Koestrel? Something to make you sleep?'

'N-no,' she managed.

'Excellent.' He lowered her onto the soft covers of his big, masculine bed and hauled his shirt over his head.

She'd seen this man's body—in swimming trunks, when he'd been seventeen.

She hadn't seen this. His body...his big, lovely body. It took her breath away.

'Ben...'

He stopped, the laughter disappearing again.

'Ginny?' His voice was tender and she knew if she said stop now, no would mean no.

Where did friendship end and love take over?

Right here, she thought. Right now.

'Come here,' she whispered, and she tugged him down to join her. 'You've done enough. The least I can do is help you get that belt unbuckled.'

He laughed and submitted. He was undoing the buttons of her blouse. It was already ripped. She should tell him to rip it straight off but he was over her, half straddling her, concentrating on each button, and her mind was doing some sort of weird shutting-down thing.

Only it wasn't shutting down. It was sort of...focussing. Every single distraction was disappearing to nothing. Earthquakes. Button. Patients. The past and the future. Nothing mattered. There was only this man carefully, painstakingly undoing buttons on a ruined blouse.

She put her fingers up and ran her palms down the length

of his chest to where his belt was unfastened. She could go lower but Ben was taking his time and so was she.

The buttons were no longer an issue. He spread her shirt wide. 'You want me to tug it free?' he asked, and she grabbed both sides of the skimpy fabric and ripped.

'Wow,' Ben said. 'You want to do that to your bra as well?'

'You have to work for it,' she said, smiling and smiling, and he did, and then a few very satisfactory moments followed while he explored what was underneath.

She was on fire. It didn't actually matter if this night wasn't consummated, she thought hazily, but then his fingers drifted further, and she forgot any thoughts of lack of consummation. Consummation did matter. She wanted him. This was here, this was now. This was Ben.

And as a faint aftershock rippled across the island, waking weary rescue workers and causing islanders to hold each other tighter, Dr Ben McMahon and Dr Guinevere Koestrel didn't notice.

In a few short hours they'd be back in the wards, back to being emergency doctors.

For now there was only this night, this heat, this need.

For now there was only each other.

CHAPTER EIGHT

SHE DIDN'T WANT dawn to come. She lay encircled in Ben's arms and she thought if she didn't move maybe time would stand still. She was spooned against Ben's body, skin to skin, warm, protected...loved?

Somewhere out there was the outside world, responsibilities, cares, life, but for Ginny right now life was solely within this man's arms, and she wanted nothing more.

He was awake. She felt him shift slightly and the tingle of naked skin was enough to make her tremble. He kissed her hair and then tugged her around so she was facing him and he could kiss her properly. Deeply, achingly wonderful.

And then, as she knew he must, he set her back, holding her at arm's length, and they both knew the world needed to intrude.

'We've had four hours' sleep,' he said ruefully.

'Three and a half,' she said, and smiled, and he kissed her again.

'I know,' he said, half-mournfully. 'A man had the promise of four hours' precious sleep and suddenly there was a seductress in my bed.'

'You didn't appear,' she said smugly, 'to take very much seducing.'

'We need to go, Ginny.'

'We do.' She needed to find Hannah and check on Button, before heading back to the hospital. With the dawn the searchers would be out again and there'd be another influx of injured islanders.

Please, let the worst of it be past, she pleaded silently, and Ben kissed her again, but lightly this time, on the lips, and it was a kiss of reassurance.

'We can cope,' he said. 'Whatever the day brings, we'll face it. Ginny, will you share my bed again tonight?'

That was one to take her breath away.

'Ben...'

'I know it's too soon,' he told her. 'We're too stressed. This is hardly the time to be making a lifelong commitment and I'm not asking that. Okay, I'm not even asking for tonight, but if you're hanging around, wondering how to fill in time, and if the pillows up at the vineyard have dust on them, think of this as an alternative.' He touched her cheek, very gently, and his smile was a caress all by itself.

'Any time, my Ginny,' he said softly. 'This thing between us... I haven't figured it out and I know you're even further behind than I am, but I do know that I want you on my pillow, for tonight and for whenever you need me. I'll take my needs out of it for now because I know that they scare you. For now. I'm here, Ginny. I'll never hurt you and I'm just...here.'

For a while after that things got crazy. The two doctors with the rescue service plus every available nurse were fully involved caring for those who made their way to the extended hospital for treatment.

The main injury was lacerations, but there were broken bones, bruises that swelled into haematomas, twists, sprains and also fear. In some cases the fear was as much an injury as a bone break—a young mum who lived alone while her husband was away on a fishing trip was almost paralysed with terror and her terror was infecting her kids.

Medics turned into social workers, calling for help as they needed it. The young mum was matched with an elderly couple who had a lovely stable old weatherboard house that had remained unscathed. Their age meant they'd seen it all and they weren't the least bit bothered about what nature could throw at them, and they were warmly welcoming.

'Come and stay, as long as you like,' they told her when Ben contacted them and asked for their help, and Ginny watched Ben reassure everyone and she thought...

How could she ever have let herself believe family medicine was beneath her?

How could she ever have let James and her father persuade her?

Things still were changing inside her. They were twisting, jumbling, like the world had yesterday.

Last night had been world-changing for her. Today, working side by side with Ben, it changed even more.

She was so aware of him. She was so...

Discombobulated. It was the only word she could think of to describe how she felt. Weird, out of her body, where the only thing that kept her feet on the ground was seeing the next patient.

But finally they ran out of patients. By late morning the number of casualties was slowing to a trickle and she was able to surface and think of other imperatives.

She glanced around and thought, *I'm not needed here. Not for a while at least.*

'Ben, is it okay if I go and find Button?'

'Of course.' Hannah had popped in early to reassure Ginny that Button was fine but Ginny had been in mid-suture and hadn't been able to stop. 'I reckon she could do with a cuddle,' Ben told her.

'She's pretty good at giving them,' Ginny said, and Ben grinned.

'She is, that. So now you have two cuddlers. Off you go, Dr Koestrel, and find your alternative.'

And he kissed her, lightly, a feather kiss, but every eye in the big makeshift casualty ward was on them and she left with her face burning. She was feeling…feeling…

Even more discombobulated.

Practicalities. She needed to focus on what was necessary rather than what she was feeling, she told herself fiercely as she headed down from the hospital towards the town.

There were people everywhere. Even now, the chaos of last night was turning into organised chaos. Debris was being removed from the road, teams were going from house to house, inspecting damage, using paint to scrawl codes on each—'Safe', 'Safe With Care', 'Do Not Enter'.

And everywhere she went, people greeted her.

'Hey, Ginny, good to see you safe. You guys are doing a great job. So glad you're back. Great to have you here, lass, so glad you're home.'

This was….home. She knew it.

This morning she felt an islander. It was a strange sensation.

She'd never felt like she belonged, she thought. Had it taken an earthquake to make her put down roots?

And then she saw Hannah, heading up the road from Ailsa's house, carrying Button, and her stride quickened. Button. How fast had this little girl wrapped her way around her heart? She'd wanted so much to be with her last night. But then… But then…

To her dismay, she was blushing again, and she reached Hannah and took Button into her arms and buried her face in the softness of her new little daughter until the colour subsided.

As she knew she would, Button's arms wrapped around her in a bear hug.

'Ginny,' she said in satisfaction. 'Cuddle.'

It was the best thing. What was Veronica about, abandoning this little one? she thought. She'd lived with her for all of two weeks and already she was starting to think that if Veronica wanted her back she'd face a fight.

She needed to get those documents sorted. She needed to get the formal adoption through so that Veronica couldn't just swan in and take her away if the whim took her.

Ben would help.

All this she thought in the moments she took out to let her colour subside, to let the warmth of Button settle her, to feel even more that this was her home.

'How frantic are you?' Hannah asked when she finally emerged from her bear hug, and Ginny smiled ruefully.

'Sorry.' On impulse she hugged Hannah as well, with Button sandwiched between. 'I haven't even said thank you yet. Taking her in last night...'

'It was the least I could do, and I always do the least I can do,' Hannah said cheerfully. 'Mum and I had six toddlers between us. But no tragedies. They're all kids of those caught up in rescue efforts, like you and Ben.' Then her face clouded. 'But I heard Squid died.'

'Yes.' There was nothing else to say.

'Ben will be upset,' Hannah said quietly. 'He loved that old man.'

He didn't try to save him, Ginny thought, but she didn't say it. Ben's reasons were sound; she knew they were, but they took some getting her head around. She should have her head around it. Her reaction was illogical but it was still there.

You fought to the end, and if you failed...

Failure. It slammed back, right there and then, standing

on the rubble-strewn main street with Hannah watching
her curiously and Button still clinging, nonjudgmental, her
one true thing.

Was that why she loved her? Because Button would never
judge her?

Would Ben ever judge her?

This was crazy. She gave herself a fierce mental shake
and turned her attention back to the question Hannah had
asked first.

How frantic are you?

'The worst of the rush is over,' she told her. 'We have
four doctors, five nurses and for the time being not enough
patients. Please, God, it stays that way.' She hesitated. 'I
thought…if I could find a car… Henry's on his own out at
his cottage behind the vineyard. I just met Ella—she's his
closest neighbour but they were in town when the quake
hit and haven't been back. Ella has a sprained wrist and
is staying put. That means Henry's on his own. Ben and I
drove down from the vineyard yesterday so I know a route
we can take and we've already chopped the fences. I might
just go and check.'

'Send a team,' Hannah said, and Ginny gazed along the
street at the organised troops of orange-clad workers moving methodically from house to house.

'It's just one old man in a tiny weatherboard cottage,' she
said. 'It's hardly worth a team and if I know Henry he'd be
furious if I sent strangers.'

'So let him be furious.'

'No.' Ginny shrugged. She'd had enough blame in her
life, she didn't need to wear this. 'It's easy enough to check
and it's safe enough. I'll take one of the hospital vehicles.'

'You can take Mum's,' Hannah offered. 'It's four-wheel
drive and it has a child seat.'

'Why—?'

'Um…that's why I was coming to find you,' Hannah said diffidently. 'There's been a bit of a drama with the school bus. Nothing dreadful,' she added as Ginny flinched. 'It was stuck between two landslips. They had a kid missing but they all seem to be accounted for now and as far as I know there's no casualties. But they're bringing them into town by boat now and lots of their mums and dads are still stranded in outlying parts of the island. So Mum and I have been asked to help. If you're sure where you're going is safe…could you take Button with you?'

She thought about it. The route she and Ben had taken yesterday had been bumpy but sound. They'd checked the farmhouses along the way so there'd be no huge dramas to find.

She could stop in at the vineyard, check the house was okay, maybe pick up a few things she would need if they were to stay in town. She'd take no risks.

And at Henry's cottage…

The worst she'd find would be an injured old man, but she was more likely to find him distressed than injured. And angry that she'd come?

Button could defuse that, she thought. She might even help.

'Take a radio with you,' Hannah urged. 'The rescue coordinator is giving them out. You'll need to tell him where you're going. Oh, and I'm off to let Ben know about the bus. He's been worried about Abby. I'll let him know where you've gone as well. Is that okay?'

She shouldn't take Button. She held her and thought there were risks. But the risks were small, and with no one to mind her… The alternative was to leave Henry without assistance he might need.

She could do this. It'd be safe.

'You do that,' she said, and gave Hannah another swift hug. 'And tell Ben I'll be fine. We'll all be fine. Let's hope we've heard the worst of the news about this earthquake. It's time to come out the other side.'

'She's gone where?'

'Up to Henry's.' Hannah suddenly sounded scared and Ben caught himself. He'd reacted with shock, and given a moment's thought he had himself together. The route they'd taken yesterday was safe enough. She had his mother's car, which was as tough as old boots. She was sensible.

'She took Button,' Hannah said, and he had to fight shock again.

But it was still reasonable. Woman heading off to check on an elderly neighbour, taking her daughter with her. Via a safe route. Taking a radio.

She was sensible and she'd be even more sensible with Button with her.

'Mum and I are heading down to the harbour to be there when the kids come in,' Hannah said. 'You want to come? Abby will be there.'

She was still matchmaking, Ben thought, humour surfacing. Ailsa and Hannah—plus half the island—had been trying to get Ben and Abby together for years.

It wasn't going to happen. They were friends but there'd never been that spark.

Like the spark of last night?

Last night hadn't been a spark, he conceded. It had been wildfire. A meeting of two bodies that ignited each other.

Ginny had ghosts.

He could lay ghosts to rest, though, he thought as Hannah waited for his reply. He could work with whatever demons she had; she lived here now and he had all the time in the world.

Except he wanted her in his bed again, tonight.

'It's Ginny, isn't it?' Hannah said cheekily.

And he wished he was busy. He needed a whole busload of casualties to come in the door this minute to stop the prying, laughing eyes of his little sister seeing far more than he wanted her to see.

'You're sure she's taken a radio?'

'Cross my heart and hope to break a leg. We walked to the co-ordination centre together. She's got more safeguards in place than you can shake a stick at. You know, Abby's been out all night with the most gorgeous rescue paramedic. You're not worried about Abby?'

'Not if she has the most gorgeous rescue paramedic with her.'

'But if it were Ginny?' Her eyes danced and she held up her hands. 'Okay, big brother, no more questions. I don't think I need to ask them anyway. I'm off to do some serious childminding.' She glanced around the makeshift casualty ward where medics were working efficiently and well. 'You know, if this place stays quiet you could even follow Ginny.'

'She doesn't need me.'

'She might,' Hannah said airily. 'You never know.'

It was kind of eerie retracing the route she and Ben had followed yesterday. Then their minds had been set to crisis mode. They'd faced fear and tragedy, and they'd known they had to get down to the hospital fast.

Now the crisis seemed to be over. It was a gorgeous autumn day. The rolling hills were bathed in warm sunshine, the cattle had gone back to grazing and only the occasional fallen tree or weird gash across a paddock indicated anything had happened.

The gashes were easy to avoid. They seemed to happen in fault lines, where the earth underneath had simply pulled apart. They didn't look deep but Ginny didn't need to find out how deep they were.

She could still see the tracks they'd made yesterday, driving the truck cross-country over the lush pastures. She kept to the tracks. She didn't deviate to the houses she passed—she knew they'd been checked. The fences were all slashed thanks to yesterday's efforts so she didn't need to stop until she reached the vineyard.

Her house was still intact.

She climbed from the car, lifted Button out and stood looking at it. The long, low homestead showed superficial damage—a couple of broken windows, downpipes skewed, the front steps to the veranda twisted away and one crumpled chimney—but nothing major.

The house had been shaken and then put down again on the same foundations and she stood and hugged Button and looked at it and felt her eyes well with tears.

Why? This had been her parents' holiday retreat. This place had only been home for her for six months.

But that's what it was. Home.

This island was home.

Ben was home?

She had a tiny flash of longing. She and Ben. Kids, dogs, family. Here?

Whoa, that was like a teenager sitting in class signing her name Ginny McMahon, over and over again. She'd actually done that when she was seventeen. Dumb. Emotional. Not based on facts.

But it might be, she thought. Last night had been real. Last night Ben had said he loved her.

So many emotions. She stood in the sun in the stableyard and for a moment she simply gave in to them. Yesterday the world had shaken, but for her, now, the world had settled, and her foundations seemed surer.

'This is home,' she whispered to Button. 'We'll fix this up. It's big and solid and safe. We can live here for ever and ever.'

And Ben? Big and solid and safe?

So sexy he made her toes curl?

That was way too much to think about right now. Ben and what had happened last night was an image, a presence, a sensation that had her retreating fast to the practical.

She and Button ventured round the back of the house to the kitchen. She turned on the hose—miraculously the water tanks were still standing and she still had pressure. Button's favourite occupation was still to stand and point the hose, and the late-producing tomatoes were wilting.

'Give them a big drink,' she told her, and knew she had a few minutes to enter the house. If she avoided standing under the beams she'd be safe enough. She needed to collect urgent belongings, things they'd needed to stay in the town for a few nights.

With Ben?

Don't go there. She was starting to feel…just a little bit foolish. More than a little bit afraid.

Get on with it. Move on, she told herself, and get back to the hospital. She might be needed. Coming up here was a bit irresponsible.

Unless Henry did need her.

She headed back out to the garage and grabbed bolt cutters for hacking through fences if needed, and then popped a happy, soggy Button back in the four-wheel drive. Henry's cottage was further out on the headland. The track seemed to be okay. There weren't any significant ruts or crevices, though at one place there was a small landslip partly blocking the way.

'Nothing to this, Button,' she told the little girl as they edged past. 'We'll reach Henry's cottage in no time. It'll be fine.'

And then they topped the next rise and saw the cottage and it wasn't fine at all.

Ben was starting to worry. It seemed simple, logical even, for Ginny to drive to Henry's. It didn't even seem risky to take Button with her. Childminders were at a premium, the way seemed safe and Ginny wasn't one to take risks.

So why was he worrying?

It wasn't as if he didn't have enough to do. The boatload of school kids had arrived, with myriad cuts and bruises to be checked. There was nothing serious but most of these kids had parents who'd spent a sleepless night imagining the worst, and every cut needed to be checked.

Besides, to a traumatised five-year-old a bandage was a badge of honour, a signal to the world that he'd been doing something dangerous. It was therapy all by itself, Ben thought as he applied a much-too-big plaster to Rowan March's grazed arm. He'd applied antiseptic with liberal abandon as well, so Rowan headed off with his parents, plus a bright orange arm and a plaster to brag about. He was all better. And suddenly there were no more kids.

'We have a bit of medical overkill.' Margy was clearing trays, keeping a weather eye on the door. 'So many helpers... The guys have been wonderful, though. Four deaths, five major injuries, minor injuries arriving slowly enough to be dealt with promptly, and teams are reporting most properties have been checked.'

'I should have sent a team out to Henry's,' Ben growled, and Margy frowned.

'Didn't Max and Ella check on him?'

'Apparently not. Their daughter's here in town. They came down in a rush and stayed.'

'I'll ask one of the rescue guys—'

'There's no need. Ginny's gone up there.'

'Has she now.' Margy eyed him thoughtfully. 'And that's why you seem distracted?'

'I'm not distracted.' Then he shrugged and grinned. 'Or not very.'

'You want to follow her up there?' Margy raised a quizzical eyebrow and smiled. What was it with the people around him? Was he that transparent? 'Surely she shouldn't be out there by herself.'

But one of the searchers was coming in now, cradling his arm. He needed to be seen to and the two fly-in doctors were taking a break. Margy and Ben were it.

'I don't have time.'

'But when the others come back on duty?'

'She'll be back by then.'

'So she will,' Margy said, pinning on a smile. 'So you can stop worrying.'

'I've got you worrying now,' he said.

'She's a sensible woman.' But Margy was starting to look worried.

'Will you cut it out? There's no reason to worry.'

'Except that if it was my Charlie I'd be worried,' Margy said. 'And the way you feel about Ginny...'

'What the...? I do not feel—'

'Sure you do,' she said, cheering up. 'You think you can sleep together on this island and not have every islander know in five minutes?'

'Margy! We were exhausted. She needed to stay in my apartment.'

'Of course,' Margy said equitably. 'But if you slept on the sofa I'm a monkey's uncle and if you're not feeling like I feel about Charlie, when you're looking the way you're looking...'

'Will you cut it out?'

'Yes, Doctor,' she said meekly. 'Anything you say, Doctor. But let's get this arm seen to and get you up the valley to rescue your lady.'

* * *

Henry's cottage was ramshackle. He'd run a small farm up here before her parents had employed him, but he'd let this place go. He'd only left the vineyard six months back, when arthritis had overtaken him, and he'd refused Ginny's offer to stay in the caretaker's residence permanently.

The old cottage, therefore, was hanging together with rotting timbers and rusty nails. Ginny had been out here a couple of times to see him. She'd been horrified but he wouldn't move.

And now…maybe the time for him to move was gone. The entire building had folded in on itself. The chimney looked as if it had crashed down, bringing the rest of the house with it.

It looked like a huge bonfire, set and ready to go.

And where was Henry?

'Stay in the car, Button,' Ginny said, handing Shuffles over. 'I need to see…'

'Henry,' Button said, and Ginny wondered how much this little girl understood. Henry had been down in the vineyard teaching Ginny to prune. He'd shown Button how to build Shuffles a little house with the clippings and then, the last time Ginny had come up here, the day after Henry came home from hospital, Henry had made Button red cordial, which she liked very much.

'I don't know where Henry is,' Ginny conceded. 'But you stay in the car while I look.'

'Okay,' Button said happily, and Ginny left the doors open so the sun wouldn't heat it up too much and turned her mind to Henry.

Somewhere in this mess, an old man…

The house was on the headland overlooking the sea. From here you could almost see to the mainland. A sea eagle was soaring in the thermals, seemingly having given up on fishing for the day just to soak up the sun. There seemed no urgency at all. How could anything dreadful happen on such a day?

Where was Henry?

'Henry?' It was a cautious call, and produced nothing. She tried again and put a bit of power behind it.

'Henry!'

And from the ruins...

'Well, about time. I've bin thinking I was going to have to chop me leg off with a penknife, only I can't reach a penknife. You want to get me out of here, Ginny, girl?'

Ginny, girl. He'd called her that all her life, she thought as she tried to get closer, tried to figure where exactly he was.

Feeling ill.

She should have insisted he stay with her. She thought suddenly that this man was more of a parent to her than her own parents were. Henry at the vineyard, Ailsa in town, her friend Ben—those were her people.

'Are you hurt?' she called, shifting to the far side of the house, calling loudly because he was far in, she could hear it from his voice.

'I'm stuck. Bloody piano came down on me ankle. I can still wiggle me toes. It got me sideways, like. I never even played the thing either. My May only got it 'cos she liked the look of it.'

He was sounding brave but she heard the pain and weakness behind the bravado. But how to get him out? She was looking at vast sheets of roofing iron topping a crumbling mess.

'I need to call for help,' she told him. 'Can you hold on for a bit?'

'Can you get me one of them intravenous line things you docs have? You could feed it down through the cracks with a bit of beer in it. A man 'd feel better with a beer in his belly.'

'You're still recovering from a stomach ulcer,' Ginny retorted. She had him pinpointed now, she thought. From the sound of his voice he was near the remains of the main chimney but completely under the roofing iron. 'No alcohol for you!'

'No, ma'am. But you're calling for help?'

'You'd better believe it.'

'Ben!'

Ben had just finished splinting the fractured arm. It was a vicious break; it'd need setting by a decent orthopaedic surgeon, but he'd done enough to make the guy comfortable. He was starting to clear up when Don Johnson, the island's fire chief, stuck his head around the door. 'Can I have a word?'

'Sure. You settle down on the pillows, Mac,' he told the guy he was treating. 'You'll be on the next chopper out of here.'

'Chopper'll be half an hour,' Don said across him, glancing at Mac with concern. 'Do you have decent painkillers on board, Mac? Can you wait until next trip?'

'Sure,' Mac said. 'Broken wing is all. I can still handle a shovel if you let me.'

'I don't need a shoveller,' Don said, but he sounded worried. 'What we need is more vehicles. Ben, Ginny's just contacted base. She's up on the headland past her place and Henry's trapped under his collapsed house. I'm hauling a team together now. Are you free as soon as we are?'

'I'm free now,' Ben said.

It was the longest wait. There was nothing she could do but sit in the sun by the ruin that was Henry's house, and cuddle Button and talk to him. If she tried to climb onto the ruin to rip up the sheets of iron that hid him from view, she could bring more down on the man beneath. She had to sit and wait, sit and wait, and Henry knew it.

'So tell me why you never came back?' Henry asked, and she shook herself and thought it was she who should be asking questions, she who should be focussing on keeping him distracted.

'I did come back.'

'From the time you were seventeen... Your parents came back every summer and played the landed gentry. Why not you?'

'I guess I didn't...like playing the landed gentry.'

'Or were you scared you'd fall harder for our Ben?' Henry said. 'That's what my May said. "She's fallen for that lad in a big way," she said. "If she comes back next summer they'll be together for life, mark my words," and then you never came back. So what was it about our Ben that scared you?'

'Nothing.' She was holding Button on her knee, making daisy chains to keep the little girl occupied. She was as close to Henry as she dared to go.

'Something did,' Henry said, and she heard the pain in his voice and knew he was trying hard to find anything—anything to distract him. 'You don't need to tell me, but May said you were as besotted with him as he was with you, and then you disappeared. It seemed dumb to us.'

'It was too hard,' she said, and she didn't say it loud enough. In truth it was barely a whisper.

'You still there?' Henry's voice rose sharply and she caught herself. This wasn't about her. This was about Henry and distraction and nothing else.

And maybe...maybe it was time to say it like it was.

'I wasn't brave enough to love him,' she said. 'I was seventeen and my parents treated this place as an escape. That summer...I told my mother I was in love with Ben, and she laughed. And then she told me exactly what would happen if...if I was stupid.'

'What would happen?'

His voice was so thin she was starting to panic. He sounded so weak there was no way she could do anything but tell him the truth.

'My dad was a powerful man,' she said. 'He was at the top of his field and he was wealthy to boot. Very, very wealthy.'

'You know, I figured that,' Henry said dryly and Ginny managed a smile.

'So he had friends all over the world. Friends in most of the major teaching hospitals. Friends in Auckland. The head of medical training for Auckland Central was a house guest here that summer. Dad said he only had to drop a word. He said nursing was a much more suitable profession for someone of Ben's background—his words, not mine. He said it was fine for a kid like Ben to have aspirations and he could have any aspiration he wanted except his daughter. And if he was to keep wanting me then his plans to be a doctor would be pulled from under his feet, just like that. So be a good girl, Ginny, he said. Let him down kindly and move on.'

'So that's what you did.'

'That's what I did,' she said drearily. 'And, of course, he was right. We were only seventeen, and it even seemed sensible. Medical school seemed exciting. The way I was feeling seemed dumb. I managed to dump Ben like it was my idea. But if I'd had the courage to maybe keep writing, keep in touch, who knows? But I couldn't write without crying and then I met James and it was the easy way out. Now I'm so, so sorry.'

There was a long silence, a silence that stretched until she got scared.

'Henry?'

'I'm still here,' he said, almost amicably. 'And Ben could have written, too. Is he sorry?'

'I don't know,' she said, confused.

'Bet he's not,' Henry said. 'He's a guy. I'm seeing a pattern here. I know it's sexist, but *women*. You know, my May once dropped her best meat platter—a plate she inherited from her mum who inherited it from her mum. So she's standing there staring down at five or six bits of broken crockery and she's welling up with tears and saying, oh, Henry, I'm so sorry, I'm so sorry. Like she's apologising to me, or to the shades of her mum and her grandma, but who's hurting? Daft woman. Hell, this piano hurts. You think they're coming?'

'They're coming,' Ginny said, and they were, at least she thought they were. In the distance she could see a Jeep, coming fast. 'At least…I hope…I think Ben's here.'

'Thank God for that,' Henry said morosely. 'A nice shot of morphine'd be useful and I hope he has tin cutters.'

'Or a crane,' Ginny said, hugging Button and climbing to her feet to wave to the approaching Jeep. 'I'm sorry I haven't been more useful.'

'Oh, for heaven's sake, you know where you can put your sorry,' Henry snapped. 'Let's put the past behind us and acknowledge all we both want is Ben.'

CHAPTER NINE

BEN WAS ALONE. Ginny had called for the cavalry and the only one who had come was Ben. That was fine, as far as it went—the hard hug he gave her when he arrived was reassuring, as far as it went—but she wanted more.

Did Wellington have these sorts of problems? Ginny wondered. Did 'Get the fourth infantry division to the front now' mean get them here after the fourth infantry division had finished dinner and put their boots on? Or after the fourth infantry had coped with a wee crisis like fighting five French divisions down the line?

Something must have happened. There must be another catastrophe somewhere, because there was no back-up in sight.

Meanwhile, she and Ben walked carefully around the ruined house, with Ginny carrying Button, while Ben tried to assess how he could get in there.

There seemed no safe way, but Henry's voice, which had risen in hope when Ben had arrived, was now a thready whisper.

And then, appallingly, Henry started to sob.

It wasn't loud sobbing, the kind of wail you'd expect to hear from loss, but the slow rasp of someone in unbearable pain, someone who'd held up as long as he could but had now reached the edge.

'I'm sorry,' he gasped. 'No, don't tell Ginny I said that. I'm not sorry, it's just this damned piano is heavy.'

Ben headed for the radio. 'Where the hell are you guys?'

'The church has come down,' Don barked at him. 'We have three old ladies trapped in the rubble. They were trying to rescue the altar cloths, for heaven's sake, in a building categorised as unsafe. It's okay, we'll get 'em out, but what's worse, the land behind has slipped and our vehicles are trapped. No, it wasn't another tremor, it was just damage we couldn't see—the rise behind the church must have been waiting to fall since the quake. We're organising vehicles on the other side but I reckon it'll be another half-hour before we get up to you.'

'I don't think he can last half an hour,' Ginny whispered. They'd gone back behind Ben's Jeep to radio where Henry couldn't hear. 'Ben, there's a sliver—a small cavity round the back. If you hold Button I could…'

He'd already seen the cavity she was talking about. It was a tiny hump in the caved-in iron. He'd shone his torch in and seen nothing but rubble, but at that point they were only maybe ten feet from where Henry was lying. If they could reach Henry… Even an arm or a leg might be enough to inject painkillers. As well as that, if someone could just be here with him it could make all the difference.

An elderly nurse, an old-school martinet, had instilled *Just being there* into Ben in his first year as an intern.

'Don't be scared of getting personal, Doctor. All these new-fangled drugs and treatments, they don't matter half as much as human contact, and don't you forget it.'

He hadn't. He wasn't forgetting it now.

They'd been talking to Henry—of course they had. Ginny had persuaded Button to sing her favourite song, *'Happy Birthday to Button'*, to Henry, and he knew it helped, but touch…

The way Henry sounded…

'You can't,' he said harshly to Ginny. 'I'll go.'

She drew back, appalled. 'No!'

'Hang on. It's okay if you go in but not me?'

'No,' she said, more urgently. 'I'm smaller.'

'And I'm stronger.'

'What if the roof comes down?'

'So what if the roof comes down?' he said. 'Ginny, you know as well as I do that if we don't get drugs on board soon we'll lose him—we can both hear it. I'm only going under iron. You suggested it. I'm the one to do it.'

'No!' It was a cry of terror.

'Yes,' he said. 'Ginny, I'll concede there's a risk. I think it's small but it's still there. With that in mind, I'm a bachelor with no dependants, and you, my love, like it or not, are a mother with a dependent four-year-old. Your job, I believe, is to keep the home fires burning, take care of the children and prepare slippers and pipe for when your man comes home.'

'Ben!' Despite the gravity of the situation she choked on laughter.

'That's right, my love, I'd like a nice Irish stew when I come out, please, with golden syrup dumplings on the side.' He was shoving gear from his backpack into his pockets as he spoke; syringes and vials, wrapping the vials in dressings to keep them unbroken. Then he gave her a swift, hard kiss, the sort of kiss a man should give his woman as he went off to battle—and he was gone.

She could help him for the first part. At the edge she helped him clear loose rubble, and then as he worked his way under the iron, he shoved stuff sideways and she reached in and helped him haul it clear.

There'd been some sort of sideboard at the side of the

room. It formed a kind of base so the roofing iron hadn't been able to reach floor level.

Once the rubble had been exposed they saw clearly what was happening. The sideboard was too low for Ben to go under it; there was no way they could shift it and neither would they want to—it could bring the whole roof down even further—so Ben had to manoeuvre his way round the sides.

It was filthy, dangerous, even foolhardy, but Henry had grown silent. Ginny had stopped protesting, but she felt sick.

She felt worse when Ben managed to get around the massive sideboard, gave a grunt of satisfaction and hauled himself further under and she could no longer see him. There was now nothing else she could do.

She went back to Button. They started making daisy chains again but Ginny was doing it by feel.

She was watching the crumpled roof and she was watching the track down the valley.

Please, let it not collapse.

Please, let help arrive.

'Talk to me,' she pleaded, and Ben grunted back.

'It's pretty hard to talk with a mouth full of grit. Henry, I know now why we haven't heard from you for a while. You couldn't, I don't know, whistle or something, just to let me know where you are?'

There was a faint attempt at a whistle and Ginny managed a smile and went back to daisy-chain-making as if her life depended on it.

'We need a conversationalist,' Ben grunted, his voice muffled almost to incomprehension. 'Go on, Ginny, tell us a story.'

'Story,' Button said in satisfaction.

Ginny thought, Story? What sort of story?

Ben was inching his way through rubble. Henry was lying trapped in pain. Button was looking up at her expectantly.

She'd been in pressured situations before, but none like this.

Tell us a story.

'Once upon a time,' she said, feeling helpless, and Button beamed and bounced on her knee.

'I like stories.'

'You need to stay quiet,' Ben growled. 'Shush, Button, we all need to hear.'

A story.

Stories don't have to be made up, though, Ginny thought, floundering for inspiration. Stories could be real.

'Once upon a time there was a little girl called Ginny,' she said, and Button squeaked in surprise, but then put her hands firmly across her small mouth as she remembered the rules.

'Ginny's mum and dad brought her to the island but she was very lonely,' Ginny continued. 'She didn't have any friends but she had beautiful clothes.'

'I remember those clothes,' Ben said, muffled, and there was a thump and grating of metal on metal and Ginny's heart almost hit her ankles. But her job wasn't to quiver with fear. She was the storyteller.

'Ginny's mum and dad were busy,' she said. 'They were always busy. So they asked someone else to take care of Ginny. The lady's name was Ailsa and she had a little boy called Ben. The first time Ben met Ginny he pointed to her pretty white pleated skirt and he snickered.'

'I did not,' the voice from under the tin said.

'What's snickered?' Button asked.

'Laughed. He laughed at my white pleated skirt.'

'That wasn't nice,' Button said.

'I didn't think he was a very nice boy,' Ginny agreed. 'But

then he offered to take me tadpoling. You've seen tadpoles, Button. We caught some last week, remember?'

'Yes,' Button said, wiggling more firmly onto Ginny's lap. 'I like this story.'

'As long as I stay the good guy,' Ben said. 'Henry, mate, could you grunt or something? I should be able to see you soon.'

'Grunt,' Henry managed. 'Will that do? Keep going, girl.'

'So he took me tadpoling,' Ginny said. 'Out the back of town there's a farmer's field with a lovely, wide pond. It's a great place for catching taddies.'

'I know it,' Henry said, sounding strained to breaking point. 'You nearly here, lad?'

'Reckon I'm three feet from your feet,' Ben said, sounding just as strained. 'Oi, storyteller, get on with it.'

She couldn't bear it. If the iron came down…if anything happened…

Get on with it.

'So Ben took Ginny to the pond,' she managed. 'And he said the best taddies were on the far side. Now, the farmer had left an old bath lying near the pond. I don't know why, but Ben said it was a good old bath and he used it as a boat. The only problem was there was a hole where the plug should be.'

'Didn't you have a plug?' Ginny asked, and astonishingly Ginny heard Ben chuckle.

'Shush, Button,' he said, mock-sternly. 'This is a very good fairy-tale and I like the ending.'

'Shush yourself,' Ginny said tartly, and it was almost as if he was standing beside her, grinning. Her Ben…

'There was clay by the pond,' she made herself continue. 'So Ben showed Ginny how to make a ball of clay mixed with grass, and shove it into the hole in the bath. Then Ben climbed into the bath and used a pole and pushed himself all the way across the pond and back. He'd obviously done it lots of times because he was very fast.'

'Old trick,' Henry muttered. 'I did that when I was a lad. Got into all sorts of trouble. Hey...'

'Yeah, that's me touching your arm,' Ben said. 'Can you see the flashlight?'

'Can I...? Answer to me prayers,' Henry said, his voice breaking. 'Lad...'

'Hold still. I can reach enough of your arm to give you a shot of something to take the edge off the pain.'

'I'm scared of needles,' Henry retorted, and the old Henry was back. Human contact...the best medicine in the world. Ben was in there with him, and Ginny heard the easing of the old man's terror.

'Be a man and put up with it,' Ben retorted. 'Quick, Ginny, get to the exciting part.'

'So then Ben brought the bathtub back to Ginny's side of the pond,' Ginny said, and for the life of her she couldn't keep her voice steady. 'And Ben made her make her own plug out of clay and grass and fill the hole. And then he pushed her out into the pond and told her how to use the pole to push herself across the pond. The pond wasn't deep but it was very, very muddy. And Ginny wasn't good at rowing. So she was slow, and because she was slow the plug in the bath slowly melted.'

'What does that mean?' Button asked, trying hard to keep up.

'It means,' Ginny said direfully, 'that Ben had tricked Ginny. The hole in the bath was open again and the water was pouring in and Ginny stood in the bath and yelled to Ben to help her but he stood on the bank and laughed while she sank into the mud. And her lovely white pleated skirt got covered with mud, and her pale pink cardigan was ruined and her nice curly hair got soaking wet and there was even a tadpole in my...in her hair. And then Ben strode into the pond and rescued...'

'Rescued Ginny,' Button crowed.

'Rescued the tadpole,' Ben said, and even Henry chuckled.

There was a long silence. This was surreal, Ginny thought, sitting in the bright sunlight on this gorgeous autumn morning, where everything seemed perfect, where underneath the ruin one man was fighting for his life and another was putting his life on the line to save him.

'And then did she cry?' Button asked in a small voice, and she had to go back to the story. To how she'd felt as an eight-year-old, standing shoulder deep in mud while this strange boy carefully disengaged a tadpole from her curls. Knowing she'd go home to her parent's disgust. Knowing she'd been tricked. Knowing she looked appalling.

'No,' she said softly, and added, because suddenly it seemed important, 'No, she didn't cry because he saved the tadpole. Just like he's saving Henry now.'

'Oi,' Henry said, and his voice was now sleepy instead of pain-filled. 'Are you comparing me to a tadpole?'

'No,' she said. 'But you're being saved by a hero and all the best stories have heroes.'

'And heroines,' Henry muttered. 'And then they all live happily ever after. Is that you, girl? You're ready for your happy-ever-after?'

'We'll get this roof off you guys first,' she said. 'And then we'll see.'

'That sounds promising,' Ben said, and there was strain in his voice now. What sort of situation was he in? He sounded as if he, too, was in pain. 'So, in your story...the heroine falls in love with her hero?'

'Maybe she did,' she said. 'Maybe he was the first person she'd met who cared more for tadpoles than for pleated skirts.'

'That,' said Henry, 'is just plain weird.'

'Maybe it is,' Ben said. 'But it's important. So the heroine might have fallen in love?'

'The best heroines do,' she whispered.

'Pardon?'

'The best heroines do,' she yelled, and she yelled too loud but it didn't matter. Her Ben was underneath a ruined house, risking his life, and nothing was more important than that.

'A truck's coming,' Button said.

Ginny swivelled and stared down the valley and a truck *was* coming—no, two trucks.

'The cavalry's here,' she told the guys under the house, as she recognised Don Johnson and his fire crew. 'Let's get you guys out and concentrate on fairy-tales later.'

'Let's not forget to,' Ben said. 'I have a feeling the end of this one's pretty import—'

And he got no further.

The aftershock was the biggest yet. It rolled across the island as a great, rolling swell. The iron of the house heaved and shifted.

Ginny heard Ben yell once, just once, and then she had to grab Button and hold her and crouch down until the land settled.

Until the world settled in its next new place.

The fire crew had to stop while the world shook but no more cracks appeared in the earth and as soon as things settled Don ordered his crew forward.

They topped the rise and saw the ruins of Henry's home. A great sheet of roofing iron was ripped almost all the way along and on top of it a woman was tearing at it with her bare hands.

Ginny.

'They're in there,' she screamed at them as Don and his crew reached her. 'Henry and Ben. Ben... The iron's come down. Get it off them. Please, get it off them. I can't bear it. Oh, Ben... Oh, Ben, my love, no...'

If it hadn't been for the dust they would have been fine. Or sort of fine. The world gave a giant heave, the mass of iron and debris above them rolled and shook and shuddered, there was momentary pressure on Ben's chest that took his breath away but then the iron shifted again and the pressure eased—and the heaving stopped.

He was fine except the torch had rolled somewhere out of reach, beaming a useless stream of light into unreachable darkness. The air was clogged with a dust so thick he couldn't breathe and Henry was rasping with ever-decreasing strength.

What was it they said in planes? Fit your own mask first and then help others around you?

First make a mask.

He was trying to haul his shirt off but there wasn't enough room to manoeuvre. He needed to rip the thing and who would have guessed how strong shirts were? Note: remember to buy cheaper ones. He couldn't get his hands apart wide enough to wrench it.

He had a sudden flash of memory of Ginny's shirt ripping...how many hours ago?

Ginny.

Above him he could hear her sobbing, ripping away at the tin, her voice filled with terror. He wanted to reassure her, to tell her he'd be fine, but he wasn't yet. It was so hard to breathe.

Finally the shirt gave way, and he wrenched again, haul-

ing the arms off so he had two long strips and large panels
front and back.

What followed was more ripping and then wriggling in
the darkness, trying to get cloth on his face and the sleeves
around to tie his makeshift mask on. But when he did, the
relief was almost instant. The appalling, clogging muck was
kept out by the barrier.

Now for Henry.

'Ben? Henry?' Ginny was screaming from above but there
was no way he could use precious air to call back. He had
to get closer to Henry. He had to.

He heaved himself forward, risked bringing the entire
sheet of rubble down on them, but he had no choice. Before
it had simply been enough to reach Henry, to get the drugs
to his arm, but now he had to get to his face; he had to fit a
mask. The drugs he'd given him would depress his breathing still more.

He was hauling at the rubble, pushing forward—and miraculously something moved, gave and he could pull himself
the last foot forward and feel Henry's head.

'Mate…Henry?'

He got no answer—Henry's entire focus was on his weak,
rasping breaths.

'Help me, Henry,' Ben managed, and swept a handful
of dust from the old man's face and somehow managed to
get the back of his shirt across it. He was clearing Henry's
mouth, shifting muck the old man was clearly unable to shift
himself. 'Breathe through the cloth. Breathe…'

'They're coming, Ben, they're coming,' Ginny called from
above, and he gave up trying to tie Henry's mask in place. It
was too hard. He didn't have enough breath left himself. He
simply lay full length in the filth and held Henry's makeshift mask in position and willed Henry to keep on living.

Ginny'd tell them where he was. Ginny'd bring in the troops.

Ginny...

The thought of her up there in the sunlight was his one true thing. He thought of her again as she'd been at eight years old, standing in tadpole territory, and he thought how he'd decided he had been stupid asking her to marry him when he'd been seventeen.

He should have asked when he was eight.

'Just keep breathing, mate,' he told Henry. 'Just keep on breathing, one breath after another. Over and over. Breathe, breathe, breathe, because Ginny's up there waiting for us, and I, for one, have unfinished business with the lady. I suspect she loves us both and, dammit, I suspect if we die she'll blame herself. She's dumb like that, but there it is. For Ginny's sake, we keep on breathing.'

Don's crew consisted of eight emergency workers, tough, work-ready men and women who were trained to cope with stuff just like this, a few who'd been in earthquakes before, who understood about risk and urgency. This was no massive collapse of stone. It simply needed strength, skill and the right equipment, all of which they had.

Ginny had been trying to haul sheets of iron back from where she'd last heard voices. Don put her aside, snapped a few incisive questions and then set his crew to work.

In less than five minutes the vast sheets of tin were rolling back, exposing what was beneath.

What was there was a massive pile of rubble, dust, grit— and two prone bodies, one almost completely covering the other.

For one appalling moment Ginny thought they were both dead. She'd backed to the edge of the ruin to give the guys

space to move but she hadn't been able to take her eyes from
what was being exposed.

Two bodies...

And then one raised his head, revealing a makeshift mask
and a face so caked in dust it was unrecognisable. But, of
course, she recognised it.

Ben.

'I'm fine,' he said in a voice that wasn't the least bit fine;
it was the merest croak through the mask. 'And I reckon
Henry'll be okay, too, once we get this piano off his leg.'

And miraculously there was a grunt of agreement from
Henry.

Ben was hauled to safety first. They tugged him to his
feet, he staggered but then stood, unhurt, whole.

Ginny started breathing again. She hadn't been aware
she'd stopped but her body sucked in air like she'd been
drowning.

Ben. Safe.

He didn't come to her. Instead, he watched as four strong
men, one at each corner of the piano, acting in unison, lifting the thing clear. And Henry was out, free.

There was stuff to do. Somehow she shifted into doctor
mode, adding to Ben's in-the-dark care, setting up IV lines
while Ben snapped orders to keep Henry's spine steady,
watch for his hips and beware of a possible broken pelvis as
they transferred him to a rigid stretcher to carry him back
across the ruins.

But Henry was giving sleepy directions himself. 'When
are you going to get a tarp here to cover this? There's stuff
here worth saving. Be careful of that piano.'

And Ginny knew, she just knew, that he'd be fine.

Finally, finally there was time for Ben to turn to her, for
Ben to take her in his arms, to hug her close.

'About time,' Henry said weakly from his stretcher. 'We've only been waiting twelve years for this to happen.'

There was laughter, filled with relief, but Ginny hardly heard it. Ben had her in his arms, against his heart. Her world folded into his; into him. Heart against heart.

He kissed her hair and then he tilted her chin and he kissed her on the mouth, a full, public proclamation that this was his woman, his love.

She melted into him. This proclamation was okay by her. What were her qualms anyway? Last night had been the beginning of the rest of her life. Why had she ever thought she wasn't brave enough to start again?

How could she not when that start was Ben?

There was slow clapping. Somehow they broke apart and found everyone was looking at them, cheering, and Henry was even leading the clapping from his stretcher.

Ben smiled and smiled at her. Her love. Her Ben.

And then he looked around, still smiling, and said, 'Where's Button?'

She'd forgotten Button. In the midst of her terror her thoughts hadn't swerved from the two men fighting for their lives in the ruins. When the second tremor had hit she'd almost thrown Button into the Jeep. She'd said stay, and she'd run.

But now…

She was standing in the arms of Ben, who was safe, safe, safe, and a little girl who depended solely on her was no longer where she'd left her.

Ginny was no longer in Ben's arms. She was staring wildly around her.

'Button!' Her yell sounded out over the valley, echoing back and back and back.

The Jeep was empty. She stared back at the ruins. Surely she would have seen… If Button had come anywhere near the ruins, she would have noticed.

She should have noticed. What sort of a mother…?

The cliff…

But Ben was before her.

'Button's missing,' he snapped to the team around him. 'Four years old. Priority one.'

Triage… When faced with an emergency, take time to assess then look at worst-case scenarios first. That meant no matter who was yelling, who was bleeding, you took the time to assess, see the guy with the grey face clutching his chest, know that even though it might simply be shock and bruising you checked that out first.

So head for worst-case scenarios first. The worst scenario was that Button was buried under the debris…but maybe it wasn't. Because Ben was turning away from the ruin and striding—no, running—towards the cliff.

The cliff. Dear God.

Below was the sea, fascinating, awesome for a little girl who had no sense of danger.

Ginny gave a sob of terror and followed, but Ben was before her.

He reached the edge.

'Here,' he snapped back at them. 'She's slipped down a bit but there's a ledge. Button, don't move. Sweetheart, I want you to play statues, don't move at all. I'm coming down.'

And just as he said it a tiny tremor, the vaguest hint of an aftershock, rocked the world. It may have been tiny but it was too much for what must have already been a weakened stretch of headland.

A crack opened between Ginny and Ben. A tiny crack, but it was widening.

Ben gave a yell of warning. 'Ginny, stay where you are.'

And then he slid over the edge of the cliff, helpless, as the crack widened still further and the land seemed to slide toward the sea.

What did you do when your life crumpled before your eyes?

Nothing?

There was nothing she could do. She stood numb with shock and terror while around her men and women leapt into action.

They'd been in earthquakes before? Disasters? They must have been for instead of standing like useless idiots they had ropes out of the truck, they were gearing up with harnesses and shackles, and Don was edging out to where the edge of the cliff was a crumpling mess of loose dirt.

Someone was holding onto her, a woman who seemed just as competent as the men but whose job, obviously, was to keep her out of harm's way.

'We're belaying down,' she told Ginny. 'Hold on, love, Don's good. If anyone can reach them, he can.'

The world held its breath. There was no way anyone else could go near the edge—the headland was still crumbling, and another tremor could hit at any moment.

Don edged out, slowly, slowly. Dirt was breaking away as he moved, but he was testing the footing each time before putting his weight on it. He was safe; they'd fastened the rope onto the Jeep and the crew was guiding it to keep it steady but the last thing they wanted was to cause further collapse.

And then Don was over the edge and lower, lower.

'They're here.' His voice crackled through the radio. 'Send down two harnesses, a big 'un and a little 'un. The kid looks okay and Ben's holding her. Ben's shoved Button against the cliff face. He looks in pain—he's hit something but he's conscious. He's kept her safe from the landfall. Harnesses fast would be good. It'd be a bit of a waste to lose them now.'

A bit of bruising and confusion—that was Button.

One fractured pelvis—that was Henry.

Pain, dropping blood pressure, possible internal injuries, that was Ben. Ginny set up IV lines, gave him pain relief, tried desperately to be a doctor rather than a woman whose man was in mortal danger.

They called in the chopper, and Dave, the doctor Ginny had met the night before, came with it. Dave took over from Ginny, examining Ben fast, concurring with what she thought—or hoped. Was it foolish to hope for the best? 'Query ruptured spleen,' Dave barked into the radio—there were directives to take them straight to Auckland—and then there was nothing Ginny could do but hold Button and try to stop shaking.

'Take Ginny down to the med centre,' Dave told the team as the chopper prepared to take off. 'She'll need something for shock.'

'I don't,' Ginny said as she watched the chopper lift. She'd said goodbye to Henry—and to Ben—but it had all been done in such a rush there'd been no time to talk. Ben had taken her hand and gripped hard, but she wasn't sure if it had been need or pain making him hold on so tight.

She wanted, so much, to go with him, but her priority had to be Button.

She'd forgotten Button once. Not again.

She felt sick to the depths of her soul.

'You idiot.' She heard James's voice echo back to her, words that had been said over and over in their marriage. 'You don't have the brains you were born with.'

She stood in the morning sun and let the words play and replay.

It was her fault that Ben could be so hurt.

Even Henry… She should have insisted he stay with her at the vineyard. She should have…

'Come on, Ginny, let's get you down to the hospital,' Don said, and she shook her head.

'I'm fine,' she said dully. 'No thanks to me, but Button and I are okay. I can still drive. Thank you all for your care, but I need to manage by myself.'

'On a scale of one to ten, how bad's the pain?' Dave asked Ben as the chopper headed out over the sea.

'Eleven,' Ben said morosely, and then at Dave's look of alarm he shook his head. 'Sorry. Seven, I guess, so, yes, I would like a top-up. There's just a few more things going on.'

'Like leaving his lady,' Henry said from beside him. They'd set both patients up with headphones so they could speak to each other. 'He'll be feeling bad because of Ginny.'

'Ginny seems okay,' Dave said, startled. 'She's a competent woman.'

'Yeah, she's a competent woman and a fine doctor,' Ben managed through his pain. 'But the lady has demons. I thought I'd slayed enough of them to break through, but something tells me Henry and I have conjured up a whole lot more.'

She drove carefully back into town, filling her mind with plans, figuring how she needed to get the house inspected and repaired, get the manager's residence liveable for Henry, persuade Henry to stay, get her and Button back to the vineyard.

Her list was vast, and she concentrated on it fiercely, because if she didn't concentrate, fears broke in. As well as that, the voices flooded back, accusing, and it was too hard to cope with.

She'd had a whole lifetime of not being good enough, and she was weary to the bone.

'I am good enough,' she said out loud, finally cracking and letting the voices hold sway. Trying to defend herself by facing them down. 'I will look after Button. I will.'

'And that's all,' she added in a less fierce voice, a voice that was an acknowledgment that she couldn't fight failure on more than one front. 'That's all I'm focussing on. I might love Ben. I might even love medicine, but I stuff things up and I won't risk it any further. I'll help Ben with emergency medicine until he finds someone else but that's all. It's Button and the vineyard and nothing else.'

CHAPTER TEN

A WEEK LATER Ben went out to the vineyard to find her. When he arrived Ginny was hammering boards onto the veranda of the vineyard manager's residence. Button had a hammer as well and was banging everything in sight. Ginny paused in her hammering as the car approached, but Button kept right on going.

His mother had driven him up from the town. She paused at the gate—there seemed to be unstable ground along the driveway and she wasn't risking driving further—and looked at the woman and child in front of them.

'You sure you want to do this? Do you want me to wait?' she asked.

'Nope,' he said. 'Ginny will drive me back.'

'You might have trouble getting her out of here,' Ailsa said worriedly. 'Okay, it's not the shaky ground I'm worried about. I know you can go cross-country. But she's wounded and retreating, Ben. More wounded even than you are.'

'What, worse than a ruptured spleen?'

'You don't have a spleen any more and Ginny still has her wounds,' Ailsa said sternly. 'Her father was a bully and a thug, and her mother was appalling. I know you love her but even when she was a kid I could see her shadows. From what I hear, her marriage has just meant longer ones.'

'I can cope with shadows,' Ben said, but uneasily because he wasn't sure that he could.

'Good luck,' his mother said, and leaned across and kissed him before he climbed out of the truck, carrying his grandfather's old walking cane for support. His ruptured spleen had been removed by laparoscopic surgery, he was recovering nicely but he'd been bruised just about everywhere it was possible for a man to be bruised. His mother had been fussing, and maybe she had cause.

'Give me a ring if you don't get anywhere,' she said now, and glanced ahead at Ginny. 'You might need more than a walking stick to get through this pain.'

'If I travelled by helicopter to Auckland with a ruptured spleen, I can get through anything,' Ben said, but Ailsa still looked doubtful as she drove away.

Ginny had seen him arrive. She'd started walking towards them, pausing to fetch Button. It seemed Button wasn't to be allowed out of her sight.

She stopped coming towards him when Ailsa drove away.

'H-hi,' she managed, and then the doctor part of her took over. 'Surely you shouldn't be out here, walking. I… Can I get you a chair?'

'I'm fine,' Ben said, and then they both looked at the walking stick. 'And I'm tough,' he said, like he was convincing himself. He managed a grin. 'Chairs are for wusses. Thanks for the flowers.'

'They were…the least I could do.'

'And you always do the least you can do? That's Hannah's line, not yours.'

They were twenty yards apart. It was slow going with his walking stick—he had a corked thigh that was still giving him hell a week after the event—and Ginny had stopped and wasn't coming any closer. 'I thought you might visit,' he said. 'I sort of hoped.'

'I phoned.'

'To enquire. And then didn't ask to be put through. Coward.'

'On the card I said I was sorry,' Ginny managed. 'There didn't seem anything else to say. I *am* sorry, Ben. I can't say more than that. So why would you want to see me?'

'To ask you to marry me.'

Marry...

The word was huge. The word was impossible, Ben thought as he watched all the colour drain from her face. Maybe his plan to put it all out there hadn't been such a good idea after all.

'Ben...'

'What happened wasn't your fault,' he said. 'Nothing's your fault. You're my Ginny and I'm your Ben. Bad things happen but whenever they do, we face them together.'

'You wouldn't want to share...my bad things.'

'Ginny...'

'I always get it wrong,' she blurted out. 'I try and try but it never turns out right. Even Button...I'm so scared of caring for Button. I know she has no choice. I know she needs me, but she'd be so much better with someone who can love without messing things up.'

'That sounds...' He sorted his words carefully, fighting for the right ones. 'As if you're seriously thinking of stepping away.'

'I can't,' she said. 'Not from Button.'

'And from me?'

'Yes,' she said. 'From you.' It was a bald, harsh statement, and he thought suddenly of the harsh things Ginny had said to him when she'd been seventeen, and how he'd believed her and had let her go.

It'd be easier to be a caveman, he thought suddenly. It'd be over the shoulder, a bit of manly exercise lugging her back to his lair and he'd have her for the rest of her life. But now…he had to make her see sense.

'Do you love me?' He asked it like it was the most natural question in the world, like it was totally reasonable for a guy who ought to be in bed to lean on his walking stick in the midday sun and wait for an answer to a question of such import that it took his breath away.

But there'd never be a better time to say it, he thought.

Maybe there'd never be a good time to say it.

He watched the doubts flash across her face, the fear, and he drove his advantage.

'Yes, my first question was marriage,' he conceded. 'That didn't get me anywhere, so let's try this from a different angle. No lies, Ginny. Do you love me?'

'Too…too much,' she whispered.

He nodded. 'As a matter of interest, did you love me when I was seventeen?'

'Yes, but—'

'So what Henry told me was true. We shared a ward in Auckland and he told me. You tossed me over because your old man made threatening noises about my career.'

'He shouldn't have told—'

'Henry shouldn't have told me?'

'No.'

It was too much, he thought. He was aching all over. She was standing there in her faded jeans, dirty from pruning grapes, holding Button's hand, and she was just as unattainable as she'd been at seventeen. Dammit, did she really expect him to walk away?

'Henry shouldn't have told?' Suddenly he was practically shouting—okay, he was shouting, and he might frighten Button but Button looked interested rather than scared. 'Henry shouldn't have told? What about you? Why didn't you say it like it was and we could have faced it down together? You don't need to fight shadows yourself. Think about the immorality of your father's threats. Think about the sheer cowardly bullying of your husband, the guy who's making you shrink now and look like a scared rabbit because somehow you think it's all your fault that I'm angry. Do you love me, Ginny?'

'Yes, but—'

'Then that's all I need right now,' he said grimly. 'Go take a shower. We're going to a funeral.'

'Ben…'

'If you think I'm letting you lock yourself away all over again, you have another think coming,' he snapped. 'I shouldn't be here. I'm incapable of driving. I'm walking wounded standing in your driveway and I promised Squid that I'd speak at his funeral.' He glanced at his watch. 'In forty minutes from now. So Hannah's meeting us at the church to take care of Button and you're going to get yourself into something a wee bit cleaner and then you're driving me to the funeral. And then you're coming in with me, Ginny, like it or not. You're part of this island. I need you, Ginny.'

And then he softened as he saw her face. She looked like a deer trapped in headlights, but he wouldn't—he couldn't— let her walk away.

'I can't do this alone, Ginny,' he said, and he held out his hand. 'One step at a time. I won't talk marriage. I won't even push the love bit, but I will push belonging. Squid knew you as an islander, as do I. You were with us when we needed you most. This is to say farewell to one of us. Ginny, come with me, just for now.'

'You mean you come with me,' she said with an attempt at humour. 'I appear to have the only set of wheels here.'

'That's why I need you, Ginny, love,' he said. 'That and

about fifty other reasons and a lot more besides. Come on, love, it's a date you can't refuse. Let's go and say goodbye to Squid.'

She sat in a pew at the back of the crowded church. Ailsa squashed in with her and gave her a swift hug.

'Ben's been asked to do the eulogy,' she said. 'He and Squid were friends. He's feeling it.'

And she fell silent as if she was feeling it, too, and Ginny was left with her own thoughts.

Love? Marriage?

She'd just hurt him, as she'd hurt him already.

That had been her cowardice talking. That had been the shades of her parents and James.

But to hurt someone else…to expose Ben to mistakes she'd inevitably make? How could she do that?

Ailsa's hand gripped hers.

'He loves you with all his heart,' she whispered. 'Go on, Ginny, love, jump.'

Was she so obvious? She dredged up a half-hearted smile as they rose for the first hymn.

Jump? And that was all she had to do. Jump, dragging Ben with her. And what was at the base of that leap?

The hymn ended. Ben was in front of the congregation, in front of the plain, wooden coffin, holding a sheet of paper before him. 'Squid asked me to speak today,' he said, and her heart turned over. 'And everyone here knows Squid. He liked to predict what would happen so he made sure. He wrote this just before the earthquake, just in case, telling me exactly what to say.'

There was a ripple of laughter, and then the room fell silent. Squid had been an ancient fisherman, a constant presence on the waterfront since childhood, and the island would be the poorer for his going. Besides, who would predict disaster now?

'It wasn't my fault.'

Ben's first words—Squid's first words—hauled Ginny from nostalgia and regret. They were her words, she thought in confusion—or maybe they weren't.

She'd spent a childhood trying to desperately defend herself with those words—*it wasn't my fault*—only to learn it was easier to appease and accept.

It was my fault.

'"Me heart's been giving me trouble for a couple of years now",' Ben read, following faithfully the script on the page. Unconsciously, his voice even sounded a little like Squid's. '"Doc's been telling me I ought to go to mainland to get one of those valve replacement thingies but, sheesh, I'm ninety-seven—I might be even older when you hear this—and who wants stuff inside you that don't belong.

'"So I'm sitting on the wharf enjoying me last days in the sun and I'm starting to tell all you fellas there's a big 'un coming. An earthquake. Be good if it did, I'm thinking, only to prove me right, but I sort of hope I'm wrong. Only then I'm reading in the papers there's two scientist fellas somewhere who are in jail because they didn't predict an earthquake and I reckon the world's gone mad. If I'm wrong then it's my fault? If I'm right is it my fault 'cos I didn't yell at you louder? Fault. Like Doc telling me I need a new valve. Is it his fault I'm lying in this damned coffin?"'

There was a ripple of uneasy laughter through the church. Ginny had heard the island whispers, and sometimes the voices had risen higher than whispers. 'Someone should have warned us. Who can we sue?'

She thought of James, apoplectic with fury because she'd tried to inject a drug he'd needed and had had trouble finding a vein. Lashing out at her. 'It's your fault I'm in this mess.'

It was totally irrational, but blame was a powerful tool. When all else failed, find someone to blame.

"'You want me to cop it so you'll all feel better?'" Squid—Ben—said from the pulpit. "'No way. That's what I want to say here. That's the reason I didn't ask to get wrapped in a tarp and tipped over the side of me fishing boat out at sea before I'd had this nice little ceremony. I reckon if I'm right about the quake and it sets me ticker off—and I know it might—you might be sitting here shaking your fist at me coffin, saying the mad old coot caused this mess.

"'So I just wanted to say stuff it, no one causes earthquakes so don't dare stop drinking beer at me wake if it's happened. I want a decent wake and I want you to pour a bit of beer over me coffin and then toss me out to sea with no regrets and say I'm done. Great life. Great times. Great island. Merv Larkin, notes on me snapper spot are written on the back of the calendar of me dunny. That's it, then. There's me legacy. See you.'"

Ben paused then. There were more ripples of laughter but Ginny still heard the odd murmur. There had been blame. Ben was watching calmly as islanders elbowed each other.

She knew the mutterings. 'If Squid knew, why didn't he say just how bad it'd be? Why didn't he talk to the mainland scientists, shove it down their throats, get official warnings out?'

'He really didn't know.' It was Ben now, Ben speaking his own words, and suddenly he was looking at Ginny. Straight at Ginny. He was smiling faintly, and suddenly she knew that his smile was meant only for her.

'A hundred years of living, and you know what Squid knew for sure?' Ben said. 'That no one knows a sausage. We can make guesses and we make them all the time. I'll cross this road because chances are a meteor's not going to drop on my head. That's a guess. It's a pretty good guess, and Squid's earthquake prediction was a pretty good guess, too, backed up by a hundred years of Squid's grandpa telling him the signs. But, still, unless Squid got underground and heaved, it wasn't his fault.

'Meteors are sitting over everyone's head and one day they'll drop, nothing surer, and we just need to accept it. Anyway that's all I need to say except we were blessed to have Squid. We should have no regrets except that even though he's left his snapper spots, his best crayfish spots die with him. We loved him, he drove us nuts and we'll miss him. That's pretty much all we need to say, except he left enough money for everyone to have a beer or a whisky on him. Bless him.'

There was laughter, but this time it wasn't uncomfortable. There was the odd sniff and the organist belted out a mighty rendition of what must surely be the island's favourite hymn by the strength of the island voices raised in farewell.

And then six weathered fishermen led by a limping Ben carried the coffin from the church, the hearse carried the coffin down to the wharf because after all this he would be buried at sea—and then the island proceeded to the pub.

'Shall we join them?' Ailsa asked, and Ginny realised Ailsa had been holding her hand all the time. Even while singing.

As if Ginny was her daughter?

She wasn't this woman's daughter.

She could be.

Courage.

'I'm a wimp,' she said softly, and Ailsa followed her gaze to where Ben was talking to the pallbearers while they watched the hearse drive slowly through the still rubble-strewn streets down to the harbour.

'You trusted,' Ailsa said. 'You trusted your father and

you trusted your husband. It's no fault to trust, child. But you know Ben would never hurt you.'

'It's not that. I just…mess things up.'

'Like Squid messed the island up,' Ailsa said briskly. 'Nonsense. You want to take that attitude, then you are a wimp. Get a grip, girl, go for what you want and stand up for yourself. Now, you want to head for the pub for a bit of Dutch courage? Squid's prepaid for the very best beer—and whisky all round.'

'I need to think,' Ginny said, and Ailsa shook her head and tugged her forward.

'Nonsense, girl. You need to belong.'

CHAPTER ELEVEN

BEN AND THE pallbearers accompanied the coffin out to sea. Ginny headed to the pub and ordered a glass of Squid's excellent whisky but only one, she told herself, because she really did have some thinking to do.

Serious thinking.

She was an accepted part of the island, she thought. No one looked askance at her; in fact, she was being treated with affection.

'Word is you've had a rough time of it,' one of the farmers who lived beyond her vineyard said. 'Doc says we're to leave you be, no pressure, but don't you bury yourself too long, girl. We need you.'

'I know the island needs a doctor...'

'Not just that,' the man said. 'I know this sounds dumb but you're an islander. You always seemed one, not like your mum and dad, but even when you were a little tacker it was like you were coming home every time you came here. And we don't like losing islanders.'

He stared into his beer and gave a rueful smile. 'We don't even like losing ninety-seven-year-olds who smell like smoked mackerel and prophesy doom. We'll miss him, like we're missing you, girl. Doctor or not, this is your home.'

There wasn't a lot she could say after a speech like that.

She hadn't brought enough tissues. Dratted funerals. Dratted islanders.

Dratted Ben.

She took her whisky and escaped out through the beer garden, through the back gate she and Ben had sneaked through when they had been under age, then out along the path that led to the island's best swimming beach.

It had barely been damaged by the quake. A few rocks had rolled down the gentle slope but the path was fine. She headed down, slipped off her shoes and went and sat on a rock and stared out to sea. Towards the mainland.

You're an islander.

She was crying good and proper now. There weren't enough tissues in the world for how she was crying, and she didn't care.

She didn't cry. Until she'd come back to the island she'd never cried. Not once, not at her father's funeral, not once when James had been diagnosed and died. So why was crying now?

Who knew? She didn't. She was so out of control she felt like she was falling, and when Ben sat down beside her and put his arm around her and pulled her into him, she had no strength to pull away.

She was falling and he was the only thing stopping her.

He took the whisky glass carefully out of her hand—the thing was half-full and one part of her still acknowledged it was excellent whisky and Squid would probably haunt her if she spilled it. Ben set it on the rock beside them, and then he carefully turned her towards him and tugged her into his arms.

'I...I'm soggy,' she managed, and it was almost impossible to get that much out.

'You're allowed to cry at funerals.'

'I don't.'

'Because you're not allowed to?'

'I don't cry. I won't cry,' she said, and cried some more, and the front of his shirt was soaked and she was being ridiculous and she couldn't stop.

'I'm...I'm sorry...'

'Ginny...' He hauled back from her then, held her at arm's length, and his face was suddenly as grim as death. 'Don't.'

'Don't...'

'Don't you dare apologise,' he snapped. 'Not once. You know what you did when I sank your bathtub?'

'I threw...I threw mud at you.' How did people speak through tears? It looked so elegant in the movies—here it felt like she was talking through a snorkel.

'And very appropriate it was, too,' Ben said, the sternness replaced by the glimmer of a smile. 'And then?'

'And then you said if I didn't tell your mum what you'd done, you'd give me your best taddy—the one that looked like it'd be a bullfrog to beat all bullfrogs.'

'A supreme sacrifice,' he said nobly. 'And I watched you care for him and skite about him to the other kids...'

'I did not skite!'

'You skited. And then I watched you let him go—my bullfrog—and I swear he or his descendants are around here still, thinking they owe their whole family lineage to you. That pond was full of ducks. He'd have been a goner but you were his lifesaver and not me. You know what? I should have just said sorry and kept the bullfrog for myself. But I didn't feel sorry. I felt...' He smiled at her then, a killer smile that had wobbled her heart when at eight years old and was wobbling her heart still.

'I felt like it was the way things were,' he said. 'I covered you with mud so you got to raise my bullfrog. But you know what? I loved watching you raise my bullfrog. There wasn't a single bit of sorry left in there.'

'Ben...'

'If we married,' he said, and the smile had gone again. 'That's what I'd want. Not one single bit of sorry.'

'You can't want to marry me,' she whispered. 'To take me on with all my baggage. To help raise another man's child...'

'It's like the bullfrog,' he said softly. 'You'd give your baggage to me and I'd take it on and you'd watch me care for it and it'd be like caring for it yourself. That's the way I see it. That's the way it's always been for us, Ginny. Not a single sorry between us, now and for ever.'

'But I hurt you.'

'And I pressured you. Pushing a seventeen-year-old to marry me... We both needed a life before we settled down. It seems like I've had a happier one—I've had some very nice girlfriends, thank you very much, all of whom sound nicer than your creepier James, but I'd prefer if you don't ask me about them, and you can tell me as much or as little about James as you want. All I'll tell you about my girlfriends is that not a single one of them would have raised my tadpole into the fine specimen of a bullfrog he turned out to be. So no sorry, Ginny. Get every tear you need to shed, shed them now and then move forward.'

She couldn't talk. What was it with tears? If she was Audrey Hepburn she'd have whisked away the last teardrop from her beautiful eyelashes and would now be fluttering said eyelashes up at her love.

Where were tissues?

'Here,' Ben said, and handed over a man-sized handkerchief.

'A handkerchief,' she said, sidetracked. 'A handkerchief?'

'I never go to a funeral without one,' he said. 'You'll note the left-hand corner is already a little doggy.'

She choked and he tugged her close again and then he simply held her; he held her and held her until finally she sort of dried up and she sort of pulled herself together and she sort of thought…that this was okay.

That this was where she belonged.

That this was home.

But to let go of the baggage of years? To let go of sorry?

'If you're still harping on sorry, then I see your duty is to catch me a very big tadpole for a wedding gift,' Ben said, putting her away from him again.

And she choked again. 'How did you know what I was thinking?'

'I just do. I always did. Like you know me, my love. You know we fit. Maybe it's time we acknowledged it.'

'Button…Button might like to be a flower girl,' she said, and his face stilled.

'I didn't know you were thinking that.'

'I'm thinking all sorts of things,' she admitted. 'So many things you can't possibly keep up.'

'So one of them might be that you'd marry me?'

'Only if I can get braver.'

'You're brave already,' he said steadily. 'You took Button on without a backward look. You didn't walk away from James, no matter how he treated you. It's not bravery that's missing, my love. It's the ability to stand over a smashed vase or a broken leg or a patient we lost no matter how we worked to save him and say, "This is life." That's all it is, life. It'll throw bad things at us, you and I both know that, but it'll also throw joy. Joy, joy and more joy if you'll marry me.'

'Ben—'

'You weren't responsible for James' death. You know that,' he said. 'Say it.'

'I wasn't responsible.'

'Or for your father's death or for his disappointment that you didn't win the Nobel Prize before he died.'

'I guess…'

'And your mother's appalling disappointment that you turned out not to be blonde.'

'Hey, I wouldn't go that far,' she said, suddenly realising her tears had gone. She wasn't sure what was taking their place—some emotion she'd never felt before. Liberation? Freedom?

'It was a heinous crime not to be blonde,' she managed, and Ben grinned.

'Yes, it was. So can you stand in the dock, look your accusers in the face and say it wasn't your fault?'

'I guess.'

'You want to have fun?'

'Fun,' she said, and the word was weird. Foreign.

'I'm not marrying you unless you turn back into the Ginny I knew,' he said. He motioned to the gently sloping rise behind the beach. The earthquake had shaken free a great swathe of loose, soft sand. It looked...sort of poised.

Poised to slide straight down the slope into the shallows beneath it.

'The Ginny I know would ride that slope,' Ben said.

'I'd get wet.'

'You're already soggy.'

'So I am.' She looked at him, her gorgeous, kind, clever Ben, her love who'd magically waited for her for all this time, who'd made her see what she should have been yelling at the top of her lungs for years.

'I believe I'm about to burst a few chains,' she said, and Ben looked startled.

'Pardon?'

'You don't know what you're getting into. If it's not my fault I'll break cups all over the place. And...' she eyed the sandy slope thoughtfully '...I'll get sand in my knickers. But I won't do it alone.'

'I don't want you to do anything alone any more,' he said,

and then added a hasty rider. 'Within reason. It seems to me you've been on your own all your life. You hook up with me, you have a whole island. We're part of a community but we're a team. You and me, Dr Koestrel. Together for ever.'

'Prove it,' she said, and he blinked.

'What?'

'Remember all those years ago when I wanted to be your friend. Prove it, you said, by rowing this bathtub all the way across the pond.'

'Haven't we moved on from that?'

'Maybe you have,' she said. 'But I'm still wary. See this slope? It's gentle sand—a gentle slope. It shouldn't hurt someone who had his surgery laprascopically and I'll kiss the bruises. Together or nothing, Dr McMahon.'

'I'll get sand in *my* knickers.'

'Yes, you will,' she said serenely, because suddenly she was serene. She was happy, she thought incredulously. She was totally, awesomely happy. She was in love, in love, in love, and miraculously the man she loved was smiling at her, loving her right back, and all she was asking was that he slide on a little sand for her.

She thought of the impossibility of asking either of her parents to do such a thing, or James, and she wondered why she hadn't seen it? The fault had never been in her. It had been in them. They'd chosen the wrong daughter, the wrong wife. Their perfect daughter, perfect wife was maybe out there somewhere but it wasn't her, and whoever it was who wanted to be blonde and perfect and servile, well, good luck to them. It wasn't her.

'Slide or nothing,' she said.

'You will kiss the bruises? Slide and everything?' Ben asked, and that gorgeous twinkle was back, the twinkle she'd first met twenty years ago, the Ben twinkle, of mischief, life and laughter.

'Everything,' she said, and turned and headed up the sand bank, and she knew he'd follow.

And he did.

Two minutes later two very wet, very sandy doctors emerged from a shallow wave, laughing and spluttering, and Ben was holding Ginny and Ginny was holding Ben, and she knew that here was her home.

Here was her love. Her life. Her whole.

And then—after all the bruises had been very satisfactorily kissed and a few other places besides—because it seemed like the right time, the right place, the right everything, Ben took Ginny's hand and led her back to the pub. Squid's wake was just starting to wind up but most of the islanders were still there.

They turned to stare in amazement at the picture of the two sodden island doctors, Ben's suit dripping, Ginny even wearing a bit of seaweed.

They stood in the doorway and Ben held Ginny's hand tightly while the voices faded and every eye was on them.

'We have an announcement to make,' Ben said to the whole pub, the whole island, the whole world. 'I'd like to tell everyone who's listening that Ginny has just agreed to marry me. And, Squid, if you're listening up there, no, it's not your fault but you lent a hand. The lady loves me, ladies and gentleman, and the next ceremony on this island's going to be a wedding.'

And so it was.

Ginny's wedding to James had taken place in Sydney's biggest cathedral, with a luxury reception in a lush ballroom overlooking Sydney Harbour.

Ginny's wedding to Ben took place in the small island chapel where they'd said goodbye to Squid, and the reception took place on the beach.

Simple, Ginny had decreed, but she didn't quite have her way. The islanders prepared a party to end all parties. Ailsa made her a dress that was breathtakingly lovely, with a sweetheart neckline, a cinched waist and a skirt that flowed out in a full circle if she spun.

And she did spin, as Ben took her into his arms and proceeded to jive instead of doing a bridal waltz.

'You can't waltz on sand,' he decreed, and she didn't think she could jive on sand either, but it seemed she could.

And did.

So did Button, dressed in a gorgeous pink dress the same style as Ginny's, jiving along with Henry, who was enjoying himself very much indeed. He was back living in the manager's residence at the vineyard now, pottering in the vineyard, falling in love with Button, deeply content with the way life was turning out. Looking forward to Ben and Ginny and Button sharing the big house.

He'd decreed Button was now his family, as was the tiny black and white kitten that followed Button everywhere. As for Button, she was pretty much in heaven. The heart specialist had decided surgery would be necessary to repair a slight abnormality but it could wait, he said. No rush. No drama. For now they could settle into what they were.

Family.

The islanders had lit the campfire to beat all campfires. Dusk was settling into night. The local band was playing its collective heart out, there was enough food for a small army, people were dancing, singing, gossiping, rolling tired children in rugs and settling them to sleep on the sun-warmed sand...

'This'll go on for hours,' Ben said into her ear, and she felt so happy she could melt.

'Let it.'

'But you're my wife,' he said. 'Is it my fault that I want you now?'

'Yes, it is,' she said serenely. 'All your own fault. I take no responsibility.'

He grinned and held her tighter. They danced on, drowsy with love and desire, knowing they had all the time in the world for each other, but there was still this desire to have that time now.

No one looked like going home. No one wanted this party to end.

'Tell you what,' Ben said. 'Why don't we have a medical emergency?'

'An emergency?'

'A serious one,' he said. 'Did you know you can make your own phone ring?' And he twirled her over to a place where the fire torches were less bright, he whirled her round so his bride was between him and any onlookers—and, lo, his phone rang.

'Uh-huh?' he said in a voice that carried. 'Goodness, that sounds serious. Really? Well, if you say so, we'll be on our way right now.'

He replaced his phone in his jacket pocket and turned to face the bemused islanders—and his bemused and brand-new wife.

'We have an emergency on the other side of the island,' Ben said. 'It needs two doctors. Sorry, guys, keep up the party, but you need to excuse…my wife and me.'

There was a ripple of laughter and more than one mutter of disbelief.

'What sort of emergency?' someone yelled.

'Heart,' Ben said promptly. 'You can't mess with hearts.'

'Whose?' someone else yelled.

'Patient confidentiality,' Ben said. 'How can I tell you? All I can say is that it's a multiple problem. Two hearts that need attention. Ginny…Dr Koestrel can care for one, and I'll take the other.'

There was a whoop of delighted laughter. 'You're making that up,' someone else yelled. 'You just want to get away all by yourselves!'

'So what if we do?' Ben said, taking his bride by the hand and then changing his mind and sweeping her into his arms to carry her up the beach, to his waiting Jeep, to the night beyond, to the future together.

'So what if we do?' he said again. 'This is my love and my life. Have you seen my bride? If we did want to get away, all on our own, it's not our fault. It's life, guys. It's life and laughter and love and it's our future, just beyond the campfire. And, fault or not, we're stepping into it, right now.'

* * * * *

LET'S TALK
Romance

For exclusive extracts, competitions
and special offers, find us online: